W9-CCJ-539

THREE WORDS
for GOODBYE

Also by Hazel Gaynor

When We Were Young & Brave
Meet Me in Monaco (with Heather Webb)
The Lighthouse Keeper's Daughter
Last Christmas in Paris (with Heather Webb)
The Cottingley Secret
The Girl from The Savoy
Fall of Poppies (with Heather Webb and others)
A Memory of Violets
The Girl Who Came Home

Also by Heather Webb

The Next Ship Home
Ribbons of Scarlet
Meet Me in Monaco (with Hazel Gaynor)
The Phantom's Apprentice
Last Christmas in Paris (with Hazel Gaynor)
Fall of Poppies (with Hazel Gaynor and others)
Rodin's Lover
Becoming Josephine

Praise for *Three Words for Goodbye*

"Utterly delightful and the perfect escape. I loved being swept away to 1930s Paris, Venice, and Vienna alongside sisters Maddie and Clara, who, despite their differences, have come together to fulfill their dying grandmother's final wish. Unshackled by family and the expectations of society, they learn a lot about themselves and each other as they uncover long-kept family secrets and discover their own talents and desires. A heartwarming and wonderful story about the power of forgiveness and the unbreakable bond of sisters."

—Natasha Lester, *New York Times* bestselling author of *The Paris Secret*

"What a treat! *Three Words for Goodbye* is an absorbing, escapist, uplifting read, with engaging characters in Clara and Maddie, and a clever plot that takes us on a tour of 1930s Europe. Reading this novel is like reclining in a comfortable beach chair with warm sun on your skin and a glass of champagne at your elbow: you won't want it to end."

—Gill Paul, *USA Today* bestselling author

"Vibrant and laced with fascinating historical references—including the around-the-world journey of journalist Nellie Bly, the approaching shadow of the Nazi occupation, and the ill-fated last flight of the *Hindenburg*—this tale of the complicated love between sisters and the mending of fractured relationships will move you, entertain you, and maybe even inspire you to seek out a truer path of your own."

—Kristin Harmel, *New York Times* bestselling author of *The Book of Lost Names* and *The Forest of Vanishing Stars*

"With three glorious locations, two different but equally engaging sisters, family secrets to uncover, and hearts to be won and lost, plus one big, shocking finale, *Three Words for Goodbye* is the very best of immersive, escapist historical fiction. I loved it from the first page."

—Liz Trenow, author of *The Forgotten Seamstress*

"Illuminating the importance of family and the power of forgiveness, *Three Words for Goodbye* beautifully renders the romance of France, Italy, and Austria with picturesque streets and culinary delights. As two sisters test the bond of their relationship on a sumptuous journey through Paris, Venice, and Vienna, both long-simmering resentments and secrets come to light while European tensions mount, challenging their perceptions of the past and their visions for the future. I couldn't stop turning the novel's pages until I'd reached the high-octane conclusion."

—Meredith Jaeger, *USA Today* bestselling author of *The Dressmaker's Dowry*.

Praise for *Meet Me in Monaco*

"With glamour, perfume, and romance, Gaynor and Webb's second collaborative novel (after *Last Christmas in Paris*) is a scrumptious concoction served up with delectable descriptions and heaps of emotion. . . . Sweet, then bitter, then sweet again, the love story is woven through with Grace's fairy-tale romance with Rainier and its devastating ending, snatching redemption from tragedy in the best Hollywood style."

—*Publishers Weekly*

"Gaynor and Webb make history come alive with a beautifully crafted and expertly paced story of one of history's most celebrated stars. Their artful blend of history and imagination is a deeply satisfying tale of love and friendship, and a reminder of the power of second chances to determine our fate."

—*Booklist*

"A sparkling tale that will delight Francophiles and fans of historical fiction alike. These characters are engaging and expertly drawn, and their story is as evocative as the lingering traces of a fine eau de parfum."

—*Library Journal*

"Everyone from shop owners to paparazzi and movie stars arrive in glamorous Monaco against the backdrop of Grace Kelly's 'Wedding of the Century' to Prince Rainier. A delightful beach read."

—*New York Post*

"Grace Kelly fans, this one is for you! . . . An absolute and utter delight."

—POPSUGAR

Praise for *Last Christmas in Paris*

"Humor, love, tragedy, and hope make for a moving, uplifting read. A winner!"

—Kate Quinn, *New York Times* bestselling author of *The Alice Network*

"Bestselling author Gaynor (*A Memory of Violets*) teams with historical novelist Webb (*Rodin's Lover*) to pen a moving and heart-felt story of love and bravery."

—*Library Journal* (starred review)

"Gaynor and Webb's first collaboration is beautifully told. . . . The authors fully capture the characters' voices as each person is dramatically shaped by the war to end all wars."

—*Booklist*

THREE WORDS *for* GOODBYE

a novel

Hazel Gaynor and Heather Webb

WILLIAM MORROW
An Imprint of HarperCollins*Publishers*

This is a work of fiction. Names, characters, places, and incidents are products of the author's imagination or are used fictitiously and are not to be construed as real. Any resemblance to actual events, locales, organizations, or persons, living or dead, is entirely coincidental.

P.S.™ is a trademark of HarperCollins Publishers.

THREE WORDS FOR GOODBYE. Copyright © 2021 by Hazel Gaynor and Heather Webb. All rights reserved. Printed in the United States of America. No part of this book may be used or reproduced in any manner whatsoever without written permission except in the case of brief quotations embodied in critical articles and reviews. For information, address HarperCollins Publishers, 195 Broadway, New York, NY 10007.

HarperCollins books may be purchased for educational, business, or sales promotional use. For information, please email the Special Markets Department at SPsales@harpercollins.com.

FIRST EDITION

Designed by Diahann Sturge

Library of Congress Cataloging-in-Publication Data has been applied for.

ISBN 978-0-06-296524-0 (paperback)
ISBN 978-0-06-308233-5 (library edition)

21 22 23 24 25   LSC   10 9 8 7 6 5 4 3 2 1

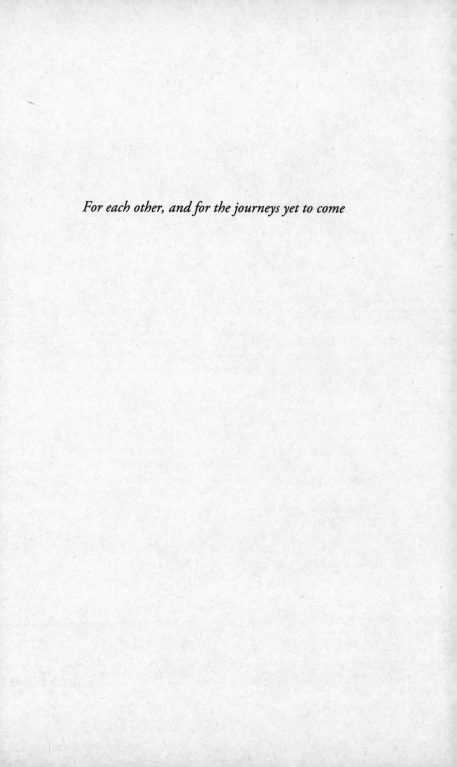

For each other, and for the journeys yet to come

I took off my cap and wanted to yell with the crowd, not because I had gone around the world in seventy-two days, but because I was home again.

—NELLIE BLY

THREE WORDS *for* GOODBYE

Prologue
Violet

✦

Veneto Estate, East Hampton, New York
January 1937

They say absence makes the heart grow fonder, and I know it to be true. I have never loved my home more than when I return to it after a trip away. I find a special joy in sleeping in my own bed again, or settling into the time-worn contours of a favorite armchair. It's why I look so fondly on everything now, as the snow settles in drifts against the windowpanes, knowing that the next time I leave my beloved Veneto, I will not return. There's a profound sadness in that knowledge, but there is also a sense of peace, of letting go. Mostly, there is a desire to have one last adventure before I take my final bow.

I smile as I push aside the velvet drapes, rest my palms against the cold glass, and recall the words of my dear friend Nellie Bly. She'd told me we must sometimes leave the places and people we love the most, so that we can return to them and love them all the more. "Why stare at the same four walls when there's a whole world to be seen? We have to leave, Violet, so we can come back." And she—more than most—knew a thing or two about leaving, about travel and the way it changes a person.

It had all started with a question to her newspaper editor: Was it possible to travel around the world in less than eighty days, and—more importantly—could a *woman* undertake such a challenge alone? Not only did she ask the question, she proved the answer was a resounding yes, on both counts. I didn't know her then of course, but oh how I admired her bravery and sense of adventure. She was a breath of fresh air, so carefree and alive as she waved to the crowds from the deck of the steamship *Augusta Victoria* in her now-famous checkered coat. How I longed to share that feeling of anticipation, of departure and setting sail into the unknown. Along with thousands of others who looked for the latest update on her progress in the newspapers over the following weeks, I studied every detail of her race around the world. Somehow, I knew our paths would, one day, intersect, but I didn't know then just how much Miss Bly's life-changing trip would change my life, too.

I return to the desk and run my hands over the embossed date on the front of my new appointment book. 1937. It's hard to believe nearly fifty years have passed since I watched Nellie's triumphant return at a New Jersey train station. I'd guessed her exact arrival time—seventy-two days, six hours, eleven minutes, and fourteen seconds—and won the *New York World*'s coveted competition prize of two tickets to Europe. There was never a question about whom I would travel with. I would go with Margaret, my sister, two young women in search of life's answers. If Miss Bly could travel alone, so could we. Our steamship tickets to France were arranged for that spring. I can still remember those elegant paper tickets, how they, and the luggage labels that decorated our trunks, held a sense of so much possibility. The same luggage is gathering dust in the attic now. All that possibility abandoned with it.

Beyond the window, the graceful sweep of lawn is already dusted with snow. Sun glistens on the blinding white and sparkles like chips of polished glass. The gardener has cleared a pathway from the porch to the little stone fence, through the hedges, and around the dormant flowerbeds I've spent years tending with care. Time is a precious gift now. Suddenly, I can't bear to be inside a moment longer.

I call my nurse, who promptly arrives in the parlor with a smile. I'm grateful for her sunny disposition. She's made the last few months of my illness far more bearable.

"I'd like to take a walk through the garden, Henrietta."

"In this cold? But your lungs, Violet."

"My lungs belonged to me the last time I checked, and they'd like some fresh air," I reply.

Henrietta is used to my stubbornness.

"What will Mrs. Sommers say?" she asks, hands on her hips.

"Mrs. Sommers is volunteering at a soup kitchen in Manhattan. She doesn't need to know." I make my way to the door. "And you've been with us long enough now to refer to my daughter as Celestine. We can dispense with the formalities."

"Of course."

We both feel the question circling around us: How much longer will I need a nurse? How much longer do I really have?

"Well," I prompt. "Are we going or not?"

Henrietta throws her hands in the air and, after bundling us both in scarves and hats, escorts me and my walking cane to the garden.

It is wonderful to be outside, even as the sharp air steals my breath away. I laugh as I slip and grip Henrietta's arm to steady myself.

"You're full of mischief today," she says. "It's nice to see you smile."

"I'm excited," I reply. "Clara and Madeleine will arrive soon, and I have a surprise for them." I don't tell Henrietta it is a surprise neither of my granddaughters will particularly like, but one that will change their lives for the better—I hope.

As we walk on, treading carefully over the frozen ground, I contemplate the impenetrable parts of my past, the secrets I've hidden from my daughter and granddaughters. Secrets I no longer want to hide. I only hope there's still time to set things right.

Henrietta steadies me as I slip again on a patch of ice. "Maybe we should go back to the house?" she says, her voice full of concern. "I'd hate for you to fall."

I look toward the ocean, steady myself, and take another stubborn step forward.

"I'd like to go on," I say. "The more interesting path always lies ahead."

PART ONE

Au revoir

Clara

Veneto Estate, East Hampton, New York
January 1937

My grandmother didn't often arrange luncheons in the middle of winter. She disliked entertaining in the colder months almost as much as she disliked the many pills and medicines Henrietta made her take every night, so I was surprised when she'd asked me to be home for noon, "on the dot." Violet was very precise about time. "Seconds matter" was one of her favorite reprimands when one or the other of us dawdled. She'd said there was something important she wanted to discuss with me, and from the brightness in her voice I could tell she was up to something. Violet was often up to something, or about to be.

I drove the familiar ocean road toward Veneto, our Long Island home. The golden beaches were shrouded in sea mist, the salty tang heavy in the air beneath moody clouds. It was a seascape begging to be captured in oils—or watercolor, perhaps—but the prospect of sitting down to paint didn't appeal to me as it usually would. All I could think about was how empty our home would be without Violet tending her beloved rose garden, or listening to jazz on her old gramophone, the clink of ice in her glass at five o'clock. Violet was a force of nature, but the doctor said the cancer had spread to her lungs and time was running out. To see her fade away was unbearable.

I drove on, more heartsick with every bend in the road until I slowed the Lincoln, turned through the elaborate filigree gates and up the driveway, past the sprawling lawns toward the pink stucco walls. I killed the engine and took a moment to quietly reflect, to remember happier times before the complicated business of death and illness had arrived. Veneto was always a house full of love and laughter. Madeleine and I had enjoyed a privileged childhood there, attending our mother's legendary summer lawn parties and Violet's afternoon teas, with a private beach to play on with our friends, and lazy Sunday sailing trips around the bay with Father. Madeleine had first broken the spell, abandoning us for the city to be closer to her beloved Newspaper Row. The rooms and corridors had become quieter still with our father's sudden passing last year. Soon, it would be a house without Violet, too. Veneto would become a house of ghosts and memories.

I stepped out of the car, walked up the driveway, and entered through the terrace door. I made my way toward the parlor, stopping to brush my fingertips against the velvety petals of a spray of Christmas roses as I passed. I pulled my silk scarf from my head and called out a hello as I pushed open the parlor door.

"Oh good. You're early," Violet announced, smiling approvingly as she checked her wristwatch.

I bent to kiss her cheek, and told her she looked nice.

She was sitting on the chaise, beside the window with the

ocean view. It was her favorite seat in the house. Mine, too. She patted the seat beside her. She'd long since dispensed with the effort to stand up to greet people.

"It's wild out," I continued. "The Lincoln was almost blown off the highway." I checked my reflection in the mirror above the mantel as I took off my gloves and hat. My hair was woefully untidy. I pinned a few loose strands back into the chignon at the nape of my neck.

"But it wasn't blown off the highway was it, dear," Violet replied. "So stop worrying about things that didn't happen, and sit down."

Violet was used to my cautious outlook on life and had long since stopped indulging it.

I sat beside her and took her hand in mine as we admired the view beyond the window. I'd painted the scene so many times, forever trying to capture the light, the shifting tones of the sky and the ocean as the weather and the seasons changed. I'd never quite gotten it right, perpetually frustrated by my limitations.

"You'll get it just right one of these days," Violet whispered, instinctively understanding my thoughts as she squeezed my hand. "You can still come and sit here when you're a married woman."

My heart sank a little at the mention of my impending wedding. I would miss Veneto terribly when I married Charles Hancock in the summer. Even though I would have a successful husband and a Hamptons home of my own, with new ocean views to paint, now that it was so close, I was nervous about what it meant: becoming a wife, a woman, eventually a mother. It was all happening so quickly, and I felt increasingly unprepared.

"I wish we could live here after the wedding," I said. "At least for a little while, until I get used to things."

Violet nudged me gently with her shoulder. "All brides have their doubts," she said. "It's perfectly natural."

"What was it you wanted to talk to me about anyway?" I asked, eager to change the subject. "You don't usually host luncheons until you come out of hibernation at Easter."

"I have a surprise for you. Two surprises, actually."

I groaned. "You know I hate surprises."

She waved my comment away. "Don't be such a bore. You could at least pretend to be intrigued."

Her enthusiasm was infectious. Her faded gray eyes looked brighter than they had for a long time, and her lips brimmed with a mischievous smile. Despite her illness, the sense of adventure she'd carried with her as a younger woman still lingered like one of her fine French perfumes.

"Well, whatever's gotten into you, you're like a child on Christmas morning!" I laughed as I smoothed my skirt, the cold air lifting from the folds in the fabric and lending a freshness to the room.

Violet couldn't contain herself a moment longer. "I'm sending you on an adventure! To Europe!"

"You're what?"

She wrapped her hands around mine and squeezed them tightly. "I'm dying, Clara, and there are some things I need you to do for me."

"Oh, Violet. Don't say it." My grandmother had always been honest—painfully so at times—and her insistence on talking about her death, while terribly upsetting, was typical of her practical attitude. Admirable, in a way.

"There's no point pretending it isn't going to happen," she pressed, sensing my reluctance to discuss it. "And at least this way I have a chance to put things in order."

"What sort of things?" I asked.

"That doesn't matter for now. First, you need to agree whether or not you'll go."

"But I can't just go dashing off to Europe. I have the wedding to organize."

She looked at me, her gray eyes searching mine. "Charles's mother will deal with the wedding preparations. You know how she likes to interfere."

"Which is precisely why I should be around to keep an eye on her." I picked at a loose thread on the hem of my skirt. "And I promised to help Edward with the new collection at the gallery."

Violet turned to look at me. "How is he?"

"He's very well."

I stood up and walked to the window.

Edward Arnold, my art tutor, owned a small gallery in the West Village. Were it not for him, I would have packed away my easel and oils long ago. Charles didn't show much interest, being a man of commerce rather than art, so I spent as much time at the gallery as I could. More time than I should, perhaps.

"I'm sorry to let you down, Violet, but it really isn't good timing for me. Can't you send Madeleine instead? With a one-way ticket, preferably."

Beyond the parlor door, I heard footsteps approaching.

Violet clapped her hands together. "Good. Now you're both here."

"Both?"

"That's the second surprise, dear. I invited your sister. You'll take the trip together."

"Madeleine? Here? You invited *her*?"

"Yes, she invited *her*. And she's delighted to see you, too, Sis."

I stiffened at the familiar voice behind me and glanced over my shoulder. I hadn't seen or spoken to my sister since Father's funeral a year ago, and here she was, back in the family home as if she'd only stepped outside for a moment to fetch something or other. I studied her face, hair, outfit. She hadn't changed in the slightest, still all angles and terrible posture and clothes that looked more suited to a man than a woman. But for all our differences, and for all the simmering resentment between us, I felt a flicker of a smile at my lips.

Madeleine raised an eyebrow in return, and laughed.

Really, she was *so* annoying.

Maddie

I never could resist Clara's smile. I hadn't as a child when she laughed at my silly antics, and I couldn't now. I laughed and returned her grin, even as hers faded.

Breezing past her, I bent to kiss Violet's cheek. "I'm sorry I'm late. A man was blocking the train platform for a stage performance of 'The Star-Spangled Banner.' A stirring rendition, I assure you. Piercing even."

Clara rolled her eyes. She'd never understood why I chose to ride the trains when I could take a car, but I liked the predictability of the schedule and the unpredictable nature of the other passengers. It was good fodder for my writing.

"You're right on time," Violet insisted. "Sit, my pet. We have something to discuss, the three of us."

"What's this all about? You have me intrigued!" I took off my hat, tossed my coat over a chair, and dropped onto the sofa across from her in a very unladylike manner, as Mother would say. Since slacks and socks had come into fashion, I'd shoved my hosiery to the back of the drawer. If I never wore a skirt again, it would be too soon. Clara eyed my slacks and saddle oxford shoes, and though she said nothing, I knew she wouldn't be caught dead in something so ordinary, or so masculine. Clara had an artistic eye and dressed like a carefully curated gallery exhibition. Look and admire, but don't touch. I, on the other hand, found beauty in words.

"Violet wants to send us to Europe together," Clara blurted out. She always had to be the one to announce important news.

I sat up, perched on the edge of the seat as if ready to leave immediately. "To Europe? Really?" Violet nodded with a smile. "Well, this is great news! But . . . together?"

While I instantly liked the idea of a trip to Europe, barreling down the tracks on some foreign train into the exciting unknown, Clara was the last person I could imagine beside me. We hadn't seen eye to eye on anything since our teenage years, and not much had changed since. In fact, things had only gotten worse. Charles Hancock had taken the last pieces of the Clara I'd actually liked and swept them under the rug for good. I glanced at her then, noticing the dark circles under her eyes, and I wondered if everything between them maybe wasn't so perfect after all.

It was probably wishful thinking.

"It's time you both took a vacation," Violet said. "Time you left America and saw more of the world!" She chuckled at her own enthusiasm. "You're going first to Paris, then to Venice, and finally, to Vienna. And you're going *together*. It's time you put your differences aside."

My mind raced. I knew things were heating up in Germany with the Nazi Party, and I suspected the ripples were being felt throughout Europe. If I was there, among it all, I could take stock of it firsthand, perhaps find some new angle, a gripping story I could submit to the newspapers here. I thought of the stack of articles I'd written and submitted the last three years. Only one had been picked up, placed in a small periodical. But I was determined to keep trying. Maybe this trip to Europe would provide new inspiration.

As my thoughts raced ahead, Violet reached beneath the chaise and lifted out a notebook filled with newspaper clippings and photographs, one of which stuck out farther than the others. I recognized the woman in the picture at once: Nellie Bly, or Auntie Nellie as we'd known her as children.

"What's all this, Violet?" I asked as I flicked through the paperwork.

"You remember Auntie Nellie," she replied.

"Of course. Who could ever forget her!"

Clara scoffed. "You were so silly the way you always trailed around after her. 'Tell me that story again, Auntie Nellie. Tell me about that time you went to Mexico.' I'm surprised she didn't get weary of you."

I ignored my sister's sniping and looked through the newspaper clippings. I'd admired Nellie from the moment she'd swept into our home in a wave of brusque determination and irrepressible ambition. I hung on to her every word, fascinated by her tales of daring trips, undercover newspaper reporting, and being on the front line of the war. It had been more than a decade since her death, but few women had matched her journalistic achievements. I was determined to follow in her footsteps. I'd worked hard the last three years, trying to do just that.

"She was a woman without equal," Violet continued. "It was a real first, you know, a woman traveling alone around the world.

Many didn't believe she would manage it, let alone break the eighty-day record Jules Verne wrote about in his novel." Violet shifted on the chaise, her sickly body not able to sustain any one position for too long. "Nellie once said, 'Jules Verne made it all up. I made it really happen!'"

"She was funny," I said. "A real straight shooter."

"She was," Violet agreed. "Just like you!" She patted my hand affectionately. "But she was much more than that. She was a complex and complicated woman, as most of us are."

The room fell silent. Clara and I both sensed Violet needed a moment to dwell in the past, the way she often did in recent months.

"Anyway," she continued eventually. "As I reach the end of my life, there are some things I need to say to three people who are very important to me. A curtain call, if you will. A chance to make my peace. I'd like you both to deliver some letters for me. One in France. One in Italy. And another, the most important of all, in Austria."

"Couldn't you mail the letters?" Clara asked. "It seems like an awfully long way to go to deliver them in person. And they would get there much faster."

I blew out a breath of frustration. Clara had a rare ability to drain all the joy out of a situation.

"Why all the mystery?" I added, ignoring my sister. "Who are these letters to?"

Violet smiled. "So many questions, girls! First, let me tell you about the planned itinerary. You'll sail from New York to France on the *Queen Mary,* visit Paris and its wonderful sights and, of course, the art galleries. From Paris, you'll take the Orient Express to beautiful Venice, with all its bridges and canals. From Venice, you'll travel to Vienna to deliver my final letter and then . . ." She paused, dramatically.

"And then?" I asked, unable to hide a smile.

"And then, you'll fly home on a zeppelin. The *Hindenburg*. The finest airship ever built! It's not quite circumnavigating the world like dear Nellie did, but you'll travel far enough, and for long enough, to figure out a few things along the way."

The prospect of such luxurious travel and visiting some of the most famous cities in the world was impossible to resist. I thought again of the shifting politics in Europe and the newspaper articles I'd read recently about Austria's struggle against the new autocratic rule, and Mussolini's regime in Italy. I'd have a front-row view of it all, unlike the many journalists here in the city. For once, I'd have an advantage.

Violet shifted on the chaise again as Clara helped her and folded a blanket over her knees. That was when the impossibility of Violet's plan struck me.

"But Violet, you aren't well," I said. "How can we possibly leave you for months when we don't know how long you've got?"

Violet smiled, her watery eyes lit from within.

"Don't worry about a thing. I will still be here when you return, my darling girls. Really, this is very important to me." She paused, seeking our gazes before she continued. "Everything will make sense when you get to each location. But I want you to know this isn't just about making the trip for me, it is also about finding the answers to your own questions: Who you are. What you care about. Where, and with whom, you will be most happy. It will all come together, you'll see."

"Well, it's tantalizing, but Clara will complain and worry the whole time," I said, knowing my comment would irritate her. "She'll take all the fun out of it."

"And Madeleine will make a nuisance of herself with others, and get us into trouble," Clara added. "She never listens or obeys instructions."

Violet held up her hand. "Hush, you two! It breaks my heart to see you bicker and argue. There is nothing more important in the world than family." She leaned back against the cushions, her energy waning as she brushed a long silver strand of hair from her face. "Besides, I already have the tickets. And I want you to promise me that you will travel and lodge together, without exception. It will mean so much to me to have the letters delivered in person, but it will mean even more to have the two of you become friends again, or if not friends, then at least not picking at each other over every little thing."

I stood abruptly, moving to the large windowpane overlooking the curve of private beach I'd played on as a child with my favorite person in the world. My sister. I could still feel the wind whipping through my hair, still smell the briny air mingle with the tinge of lavender from Clara's favorite soap as she bent over a mound of sand with shovel and pail. There was a time we'd gotten along so well. Though we were different, our personalities complemented each other, but as adults, we were as opposite as the sun and moon, Broadway and Park Avenue. All my life, I'd wanted to throttle my sister as often as I'd wanted to embrace her, only the embraces had grown fewer over time until they'd disappeared entirely. Now, we were to travel together for nearly three months? It would be a horror show.

I turned and met Clara's stormy eyes.

She crossed her arms over her chest. "Well, what do you think? I seem to remember you usually have all the answers."

As colorful images of the Eiffel Tower and the Piazza San Marco filled my mind, and the chance to study the political situation in Europe, up close, became a reality, a smile spread across my face.

"I think it's an excellent idea."

Violet grinned. "It's settled, then."

"Not quite," Clara added. "Charles will never agree to it."

"Ah, but he already has, dear," Violet said. "I spoke to him yesterday. He thinks the trip will do you the world of good."

For once, Clara was rendered speechless. I was as surprised as she was to learn of Charles's reaction, and I didn't trust it, not one bit. Clara's fiancé was undeniably handsome with his blond hair and striking build, but his overbearing charm grated on my nerves. He always had a gaggle of self-important people around him that I found tiresome, never mind his questionable business dealings. Despite our differences, I wanted more for my sister. My mistake, along with many others, had been to tell her as much.

"By the way," I added, turning back to Violet. "Who are we taking these letters to? You didn't tell us."

"All will become clear along the way." She turned to face us both. "Trust the journey, girls. Trust each other."

When it came to Clara and me, that was far easier said than done.

Clara

The unexpected confrontation with Madeleine, and Violet's outlandish plans for our trip to Europe, had left me rattled. I arrived for dinner with Charles that evening in a fractious mood.

"It's a silly idea," I said as we took our usual table at the yacht club. "I understand Violet's desire to put things right, but she knows how strained things are between me and Madeleine. And there's a wedding to organize."

"Yes, darling. It all came as a bit of a surprise."

He wasn't really paying attention. He was in a sour mood after a difficult day of business wrangling, something to do with tenements he was trying to purchase in Manhattan, and I knew I was irritating him with my incessant chatter. He studied the menu and signaled to a waiter without looking up.

"Why did you tell Violet you approved of the idea without discussing it with me first?" I pressed. "Even if I enjoyed Madeleine's company—which I don't—the idea of two women traveling through Europe is absurd, not to mention dangerous, particularly at the moment. You were telling me yesterday about the Nazi Party becoming ever more powerful. I don't know why Violet can't just mail the letters. I really don't like the thought of crossing the Atlantic, either. You know how seasick I get."

Charles glanced up. "Do you?"

I didn't reply. Having often sailed with him on his yacht, I'd have thought he knew this already.

He ordered for us both and lit a cigarette. I didn't like him smoking, but hadn't told him so.

"The new liners are very safe, darling, and the *Queen Mary* is the best of the best. I'm actually quite envious I won't be joining you." He smiled over the top of his newspaper. "I thought you would enjoy the opportunity to see Europe. You've often said you'd like to experience the Orient Express, and you're not going to spend time in Germany, so I don't think we need to be concerned about the political unrest there."

"You sound as if you're almost keen to get rid of me." I circled the rim of my water glass with my fingertip so it hummed.

Charles folded his newspaper and placed it on the table. "I'm not *keen* for you to go, darling, I'm simply offering reassurances. Your grandmother put me in a difficult position, talking about her dying wishes and what have you." Our conversation paused as the waiter returned with a bourbon for Charles and a sidecar for me. I wondered if they had different cocktails in Paris. "Go and have your European adventure," Charles continued when the waiter left. "When we're married, we'll have the rest of our lives to spend together. Morning, noon, and, most importantly, night." He winked seductively as he drank half his bourbon in one gulp.

"Charles!" Color rushed to my cheeks. "Stop it."

He put down his glass. "The way I see it, you and Madeleine already can't stand the sight of each other, so it can't get much worse. You can stay out of each other's way as much as possible, deliver Violet's letters, enjoy a little sightseeing, and you'll be on your way home before you've hardly had time to miss me. You might even enjoy yourself. They say Paris is wonderful in the spring."

I stared at him, wondering what had come over my fiancé. He made it sound so simple when I'd expected him to dismiss the entire scheme as nonsense.

I leaned back in my chair and peered out of the window at the narrow strip of midnight blue where the ocean met the horizon. Cotton wool clouds drifted across the sky, nudged along by a brisk wind. Ours was the best table in the restaurant. It offered uninterrupted views of the water but was positioned so that Charles could keep a careful eye on the other patrons coming and going, in case there was someone's hand he needed to shake. There often was. Charles Hancock was someone everyone wanted to meet.

We'd fallen in love quickly, too quickly according to my sister. Charles had easily dazzled me with his charm and good looks. His status among the most prominent families in New York had impressed my parents, and while his proposal had come as something of a surprise, my father had already given Charles his permission, and I'd accepted without hesitation. I knew I'd ruffled a few feathers, and that many other society women had hoped Charles would put a ring on their finger, instead of mine. I glanced at the ring now and wondered if I would ever tell him I wasn't especially fond of sapphires.

"But there's still the matter of the wedding," I said eventually. "I can't very well organize things from the *Queen Mary*, can I?"

Charles reached across the crisp linen tablecloth and took my hand in his. "My mother will be only too happy to step in and help with arrangements while you're gone." I resisted the temptation to tell him that was precisely what worried me. "Go and have some fun. You're so serious recently. It seems silly to throw the opportunity away just because of a little disagreement with your sister."

I pulled my hand from his. "Mine and Madeleine's differences are more than a little disagreement. You know how stubborn she can be."

"Yes, I do. She's damn hard work. Is she still trying to be taken seriously as a writer?" He laughed, a little unkindly. "God loves a trier, I suppose. But listen, darling, since you'll be spending a lot of time with her, don't let her bad-mouth me. You know how she loathes me, for no reason at all. She just can't accept you've found someone who treats you as you deserve, rather than deriding you all the time, the way she does."

To my surprise, I found myself wanting to defend Madeleine.

"Well, she has every reason to want to take this trip," I concluded. "I have every reason not to."

"Why not sleep on it? I really do think you should honor Violet's dying wish. The old dear doesn't have much time, and these letters seem to be important to her. I could always meet you in Austria at the end of your trip? I have a few business arrangements in the country so it would make sense for me to come. We can travel home together on the *Hindenburg* and be the envy of all our friends. What do you say to that?"

He raised his glass to mine, but his attention was caught by the arrival of friends of ours, the Strausses. Charles waved to them, put down his napkin, and stood up.

"You don't mind, do you darling. There's something I need to discuss with Robert." As usual with Charles, it was a statement, not a question. He didn't often ask for others' opinions.

As he went to join his business colleague at the bar, Lacey Strauss made her way over and sat in the empty chair beside me.

"Penny for them? You look like you have all the troubles of the world on your shoulders."

I smiled. "World is right."

Lacey was one of the older wives in the yacht club, and someone I trusted. I was glad of her company.

"Tell me to mind my own business if it's something you'd rather not talk about."

I didn't want to talk about it, and yet I couldn't stop thinking about it, about what to do.

"It's my grandmother. She's concocted a plan for me to travel across Europe with my sister. Live a little before I commit to a life of marriage and children. I'm really not sure about it at all."

Lacey laughed. "Sounds very sensible to me. You'll be married a long time, Clara. I'd grab the opportunity with both hands if I were you. What does Charles think about it?"

"He says I should go. He's actually quite insistent."

I took a long sip of my sidecar and thought about the itinerary Violet had created. She knew exactly how to entice me. I'd always wanted to visit the Louvre and the Gallerie dell'Accademia and the dozens of other European art galleries and museums that held some of the world's most beautiful masterpieces. Spending time with Madeleine would be worth it to see the *Mona Lisa* in person.

Lacey looked at me knowingly. "Well, as your husband, Charles

will decide what you can and can't do, so there's little point in dis-
agreeing with him."

"I suppose you're right," I replied.

Lacey leaned a little closer. "Go to Europe, Clara. Have an adventure. Who knows, you might see everything quite differently
when you get back. Traveling has a way of doing that to people."

"Doing what?"

"Showing them what it is they *really* want."

Lacey's words swirled around my mind as the ice in my drink
cracked and Charles and Robert Strauss laughed loudly over a
shared joke.

"To adventures," I said as I raised my glass to hers.

"To you," she replied. "Go and have a little fun. What's the
worst that can happen?"

Maddie

New York
March 1937

It took two months of disagreements to figure it all out, but in the end we agreed to go, for Violet's sake. Her doctor assured us, as best he could, that we could make the trip and still spend time with Violet when we returned, before the inevitable happened.

Planning began in earnest, though Clara and I couldn't agree on a single detail. Every time we met to discuss something, we parted under a cloud of dissent and renewed animosity. She said my smoking irritated her, that my casual attitude was all wrong, and my laissez-faire approach would get us lost, or worse. Clara was even duller than I remembered. Had she always been so straitlaced and conservative? Everything she said was peppered with caution and pessimism. Her insistence on following rules and schedules made me break out in hives.

Eventually, Violet intervened and made most of the decisions for us. She was a stubborn old mule once she set her mind to something. I was a mirror image of her in that way. In fact, I had more in common with Violet than with either of my parents or my sister. It had always bothered me, that sense of being in the wrong family. I'd once asked Mother if she was sure she'd brought the right babies home from the hospital. She'd told me not to be ridiculous. "There isn't always a shocking story, Madeleine. You're just . . . different from the rest of us. That's all." But she was wrong. There *was* always a story. You just had to know where to look.

At last, departure day came, and I arrived early at the Cunard-White Star pier in New York City. Thankfully, the early spring rain held off for the first time in days, and my gloves and hat kept me warm in spite of the chilly March breeze. I wondered how cold it would be on the sun deck of the *Queen Mary* as we made our way across the Atlantic, to Cherbourg, and then on to Paris by train. Violet had chosen our first stop wisely. As a city of art, Paris would make Clara happy, and as the home of writers like Hugo, Voltaire, and George Sand, it would also make me happy.

I held a hand to my eyes and peered up at the mighty *Queen Mary*. Smoke already billowed from her three funnels that reached proudly into the clear sky, and colorful flags fluttered from her masts. She was magnificent. I turned my gaze to the crowds gathered on the dockside: elegantly attired passengers greeting each other with kisses and handshakes, flustered-looking lady's maids, and porters pushing luggage carts loaded with trunks and hatboxes. The noise was deafening, the anticipation for our departure palpable as my mood swung from excitement to uncertainty. Where was Clara? It wasn't like her to be late. I wondered if Charles had talked her out of the trip, after all. It would be just like him.

I hadn't told Clara where I'd seen Charles, only last week. I'd been donating time at the soup kitchen and among the breadlines on the Lower East Side. I shouldn't have been surprised to see Charles there, doing just the opposite. I wanted to help those who were still suffering immeasurable poverty after the market crash years before, but I was also looking for a story, or something to inspire one.

Charles wanted to buy property, to demolish it, and erect a new building at the site. The only problem was that the tenements on the land he wished to purchase still lived there. But I suspected he, and the landlord, had a plan about that. We'd exchanged a few choice words before Charles left with a final threat, telling me to stop interfering and poking my nose into things I didn't understand. I considered it a job well done to have made him angry. He was difficult to ruffle, being an opportunist and a ruthless businessman, but he knew I was onto something, and he didn't like it. The only good thing I could say about him was that he did seem to care about Clara, at least in his own way, though I still didn't believe it—he—was enough for my sister.

Intent on beginning the day in a happy mood, I pushed Charles Hancock from my mind. I'd figure out how to tell Clara later what he was up to, *if* I decided to tell her at all.

Eventually, I spotted her in the crowd and breathed a sigh of relief. As much as I was looking forward to the trip, I really didn't want to do it alone. Still, I'd rather miss the boat than admit as much to Clara.

She hobbled along the dock, carrying two enormous handbags. A porter walked behind her, dragging two large trunks. Typical

Clara. She'd probably packed a dozen pairs of shoes and three
dresses for every occasion. I watched in disbelief as I took in her
wool overcoat trimmed with fur, an elegant hat, and diamonds at
her ears. The hem of a blue silk dress fluttered around her calves
in the wind. I had to suppress a laugh. She looked more like she
was heading to an evening gala than about to set sail across the
Atlantic.

I waved my arm overhead to grab her attention, but the dockside was too crowded for her to see me. I stuck my fingers in my
mouth and gave a loud piercing whistle, just as Auntie Nellie had
taught me when I was a girl. "It's the only way to get anyone's attention on a crowded street," she'd said. "That's why the bellboys
whistle to hail a cab in Manhattan. No point standing around
waving like a helpless woman for hours on end."

Clara turned her head, her face creasing into a disapproving
frown when she saw that it was me who'd made the noise. I stuck
out my tongue, and while I knew I'd already embarrassed her, I
saw her lips curve into a smile. I'd forgotten how easily I could
make her laugh, how a smile changed her face from prim and
pretty to charming and radiant. As she made her way toward me,
I was also reminded why everyone loved her and that I'd always
been the other girl beside her, the younger, difficult sister skulk-
ing in the background.

While we hadn't been so different as young girls, adolescence
and adulthood had emphasized Clara's petite beauty and my
gangling awkwardness. More and more, I'd noticed how everyone's gaze alighted on her while I was ignored until eventually,
I'd stopped caring, stopped trying to impress and be someone I

could never be. The question now, I supposed, was: Who *could* I be? Who *was* Madeleine Sommers?

Violet said I was a work in progress. "You'll figure it out, Maddie," she'd said as I'd kissed her goodbye. "You'll find your chapters and your epilogue. While you're busy delving into everyone else's stories, don't neglect your own."

But other people's stories were so much easier to write.

Clara

$\mathscr{I}$ was as surprised as anyone to find myself at the pier in New York, the mighty *Queen Mary* soaring into the sky beside me. Although I'd made it this far, I was still apprehensive about the prospect of traveling to Europe, especially with Madeleine. Even as I'd packed the last of my things just an hour earlier, I still wasn't sure if it was the most ridiculous thing I'd ever agreed to, or the most thrilling. In the end, I'd agreed to go because there were more reasons to undertake the trip than not. More reasons than I was prepared to admit, even to myself.

Madeleine beamed an annoying self-satisfied smile when she saw me weaving through the crowds. I left my luggage in the care of a porter who assured me, twice, that he would take it directly to our stateroom, and I joined my sister in the line for first-class ticket holders.

"Must you really make such a spectacle, whistling like a hotel bellboy?" I chided.

"You came, then?" she said, ignoring my admonishment and making no attempt to conceal her sarcasm.

"Of course I came. You didn't really think I'd let you travel to Europe alone?"

"Actually, I didn't think you could bear to be away from Chuck for so long."

"I am perfectly capable of making my own decisions, Madeleine. And please don't call him Chuck. His name is Charles." I turned to face her. "I'm here because Violet asked me to be, and whatever reservations I have about spending the next few months in your company, I would go around the world with you twice if it was what Violet wished. Besides," I continued, tipping my chin to take in the sight of the majestic *Queen Mary,* "the chance to see Paris and Venice was far too tempting. I doubt even you will be able to spoil such beautiful cities."

"Oh, you underestimate me. I'm sure I'll do my best." She lit a cigarette. "I see you dressed for the occasion," she continued, eyeing my outfit with a bemused expression.

"I did. And I can see that you most definitely didn't. Really, Madeleine, you'd think you were traveling in steerage." I shuddered at her poor choice of navy slacks and sensible shoes, and the untidy curls of strawberry blond hair she hadn't bothered to pin properly beneath her hat.

She laughed. "I dressed as someone about to travel across the Atlantic. I give you ten minutes on the promenade deck in that flimsy dress before you'll be running to the stateroom for an extra coat."

I decided to ignore her. Madeleine knew nothing about fashion. If she wanted to dress like a pack mule there was very little I could do about it. Soon, I would be walking through the great halls of Europe's finest art galleries and museums. I would focus on that, not on how easily my sister soured my mood.

"I half expected Chuck to have a change of heart," Madeleine remarked as we moved forward in the line. "I know he doesn't like you to be more than a few feet away from him at any given time."

I bristled. Why must she always be so condescending? "I have Charles's full support for the trip. He thinks it will be good for me to see a little of the world before I become a wife and mother."

"Mother?" Madeleine's eyes widened with exaggerated surprise. "You should have said, Clara. I'd have brought my crochet hooks to make a bonnet."

Color rushed to my cheeks. "Don't be ridiculous! I meant, in time."

Thankfully, our conversation was interrupted by the announcement that we could start boarding. My stomach lurched. This was it, then. No going back.

"Charles only wants what is best for me," I added as we prepared to board. "And he'll join me in Vienna so we can travel home together on the *Hindenburg* and then we'll be married and there's not a thing you can do about it. I don't know why you must be so entirely against him."

Madeleine smirked. "I see him for who, and what, he is. I'm not blinded by his slicked-back hair or his dreamy blue eyes. Where is he, anyway? No tearful farewell?"

I huffed at her reply. "We've already said our goodbyes. In private."

The truth was, I'd asked Charles not to come to the pier. I'd told him it would only make me emotional.

Madeleine turned her attention to a slim volume in her hands.

"What's that you're reading?" I asked, glad to change the subject.

"Jules Verne's *Around the World in Eighty Days*. I thought I should read it since we're here partly because of it. This copy belonged to Auntie Nellie. Look. She inscribed her name inside and crossed out the eighty on the title page and changed it to *Around the World in* Seventy-Two *Days*! She left the book to Violet when she died. Violet gave it to me for good luck."

I placed my hand in my coat pocket and felt for the pocket watch Violet had pressed into my hands that morning. "It belonged to dear Nellie," she'd said. "She took it with her on her race around the world, so that she would always know what time it was back home. She gave it to me just before she died, said it had always brought her luck. I think she'd like for you to have that luck now." I decided not to mention it to Madeleine.

"I've taken the liberty of writing out some rules," I announced, changing the subject before Madeleine launched into another of her monologues about Auntie Nellie and how inspired by her she was. As the line inched slowly forward, I fished in my handbag for the page of writing paper I'd folded neatly inside and handed it to Madeleine.

She scrunched her nose in disdain. "Rules?"

"Yes. I thought it would be helpful to establish some dos and don'ts. So we know where we stand."

She took the piece of paper from me and began to read aloud. "You must refer to me as Clara, not Sis. You must let me do the talking in any difficult situations. You must avoid eye contact with strange men. You must not refer to Charles as Charlie, Chuck, or *him*. You mustn't mention the wedding, unless you have something good to say about it."

Madeleine looked at me and rolled her eyes. "Really, Clara? You couldn't resist, could you?" She folded my page of rules and proceeded to tear it into pieces.

I stared at her in shock. "What on earth are you doing?"

Ignoring me, she walked to the edge of the pier and scattered the torn fragments onto the water.

"I'm feeding the fish." She brushed her hands against her slacks. "How about this for a rule," she continued. "There *are* no rules. We make it up as we go along. Let fate, luck, and chance be our guides." She turned back to face the ocean, her hands on her hips, her feet splayed inelegantly. "Who knows what's waiting for us out there, Clara." She swept her arm in a long arc across the vast expanse of the Hudson stretching out ahead. "Aren't you excited? We're free women! We can be whatever and whomever we choose. This is the one time in our lives when we don't have to abide by anybody's rules! I say we embrace it."

Her enthusiasm was hard to ignore. A shiver ran across my skin as I gazed at the water, the horizon beckoning.

"You're starting to sound like her," I said.

"Like who?"

"Auntie Nellie. Next you'll be telling me you only brought one bag and one dress for the entire journey."

She laughed. "You know me too well."

"You didn't? Really?"

"No. I didn't. I brought two bags, and two dresses. How many pairs of shoes did you bring anyway? I saw the poor porter struggling with your trunks."

I was about to chastise her for teasing me when I heard my name being called.

"Clara! Clara, wait!"

I turned and reached up onto my tiptoes to see who was causing such a commotion.

"Isn't that Edward Arnold?" Madeleine said. "Your art tutor? What's he doing here?"

I stared in disbelief, my heart clattering as Edward threaded his way through the line, apologizing and excusing himself as he sent people scattering. He was tall and easy to spot, and the sun glistened against the gray in his hair. He said it made him look old, although he had only just turned forty. I thought it looked distinguished.

His mouth broke into a wide smile when he saw me. "Oh good! I made it! I thought I was too late."

Too shocked to speak, I was glad of Madeleine's interjection.

"Edward, what a surprise!" she said. "Did you run all the way from the West Village?"

He gripped his sides as he caught his breath. "Nearly all the way! I'm not as fit as I used to be!"

"Are you traveling to France, too?" she added since I was still unable to find my tongue.

He shook his head. "Unfortunately not, Miss Sommers. But hopefully to Venice." He turned his attention to me then. "I wanted to give you this, Clara. For the trip. I meant to give it to you when I saw you yesterday, but I found it still sitting on the countertop when I opened the gallery this morning." He handed a book-sized parcel to me, wrapped in brown paper and tied with string.

"For me?" I asked. "But whatever—"

"Just something small. Watercolors, to encourage you to paint the sights. You said you might. Now, I hope you will."

I didn't know what to say, what to do, where to look. To see Edward here, with such a thoughtful gift and the light dancing in his eyes . . . I felt the heat rise in my cheeks, despite trying to present an air of casual calm. "That's terribly kind of you, Edward, but really you shouldn't have. . . . I . . . thank you."

We were holding up the line. The passengers behind us began to grow impatient.

"We have to board," Madeleine urged. "Come along, Clara."

Edward looked at me, a broad smile on his lips. I smiled back, unable to hide my delight. Nobody had ever done anything so unexpected and thoughtful for me.

Someone behind us grumbled about the holdup and another shouted about being left behind on the docks.

"Clara," Madeleine repeated, a warning note in her voice.

"Have the most wonderful time," Edward said. "They say the light in Venice is the best anywhere in Europe. I can't wait to see it for myself."

"You're going, then?" He'd told me about an exhibition he was due to attend in Venice later that month but hadn't decided if he would go. Things were a little strained between him and his wife and he'd worried that spending time apart might prove to be the final nail in the coffin.

"Yes," he replied. "I'm going. How can I not?"

He paused, holding my gaze before stepping aside to let the

passengers behind him move forward, and I found myself propelled up the gangway toward a narrow door in the side of the vessel.

I turned at the top before entering the ship. Edward stood in a pool of sunlight, his rumpled hair waving in the breeze, the sleeves of his shirt rolled to his elbows as if he'd just put down his brush. He hadn't worn a hat or a jacket. Edward wasn't bothered by such things. He was a true artist, his mind too busy working through a palate of color combinations, or the details he'd add to his latest tableau, to worry about things like hats and propriety. I smiled, all thoughts of arguments with Madeleine forgotten as I waved a final farewell and followed my sister inside.

"Yesterday?" she said, eyeing me suspiciously. "What were you doing at Edward's gallery yesterday? I'd have thought you'd be too busy saying goodbye to Charlie."

I studied a sign on the wall, deep in concentration as I checked which direction our stateroom was in. The detailed labyrinth of decks, restaurants, leisure rooms and lounges, corridors, and stairwells was both exhilarating and alarming. How would we ever find our way around, and—more to the point—if the deck map of a ship was overwhelming, how would we ever manage with a map of Paris?

"That's none of your business," I said as I set off down a long corridor to the left. "But, if you must know, we were working on pointillism. Paintings made up of lots of tiny dots. It's a fascinating technique. Seurat and Signac became famous for it. I think it may become a favorite of mine. Not that you'd care about any of that." I was talking too much in my attempt to distract her. Madeleine was tenacious. When she detected a story, she pursued it relentlessly, and I really didn't want her poking her nose into my private life. "I hope the porters have been efficient with the luggage," I continued. "I'd like the stewardess to unpack my dresses before they get too creased."

As I pressed on, Madeleine remained unusually quiet, and the question of my visiting Edward's gallery yesterday hung in the air around us. If I knew my sister at all, she was simply biding her time to raise it again. When she did, I would hopefully have a suitable answer.

Maddie

Clara was hiding something, I could tell. She'd lit up the moment Edward arrived with his gift, though she'd tried to play the polite art student. Edward was an older man, and a married man. It was a delicious nugget of gossip. I wondered how much time she'd spent with him since I'd last seen her a year ago, and—more to the point—whether Charles was aware of the obvious attraction between the two of them. He was so self-absorbed he probably hadn't noticed.

After getting hopelessly lost, for which I blamed Clara, we enlisted the help of a steward to direct us to our stateroom. The long passageways were elegantly decorated with sconces along the walls in the style of Art Deco and plush carpeting. Seascapes and other nautical art hung from a gilded picture rail. Clara stopped to study the paintings, drawn to pictures as naturally as I was drawn to words and stories. As she clutched Edward's parcel to her chest, I wondered what particular story might be revealed from the contents inside.

At last, we reached our stateroom. It was similarly decorated with luxurious carpets and rugs, rich mahogany paneling, and two large beds made up with silk sheets and colorful bedspreads. We hadn't shared a room since we were little girls, giggling in the dark about Father's stern words over supper, and planning our futures in whispered secrets, imagining the house we would live in together because we couldn't imagine spending a moment apart.

"Will it do?" I teased as I threw my smaller bag, and myself, onto one of the beds. Violet had spared no expense. I already felt a million miles away from my small Manhattan apartment.

"It's beautiful," Clara replied as she reappeared from inspecting the en suite bathroom and ran her hand over the smooth bedspread. "It's still a shame it has to be on the water. They say the Atlantic is a mile deep in places."

"Well, it would be difficult to see Europe if we stayed anchored beside the pier." I opened my suitcase, tossed everything onto the bed, put my toiletries on the dressing table, and set a stack of the morning's newspapers on the writing desk to read later. "Why do you always think something bad is going to happen? Try to relax and enjoy yourself. For once."

Clara glanced at my side of the room and exhaled an exasperated breath. "We've been here three minutes and you've already made the room look as if it has been ransacked. I might like to put my toiletries on the dressing table, too."

I knew my disorganized clutter bothered her, and always had, but I didn't intend to waste a minute of precious time aboard this amazing vessel putting everything neatly away. She'd have to learn to live with it.

"Move things around, if you must," I said as I stretched out on the bed and placed my hands behind my head. It really was exceptionally comfortable.

After watching Clara rearrange her potions and powders for a good ten minutes, I couldn't stand it anymore. I leaped up from the bed, stuffed my journal, pens, and Violet's notebook into my handbag, and grabbed my coat. "I'm going up to watch our departure," I said. "Are you coming?"

Clara glanced at the unopened parcel from Edward that sat on the end of her bed. "I'll follow you up in a bit," she replied. "You go ahead."

So, she was waiting for me to leave, for some privacy.

I didn't bother to hide a knowing smile as I left her alone and made my way back along the corridors and up several stairwells until I found the exit to the sun deck. Crowds of passengers were already gathered around the ornate iron railings, ready to wave a final farewell to loved ones and well-wishers. I savored the buzz of anticipation, the anxious glances at pocket watches and wristwatches. Everyone was eager to set sail and yet there was the inevitable pang of leaving loved ones, and the sense of trepidation that always accompanies the start of a new journey. My thoughts turned to Violet. This was her last wish, but I still felt torn by going so far away when all I truly wanted was to stay close to her.

I held my hand to my head to save my hat from the breeze. Just as I was beginning to feel a little chilly, the ship's whistle signaled our leaving, the anchor was lifted, and slowly, gracefully, *Queen Mary* slipped her moorings. My stomach dipped in excitement. At last, we were on our way.

"I guess there's no going back now, is there." Clara's voice came from behind me.

I glanced to my right as she joined me at the railing. "Nope. You're stuck with me, Sis."

"I really wish you wouldn't call me that," she said as she gripped the railing tightly. She tilted her head back, her face open to the cold breeze.

"And I really wish you wouldn't nag me all the time, but here we are."

Clara looked down at the water, before wincing and turning away. "I think I'll take a walk inside, see what all the fuss is about. Apparently there's a tennis court somewhere, and Turkish baths."

"You go on. I'm going to stay up here and write a little while everything is fresh in my mind. I'll meet you at lunch."

That was the partial truth, anyway. I already felt the urge to write, to capture the sense of departure on the page, but I also wanted to explore the ship on my own. We might be traveling together, but we didn't have to spend every moment together. I knew we both preferred it that way.

Before long, New York faded from view, the familiar skyline steadily shrinking to nothing more than a stack of gray blocks tumbling into the sea. I scribbled a few lines in my journal. I planned to document every interesting thing I saw on our trip, and to capture every farewell and arrival along the way. As for articles, I already had a few ideas brewing: Women traveling alone. Following in Nellie Bly's footsteps. How Europe was coping with the rise of dictatorships. This was a chance to write about something that I couldn't do justice to from New York, a chance to really get under the skin of a place, to experience things firsthand, just like Nellie had always tried to do. First and foremost, we were making this journey for Violet, but I couldn't deny the fact that it was also an opportunity to write something powerful, to really kick-start my career. The *New York Times, New York Post, Cosmopolitan* . . . they all awaited. I lit a cigarette and let a determined smile linger at my lips.

Settling in one of the many deck chairs, and grateful for the wool blanket I draped over my knees, I pulled Violet's notebook from my bag, and ran my hands over the faded ink on the first few pages. She'd carefully documented each step of Nellie's race around the world, every stage of the journey meticulously dated and labeled alongside a newspaper clipping.

Departure on a steamer from New York—November 14, 1889

Halfway around the world—December 19, 1889

Triumphant final train ride into Jersey City—January 25, 1890

She'd even included a blank coupon from the *New York World*'s guessing competition. I smiled at the image of a young woman lassoing the globe. How apt for an adventurer like Auntie Nellie, and now I would follow suit. Turning the page, I saw that Violet had also copied snippets of Nellie's writings from her trip:

My head felt dizzy and my heart felt as if it would burst. Only seventy-five days! Yes, but it seemed an age and the world lost its roundness and seemed a long distance with no end, and—well, I never turn back. . . . "I am off," I thought sadly, "and shall I ever get back?"

I became lost in Nellie's words, her bold voice speaking to me as clearly as if she were standing beside me, encouraging me in her forthright way. *Get on with it, Maddie. If you don't write it, you can be sure as hell somebody else will.*

She was right. It was time to get on with it, time to become the journalist I really wanted to be.

Clara

Edward's arrival at the dockside had come as such a shock that the contents of his gift—the most beautiful set of Winsor & Newton watercolor paints and brushes—did nothing to calm my emotions. But it was the accompanying letter that surprised me the most.

Glad to have a few moments alone in our cabin and away from Madeleine's prying eyes, I read his words over and over, my hands shaking as I tried to come to terms with his honesty, his passion, and his intent.

I find myself unable to imagine the weeks passing without our usual lessons and laughter. Your going away has made me realize how much I enjoy your company, Clara, and I will miss you terribly. Which is why I have settled on attending the exhibition in Venice after all, despite Annabel's lingering resentment about my career, and my desire to see it grow. Perhaps we were always meant to be in Venice at the same time? Perhaps fate, and your dear grandmother, have intervened! The truth is that life with Annabel lately feels like sitting at an old canvas, a

*tired thing to be reused over and over. When I'm with you,
there is only purity and newness and such wonderful possibility.*

*I have included, below, the address of the hotel I'll be staying
at while I'm in Venice. It would make me so happy to hear from
you while I'm there.*

I didn't know what to think, what to do. I was marrying
Charles in a matter of months. There could never be anything
more than a mutual love of art between Edward and me. Could
there?

A knock at the door disturbed me.

Quickly, I put the paints and brushes on the writing table and
pushed the letter among the pile of newspapers Madeleine had
infuriatingly left lying around. Flustered, I opened the door to a
stewardess carrying an enormous bouquet of white roses.

"For you, Miss Sommers," she said as she bustled inside, filled
a vase with water in the bathroom, and proceeded to arrange the
roses. "Someone must be missing you already, and we've only just
departed!"

"Gosh. There are a lot," I replied as I gazed at the obscene
amount of flowers. I was a little embarrassed by the extravagance
and waited patiently for her to finish her job and leave. "Here," I
said, pulling a stem from the vase and handing it to her.

"Oh, I couldn't, miss."

"I insist. I'm not exactly going to notice one less, am I?"

Muttering a thank you, she took the stem and left with a smile
on her face.

My smile, meanwhile, dissolved as soon as she closed the door
behind her. I knew the roses were from Charles even before I

picked up the accompanying note. *Darling Clara. Have a wonderful trip. I will be thinking of you.*

I'd never told him I didn't care for roses, and he'd always assumed that, like most women, they were a favorite. As I stared at the impressive display, and Edward's thoughtful art supplies beside them, it struck me that I preferred the wrong man's gift.

Overwhelmed by the heady perfume of the flowers, and by an overwhelming sense of guilt, I left the cabin in a hurry.

THE ILLUSTRIOUS *Queen Mary,* the pride of the Cunard-White Star Line, was enormous and I found myself tiring as I ascended yet another sweeping staircase. It would have been easier to take one of the many elevators, but I didn't trust them, so I continued my exploration without their assistance.

Options for entertainment, exercise, and dining on board were seemingly endless, the deck plans dizzying in their detail of indoor swimming pools, beauty salons, libraries and public rooms, outdoor paddle tennis courts, and dog kennels. The dining room for first-class passengers was three stories in height. It was almost inconceivable to think that such a construction was possible on a liner, floating on the ocean. I gave myself an ache in my neck from staring up at the columns and decorative ceilings.

Having explored as much as I wished to for the time being, I began to make my way back to the cabin, pausing briefly to admire the art in the observation lounge. I wasn't familiar with the work of the artist but recognized the style as Cubism. I admired the abstract imagery and the unusual use of texture and color. It was a technique I hadn't attempted yet, and I wondered if I might try it once we arrived in Paris.

In the weeks after Violet had announced her plan for our trip, she'd talked a lot about the great works of the Renaissance and Impressionist masters I would see. She knew that the prospect of seeing Canaletto's views of Venice and Degas's beautiful ballet dancers might just make up for the fact that I would have to spend time with Madeleine, and time away from Charles. "Imagine seeing some of the most famous paintings in the world! I don't know many artists who would turn down such an opportunity." While she had diminished in height over the years, Violet certainly hadn't lost any of her powers of persuasion.

I continued on to the first-class restaurant but stopped as my attention was drawn to an enormous painting titled *Birds of the Old World*. It depicted peacocks in the most glorious colors, and I couldn't take my eyes off it. Something about their beauty and freedom spoke to me.

"Beautiful, isn't it?"

Startled by the voice at my shoulder, I turned to see an elderly gentleman admiring the painting beside me.

"Yes. It's striking," I agreed. "The use of color is so interesting."

He studied me with narrowed eyes. "You must be an artist."

I nodded. "Trying to be. I'm hoping to find inspiration from the masters in Paris and Venice."

"I envy you," he said with a sigh. "I'm afraid my journey isn't quite so romantic."

"Oh?"

"I'm returning to my family in Austria, but I'm not entirely sure what I'll discover when I get there." He pointed to his skull-cap. "My religion is not tolerated there as it once was."

"Ah." I fidgeted with my hands, unsure of what to say. "I'm afraid I don't know too much about it, only what I hear from my sister. She's a journalist, of sorts. She's been following the rise of the Nazi Party. She rather obsesses about it."

He smiled thinly and rubbed the whiskers on his chin. "She is right to be informed. With knowledge comes power."

"Well, when it comes to my sister, knowledge more often comes with trouble."

He chuckled softly. "Sisters, huh. No greater friends or more loathsome enemies!" He held out his hand. "A pleasure to meet you, Miss . . ."

"Sommers," I replied, shaking his hand.

"I hope you and your sister can enjoy your travels safely." He pulled a prayer book from his coat pocket. "I will include you both in my prayers. The *Queen Mary* is the first liner to have a Jewish prayer room, a stance by the shipping line against anti-Semitism in Nazi Germany. Let's hope others will follow."

He tipped his hat and bid me farewell. As I watched him walk away with the assistance of his cane, I worried anew about traveling through Europe when it was clearly heading in the direction of another war. I decided to share my concerns with Madeleine over dinner, even though I disliked talking to her about politics and there was very little we could do about it now that we were already en route.

The motion of the ship, while minimal, was enough to make

me unsteady on my feet and I braced myself against this wall and that wall as I made my way back to our stateroom, only to discover that I was on the wrong side of the ship.

A young steward, whom I stopped to ask for assistance, looked amused as he explained that I was on the starboard side of the vessel.

"Your cabin is port side aft, miss." He threw nautical terms at me as if I were a sailor and had any idea what he was talking about. "Would you like me to escort you?"

I assured him I was perfectly capable of finding my own way, but quickly regretted my decision as I took another wrong turn and found myself back at the observation deck in front of the birds again.

Tired of getting lost, I ordered a ginger ale to help settle the queasiness that had come on suddenly, took a seat beside the window, and thought again about Edward's letter and his planned visit to Venice. Would it be improper for us to meet? We were simply two friends visiting a couple of art galleries, that was all. What harm would there be in that?

As my thoughts wandered, I gazed at the painting and the sense of freedom among the birds, and I wondered if Madeleine was right in what she'd said about us being free for once, at liberty to go where we liked and do as we pleased. Perhaps I should embrace it while I had the chance, before I became Mrs. Charles Hancock, and the duties of marriage and motherhood closed around me. Violet and Mother both said my doubts were perfectly normal and that all brides-to-be felt that way. Despite my apprehension, I was very fond of Charles. He had his faults, certainly, but I wasn't without fault myself, and I'd never want for anything with him as my husband. Besides, it was too late to start second-guessing myself with the wedding already planned and the invitations sent.

Like the *Queen Mary* conveying me across the ocean, some things, once set in motion, were very difficult to stop.

Maddie

After a few hours, we'd sailed far out to sea, and my grumbling stomach reminded me I needed lunch. I closed Violet's notebook, careful to mark my place, and returned to our cabin to stow my things and collect Clara before heading to the restaurant. But Clara wasn't in our cabin. She'd probably gone to chastise one of the stewardesses, or to complain about bed linens. She was such a nag. The fact that I found her endless complaining amusing seemed to irritate her all the more.

Without Clara casting a critical eye over my every move, I looked around our room properly, pulling open all the drawers and cabinets to see what was what. Her pressed clothing hung from hangers or sat in neat folds in the drawers, and her makeup creams and powders were arranged in a perfect row on the vanity. *Of course* they were. I pushed one out of line to see if she would notice and walked to the desk to store my writing things in the drawer. As I pulled it open, I was surprised to see Auntie Nellie's old pocket watch beside Clara's lace handkerchiefs.

What was Clara doing with Auntie Nellie's pocket watch? I

picked it up and read the inscription: *Never turn back. November 14, 1889.* Violet must have given it to Clara the same way she'd given me Nellie's copy of *Around the World in Eighty Days.* Still, I felt a pang of jealousy. Why would she give it to Clara rather than me, the one who admired Nellie most? Clara didn't even like Nellie very much. She'd always found her brash and intimidating. Frowning, I returned the watch to the drawer and made a mental note to ask Clara about it later.

As I straightened, I noticed the package from Edward had been opened, the contents lying loosely on the desk, the brown paper and string crumpled in the wastebasket. It was unlike Clara to leave her things lying about in this way. She must have been interrupted by a stewardess, or perhaps realized lunch was being served and left in a rush.

I glanced at the door. Clara had cleverly avoided my question about her being at the art gallery with Edward yesterday morning, but I wasn't ready to let the issue drop. Working quickly, I riffled through the things he'd given her: a set of watercolor paints, brushes, and a small sketchbook. Nice of him, really. He clearly knew what she liked.

I pushed aside the gift and reached for my stack of newspapers. As I lifted them up, a pale blue envelope fell out from between their pages. It was addressed simply: *Clara.* I turned it over. The seal was already broken, the letter having been read and stuffed back inside.

I looked over my shoulder at the door again. I'd dug through Clara's things more than a few times as a child. An older sister's belongings were always fascinating to the younger, and apparently that hadn't changed. She would accuse me of being a snoop if she ever found out, but didn't that come with the territory of having a journalist for a sister?

It took only a moment to decide to read the letter.

As I skimmed over it, my eyes widened, but as I reached the end, I heard the turn of a key in the door. I quickly shoved the letter into the pocket of my slacks and rushed into the bathroom.

"They're serving lunch, Madeleine." Clara had returned. "We'd better hurry or we'll miss it."

"Coming," I replied. "I was just powdering my nose."

It was a ridiculous thing to say. I never powdered my nose, and Clara knew it. Luckily, she seemed too preoccupied to notice.

I pulled the letter from my pocket, folded it neatly, and returned it to the envelope. I would slip it back into the stack of papers as soon as I had the chance. Clara would never know I'd read it. Until, that was, I decided to confront her about it.

AFTER LUNCH, DURING which we disagreed about the wine, how best to cook steak, and which cheeses to request for the cheeseboard, I told Clara I wanted to spend some time in the library.

"What will you do for the afternoon?" I asked as I stuffed a few after-dinner mints in my handbag, earning a disapproving scowl from Clara in the process.

"I'll come with you. I spotted a few art books earlier I'd like to read."

I'd really hoped she would make herself scarce, but I shrugged and told her to hurry up with her coffee.

The library was empty except for one man who sat on a long

couch beneath the large picture windows that offered impressive views out over the ocean. On the opposite wall, bookcases ran the length of the room. Clara set out to find her precious art books while I made my way to the newspaper rack in the corner. I sorted through them and carried several to a table, where I spread them out in front of me.

After reading the *Washington Post* and the *New York Times,* I flicked through those I'd found from other countries, in particular Germany's *Berliner Tageblatt* and France's *Le Figaro.* The French I'd learned in school held up surprisingly well, and though I didn't speak German, I studied the headlines and photographs, piecing together the information with the help of a German dictionary I'd cleverly brought with me.

There was nothing particularly concerning happening in France of late, though Hitler's name appeared in several headlines, including one about the Maginot Line, the wall of concrete and steel that had been extended in February, and which the French believed would stop the Germans attempting an invasion. I wondered if it could really prevent tanks from smashing through the border and found myself hoping, for France's sake, it would work. I found several mentions of Italy's involvement with the Spanish Civil War as well, and Mussolini's admiration of Hitler's military might. It was clear that Italy would join forces with Germany if things did escalate as far as another war. Dictatorships seemed to be on the rise, a frightening development for Europe.

I made lots of notes, completely losing track of time until Clara touched me on the shoulder. Engrossed in my reading, I jumped, and then laughed at my edginess.

"It's the Jewish man I met earlier," she said, tone hushed. "The one I mentioned to you over lunch. Do you mind if I invite him to sit with us?"

I perked up. "Actually, I'd like to talk to him."

Clara walked over to him and showed him to our table. I felt myself thaw a little toward my sister. She was capable of being kind when it mattered.

The older gentleman was hunched slightly, wore a dark blue suit and tie with a gleaming gold tie pin, and his hair was snow white and bushy around his ears. As he sat across from Clara and me, he smiled.

"I believe you are Miss Sommers's sister," he said, as he extended a hand in greeting. "I'm Jacob Klein."

"A pleasure to meet you," I said, shaking his hand. As was true to my nature, I dove right in, not holding back from the question on my mind. "I hear you're traveling to Austria. I've been following the events there, and in Germany, the last few years. Things look potentially unstable."

He nodded solemnly. "We are in trouble, I fear. Hitler is a powerful man, and he's gaining momentum in Europe."

"Yes, it seems so," I said gravely. "Backing Franco in Spain with aid for his civil war and palling around with Mussolini in Italy."

"My, you *are* following the news."

"I'm a journalist," I said, feeling a rush of pleasure at claiming the title though I didn't yet have an official position with a newspaper, not even as a paper runner. Still, I'd written enough articles to earn the right to call myself one, and Clara didn't refute me. I felt an ounce of gratitude for her quiet acceptance.

"Very good," he replied. "We need more female journalists."

I took his encouragement as an invitation to talk about it more. "Mr. Klein, have you heard anything about the Nazi concentration camps?" My tone turned somber. "I know about Dachau near Munich, but there are rumors more are being built."

"Hitler sends whomever he likes there," the old man said, nodding soberly. "Political prisoners who are beaten to death. People who oppose his ideas, even if indirectly. And you are correct about the rumors. My family in Vienna have already warned me about the German soldiers harassing Austrian Jews. For one reason or another, the man despises us."

"Please be careful, Mr. Klein," Clara said, her brown eyes wide with concern.

"I am an old man," he said. "They won't want anything from me. It is the younger generation I am worried about. Our women and children."

As the conversation continued, I found myself captivated by this gentle man who seemed to carry such worry on his stooped shoulders. After a while, we switched to less serious topics, including our plans for delivering Violet's mysterious letters.

"I'd like to know if you manage to locate everyone. I feel quite invested in the outcome!" He smiled. "If you'd like any assistance when you are in Austria, please do look me up. I'd be delighted to help, or just to meet you both for coffee." He gave us his card. "This is my office address, near the Stephansplatz. There are many wonderful *Kaffeehäuser* nearby."

"Thank you, sir," I said, accepting his card. "We'd be delighted. I'll send a telegram when we arrive."

"Very good." He wished us luck, and bid us farewell, for now.

"What a lovely man," Clara remarked.

"Yes, he is, but did you hear what he said? Things are worse than I feared. There are German soldiers in Austria!"

I hoped, for his sake, Mr. Klein was right, and that the Germans would leave him and his family be. Yet my instincts warned me that danger lay ahead, and an unsettling feeling lingered.

"Can't we just forget about it?" Clara said, hugging her art books to her chest. "It's not as if two American women will be of any interest to these so-called regimes. I'd like to take your advice and enjoy the trip now that I'm here, not be looking over my shoulder everywhere we go."

I arched an eyebrow at her and folded the newspapers in exasperation. Even if the danger wasn't immediate, I couldn't understand Clara's insistence on sticking her head in the sand and detaching from the reality around us. But she'd always been that way, and while we probably didn't have any real reason to worry, the world wasn't a carefree place anymore. Like Clara, I wanted to enjoy our trip, too, but I also hoped we might find a little danger along the way. Fun and enjoyment were all well and good, but danger was far better inspiration for a journalist's pen.

"I'm going to lie down," Clara added suddenly. "I think I might be a little seasick."

"Already? We're hardly off the Hudson." I had an iron stomach apparently, just one more difference between us. "Who sent the roses by the way? Chuck, or Edward?" I asked, unable to resist needling her about the extravagant display that had arrived in our room.

Clara glared at me. "They're from Charles, of course."

"I thought you didn't like roses."

"I don't." She looked, for a moment, as if she might say something else but changed her mind. "What are you planning to do for the rest of the day, apart from convincing yourself we're heading for war?"

I tossed my handbag over my shoulder. "I'm going to gamble away my fortune with some unseemly men. Get a little drunk, perhaps."

She rolled her eyes at me. "Really, Madeleine. Must you?"

"Yes, Clara. I must. You should try it sometime."

"What? Gambling and drinking!"

"Living a little."

We parted ways, each with a frosty look.

I stalked off in search of the games room. I could hear it before I found it, the sound of laughter and good-natured shouting drifting down the corridor.

I paused in the doorway and took in the scene. The room was hazy with cigar smoke and though tables filled the space, there were only three players, all of them men. I smiled. This was the kind of adventure I was looking for, not gilded wall sconces and polite conversation over expensive white wine.

I strode nonchalantly to the table. All eyes turned to me, surprised to see a woman from the upper crust who dressed more like a man. I'm certain they didn't know what to make of me.

"Hello, gentlemen. Mind if I join you?" I didn't wait for an invitation and sat in the empty chair.

One of the men stared at me, openmouthed. "You know how to play?"

"Do I ever! Deal, mister."

Ten minutes later, I'd already earned their respect and found myself with a whiskey in hand and a pile of winning chips in front of me. Clara would have been absolutely scandalized by my behavior, which only made it all the more fun.

After my third round of blackjack with an Irishman and a jovial fellow from Ohio, an impressive gentleman named Daniel Miller joined the table, and the game changed to poker. He was from Boston, he informed us, but lived in New York City, and was headed to Paris to visit a cousin. He shared a lot of personal information too easily, and I resisted the invitation to share anything in return. All I offered was that I was traveling to Paris with my sister.

"Will you remain in Paris?" Mr. Miller inquired. "Or do you and your sister have extensive travel plans?"

I regarded his dark eyes and thick frame. He was handsome, though a bit stiff around the collar.

"That's none of your business, sir," I replied, laying down a flush. Everyone around the table goaded each other for losing to a woman. Again. I flashed a devilish smile. "Really, gentlemen, can't you do any better?"

The Irishman stubbed out his cigar. "You're impossible to read, Miss Sommers."

"And your mustache twitches when you lie, sir."

The Irishman guffawed and Mr. Miller laughed, pulling a cigar from his pocket. He lit it with a match and puffed on the end until a tiny flame caught on the dried tobacco. I smoked a cigarette from time to time when the situation warranted it: when I was frustrated with my writing, after a particularly nice meal, or, especially, when I wanted to irritate Clara. Now, I wondered what a cigar tasted like and decided I'd try one before the trip was over.

"They say Paris is the city of romance," Mr. Miller said, propping his cigar in an ashtray.

"Is that so." I accepted a new hand of cards, freshly shuffled. I kept my expression blank—I had another excellent hand.

"Maybe you'll fall in love in Paris, Miss Sommers," the Irishman said, a grin on his face.

I snorted. "Perhaps you'll fall into the Seine. Women do think about things other than romance."

The Irishman laughed.

"Not much for men, are you?" Mr. Miller added.

"They're all the same, so, no, I'm not interested, thank you very much."

Amusement stamped his features, though I couldn't be sure if it was because of my reply or the jovial ambiance in the room.

"What'll you wager, Miss Sommers?" he asked, straightening his stack of poker chips.

Grateful for the change of subject, I glanced at my pile of winnings. I was up considerably. "I'll double whatever you add to the pot."

He tossed two poker chips in the middle of the table.

I added four.

"The gauntlet has been thrown!"

The game lasted longer than the others before it, and with each turn around the table, the tension grew until no one spoke. Mr. Miller scrutinized my face, my hands, my every movement. He was watching me for signs—my tells—but I had none, just as I'd been taught. I hardly breathed. At last, when his turn came again, he played a winning hand.

I frowned, wondering how I'd slipped.

"You don't like to lose, do you Miss Sommers?" Mr. Miller said, his tone teasing.

I smiled sweetly. "I wouldn't know. I rarely do."

He grinned, pulling the spoils toward him. "Where did you learn to play poker?" he asked as he reached for his nearly empty glass.

"My grandmother."

He nearly spit out his scotch. "Your grandmother taught you to play poker?"

"Does that surprise you?" I laughed at Mr. Miller's bemused expression and thought how Violet would have been amused to see me put her well-taught skills to good use.

"Everything about you surprises me," he replied as he finished the last of his drink.

Standing, I reached for my handbag. "It was fun, gentlemen, but if you will excuse me, I should check on my sister."

"I've never been bested by a lass, but the pleasure was all ours," the Irishman said, winking.

"It's getting late, isn't it." Mr. Miller glanced at his wristwatch. "Nearly time for dinner." He stood as well, reached for his hat, and tipped it toward me. "You make fine company, Miss Sommers—"

"Maddie," I said. "And thank you, Daniel. You aren't a bad player yourself, though your bluff could use a little work."

The trio of gentlemen chortled and exchanged a few choice words as I closed the door behind me.

I smiled to myself as I walked back to the cabin. I must have seemed like a curious creature to them—playing poker, drinking whiskey with men I'd just met, my hair wild after fighting with the sea breeze. No lady to be sure. But who cared what they thought of me? I would most likely never see them again, and that was fine by me.

And yet, Daniel Miller's expression of amusement lingered in my mind.

Clara

$\mathcal{U}$nsettled by the motion of the ship and irritated by my sister's insistence at trying to shock me with her unladylike behavior, I was glad to return to the cabin. Our stewardess was changing the bedsheets from silk to cotton as Madeleine had requested, but thankfully she was just finishing.

"Back already, miss?"

"Yes. I feel a little unwell. I'll take a rest when you're done."

Realizing I'd left Edward's gift lying around earlier, I went straight to the desk, but it was nowhere to be seen.

"Did you see some paints here?" I asked.

"I tidied a few things away, miss. I put them in the drawer."

They were, indeed, neatly placed inside the desk drawer beside the pocket watch and my handkerchiefs, but Edward's letter wasn't with them. The stack of newspapers was gone.

I turned to the stewardess. "You haven't seen an envelope anywhere, have you? It was right here. On the desk. With some newspapers."

I had left it on the desk, hadn't I? I couldn't quite remember.

The stewardess looked confused. "An envelope? No, miss. I

took out the old newspapers earlier with the garbage." She reddened. "Perhaps I've thrown it away by mistake. I didn't see it, but . . . I'm terribly sorry, miss. Is it something important?"

I told her it wasn't and dismissed her.

When she'd gone, I let out a sigh of enormous disappointment. The letter *was* important, though I hadn't realized quite how much until now.

I took Edward's gifts from the drawer, and pushed my hands to the back, feeling around with my fingertips in the hope of finding the letter there. But I found nothing. It was gone, and now Edward's words, and the address of the hotel he would be staying at in Venice, were lost. How could I contact him when I arrived? Perhaps I was never meant to.

I sank onto my bed, utterly deflated. I only hoped the stewardess *had* thrown the letter out because the alternative was far worse. If Madeleine had found it and read it, how could I deny anything if she started asking awkward questions? Worse still, who might she tell? She wasn't known for her discretion and it would please her greatly to cause trouble between me and Charles.

My stomach lurched and my head thumped. I was relieved to slip into bed, pull on my eye mask, and hope I would feel better the next day.

I FELT WORSE.

Even the luxury and comfort of the *Queen Mary* couldn't prevent a dreadful bout of seasickness. The world tilted and swayed as wave after wave of nausea washed over me, and I dashed to the bathroom, before staggering back to my bed.

"It's a pity you're marrying a man who loves to sail," Madeleine teased. She didn't feel the least bit seasick and was enjoying making new acquaintances and eating like a horse, while I stayed in bed, feeling like death and willing the relentless seesawing motion to stop. "And to think you brought all those fine dresses for the captain's dinner. Such a shame to leave them hanging in the closet."

I groaned as I slumped against the pillows and told her she was welcome to borrow my dresses, if she could bear to look feminine, for once.

"I'll surely die before we ever reach France," I added.

Madeleine pressed a damp cloth to my forehead. "Don't make promises you can't keep. Now, drink this. Ginger tea. Apparently, it helps."

I was surprised Madeleine was so attentive. It had been a long time since we'd spared a kind word for each other, let alone a kind gesture.

"Daniel says you'll be perfectly well when we're on dry land," she continued.

"Daniel?"

"Mr. Miller. A theater critic from Boston. We met over a game of poker."

I groaned again. "Oh, Madeleine, really."

"It's funny how quickly you can get to know people when you're stuck on a ship together."

I pulled the covers over my head, unsure of which made me feel worse: my seasickness or my social disgrace of a sister.

"Please be careful," I added as I peered out from the covers. "You don't know anything about the man."

"Don't be such a wet blanket," she said, waving away my concern. "I'm never alone with him, and as soon as we get to France, I'll never see him again."

I nodded with a sigh but couldn't help thinking that nothing good would come of her mingling with strangers. My sister had a nasty habit of attracting men who didn't have her best interests at heart. I didn't trust this Daniel Miller, even though I'd never met him.

Over the next two days, I watched enviously from my sickbed as Madeleine came and went, leaving for dinner dressed to the nines and returning from the Starlight Club at some unmentionable hour, smelling of whiskey and fine perfume. She'd slid into life on the ocean like a well-seasoned traveler, thriving and vivacious, where I'd faltered and failed at the very first hurdle. The truth was, I envied Madeleine as we steamed toward France. I envied her refusal to conform, her insistence to go her own way. Mostly, I envied her ambition. She wanted to write about more interesting things than knitting patterns and homemaking and the frivolous subjects most female journalists were asked to write about, and she stuck with it, ever hopeful of some other, better opportunity to use her writing talents. I might not approve of her choice of profession, but I had to admire her tenacity.

As young ladies, we'd often performed for our parents' dinner party guests. My piano recitals were always enjoyed, and my better paintings drew gasps of admiration, while Madeleine's dark poetry was considered odd and left everyone grasping for the right words in response. Perhaps that had been the start of the resentment between us: I was praised lavishly while Madeleine rarely received a word of encouragement.

Our father had always blamed Auntie Nellie for stirring Madeleine's journalistic interests. He'd accused Nellie of putting silly ideas in her head and Nellie, in turn, had told him exactly what she thought of his archaic opinions of what was, and wasn't, suitable for his daughters. "Your daughters are smart girls, Mr. Sommers. Smart girls who can do anything they set their minds to. You shouldn't set limits for them." We'd often pressed our ears to the door and listened to their heated exchanges. We heard things we weren't meant to hear, and which Madeleine had never forgotten.

Our father's sudden death a year ago had left the family reeling. It had also driven a deeper wedge between Madeleine and me as we disagreed over our memories of him. Madeleine remembered a disapproving, distant man. I remembered a man of principle and firm encouragement. We'd left his funeral more divided than ever and the announcement of my marriage to Charles soon after had been the final straw. We hadn't spoken to, or seen each other, since. Not until Violet's summit at Veneto.

Madeleine increasingly lived a life without limits and without any regard for societal expectation. Ambition and possibility stretched ahead of her, while I lived a life of convention and duty, and now had the confines of married life to look forward to when we returned.

As I lay in bed, willing the heaving motion of the ship to stop, I found myself, once again, questioning if it was enough. Was there more to Clara Sommers than becoming Mrs. Charles Hancock? Was there something else I was meant to do? Someone else I was meant to be?

ON THE FOURTH morning at sea, I finally felt well enough to dress, eat a light breakfast, and sip a cup of coffee brought by the stewardess.

"You look a little better this morning, miss," she chirped as she set the tray beside the bed. "You might feel up to taking a stroll on the promenade deck later. It's a lovely morning. The sea is flat as a mill pond."

I'd never seen a mill pond but said I would take her word for it and that I would do my best to get some air.

"And would you remove the roses?" I added. "The petals are already browning."

"It's the sea air, miss. The salt. Fresh flowers don't do very well in it."

I offered a wry smile. "I know exactly how they feel."

By noon, I was able to take a walk without rushing to the railings every few minutes. The sea breeze was invigorating, and despite being a little chilly, I settled in one of the deck chairs and took out my sketchbook and pencils. I hadn't sketched for a while, and it felt good to move my pencil across the blank page, capturing interesting shapes, forms, and depth.

It was Violet who'd first encouraged my love of art, setting up arrangements of tea roses and peonies she'd cut from the garden, which I carefully studied, my brows knitted into a concentrated frown, my tongue poking out of the side of my mouth as I tried to replicate their image on my page. It was Violet who'd first arranged for an art tutor to visit Veneto during the school holidays, to teach me formal techniques and improve my natural talents. I'd loved those summers. Behind the easel, there was no need to impress or to be beautiful, clever, charming Clara. When that first tutor, dear Miss Ingram, passed away just a few years ago, Edward Arnold had taken her place. I'd found him intimidating at first, his demonstrative enthusiasm so different from Miss Ingram's gentle encouragement, but my initial shyness around him had mellowed quickly into admiration and then to anticipation as I found myself looking forward to our lessons.

Now, as I sketched a charming young family playing a game of shuffleboard on the deck, my thoughts turned again to Edward's lost letter as I tried to recall his words: *Your going away has made me realize how much I enjoy your company, Clara, and I will miss you terribly.... When I'm with you, there is only purity and newness and such wonderful possibility.*

I became so absorbed in my thoughts and my sketching, I didn't notice the gentleman standing at my shoulder, watching me work.

"It's a very good likeness," he remarked.

Startled, I dropped my pencil.

"I'm so sorry," he said, bending to retrieve it from beneath my chair. "I didn't mean to alarm you!"

"Thank you," I said as I took it from him. "I didn't notice you there. You gave me a fright!"

He apologized again. "It's hypnotic, watching you sketch. You do it very well."

I shrugged off the compliment. "It's something I dabble in now and again. That little boy has such an endearing face, I couldn't resist."

"Well, I'm sorry to interrupt you. Please, carry on."

I closed my sketchbook. "I couldn't possibly. Not with an audience. Besides, my hands are numb from this breeze."

"Daniel," he said, offering his hand. "Daniel Miller."

So, this was Madeleine's mysterious gentleman friend. "Clara," I replied, shaking his hand. "Clara Sommers. I believe you've met my sister. Madeleine."

His lips curved into a broad smile. "Aha! Yes. Your sister is quite the poker player. She'll have me bankrupt by the time we reach Cherbourg." He motioned to the empty deck chair beside me. "Do you mind if I join you for a moment?"

I did mind but was too polite to say so. I nodded toward the chair. "I must apologize for my sister. She's rather . . . unconventional."

At this, he laughed. "She's a breath of fresh air. Madeleine has made the journey almost bearable."

"You're not one for ocean travel?"

"Not really. I get a little restless after a day or two." He ran his hands through his hair to smooth it against the breeze. "She tells me the two of you are spending time in Europe together before returning to America on the *Hindenburg*. I'm quite envious! I find the airships fascinating."

I pulled on my gloves. "I wonder, is there anything my sister hasn't told you?"

He smiled. "Plenty, I'm sure, but a gentleman doesn't pry."

He was charming, granted. It was easy to see why Madeleine had encouraged the friendship. "And what is the purpose of *your* trip, Mr. Miller?" I asked in an attempt to change the direction of the conversation. "Culture? Business? Poker, perhaps? Madeleine mentioned that you work as a theater critic for the newspapers."

He cleared his throat. "Yes. I have a commission to review the new show at the Moulin Rouge."

"The Moulin Rouge? Isn't that rather . . . immoral?"

"I certainly hope so!" He laughed. "But my trip isn't all pleasure. I'm also visiting a cousin in Paris."

"Well, I'm sure he will be very pleased to see you."

"She," he corrected. "And perhaps not."

The man was a riddle.

I gathered my things and stood up. "It was a pleasure to meet you, Mr. Miller," I said, offering my hand in farewell. "If you'll excuse me, I must change for the captain's dinner tonight. I find I have an appetite, at last."

He stood also. "My apologies again for interrupting you." He nodded toward the sketchbook tucked under my arm. "I do hope you'll finish that. You clearly have a talent."

"I have an interest, Mr. Miller. Talent is too generous an accolade."

"We all have a talent for something, Miss Sommers."

"And what is your talent, Mr. Miller? Pressing compliments upon unsuspecting lady travelers?"

He laughed, tipped his hat, and strolled away.

I put the enigmatic Mr. Miller from my mind as I returned to our stateroom to change for the captain's farewell dinner. I pinned my hair into a chignon, refreshed my makeup, and decided on the champagne-colored gown I'd packed. It was perfect for the occasion. Even Madeleine said it looked "nice, the way it shimmers beneath the lights." She'd at least worn one of her better dresses, a red silk that made her look almost like a woman for once, not that she was too happy about it.

"Stop tugging at your slip," I scolded as we made our way to the first-class ballroom. "And pull your shoulders back. It'll hang properly then."

She muttered something about preferring me when I was bedridden, but I was in a good mood and ignored her.

Over a fine meal of turbot in lemon wine sauce, rack of lamb, and a decadent dessert of dark chocolate mousse and orange blossom cream, we chatted politely with the other guests at our table and took turns dancing with the captain and other senior members of the crew. I was relieved to see Madeleine mostly behaving herself, although things deteriorated as the night wore on and Daniel Miller appeared. He whisked Madeleine away for a dance or two before she became involved in a heated political discussion with several men I hadn't seen before. One by one, their wives stepped away to talk among themselves, but Madeleine carried on, refilling her glass too often.

I enjoyed a few dances myself, as Daniel proved to be the gallant sort, not leaving a lady on her own, but I eventually grew tired and returned to the cabin just after midnight.

"We disembark tomorrow morning, Madeleine," I said as I was leaving. "Don't stay up too late."

She didn't listen. Madeleine never listened. She always thought she knew best and didn't need anyone else's advice. Not our father's or our mother's, and certainly not mine.

I wondered if Violet had expected too much from us, if her scheme to send us off to Europe together might only widen the scar between us rather than heal it, as she hoped. I pictured her, propped up against her pillows in bed, her nurse administering some medicine or other. I hoped, at least, she was comfortable, and I hoped the doctor's optimism would prove to be right, and that we had time to undertake this journey and return home to Violet to say our goodbyes.

As I slipped into bed for the last time on the *Queen Mary,* I wondered what lay ahead for us all.

Maddie

The captain's dinner was unexpectedly enjoyable, the conversation excellent, but I had overindulged on the delicious Bordeaux wine and woke with the most phenomenal hangover. Clara found it highly amusing.

"Some ginger tea might help?" She laughed. "Or how about a hearty breakfast? Smoked salmon? Eggs?"

"Stop it," I groaned. Fish was the last thing in the world I could stomach at that moment. "It isn't funny."

"It is," she countered. "It's very funny. We finally arrive, and now it's you who is sick at sea. We're pulling into the port now, Madeleine. We're in France!"

I moved around the cabin like a sloth, throwing my things into my case and insisting Clara leave the drapes closed as I sipped an Alka-Seltzer and wished I'd refused the final glass of wine Daniel Miller had insisted on pouring as a toast between friends.

We went up on deck to watch our arrival into the bustling French port of Cherbourg. There was something thrilling about arriving to a new continent, and my hangover eased as I took it all in.

Though the skies were as gray as wool, there was a buzz of excitement as the disembarking passengers scurried to waiting cars or to meet family. I looked out at the large array of vessels: clippers and motorboats, and another ship nearly as large as the *Queen Mary*. Seagulls searching for scraps swooped overhead, and salt and seaweed tinged the air. It wasn't dissimilar to a port in America and yet, it felt entirely new, different.

"It was great to meet you, Maddie. Have a wonderful time in Paris," a male voice called from behind me as we descended the gangway and stood on solid ground for the first time in five days.

I turned and looked up to see Daniel, standing at the ship's railings. He smiled. I felt the smallest rush of regret that our poker games had come to an end. He was an excellent player, and it had made for good sport. Now it would be just me and Clara again, and that, I wasn't looking forward to at all.

"Bon voyage, as the French say," I called in reply, shielding my eyes from the sun that poked through a gap in the clouds.

"Adieu!" he replied.

"Would you please stop shouting, Madeleine," Clara whispered as she tugged at my arm. "We have to collect our luggage, and the Paris train won't wait for us."

All too soon, the *Queen Mary* was a distant memory, and the next stage of our journey was upon us.

The *Queen Mary* had been wonderfully lavish and grand, and the Paris train was significantly less so in comparison. Clara grumbled about the lack of space as we settled into our cramped compartment seats, but I liked it. Now we were really traveling. Now I felt like we were following in Auntie Nellie's and Violet's footsteps before us, when things were dirtier and more crowded and decidedly less comfortable.

"What are you smiling about?" Clara asked. The color had returned to her cheeks at last and she was much more conversational since we'd left the ship.

"Just enjoying the experience," I replied. "I've never been on a French train before."

Clara fussed with her gloves and glanced around the compartment. "It isn't very different from an American train."

"But it's a *French* train," I countered. "*Le train, oui? C'est spécial, Clarabelle!*"

Clara shook her head at my grade school foreign language skills, but I noticed a flicker of a smile at her lips. I hadn't used her childhood nickname for so many years and was surprised at how easily it had come to me.

"You like the oddest things," she said. "Truly, it's a wonder we're related at all."

She turned to look out of the window and I left her to her thoughts as I pulled out another of Jules Verne's books, *Twenty Thousand Leagues Under the Sea*. When I tired of reading, I played solitaire with a deck of cards Daniel had given to me after I'd beaten him again. "A lucky deck," he'd said. I hoped he was right. I had a feeling we could use a bit of luck along the way.

I finally enticed Clara to play a few games of Old Maid to pass the time, and although she feigned disinterest at the start, she soon slipped back into the competitive Clara I'd known as a child. She sulked when she lost a hand and gloated when she won, just as I remembered. We only disagreed once, thankfully, and some hours later, the locomotive came to a lurching halt at the station platform in the Gare Saint-Lazare.

A uniformed guard threw open the compartment doors, sending travel-weary passengers spilling out onto the platform and scattering like marbles from a dropped bag. The station was enormous—one of the largest and busiest in Paris—with dozens of platforms and multiple stories. Signs arched over every doorway, indicating directions for the Métro, while several small cafés advertised their croissants and café au lait and croque monsieur sandwiches.

We slid into a taxicab, jamming Clara's ridiculous trunks in with us. In spite of my fatigue, I put my French into practice as I explained to the driver where we needed to go. His reply was like music.

I glanced at Clara, who appeared equally enchanted, her gaze firmly fixed on the passing sights. For a while, we forgot about our differences and enjoyed our discovery together, both of us spellbound by the grandeur of one of the most beautiful cities in the world.

Eventually, the taxi turned down a narrow street and pulled up outside a charming hotel.

"What a dreadful state to arrive in," Clara said as she stepped from the car. "Look at how wrinkled and creased I am. I've never looked so disheveled."

She looked perfect to me, but I couldn't bring myself to say so. "I don't think anyone will be looking at your outfit, Clara. Anyway, who cares how creased we are. We're in Paris!"

"Paris is the fashion capital of the world, Madeleine! Of course people will notice my outfit."

Travel weary but thrilled to be in this beautiful city, we were greeted by the concierge and shown to our suite, a bright airy space that overlooked a small courtyard with a garden shared by the tenants of the adjacent buildings. The bedrooms were cozy, each furnished with a large bed covered in floral silk, dainty bedside tables, and a chest of drawers that gleamed as if the wood had just been polished. I threw my coat and handbag onto the bed in the room overlooking the street, glad to be first to stake my claim to our sleeping arrangements, just as I always had when we were children. I remembered how Clara would say it wasn't fair, and how our mother would tell her not to be so silly and to take the other bed.

"Madeleine, come and look," she called from the sitting room.

The surprisingly spacious room showcased a set of chaises, a polished mahogany desk, and a quaint window seat with a direct view of the Arc de Triomphe, just visible in the distance. I moved to the window to take a closer look.

"It's beautiful, isn't it?" I gasped.

Clara agreed that it was very pretty, but her mood turned serious. "I just wish we were here under different circumstances," she said as she took off her velvet-trimmed gloves and perched in one of the chairs. "This isn't a sightseeing holiday. It's a duty we are carrying out for Violet."

I sprawled over the chair opposite her. "It *is* a duty, yes, but Violet also wants us to experience the cities we're visiting. She wants us to go sightseeing! You know how she is. She would hate to think of us being all sad and serious and having no fun at all, especially when Paris is outside, waiting for us to discover it. In fact, she'd be furious!"

Clara offered a small smile. "I suppose so. Should we read her first letter to us? She said we should as soon as we arrived in Paris."

"Over lunch? I'm famished and it's always better to digest important news on a full stomach."

Clara stood up. "Fine. Over lunch. But I'll need to take a soak first."

"Well, make it a quick one, before I pass out. I know how many hours you spend in the bathroom."

As Clara ran her bath and put a record on the gramophone player, singing along to a Benny Goodman number, I peered down at the pedestrians and out across the patches of emerald lawn to the left of the building. The trees in early spring were blossoming and the pale afternoon light illuminated the ornate buildings. I took my journal from my bag, eager to capture my first impressions.

PARIS

As the sky shifts from gray to brilliant blue, fresh raindrops coat everything and shimmer in the sun. Stone buildings carved with elegant frescoes line the streets, their curled-iron balconies fitted with a table for morning coffee or for watching the passersby in the street. Some look like a small city garden with their potted flowers in red and white and purple.

As we rode from the train station, we alternately glided over cement and bumped over cobblestones. We took in the sights of gleaming storefronts graced with perfumes and beautiful fabrics, glistening pastries and fresh meats, and a thousand things between. Bicyclists joined the flow of cars along the boulevards, their happy bells chiming and mingling with the roar of motor-car engines. As we turned onto the Champs-Élysées, I absorbed every sight, every sound, every smell: fresh bread, soot mingling with damp air, and the hint of greenery on the breeze.

The skyline here is so unlike New York's. Paris doesn't have any monoliths of steel and glass blocking the sun. The light here is different, rosy gold when the sun shines, and from the lattice window where I now sit, the Arc de Triomphe de l'Étoile beckons in the distance, a gateway to the city beyond.

Satisfied, I put my journal away and pulled the packet of Violet's letters from my suitcase. Three were marked *Clara and Madeleine,* along with our instructions for each city, to explain more about each person she wanted us to visit and where exactly she wanted us to go. Three other letters were marked with the names of those she'd written to: *Frank, Matthias,* and *Margaret.* But there was another letter stuffed among my belongings. Edward's letter to Clara.

I'd forgotten all about it with the endless schedule of entertainment and distractions on the *Queen Mary.* And Clara hadn't mentioned it. Presumably, she thought it was lost, tossed into the wastebasket along with the newspapers among which she'd hidden it.

As she hummed happily to herself in the bathroom, I paused. Should I tell her I'd found it and claim complete innocence? Or would it be better to save it for another day? I didn't want to spoil things when we'd only just arrived.

As any good journalist knows, there's a wrong time and a right time to pursue a story.

After a moment of hesitation, I slipped the letter between the pages of my journal.

For now, this one could wait.

ONCE WE'D REFRESHED ourselves, we ventured out for lunch, walking along the streets near the hotel and through the adjoining neighborhoods, past little markets and the occasional vendor and a wineshop with a black awning fluttering in the breeze. I gazed at the buildings, admiring the early-nineteenth-century style, and commented on the beautifully manicured trees and pristine sidewalks. Mothers pushed their children in strollers decorated with lace trim or walked their little city dogs on dainty leashes. It was all so picturesque. Though I was grateful to be staying in such a beautiful neighborhood, I also longed to see the real Paris, where the less fortunate lived and worked to scratch out a living. I wanted to see what was happening behind the city's elegant façade. As always, I wanted to find the grit, the truth of the place.

We chose a quaint brasserie several blocks from the hotel. A menu board outside the door advertised a prix fixe meal that we couldn't resist. After being seated at a cozy table by the front window, we ordered a bottle of Bordeaux and dug into a delicious vegetable terrine, followed by steaming plates of coq au vin. I'd never tasted a chicken stew like it; the meat was tender, and bright herbs flavored the rich wine broth. I sopped up every last drop with a piece of crusty bread.

While we waited for dessert, I took Violet's first letter to us from my handbag. I recalled how she'd hesitated for a moment before pressing the little bundle of letters, tied with a red ribbon, into my hands. "Take care of them," she'd said. "And of each other." I glanced at Clara across the table now, lost in her own thoughts. Were we taking care of each other or merely tolerating each other?

"Do you want to read it, or should I?" I asked.

"You read this one. I'll read the next."

I opened the envelope and took out two sheets of folded writing paper, and an old photograph.

My dearest girls,

If you are reading this, then I presume you are already in Paris. Isn't it the most beautiful city? I could hardly believe it was real when I first saw it.

I chose the beautiful Hotel George V for the duration of your stay. It is one of the city's most prized hotels, and I only want the best for my girls.

The next stage of your trip is to Amiens. I traveled there, too, with my sister, Margaret, all those years ago. It was a silly idea really, to follow in Nellie Bly's footsteps and meet the writer Jules Verne at his home there. But he was ever so kind and didn't seem to mind at all that two excitable American girls had landed on his doorstep. He said, "Any friends of Miss Bly's are friends of mine." He took us ballooning over Paris with a marvelous gentleman called Monsieur LaChambre. I felt like I was flying. I don't think I've ever felt so free.

Monsieur LaChambre's great-nephew, Monsieur Malraux,

is expecting you at his ballooning factory outside Paris, when
you return from Amiens. He will take you on an ascent in a
tethered balloon. I hope you will enjoy the experience as much
as I did. It really does change your view of the world when you
see it from the clouds.

At this, I stopped reading and looked at Clara. "We're going on a balloon ride! Good old Violet!"

"You might be," Clara countered. "I'm not stepping one foot into a balloon basket."

I rolled my eyes at her. "Don't be such a bore. It'll be fun. Anyway, that's for another day. Let's see what else Violet has to say."

But there is another reason I want you to go to Amiens. A
far more important reason than visiting the homes of famous
novelists.

It is strange that my life should circle back to this little corner
of France, so many years later. You see, your dear grandfather
Frank was billeted in Amiens during the Great War. He was
considered too old to fight, but volunteered with the American
Red Cross to use his medical knowledge. He was happy to do his
part when America entered the war.

I will never forget the day the letter arrived announcing his
death. So many years have passed since, and yet it only feels like
minutes. He was killed by a German sniper as his unit was on
the march to a field hospital somewhere near the Somme river.
He hadn't been away long, and the armistice was announced
soon after. It still catches me by surprise when I reach for his

hand at sunrise and discover his side of the bed empty. How can he not be there? How can he be gone forever, snatched from me so cruelly in the last months of the war? There hasn't been a single day since I waved him off that I haven't thought about him, when I don't miss him terribly.

He called me his best girl.

One of my greatest regrets in life is that I never traveled to France to visit his grave, to say my final farewell. Part of me couldn't accept that he was gone, you see. I felt that if I didn't see his final resting place, there was a chance he would walk through the door and lift me up into those big arms of his and plant a kiss on my cheek and tell me he loved me more than all the steel girders in Manhattan.

Frank Bell was the sweetest, gentlest soul and he loved you both dearly. I only wish he had lived to see you grow up into the wonderful women you've become. I have enclosed a photograph of him.

He was laid to rest in a military cemetery just outside Amiens. That is all I know.

Please read my letter to him when you find him.

Violet
X

We sat in quiet contemplation before Clara broke the silence.

"Do you remember Grandpa Frank?" she asked as she studied the photograph.

"I have vague memories. You?"

She nodded. "The same."

The last clear memory I had of him was a sunny afternoon when he'd given us cherry lollipops, his large warm hands in mine as we'd walked on the beach. I recalled how I'd missed him when he left to go to war. I'd never had to work hard for his love like I had for my father's; Frank never scolded me for coming home with scraped knees or climbing on the furniture when I shouldn't, and he admired the crabs I brought back from the beach and let crawl around the garden. He'd always been proud of me, just as Violet had. The rest of my family . . . well.

I put the letter and photograph away as our waiter arrived with a dish of crème caramel. Our conversation lulled as we dug into the creamy dessert and thought about Violet's words.

"How is your writing going?" Clara asked when we'd nearly finished.

I was surprised by the question and wasn't quite sure how to respond. Was it just small talk, or did she really want to know?

"It's going fine," I offered.

"Are you still in touch with that work colleague? Bill some-body. A journalist?" She took a sip from her coffee cup, peering over the rim, watching for my reaction.

Clara had always assumed Billy Jenkins was more than a friend, but I'd never had any romantic interest in him. I'd never explained what had happened between us and preferred to keep it that way. Clara would only say I told you so and scold me about trusting strangers.

I'd met Billy at the public library when we'd both approached the circulation desk for assistance with research on the same story. He seemed pleasant enough, and it was always nice to meet someone in the same line of work. We'd struck up a conversation about politics over coffee and cigarettes, and met again the next day, and then the next week and so on, until we met regularly to swap ideas and opinions and share progress—or lack of—on our submissions. I'd thought we were friends, two writers trying to help each other break into the world of journalism—until the day he pitched a story I'd shared with him in confidence. The editor at the *New York Times* was impressed enough to offer Billy a position as a regular on their staff. The deceit and betrayal still stung, but at least I knew my ideas were sound. Now I was more determined than ever to succeed without anyone's help, least of all a man's.

"Bill nobody," I replied, and changed the subject. "How about a stroll along the Seine to walk off some of this food."

"I'd like that," Clara replied. "It will be nice to enjoy the water without feeling nauseous."

I pressed my hand to my mouth in a faux exclamation of surprise. "We agree on something?"

Clara crossed her arms over her chest. "Don't get used to it."

But I wondered if I could get used to it. If I wanted to get used to it. I certainly didn't need Clara back in my life, especially if it meant bringing Hancock with her, but I couldn't deny that there was something right about being around her, even if she drove me crazy with her airs and graces and misplaced fears. She was, after all, my sister, and like her or loathe her, I was stuck with her.

Clara

$\mathcal{P}$aris was like an Impressionist painting, all gentle color and romantic detail. I couldn't wait to capture it on canvas: sunrise over the Seine, the bustle of the Champs-Élysées, the delicate curves of the Sacré-Coeur. As I admired a copy of Degas's famous *Danseuses bleues* that hung in our suite, it struck me that Paris was like a ballet itself. Everyone moved as if carefully choreographed, dancing around each other with a delicate energy, so different from New York with all its noise and determined bustle. Paris drew me in, and I felt the last remnants of concern and hesitation about the trip dissolve as I slid beneath the bedcovers that evening, full of good wine and hearty food, and relieved to be free of the sensation of everything swaying beneath me.

I slept like the dead and woke refreshed.

"I'd like to visit the Left Bank today, watch the artists at work," I said as I applied rouge to my cheeks. I needed only a little, my skin having taken some color from my hours sketching on the sun deck of the *Queen Mary*.

"Well, I can't be in Paris a minute longer without visiting the

Eiffel Tower," Madeleine replied. "Imagine the views from the top! Why don't we do that first, and have lunch in the Latin Quarter by Notre-Dame after?"

I shook my head. "You know I can't stand heights. I have absolutely no intention of going to the top of that tower."

Madeleine's chin nearly hit the floor. "But it's one of the most famous landmarks in the world, Clara. You *have* to climb it, see Paris from above!"

"I'm perfectly happy to see Paris from the ground," I insisted. "But you go, if you must."

"I must," she replied.

And that was all there was to be said on the matter.

"Are you going to wear your new French *parfum* today?" Madeleine asked as she ran her fingers through her hair and considered it styled for the day ahead.

I glanced at the ornate perfume bottle on the dressing table. A second gift from Charles that had arrived while we'd been at lunch the previous day. *Only the sweetest scent for my young bride-to-be. Only the best for my Clara.*

"I'd rather not walk around Paris smelling like Charles Hancock's mother," I said with a huff, and immediately regretted being unkind about Charles in Madeleine's company.

Madeleine burst out laughing. "It isn't one of her favorites, is it? Poor Chuck! He seems to have a talent for giving you things you don't like."

I folded my arms. "Charles has given me plenty of perfect gifts," I snapped. And yet, even as I defended him, I had trouble remembering anything I'd truly loved, and my thoughts strayed again to the gift from Edward, and then to his lost letter.

"Like what?" Madeleine pressed. "You don't even like your engagement ring."

I glared at her. "Of course I like my engagement ring! Don't be absurd."

"Then why do you seem so serious when you look at it?"

Her words stung. A surge of anger brought color rushing to my cheeks. "What a ridiculous thing to say! You're just jealous, Madeleine. You can't stand for me to have nice things and a husband. Poor little Madeleine, always trying to keep up."

Now it was her turn to look furious. "I don't need to keep up with anyone, and most definitely not with you. Besides, if husbands are all as ruthless and heartless as Charles Hancock, I'm fine without one. More than fine! You hardly know the man, Clara, and he clearly doesn't understand you. Do you really intend to spend the rest of your life with him?"

For a moment, I was speechless. How dare she! "I know him perfectly well."

At this she laughed cruelly. "Oh, Clara. You don't know the first thing about what he's up to with his business schemes, the people he's happy to trample all over to get what he wants."

"I don't know what you're talking about, but I don't believe a word you say. You're mean and spiteful. Always have been. Always will be."

I stalked into my bedroom, pulled my case from the closet, and flung it onto the bed.

"What are you doing?" Madeleine asked, her face a picture of surprise as she appeared at the bedroom door.

"Packing my things. I'm not staying here with you a moment longer." I stood up tall and placed my hands on my hips. "I knew this was a terrible idea. You can see Paris on your own. The way you're going, you'll spend the rest of your life doing things alone. You make it impossible for people to love you, Madeleine."

For once, I had stunned her into silence.

She glared at me for a moment before taking her coat from the stand and striding across the suite. She slammed the door behind her for good measure, sending the Degas tumbling to the floor.

I turned and stared at the empty case on my bed. I'd only just unpacked it and hung everything in the closet with such determination to enjoy myself here. I thought about the inscription on Nellie's pocket watch: *Never turn back.* Why should I rush back to America just because my sister could never be happy for me? She was wrong about Charles, and she was also wrong about me. She expected me to flounder and worry. She expected me to fuss and fret and give up easily. So, I would prove her wrong. I would show Madeleine Sommers what I was made of.

I waited awhile to make sure she'd actually gone, then pulled on my gloves, studied the Paris street map on the wall, and set off for Notre-Dame cathedral. I was glad to be on my own, despite the daunting prospect of finding my way around an unfamiliar city.

Using a map as my guide, I walked on, until eventually I turned a corner and the majestic Notre-Dame cathedral filled the skyline. I craned my neck to see the highest point of the two bell towers that flanked the great door, the famous rose window above it. Tiny dogs barked insistently beside me as friends stopped to greet each other with a kiss on each cheek and proceeded to converse in a language so beautiful I could almost paint their words in my mind. I let out a long sigh and felt my shoulders relax. I was in Paris, and I mustn't let my spiteful sister spoil it.

I found an empty bench and took out my sketchbook and pastels, working quickly to capture the cathedral's majestic outlines and taking my time on the more intricate details. I turned my attention then to the scene around me: couples holding hands, family and friends flitting around like butterflies, pollinating each other with love and good humor. Hours passed in a happy daydream, marked only by the regular chime of Notre-Dame's bells.

When hunger began to distract me, I gathered my things and studied my map, tracing narrow streets and bridges with my fingertip to remember my route back to the hotel.

As I set off, buttoning my coat against a light breeze, a gentleman bumped into me.

He apologized with a *"Pardonnez-moi, mademoiselle!"* but as I looked up to acknowledge his apology, I found myself staring at a familiar face.

"Mr. Miller?"

"Miss Sommers! Goodness. What a surprise."

"It is, indeed."

"Did you lose your sister already?" he asked with a smile.

"Unfortunately not. We wanted to see different things today." I closed the last button on my coat. "Your cousin is well, I hope?"

He looked a little confused. "Ah, yes. He's perfectly well. And the show at the Moulin Rouge was everything you would hope for. Or not. Depending on how easily offended you are I suppose."

Hadn't he said his cousin was a woman? Yes, he'd even corrected me when he'd mentioned it during our conversation on the *Queen Mary*.

I forced a smile. "Well, I must be getting back to the hotel before Madeleine thinks I've fallen into the Seine."

"Of course. Are you staying nearby?"

"In the eighth arrondissement. Not too far. And you?"

"The same. I wonder if . . ."

"Hotel George V?"

He laughed. "Yes! What are the chances! Can I walk you back?"

I politely declined. He might be charming, but his slipup over his cousin bothered me. "I'm happy to walk by myself, thank you. One has to get a little lost, now and again. It is, after all, the best way to explore a new city."

"It is indeed, which is precisely what I intend to do right now." He pushed his hands into his pockets and we bid each other farewell. "Send my regards to Madeleine," he added.

"I will," I replied, although I wasn't sure I was even speaking to Madeleine let alone passing on other people's regards to her, and especially not Mr. Miller's. He had definitely referred to a female cousin when he'd spoken about it previously. What on earth was he up to?

The late morning sunlight scattered diamonds across the rolling wake on the water as boats slipped beneath the many bridges, and followed the gentle curves of the Seine. I imagined Violet standing here, watching the light in the same way when she was a young woman, her future stretching ahead of her. I wondered if the impact of my time in Europe would be as lasting as it had been for her. Like a fine French perfume, Paris had already settled against my skin.

As the church bells chimed the quarter hour, I turned from

the river and made my way back to the hotel, steeling myself to confront Madeleine and her misplaced notions about Charles. I decided I wouldn't tell her about bumping into Daniel Miller. She'd said he was nothing more than a passing amusement on the *Queen Mary,* although I didn't believe for one second she was as unimpressed by him as she claimed.

MADELEINE HAD RETURNED before me. We studiously ignored each other as I hung up my coat and took off my shoes.

"I thought you were leaving," she said eventually.

"I thought you should apologize first," I bit back as I crossed my arms over my chest.

"You're always telling me I should apologize first. Did it ever occur to you, Clara, that you're not perfect, either?"

We glared at each other, but there was a hint of a smile at the edge of Madeleine's mouth, and I felt one pull at my own.

"You are absolutely infuriating," I huffed as I turned my face away from her, picked up the perfume from Charles, and dabbed it liberally against my wrists and neck. It really did smell dreadful.

Madeleine wafted the air away from her dramatically. "And you're as stubborn as hell. But if you're staying then I suppose we should call some sort of truce, for Violet's sake."

As she leaned against the window, the light caught her perfectly.

"Don't move," I said as I rushed to fetch my sketchbook. "Stay exactly where you are."

"What for?"

"So I can draw you. The light is exquisite. It makes you look . . ." I fished around for the right word. "It makes you look nice."

"Nice? Is that all?"

"Nice is a vast improvement on insufferable."

Madeleine did as I asked, sitting patiently while I captured her on the page, the Arc de Triomphe just visible in the distance. The silence enveloped us as I studied her features, properly considering her for the first time in a year. I detected an air of dissatisfaction in her, a longing for something she couldn't grasp and which she covered up with her breezy confidence and compulsion to shock and go against expectations.

I tried my best to capture her but I couldn't get it quite right. I balled up my first attempt before pulling another piece of paper toward me and starting again, and again, but on every blank page I felt the gaping distance between us more keenly, a void filled with too many years of resentment and jealousy.

After an hour she grew bored and fidgety. "Are you ever going to finish? This is unbearable."

"These things take time," I said, letting out a frustrated breath. "But I suppose it'll have to do."

I closed my sketchbook, the likeness incomplete. Half a sketch. Half a person. Half a sister. Always some part of her I couldn't fully grasp.

Maddie

$\mathcal{T}$he next morning dawned with a sleepy sky, blanketed with clouds. I woke early, dressed, and slipped out of the hotel before Clara had stirred. I'd committed to taking a morning walk of the city each day, determined to enjoy every single moment while in Paris, even if the weather wasn't the best.

A pervasive damp chilled my skin as I strolled alongside the silvery waters of the Seine. I rubbed the goose bumps from my arms as my thoughts turned to Clara. Our argument the day before had cut me deeply, her words too close to the truth. *Poor little Madeleine, always trying to keep up. . . . You make it impossible for people to love you.* Maybe I did make it impossible for people to love me, but only because if I let them in they eventually betrayed me. It seemed I was too difficult, that it was too hard for people to understand my brashness and unconventional ways.

I listened to the lonely cry of a mourning dove, its song echoing through the quiet streets. As I walked over a bridge dotted with ornate iron lanterns, I thought about Charles Hancock's unscrupulous business dealings, and the troubled tenement neighborhoods in lower Manhattan. I'd been disgusted to discover what he was up to, and wondered how many other less-than-ethical dealings he was trying his hand at. I also wondered what Clara would say if she knew. Perhaps it was time to tell her.

On the other side of the bridge, I turned south, past a *tabac* that sold cigarettes and candies, and newspapers. The headlines that morning were troubling. Chancellor Kurt von Schuschnigg was running Austria more or less like his predecessor, as an autocrat, but he was emphatically anti-Nazi. In fact, he'd staved off more than one coup, or so the article I skimmed seemed to say, yet he was still playing nice with Hitler—and also with Mussolini to the south.

"What a mess," I murmured to myself, paying the vendor with the correct combination of the little franc coins, and tucking the newspaper under my arm. It all made me anxious. Anxious enough, in fact, that I began to scrutinize faces in the street and couldn't help but look over my shoulder when a policeman passed or someone acted, to my mind, suspiciously. It was absurd, I knew, but I was beginning to feel a little on edge. Perhaps I shouldn't read the news for a few days.

I tried to bridle my thoughts and enjoy the rest of my walk.

After warming myself with a *chocolat chaud,* I took the Métro to Montmartre. Clara had questioned my intentions to go to the seedier side of the city and cautioned me about how unsafe it was for a woman to go alone. Admittedly, Montmartre was run-down and known for its pickpockets, but I wanted to see this village of struggling artists and dance halls for myself. At last, she'd given up, and said she would let me make my own poor choices. She planned to visit the Jardin du Luxembourg that morning to work on a collection of portraits she'd begun of our travels, and which she intended to give to Violet. It was a shame we couldn't experience more of the city together, that each of us pulled in a different direction, but it wasn't a surprise. Sharing a hotel suite and eating together was far more than we'd managed in the last twelve months.

When I emerged from the Métro into the daylight, I chose a table on the sidewalk, ordered a *café crème* and a *crêpe au jambon,* and watched the colorful Parisians and artists hawking their wares. Everyone was less polished here, humbler, more unique and distinctive than those I'd seen along the Champs-Élysées. As always, I was looking for inspiration, to find something— anything—newsworthy.

After a while, I opened my journal. Sheets of typed pages were stuffed inside, the contents of which I knew by heart: polite rejections from the *New York Post,* the *New York Times,* and *The New Yorker.* Exhaling, I gathered them into a neat stack and thumbed through them once more.

> *We regret to inform you . . .*
> *Your article isn't right for our publication.*
> *We aren't accepting unsolicited articles at this time.*

I sighed and read a more encouraging letter from *Ladies' Home Journal.*

> *While this article isn't right for our publication, we're currently seeking new writers for our Home Advice column, and would like to extend an invitation to submit your résumé and a sample.*

I hadn't applied. Domestic advice columns weren't the sort of thing I wanted to write, and though Billy-the-Traitor told me I was foolhardy to turn down work, I couldn't stand the thought of answering questions about things of which I knew little— motherhood, cookery, linens. Family. I wasn't qualified for any of it, nor did I want to be.

But a more recent letter from the *New York Herald Tribune* had given me a real glimmer of hope:

Miss Sommers, you write with authority and a style befitting our publication. Though we aren't able to place your article at this time, we invite you to submit again. Please direct your inquiries specifically to me, Gerald McDougal, at this address.

I felt a surge of determination every time I read it. I could do this. I would keep trying until I got the yes I was looking for.

There was another letter among the others: Edward's letter to Clara. I still hadn't talked to her about it, still hadn't decided how to get myself out of the awkward situation I'd gotten myself into by taking it in the first place. Not wanting to spoil my morning by worrying about it, I slipped it back inside the journal, and tried to forget about it.

I cut a piece of crepe with my knife and forked a steaming bite into my mouth. I sighed as the melted Gruyère paired perfectly with the cured ham and tangy onion. Even the simplest of foods in Paris were better than any extravagant meal I'd been served back home. I savored every mouthful and silently thanked Violet for sending me to a city that tasted so damn good.

Energized, I strolled through the village past the majestic Sacré-

Coeur, down the hill to a row of shops showcasing their wares on rotating racks: scarves in lavender and dove gray, lemon yellow and pale pink, and a collection of change purses printed with images of Marie Antoinette and the Eiffel Tower, and little French phrases I'd learned in school. *Vive la France! C'est bon. La Ville Lumières.* I continued on, winding through the narrow streets. Notably absent were the elegant boutiques and lace-covered strollers I'd seen on the other side of Paris. Here, beggars squatted on benches or hunched beneath the overhang of a doorway. Women with a cigarette dangling from their lips and in too-high heels rushed to some questionable establishment that looked as if it only came alive at night. The infamous Moulin Rouge appeared empty, at least for now, but I suspected that wouldn't last for long. I was glad I'd ventured to the part of town Clara considered seedy and dangerous. It had character all of its own.

I stopped to peer over the shoulder of an artist as he worked diligently at his easel. Impressed by his work, I bought a small painting of the Sacré-Coeur for Clara, as a peace offering, and a replica of a Toulouse-Lautrec dancing girl for myself. As I pulled out a crisp bill of twenty francs to pay for my purchases, the artist smiled, revealing a large gap between his two front teeth.

"*Merci, mademoiselle.*"

As he handed me the change, I said, "*Non. C'est pour vous.*" I didn't need the money as much as he did. I returned my change purse to my coat pocket. The artist thanked me several times, and wrapped the portraits in brown paper.

I tucked them under my arm and continued on my way. As I took a left down a narrow side street, someone behind me whistled loudly. I turned to see a man in brown workman's slacks and boots, and a filthy dark coat. He whistled again and shouted in French, but I didn't understand him.

I picked up my pace, heading to the end of the street where I knew I could find a taxicab, but as the man called out again I turned, and in that instant, I felt a tug on my pocket. Before I had time to react, another man sprinted away.

"Stop!" I shouted. "That man stole my money!"

A few people glanced in my direction but went about their business, no doubt used to seeing this sort of thing all the time, so I took off to chase the thief myself. He must have watched me buy the paintings and seen me slip my change purse into my pocket. The whistling man was purely a distraction. I cringed at my naivety and continued to chase the thief to the end of the street, but he was too fast. He ducked behind a building, and disappeared.

I gave up, bent over to catch my breath, and then started to laugh. I'd gotten the proper French welcome after all.

I RETURNED TO the hotel resigned to the loss of the hundred francs I'd foolishly kept in my change purse and made my way to the lounge for a much-needed drink. I knew I shouldn't sit at the bar if I were any kind of lady, especially in Paris, but I didn't care. My feet were sore and I wanted a glass of hard liquor, tout de suite.

There was only one other customer at the bar, a man sitting alone. I offered a friendly bonjour as I smiled at him—and did a double take.

"Daniel?" I said, my eyes wide. "What are you doing here?"

"Madeleine!" He stood up from his stool, a broad smile on his face. "I'm staying here, too. Didn't Clara tell you? We bumped into each other yesterday."

"No. She didn't mention it. It must have slipped her mind." I wondered why she hadn't told me. "But anyway. What a surprise! Of all the hotels in all of Paris!"

"Well, the George V is the only place to stay, isn't it?" he replied with a playful wink. "But it's a happy coincidence."

"Do you mind if I join you?" I asked. "I could really use a drink."

"Please," he said, pulling out a stool beside him. "I could really use the company."

I set down my purchases on the bar and ordered a brandy.

"Good choice. You look like a woman with Paris running through her veins. France clearly suits you."

I smiled. "I like it here. I spent most of the day in Montmartre."

He looked surprised. "Alone? I've heard it can be a little rough there."

"Nothing I couldn't handle." I decided not to bring up the pickpocketing incident, especially if he was crossing paths with Clara. "I passed the Moulin Rouge earlier. Did you see your show there yet?"

He shifted on his stool and took a sip of his drink. "Not yet. That end of Montmartre is the worst. The beggars and nightclubs and all of that."

I felt myself brighten. "I'd love to go back at night, go to a club. Drink absinthe with the literary set."

At this, he laughed. "I'd be very happy to accompany you."

"Clara would be horrified." I grinned. "Let's do it!" I took a warming sip of brandy as soon as the bartender placed the glass in front of me.

"It would certainly give you something to write about," Daniel continued. "What is it that you write, exactly? You never really said."

"I write news articles that are mostly never published, except for one. I had a few ideas stolen by a so-called friend, or should I say, ex-friend. He's built up an enviable reputation now, while I continue to receive rejection letters. The curse of being a woman trying to make a name for herself." I caught my reflection in the mirror behind the bar. My cheeks were rosy from too much sun and the light spray of freckles across the bridge of my nose had deepened. To my surprise, my hair was still pinned into a relatively neat knot for a change.

"Have you ever considered writing under a male pseudonym?" Daniel asked, his dark eyes on mine. "You might have better luck. I know we're supposed to be living in progressive times, but I'm not sure all that much has changed for women in the last few years."

I stared at him a moment, both intrigued by his suggestion and impressed he should take an invested interest in women's rights. "You might be right," I said at last. "The Brontës did it. George Sand. Even Colette for a time. Auntie Nellie used a pen name, though it was still a female name."

"Auntie Nellie?"

I laughed. "Not technically an aunt. More of a family friend. You probably know her as Nellie Bly. Elizabeth Cochran was her real name."

"You knew Nellie Bly? Well, that's quite the claim to fame. Was she as brazen and outspoken in real life as her reputation would have us believe?"

"She was worse, in the best way possible! Nellie didn't leave anything left unsaid. She was a friend of my grandmother's. She's part of the reason we're making this trip across Europe." I paused. "And she's one of the main reasons I'm a writer."

He nodded. "We all need role models. My youngest sister has struggled to find work as a mathematician, even in Boston where things should be a bit easier than in a small town. It's a crime, really. She isn't the type to be confined to the home. You remind me of her a little, actually, only taller."

Daniel was a little on the short side, barely reaching my height. He was broad rather than lanky, but he moved with a certain confidence and grace. It struck me how little I knew about him, even though I felt as if I'd known him for some time.

"I'm serious," he went on. "You should consider a pen name. You're an intelligent and capable woman. Once you remove the female stigma, I'm certain you'll have more luck."

A stigma indeed. It infuriated me. I finished my brandy and placed the glass on the bar.

Perhaps I *should* consider using a man's name, or even my first initial and last name. *M. Sommers. Journalist.* No one would know whether the *M* stood for Mark or Michael or Madeleine, and frankly, it was none of their business. As a man, they'd have one less reason to turn me away. A sudden lightness came over me. Now, if only I had a great pitch.

"Care to join me in another?" Daniel asked.

"Why not." As the bartender poured another brandy for me and a Lillet for Daniel, my eyes strayed to the folder on the bar top. "Working on something?" I asked. "A review of a show?"

Daniel cleared his throat. "Well, no. It's—"

"Let's see," I said, pulling the folder toward me without waiting for his permission. The alcohol had gone straight to my head.

"They're drawings," he blurted, his ears going red. "I'm fascinated by architecture, you see. Buildings and structures in Paris range from Roman times to Gothic, to the more modern style as they call it, from the early nineteenth century. And then there's Art Deco. The skyline is so open here compared to New York. Paris is preserved in time, really. I've enjoyed studying them and thought I'd sketch a few."

"Are you an artist, too?"

He looked a little embarrassed. "In a way, but not like your sister. She has a real talent. I just . . . dabble."

I flipped through the drawings, noticing the dimensions listed in the margins, the perfect lines clearly drawn with a ruler. "Daniel, these are very good. I'm no expert, but have you considered work as an architect? Clara's fiancé works in that line of business. Perhaps he could offer some advice."

He swallowed a sip of Lillet and, after a moment, met my eye. "I have. In fact, I'm not sure how long I'll remain a theater critic."

"That's wonderful! Good for you. Funny how sometimes you have to get away from your regular day-to-day to realize what you should be doing with your life. That was partly why Violet was so intent on us taking the trip. She has a modern way of thinking for someone born in the last century."

"So, what's next on your itinerary?" Daniel continued. "You'd mentioned some letters of your grandmother's?"

"Yes. We're headed to Amiens."

"Oh? And what's there?"

"A war cemetery. Our grandfather is buried there, apparently. I'm not sure how I feel about going to be honest."

Daniel took a long sip of his drink. "I'm sure it will be difficult, but a wonderful thing to do for Violet. You know, you light up whenever you talk about her. It's nice to see."

Not used to compliments, I sputtered on my drink, turning a sip into an inadvertent gulp. "Do I? Thanks."

"You're an intriguing woman, Madeleine. Quite different from how I'd imagined."

"How you'd imagined?" I frowned, uncertain by what he meant.

Guilt flashed across his face an instant before he composed himself. "You're so different from your sister, I mean."

I looked at him, wondering what the strange behavior was about, but rather than point it out, I shrugged. "Yes. That's a fact."

He stared back at me, a serious look on his face.

I stood abruptly and gathered my things.

"I should be going. Don't want to make dear Clara worry." I downed the rest of my drink in one gulp. "Thank you for the drinks."

"I'm sorry. I hope I didn't offend—"

I waved dismissively. "Not at all. See you around, Daniel."

I darted for the elevator, leaving a bewildered Daniel behind. Yet as I walked to my room, his words reverberated in my mind:

You're an intelligent and capable woman. Once you remove the female stigma, I'm certain you'll have more luck. Though he hadn't read a single piece of my writing, he believed I had what it took to be successful, that I had gumption, and that meant something to me.

Once in the suite, I headed straight for the writing desk, opened my journal, and began to write.

Clara

𝓜adeleine surprised me with a reconciliation gift she'd purchased from an artist in Montmartre, proving she had a heart after all. It helped to thaw some of the previous days' tensions and after an argument-free dinner together, we'd ended the evening with an unexpectedly companionable stroll along the Seine.

I woke the next morning feeling content and refreshed, my mood brightened further by birdsong and the melody of French conversation beyond the window, but the sight of Violet's letter to Frank reminded me of the difficult events the day held for us. It seemed especially sad that this was how she would say goodbye to him, but at least she'd been given the chance to put her affairs in order. I supposed Charles would manage all of those things when we were married. As I dressed for the journey ahead, I wondered what life would be like as somebody's wife. It would be different, but would *I* be different, too?

I dressed quickly and headed to the breakfast room, where I found Madeleine already at our table.

"The croissants are to die for," she said, her mouth full as she took another bite of the flaky pastry and ignored the crumbs that fell onto the tablecloth. "You should try one."

I tried not to comment on the mess she'd made on her side of the table, ordered a boiled egg, and stirred sugar into my coffee. "You seem in good spirits. You obviously slept well given how loudly you snored. I could hear you through the wall."

At this, Madeleine shrugged. "Not much I can do about that when I'm asleep," she added as she spread an alarming amount of cherry jam onto her croissant. She glanced at my outfit of an olive-green crepe tea dress and matching shoes. "You're not traveling to Amiens in that, are you?"

"Yes. And what's wrong with it?" I noticed she'd attired herself like a packhorse again.

"We're going to a cemetery, Clara. We'll essentially be walking through a field."

"Well then, you'll be glad you dressed like a farmer."

Ignoring me, Madeleine pulled something from her handbag. "Remember how I told you I ran into Daniel Miller at the bar yesterday?"

"Yes. What about it?" I was embarrassed to have been found out about not telling her I'd bumped into him myself.

"Well, read this." She pushed a page of the hotel's stationery toward me. "I told him about our trip to Amiens and it turns out I've inspired him to visit the cathedral there. Today! He's invited us to join him for lunch when we're finished visiting the cemetery."

"Really?" I skimmed the note, my mood souring with every line.

Dear Maddie,

After our conversation last night, you've inspired me to visit the cathedral in Amiens. I went to the station early this morning to buy my ticket and took the liberty of picking up tickets for your trip as well since I was already there and the timetables are impossible to decipher. I hope you don't mind.

I won't infringe upon your important plans with your sister. However, should you two find yourselves hungry, I reserved a table for lunch pour trois *at La Cave, an excellent little restaurant beside the cathedral. The food is rustic, but you'll never taste a finer rabbit stew and you strike me as someone who will appreciate the local cuisine.*

I hope things go well for you both at the cemetery. I imagine it will be a poignant experience.

Sincerely,
Daniel

I was horrified. How dare he be so presumptuous! We were perfectly capable of booking our own travel, and at the time we chose. He further insulted us by assuming we'd want to dine with him!

"Does your friend intend to make all our travel arrangements?" I remarked as I pushed the note back to Madeleine. "I'm surprised. I'd have thought you would be offended by him feeling the need to interfere. I suppose he'll expect to sit with us on the train, too?"

"He'd better not!" Madeleine said. "I like the man just fine, but this is our trip. At least we don't have to go to the bother of figuring out the tickets, but what do we do about lunch? It feels rude to decline."

I shrugged. "I don't suppose there's much we can do about it now."

"No," Madeleine agreed. "I don't suppose there is."

Although she was saying all the right words, I got the distinct feeling Madeleine wasn't quite as put off by the idea of meeting Daniel Miller for lunch as she pretended.

"Anyway, the important thing is to find Grandpa's grave," I added. "The rest of it is incidental."

We finished our breakfast in silence until I noted the time and stood up suddenly.

"We'd better get going if we want to make the train Daniel has arranged for us. I'd hate to miss it."

Madeleine insisted we had plenty of time, and that I worried too much, but I was pleased to prove her wrong when a traffic jam in the center of the city caused a significant delay and meant we made the Amiens train with only minutes to spare.

"You won't be traveling with us, Mr. Miller?" I asked when we saw him on the platform and began to board. "It was kind of you to buy our tickets, but there really was no need."

"I assume you ladies would much rather gossip about me than have me sit beside you. I hope your search is successful. Join me for lunch, if you wish. Or not. The stew is delicious, though, I promise!"

He wished us a pleasant journey and boarded a few cars down from us.

He was charming to a fault and certainly made it difficult for me to sustain my initial dislike for him.

"At least he had the decency to travel in a different compartment," I remarked as we boarded and took our seats. "I was dreading spending the journey making polite conversation and forcing pleasantries."

"Yes. Imagine," Madeleine added with more than a hint of sarcasm. "That would be awful."

Once we were on the way, I reread Violet's first letter to us, and studied the sepia-colored photograph. Grandpa Frank's face was familiar to me from old photographs Violet had on display around Veneto, but she didn't talk about him much, and we somehow knew not to ask, afraid of upsetting her.

"I hadn't thought about him much until this trip," I said as I studied the photograph again. "He looks like he was a lot of fun."

"He was a handsome devil," Madeleine said. "No wonder Violet fell madly in love with him."

I pictured Violet as a young woman in love, and thought about my feelings for Charles. Would I miss him every day if he weren't here, as Violet had said she missed Frank? Would my hand still reach for his at sunrise, twenty years after he'd last slept beside me?

I returned the photograph to the envelope, turned my face to the window, and hoped Madeleine hadn't noticed the tears I blinked away.

WE ARRIVED TO a dreary morning in Amiens, the brooding sky threatening rain. Nonetheless, it was market day and everything

was bustle and noise, the stalls adorned with fresh fruit and vegetables, rustic breads, cured meats, and cheeses. My artist's eye
was more alert to beauty than it had been for a long time. Some
invisible restraint had fallen away within me, and I felt more open
since leaving New York. I was more aware of my surroundings, of
my urge to draw and paint.

"It's hard to imagine there was ever a war going on in such
a pretty place," I said as the bus taking us to our final destination rumbled over cobbled streets and crossed a bridge above the
Somme river.

"Violet said Frank's unit was billeted here," Madeleine added.
"I wonder which house was his."

I stared out of the window, pressing the images onto my mind
so I would be able to capture them in my sketchbook later. I
dozed a little then, soothed by the motion of the bus. For once,
my mind was free of all thoughts of weddings and whether I
would ever find Edward in Venice.

After twenty minutes or so, the bus came to a stop and the
driver explained that we had arrived at our destination. We were
the only people for miles around, it seemed, as the bus pulled
away and we found ourselves entirely alone.

The cemetery was both beautiful and heartbreaking. A sea of
white crosses stretched as far as I could see, each one a precise
distance from the next. Such care had been taken, such respect
shown to the fallen.

"Where shall we start?" I asked. Violet hadn't given us a plot
number. Perhaps there wasn't such a thing.

"I'll start at the far end," Madeleine suggested. "You start here.
If you find Frank's cross, whistle."

"If I find Frank's cross, I'll wave until you see me. This isn't the docks in New York, Madeleine."

Our search took much longer than I'd anticipated. Not just because of the sheer number of graves, but because I found myself stopping to read each name inscribed on the simple white crosses, and the shockingly brief period of the dates between birth and death. I walked along row after row, some of the crosses marked only with the words "A Soldier of the Great War." Too many fallen and unidentified men to comprehend.

I glanced up occasionally to see if Madeleine was faring any better. Like me, she was peering at each headstone, reading the inscription, moving on to the next. It would take us days to find Grandpa Frank at this rate.

After an hour, the sky grew darker and a steady rain began to fall. I made my way over to Madeleine, my feet soaked from the wet grass. I wished I'd taken her advice and worn more practical laced boots, after all.

"It's miserable," I said as I reached her. "Maybe we should come back when the rain stops?"

She looked up, her natural curls sagging in the rain, which was falling heavier and heavier by the minute. "We're already wet," she said. "We may as well finish the job."

I pulled my coat up over my head. "We'll be drowned. Let's come back after lunch, preferably with an umbrella."

"Don't be such a baby. This is part of the challenge!" she replied. "Besides, does it really matter if we're drowned? You're always so caught up in appearances."

"I may be a baby, but I'd rather not catch a cold and spend the rest of our trip in bed sick!" I had to raise my voice to make myself heard against the hiss of the rain that now pelted us both. "This is ridiculous, Madeleine. I'm heading back into town. We can come back later."

Stubborn to a fault, my sister refused to listen to me. "You go back if you like," she shouted in reply. "I'm staying."

My coat was drenched and soon my clothes would be, too. I hurried as fast as I could in skirt and heels to the bus stop at the edge of the cemetery, fuming all the way. Why did Madeleine insist on turning everything into an argument? She never used her common sense. Ever.

Thankfully, a bus came along in minutes. As I boarded, relieved to be out of the rain, my anger cooled a little. What if Grandpa Frank wasn't here after all? Violet would be devastated if we had to tell her we couldn't find him. She'd sent us all this way to wrap up the loose threads of her life, and it looked like we were already set to fail. After everything she had done for me, I couldn't bear to let her down.

Taking a seat beside the window, I sighed wearily, rubbed the condensation from the glass, and searched for Madeleine. There she was, doggedly tramping among the endless rows of crosses as the rain fell in curtains around her. Her obstinacy served her well sometimes.

If anyone could find Frank, Madeleine could.

Maddie

I didn't find Grandpa Frank, despite searching the remaining rows. As the rain eventually eased, I even went back through the rows Clara had already checked. Just as I'd resigned myself to the fact that his grave wasn't here, I noticed a groundskeeper tending to the graves, removing old flowers and weeds. I approached him and explained in rusty French that I was trying to find my grandfather's grave, and was there anything he could do to help? Fortunately, he spoke good English, and what he told me gave me hope.

Not caring that I looked like a drowned animal, I caught the next bus back into town and, after stopping at a hotel to place a phone call home, hurried on to the restaurant to find Clara and Daniel already there.

Daniel laughed when he saw me, and took off his jacket, insisting I swap it for my sodden coat.

"Well?" Clara said as I sat down. "Was it worth it? Did you find him?"

"No." I reached for the bread basket, taking a crusty piece and dipping it in the bowl of steaming rabbit stew that arrived within seconds of me sitting down. "But I did find some information that might help us." I took a few hungry mouthfuls of the stew. "You weren't wrong, Daniel. This is delicious."

He smiled. "I told you so. It's an old family recipe, dating back to . . ."

"Never mind the stew," Clara interrupted. "What did you find out?"

"We were at the wrong cemetery, in the wrong town," I explained. "Violet sent us to the wrong place."

"What? How do you know?" Clara asked.

Daniel looked confused. "The wrong cemetery? How many are there?"

"I spoke to a groundskeeper. Apparently there are dozens of cemeteries and war memorials in different towns in the area, and listen to this! The cemeteries in Amiens are dedicated to British soldiers and those from the Commonwealth, or France. *Not Americans.* The groundskeeper was something of an expert. He gave me the names of several American cemeteries not far from here."

Clara looked impressed but refused to say as much as she put down her spoon. "But how could Violet get it wrong? She's usually so careful and organized."

"Grandpa Frank's death was almost twenty years ago, and let's face it, she hasn't been herself lately."

We both fell silent a moment, thinking of how ill Violet was and remembering why we were here in the first place.

Daniel remained respectfully silent and refilled our wineglasses.

"Anyway," I continued, "I stopped into a hotel in town and put a telephone call through to Mother. She was still half asleep and I spent an absolute fortune on the call while I waited for her to check Violet's memory box where she keeps all of Grandpa Frank's things."

"And?" Daniel and Clara prompted at the same time.

"Sure enough, Frank Bell was buried in the Somme American Cemetery. He was *billeted* here in Amiens but was killed while his unit was on the march to assist at a field hospital closer to the front line. The hotel concierge said we can get to a town called Saint-Quentin easily enough by train and take a bus from there. The journey should take less than two hours, but unfortunately trains don't run there on a Monday from Amiens, so we can't go today. Oh, and the graves are arranged in alphabetical order. We should be able to find him easily."

Clara ran her finger over the rim of her glass, making it sing. "Your prying turned out to be useful after all."

"I prefer to think of it as investigating rather than prying," I countered.

"Will you return to Paris tonight and go tomorrow?" Daniel asked.

I'd almost forgotten he was there, I was so caught up in relaying what I'd discovered. "I think we should stay here for the night," I volunteered, looking at Clara for agreement. "We could leave on the first train tomorrow. Give us the full day."

"Stay? Here?" Clara's mouth fell open in shock. "But where? And we have nothing with us. No change of clothes. Nothing!"

I took a long sip of wine and smiled at her. "Exactly. We're changing our plans, Clara. Rethinking and adjusting. You didn't really expect everything to go perfectly according to Violet's schedule, did you?"

She looked thoroughly miserable. "I did, actually. If anything had to fall by the wayside, I was hoping it might be the balloon ride."

"Balloon ride?" Daniel looked intrigued.

"Something Violet did when she was here," I explained. "She's arranged for us to visit a ballooning factory outside Paris, for a tethered ascent. Clara is terrified by the idea."

"It's perfectly safe, Miss Sommers," Daniel assured her. "I've been ballooning several times, at various festivals and world fairs and the like. It's tremendous fun. I'd be happy to go with you, if it would help to calm the nerves."

Clara agreed to the idea, reassured by the thought of having someone else there besides me, who, she remarked, "enjoys putting us in danger."

She was also persuaded, after a little prodding, to stay overnight in Amiens, especially with us both already soaked and preferring not to stay in our damp clothes all the way back to Paris. Without much difficulty, we found a room at a charming little pension near the center of town. A ladies' clothing shop nearby had plenty for us to choose from, although Clara muttered about the way all of the styles were in dark colors, and I grumbled about their apparent lack of knowledge that it was now 1937 and women could wear slacks.

Daniel returned to Paris to catch the show he was reviewing that evening. I was a little sorry I hadn't given him more attention, but I had more important things on my mind. He'd wished us good luck and said he hoped to see us at the hotel when we returned to Paris.

Without the usual distraction of our books, sketch pads, and

writing journals, we were left with only each other for entertainment for what remained of the afternoon and the evening.
When the rain let up, we walked along the Somme, which curved
through town and shimmered in the fire of the setting sun, winding up at the famous cathedral. We stopped to admire the High
Gothic style so similar to that of Notre-Dame de Paris with its
stained glass windows and breathtaking statuettes carved into
the ancient stone. We continued, drifting along the streets, taking in the beautiful homes in stucco or stone with slate roofs,
and storefronts overlooking the canals. We even stumbled across
Jules Verne's old house, which made us both smile. The town felt
so intimate compared to the bustle of Paris, and a million miles
away from the chaos of New York. Surprisingly, we didn't argue,
though neither did we pretend to be the best of friends.

As the light fell, we returned to our cramped room and
changed into our newly purchased nightclothes. A frumpy-
looking nightdress for Clara, and pajama pants and shirt for me.
I wondered what tomorrow would bring. Even with the new information about the American cemetery, I worried we might not
find Grandpa Frank, or the other people Violet wanted us to find
in Venice and Vienna. I hated to think we would return home
without success, and that my relationship with Clara would remain as fractured as ever.

I hoped our trip wouldn't prove to be a waste of time.

I hoped, like Violet, it would be a journey I still thought about
many decades later.

Clara

Our unscheduled overnight stay in Amiens wasn't as terrible as I'd thought it would be, and a small part of me was proud to have coped so well with the last-minute change of plans and impromptu change of clothes. Madeleine lived for such impulsive chaos, while I found it deeply unsettling. I hadn't realized just how much I needed order and routine until we'd set out on this trip. Perhaps a small part of me was beginning to enjoy the sense of unpredictability, of not quite knowing what the day would bring.

We rose and breakfasted early, and although I wasn't the tidiest or cleanest I'd ever been, I was at least dry, and full of renewed hope of finding Frank. It was unlike Violet to make a mistake, and it only emphasized how fragile her memories had become. We were the custodians of those memories now. The importance of our journey had never felt clearer.

Fortunately, there was a morning train to Saint-Quentin and a warm spring sun warmed my face as I enjoyed the gentle sway of the locomotive. Madeleine scrutinized the morning newspaper she'd picked up in Amiens, scribbling furiously in her journal as she found another report about the Nazi Party. I didn't understand her obsession with politics. It was almost as if she was looking for trouble, seeking out the very worst of the day's news. I left her to it and relaxed in my small puddle of sunlight.

After a short bus journey from the station in Saint-Quentin, we arrived at the cemetery outside of town where we believed—and hoped—Frank was laid to rest. This time, we were graced with blue skies, and a sunny warmth flirted with the cool spring air. This time, Madeleine and I agreed to search with a strategy; we made our way to the rows of pristine white crosses where the surnames of the fallen began with a *B* and started at opposite ends of each row, meeting, eventually, in the middle.

After only a few minutes, I glanced up to see Madeleine waving from a dozen or so crosses away. I took a deep breath and made my way over to her.

"Frank?"

She nodded and pointed to the simple white cross in front of her.

DOCTOR FRANK DAVID BELL
American Red Cross
1872–1918

We bowed our heads in silent respect, each of us lost in memories of Grandpa Frank: the way he always carried cherry lollipops in his jacket pocket; how he'd bounce us on his knee until we'd squealed. Doctor Bell, renowned surgeon, had felt it his duty to help at the Front and volunteered for the American Red Cross. Violet—strong, loving, vibrant Violet—had wept quietly on the day he left, while Madeleine and I held hands under the shade of the apple tree in the garden, not fully understanding what was happening, but knowing, somehow, things would never be the same.

"We found him," I whispered. I laid a bundle of dried rosemary next to the cross. "Rosemary, for remembrance."

Madeleine placed a bunch of violets beside the rosemary. "Violets, for your best girl," she added. "She misses you so very much. We brought a letter for you, too. She wanted to say farewell."

I noticed Madeleine's eyes were misty and felt my own begin to fill with tears. The number of graves—of men lost—and the beautiful solitude of the cemetery affected us both.

"Go on then," Madeleine whispered. "It's your turn to read it."

My eyes blurred with tears as I opened Violet's letter and began to read her words.

My darling Frankie,

How can you possibly have been gone for so long? How have so many sunrises and sunsets passed without you by my side? But it won't be long now until we meet again. In that, I take comfort from my last months. Whenever I feel any pain, I think of you, and I am soothed.

It's my greatest wish that the girls have found your final resting place and can leave this small token with you. Do you remember sending it to me? A poppy from the roadside? I kept it all this time, pressed between the pages of my Bible. It is fragile now, and yet its beauty remains.

I was fragile once. Lost and alone after I returned from Venice. When everyone else turned their backs on me, you of-

*fered nothing but love and compassion. You took me—us—
into your life without question, and the years I spent with you,
although far too brief, were the happiest of my life.*

*You told me when you left for France that it wasn't goodbye,
but au revoir. "Until we meet again."*

Until we meet again, sweet Frank.

Au revoir.

Your best girl,
Violet

I placed the dried poppy against the marble cross, and we both
stood in silent thought as a bird sang his lament on the branch of
a hawthorn tree behind us.

Madeleine tentatively looped her arm through mine, just as she
used to when we were little girls tucked up together on a blanket
on the sand while Mother, or Violet, or sometimes Auntie Nellie, read us a story. The made-up stories were always the best, the
wildest adventures that sent our imaginations racing. In that moment, I realized I'd missed that closeness to Madeleine, the sense
of completeness that came from being beside her. It was a gentle
moment of togetherness, when everything felt at peace: us, and
the world. I think Madeleine sensed it, too.

We took our time, but eventually I suggested we make our
way to the train station and begin our journey back to Paris. Saying goodbye to Grandpa Frank had been more emotional than
we'd expected, and I found myself lost in memories of him as we
boarded the train. Soon, my thoughts turned to Violet's letter, the
love she still felt for Frank after all these years.

"What do you think Violet meant by people turning their backs on her when she returned from Venice?" I asked.

"I wondered the same," Madeleine said, staring out the window. "And what did she mean by 'you took us into your life'? Who was 'us'?"

Whatever it meant, I felt a sense of quiet contentment as the train raced across the verdant countryside. Our time in France was almost at an end, and Venice beckoned.

Maddie

$\mathcal{U}$pon our return to Paris, we drifted to our own rooms, this time not out of frustration with each other, but for space to think about the last two days, and to rest after our extended travel. Grandpa Frank had brought Clara and me together, and it felt surprisingly good to have my sister at my side for now, even if our truce was tentative. Seeing the impact of war in such a tangible way as we'd gazed at the rows of white crosses had changed my perspective. It was difficult to comprehend loss on such a scale, especially knowing there were so many cemeteries like it all across France. The possibility of another war with Germany suddenly felt more immediate, more real somehow, and not just a distant threat.

With only three days left in Paris and still a long list of things I wanted to see and do, I cut my rest short and set out for Les Halles, a famed marketplace dating to medieval times. It wasn't the safest area of Paris, or so I'd read, and that was precisely why I wanted to go. On the main thoroughfare, as I browsed the stalls of colorful fruit and vegetables, clothing, soaps and lotions, a riot of smells filled the air, from roasted lamb to heady spices to pungent cheeses. After a couple of hours, I took the Métro to Montparnasse to visit the Café du Dôme, made famous by Hemingway and Fitzgerald. I ordered a *vin rouge* and a crepe drizzled with chocolate.

Thoroughly exhausted but happy, I returned to the hotel, stopping by the desk for any messages that may have come while I was away. There was only one note, from Daniel.

Maddie,

I hope you were able to find what you were looking for on your trip, and that all went smoothly on your return. If you're still ballooning tomorrow, I'd be glad to join you. I'll meet you in the lobby at eight?

   Thank you for the invitation.

Daniel

I was surprised he'd remembered, let alone thought to leave a note. Truthfully, I was surprised by Daniel Miller, period.

"Ballooning tomorrow," I said as Clara and I dined together that evening. "I bet you can't wait!"

She groaned and left her steak unfinished. "Must we? Really?"

I nodded and said yes, we must, and finished her steak for her.

THE NEXT MORNING, I rose with the birds and felt refreshed, enjoying a coffee on the narrow little balcony off the study window before I dressed for the day ahead. I chose a heavy sweater and overcoat, and a pair of leather gloves. Though I was practically on the verge of heatstroke, I knew I'd need warm clothes when we ascended into the clouds where the air became thinner and colder with each additional foot climbed. I couldn't wait! For all intents and purposes, we were going to fly, free as birds in the sky.

"Clara!" I called, deciding she'd been in the bathroom long enough. "It's time to go. Are you ready?" I double-checked my handbag, making sure I had my journal to capture the experience on the page.

Clara eventually emerged, her face washed of all color and none too happy about the day's excursion.

"Let's get this over with." She sighed.

"Cheer up," I said, nudging her playfully. "It'll be fun, I promise."

Daniel met us in the lobby, as arranged, and we rode a taxicab together to the balloon factory in Vaugirard. The journey passed almost entirely in silence, Daniel and I exchanging the occasional playful grimace about Clara's palpable nerves. It didn't feel odd to have Daniel with us, and with Clara so anxious, I was glad of his company. I watched him occasionally pen something in a small leather-bound notebook and return it to a pocket inside his jacket. I wondered what he was writing, if he was sending letters to a lady friend at home, or if he was merely, like me, taking notes in a travel journal. Clara, on the other hand, looked thoroughly miserable. Her lips were tight, her features drawn, and in spite of myself, I almost felt sorry for her.

When we arrived, we pulled up to a large wooden building that looked more like a barn than a factory, and threaded our way through a rough-and-tumble lawn to the main door. It was deliciously rustic. I knew Clara hated it the minute she saw it.

"I hope this is the right place," Daniel said, sliding the large door aside.

"I hope it isn't," Clara countered.

It *was* the right place.

"Welcome! *Entrez-vous!*" A young man waved us inside, a jovial smile at his lips. "You must be the Miss Sommers? I am Monsieur Malraux. Your grandmother told me to expect you. Have you had an agreeable trip so far?"

Clara and I exchanged a look.

I tempered my reply. "Paris is beautiful." There was no need to tell him about our squabbles, about going to the wrong cemetery, or fighting over which sights in Paris were the most important. "We've both enjoyed the sights."

It was the truth. We'd just enjoyed the sights *separately*.

"Shall I take you on a tour of the factory before we go for our ascent?" Monsieur Malraux continued. He reminded me of a fox with his piercing blue eyes, sharp smile, and red hair that waved over his forehead.

"That'd be just dandy," I said at exactly the same time Clara said we didn't want him to go to any trouble for us.

He laughed and said it was no trouble at all.

The factory really was an enormous barn. Large swathes of multicolored silk, designed with an appealing array of stripes and polka dots, floated from the rafters. I grabbed Clara's arm as I pointed at the beautifully detailed animal balloons; tigers with stripes and monkeys with smiles, and even a bright green crocodile that hovered overhead. Several pirates, and what looked to be a collection of court jesters, lay strewn across a worktable. On the far side of the room, two men worked diligently on some sort of motorized mechanism. In the opposite corner, a woman sat behind an industrial-sized sewing machine, where she carefully stitched pieces of balloon fabric together. When we reached the back door, Monsieur Malraux led us outside. A magnificent balloon made of bright yellow silk was tethered to several pegs in the ground.

"It's beautiful," I gasped.

Clara shook her head as she stared up into the clouds. "It may be beautiful, but I am not going up there in that thing."

"Come on, Clara," I said. "Live a little. It's perfectly safe."

"This way, ladies." Malraux directed us to a ladder beside the basket of the balloon. "Mr. Miller, perhaps you could climb in first and lend a hand to the ladies while I assist them on the ladder."

Daniel climbed inside effortlessly, and I followed, clambering over the edge of the basket with ease—but I'd underestimated the distance to the bottom of the basket. With a thud, I landed in a heap. I laughed at myself as I dusted off my slacks.

"Let me help." Daniel held out a hand. I took it and let him haul me back onto my feet.

Suddenly he was very near—near enough for me to see the thick fringe of lashes framing his dark eyes. Near enough to pick up the scent of his cologne: bergamot and leather.

As he met my eye, I stepped back quickly.

"We need to help Clara," I said, looking over the edge of the basket.

I held out my hand to my sister. Her forehead was creased into a worried frown, and I felt another wave of sympathy for her. She was trying to be brave, despite how difficult it was for her.

"Must I really?" she said. "Can't you two go without me?"

"It'll be great fun, you'll see," Daniel encouraged. "And it really is perfectly safe. Look, we're tethered to the ground."

She glanced at the tether rope but shook her head. "I don't think I can do it."

"You can, Clara," I encouraged. "Come on. I'll be right here and so will Daniel." I watched her shift from one foot to the other, her golden-brown eyes fixed on the large balloon overhead. Desperate, I tried another tack. "Do it for Violet. You promised, remember?"

In seconds she had climbed the ladder and hoisted herself up over the edge of the basket, crashing into me. I caught her in my arms as we both stumbled backward.

"Alright, here we go, everyone," Monsieur Malraux said, pulling a lever.

A roaring sound erupted as a flame poured from a spout overhead, and slowly the balloon began to lift into the air. Our guide chattered on politely, giving us details about the impressive engineering, a little about the history of balloon flight, and other interesting facts.

"The frame is made of aluminum," he remarked. "The balloon canopy is pure silk. There's a simple gas contraption here that fills the balloon with heated air. This"—he gripped a lever—"is how we control how much air goes in and out of the balloon, and in turn determines how high or low we are."

As we climbed higher, I was glad for my scarf and warm overcoat. Just as we'd been warned, the air grew colder as we ascended and the soft breeze turned to more of a steady wind. I gazed down at the distant Paris skyline. The Seine glittered in the sunlight and the magnificently shaped steel of Eiffel's tower gleamed. My heart filled with gratitude for Violet's wonderful gift and her insistence we see the world. I felt myself changing, my view expanding, and I knew it would make me a better journalist.

"It's marvelous!" I shouted, my cheeks stiff from cold and from smiling. I peered down at the factory and the assistants waiting near the pegs, ready to pull in the ropes should we need help. I took in the treetops that looked softer and smaller, the verdant sloping hill behind the factory on the outskirts of the city.

"This is wonderful, don't you think, Clara?" Without tearing my eyes away, my hand reached for hers. Only she wasn't beside me. She was cowering in the corner, hunkered down. "Oh, Clara, you're missing it! You need to see this. For your sketches."

She shook her head. "I can't."

"Take my hand," I said, reaching for her.

Daniel crouched down beside her. "Why don't we have Maddie stand on one side of you and I'll stand on the other," he said softly. "Make you feel a bit safer, perhaps?"

Clara glanced up at me and after a moment of searching my face, looking for the sister she knew would protect her even if we didn't always see eye to eye, she nodded and stood. She gripped my hand tightly and allowed Daniel to stand at her elbow to steady her.

As she caught sight of the view she gasped. "It's beautiful."

I beamed at her, so proud she'd beaten back her fear and so happy to share the moment with her.

I looked at Daniel, who winked to acknowledge our shared success, and I felt my smile broaden.

"Thank you," I mouthed silently.

He nodded, his own happiness evident from the gleam in his eyes.

We floated for some time, suspended above the ground, until at last we began to descend. Clara returned to her protected corner but remained standing this time.

I took out my journal, wanting to capture the sensation of flying on the page. My writing didn't have to all be hard politics and scheming businessmen; sometimes I liked to write more elegant prose, as I'd done in my descriptions of Paris. Perhaps, one day, I would surprise everyone—surprise myself—and turn my hand to writing a novel.

"What's that?" Clara asked as I pulled the journal from my handbag.

"My journal. I wanted to write down our experience," I replied.

She moved toward me and reached out. "Not your journal. That!"

I followed her gaze but saw it too late: the corner of a pale blue envelope, peeping from between the pages of my journal.

Edward's letter.

I'd forgotten I'd put it there. How could I have been so stupid?

Before I could stop Clara, she'd yanked the envelope free.

Her eyes widened as she flushed a deep shade of red. "*You took it?* And I assume you read it, too."

Cringing at my carelessness, I edged around the basket to

stand beside her. "I didn't mean to take it, and then I forgot about it. I'm sorry."

"You had no right, Madeleine! I thought it was lost!"

Embarrassed to have been caught, and with really no defense, I changed tactics. "He cares for you, doesn't he?" I pressed. "But do you care for him the same way?"

"Of course I care for him. He's a friend," she replied, exasperated. "It's just a letter, Madeleine. Just words on a page. That's all."

She didn't look angry—she looked devastated, betrayed. And I felt sick to my stomach. We'd started to build something between us, if only a little, and I'd ruined things. Again.

She pushed the envelope into her coat pocket. "Don't talk to me!" she said, moving to the other side of the balloon next to Monsieur Malraux and Daniel, who both politely tried to pretend they hadn't seen the entire drama play out between us.

"You're always interfering, Madeleine," she continued. "Even with your Manhattan apartment and your so-called ambitions, you haven't grown up at all, have you? You're still a child, poking through your big sister's things. What actually is it that you want from life anyway, because whatever it is, you don't seem to be getting very far with it."

Her words stung.

I wanted to be taken seriously by a proper newspaper. I wanted to prove to my family that I wasn't the oddity or the perpetual disappointment they'd always believed me to be. I wanted, for once, to make them proud, to have them turn to their friends and say, "That's my daughter," and "That's my sister."

I closed my eyes and felt the breeze tug at my hair as the silence enveloped me. I'd enjoyed the thrill of the balloon ascent, but it was, after all, just a passing distraction. An amusement. Reality was waiting for me below, back on solid ground, and Clara was right: I might know what I wanted from life, but I wasn't getting very far with it.

Something had to change. *I* had to change, no matter how difficult that might be.

Clara

$\mathcal{A}$fter the events of the balloon ascent, Madeleine and I spent our final few days in Paris apart. I didn't know—or particularly care—what she was doing and enjoyed my last peaceful hours in the Louvre and the Musée d'Orsay. While I was pleased to have Edward's letter back, not least because I now had a way to contact him in Venice, I couldn't believe Madeleine's betrayal—and yet part of me wasn't in the least bit surprised by it. She'd often been caught going through my things when we were younger. Why would that change now? I'd been silly to believe—to hope—she would act differently, and while I was furious that she'd been so deceitful, and mortified to think of her having read Edward's intimate confession, my greatest reaction was one of bitter disappointment that she'd proved herself to be exactly the same interfering Madeleine she'd always been. I wished I could share more of Paris with her, just as Violet had shared the city with Margaret so many years before us, but perhaps I wished for too much.

"Can you ever forgive me?" Madeleine asked as we ate dinner in silence at the hotel restaurant on our final evening.

I was surprised by her emphatic apologies. It wasn't like Madeleine to admit she was at fault so readily.

"I don't think I can, actually. No," I replied without looking at her. "What you did was unforgivable."

"Please, Clara. I shouldn't have read the letter or kept it from you. It was just there, among the newspapers on the desk, and then you came back into the room and I took it without really thinking, and before we . . . well, before we became friends again. Then I just forgot about it."

I dabbed at my mouth with my napkin, pretending I wasn't affected by the use of the word "friends." In truth, I wanted to let go of some of the bitterness of the past. But I wouldn't give her the satisfaction of letting her off the hook so easily. Not yet.

"When will you ever learn not to go digging through other people's things?" I asked stiffly.

"I'll never go through your personal things again. I swear," Madeleine replied, raising her hands in defeat. "Even if you do leave them lying around to tempt me. But going through other people's things . . . come on, Clara, I'm a journalist. I dig for information. It's what I do."

"You don't have to do it at another's expense!" I countered. "You upset people and cause difficulties for them. Surely there are ways to go about it that aren't quite as deceitful."

Refusing to meet my gaze, Madeleine pushed a wedge of roasted potato around her plate. She'd hardly touched her meal. It was unlike her not to finish every last bite, and more often than not, mine, too. A sure sign that she really was sorry.

"But I don't suppose there's much to be gained by prolonging the argument," I conceded at last. "What's done is done, and we still have to take the rest of the journey together. I'm prepared to put the incident aside, for Violet."

"So, I'm forgiven?" She raised a hopeful eyebrow.

"Not forgiven, but I won't bring it up again because Violet would want us to bury the hatchet and try to get along." I put my napkin on the table. "Even though you make it exceptionally difficult," I added.

"If you want to tell me about Edward, I . . ."

"I don't," I said, holding up my hand to end the conversation. "I don't want to talk about the letter, or Edward, again."

I might not want to talk about it with Madeleine, but the truth was, I couldn't stop thinking about Edward or the fact that he planned to be in Venice the following week. It was too late to try to put him off, not that I really wanted to. Was it so wrong for two friends to spend a morning at an art gallery together?

As we were finishing our meal, Daniel spotted us and approached our table.

"Ladies, I'm so glad I caught you. I wanted to wish you both farewell and a happy journey to Venice."

I thanked him for his help in the balloon, and Madeleine shook his hand.

"Where to next, Mr. Miller?" I asked.

"I'm not entirely sure. I'm waiting for a new assignment at another theater, somewhere in Europe. Possibly something in Austria, but there's also a chance I might return to America."

"Oh?" I didn't mention that we also planned to be in Austria. I'd enjoyed Mr. Miller's company but didn't want to see him turning up at every place we visited.

"Things are becoming increasingly unsettled in Europe," he

added, "and while there's no need for alarm, I'd advise you ladies to be careful."

Madeleine nodded her understanding, and I got the impression she wanted to speak to him in private. They'd gotten along like Laurel and Hardy, and I suspected they were sorry to say goodbye. I excused myself for a moment, and took longer than necessary in the bathroom.

By the time I returned to our table, Mr. Miller had gone.

"Say your farewells?" I teased.

"You didn't need to excuse yourself," Madeleine said. "I'm perfectly happy to see him go. I enjoy his company well enough, but I certainly don't need him hanging around all the time."

I didn't believe her for a minute.

I arched a brow at her but changed the subject. "Do you think he's right about things becoming increasingly unsettled? Are you sure it's safe for us to stay in Europe?"

Madeleine hesitated.

"I wouldn't say it's perfectly safe," she replied at last. "But neither is New York City. We're being sensible, and careful. And I also think Daniel is being overly cautious. A lot like you. I'm following the news closely. If I think we need to leave, I'll say so. Until then, let's keep going."

I really did want to keep going. Paris had already surprised me, but not in the way I'd expected. The sights were awe-inspiring, the food and wine delicious, the lights on the Seine made the city shimmer, but what had surprised me most was the way I felt about being away from home. I recalled Auntie Nellie once saying her trip around the world wasn't remarkable for what she'd seen and experienced along the way, but for how she'd felt when she returned home. I hadn't understood the sentiment when I was a young girl, intimidated by this brash, outspoken woman who was a friend of my grandmother's, but I was beginning to appreciate what she'd meant. I thought about the pocket watch Violet had given me for luck before I'd left New York. I had looked at it at least a dozen times during our time away from home, the inscription *Never turn back* seeming to speak directly to me, urging me on even when I doubted myself.

I studied Madeleine's expression and decided that I'd have to trust her to look out for us both, despite my reservations. For all her faults, I knew Madeleine wouldn't put me in harm's way intentionally.

"We need to think about Venice, then," I said, changing the subject as I placed Violet's second letter to us on the table. "Shall we?"

Madeleine nodded.

Opening the envelope, I removed a single sheet of paper, and began to read the letter out loud.

My dearest girls,

You are ready to leave Paris and move on, to bella *Venezia! A city that has my heart, and I hope it will enchant yours, too.*

Life doesn't always run in straight lines, and you must never believe anyone who tells you otherwise. Frank Bell was the love of my life, but there were others. One in particular, who also touched my heart. Most women will tell you (if they're being honest) that they have loved more than one man in their lifetime. Despite the commitments of marriage, most of us also hold a flame for another. We make our decisions and choices, and we live with them. I wouldn't change my marriage to Frank for all the world, but I wouldn't change what came before it, either.

Frank knew all about Matthias Morelli—there were no secrets between us—although perhaps he never fully understood how important Matthias was to me, or how he changed my life so completely. We met in Venice, during the trip I won to Europe. Margaret wanted to visit Rome, but I insisted on Venice. It's as if I knew I had to go there, that I knew Matthias was waiting for me.

I don't know if he is still there—if he is still alive, even. I do hope so. It will mean the world to me to know I have this last chance to say the things I should have said to him all those years ago.

With all my love to you both,
Violet

Madeleine's mouth fell open in shock. I stared at her, too stunned to speak.

"Violet had a love affair before she was married to Grandpa Frank," she said eventually. "Well, I didn't see that coming!"

Violet was a beautiful young woman in the old photographs she'd shown us, prettier even than our mother, so it wasn't unexpected that men should find her alluring, but she'd never once mentioned this other man. Why would she, I supposed.

"I'd assumed Matthias must be an artist Violet admired, or someone who'd helped her and Margaret on their journey," I said. "But if that were true, why would she go to the trouble of sending us to find him?" I shook my head. Perhaps we had underestimated her.

"We don't know her at all, do we?" Madeleine stole the words right off my tongue. "We thought we knew everything about her, but we don't know what she keeps hidden inside her heart, or who she was before she became a mother and grandmother. I wonder what else she's been keeping to herself all these years. What a woman!"

"I guess we all have our secrets," I agreed.

"But given how much she loved Grandpa Frank, it's hard to imagine there was ever anyone else."

My thoughts flickered to Charles, and then to Edward. "Oh, I don't know that it's such a surprise. Is it really possible to fall in love only once?"

Madeleine grinned. "Well, now I'm looking forward to Venice more than ever. I want to meet this mysterious Matthias Morelli. See what he's all about. To Venice, then!" She raised her glass in a toast.

I raised my glass in return as the setting sun cast a golden glow over the table. "To Venice. And whatever might be waiting for us there."

Madeleine leaned back in her chair. "I think a delicious story is what's waiting for us."

I bit back a smile. "You sound just like Nellie Bly."

She folded her arms across her chest and smiled. "I know. And hopefully I'll soon be writing just like her, too."

PART TWO

Arrivederci

Violet

❈

I think of the girls every moment of every day. I go over their itinerary and imagine where they are at that exact minute, what they're doing, what they're thinking in private. After so much time together, I wonder what secrets they still keep from each other, as every woman does, even from her sister.

It's a perfect spring day, and Henrietta insists we do something nice outside.

"A picnic at the beach," she announces. "Like those you're always telling me about when the girls were younger. It's such a nice day, for April. Do you think Celestine would like to join us?"

"Not today," I reply. "She's running errands. She'll be sad to miss it, though. Our beach picnics were always a favorite." They were such happy times, languishing beside the surf, the roar of the ocean the only music we needed.

"It's a pretty name, Celestine," Henrietta continues. "Unusual."

"It was her father's favorite," I say, and I picture him, telling me in that animated way of his about the painting above his fireplace, and the artist who'd captured the beautiful young woman playing among the stars. "It means 'heavenly,'" I add, recalling how he'd first said the same to me all those years ago.

Henrietta packs the perfect spread—tea sandwiches, fruit, cakes, and lemonade, the basket filled to bursting—but I find I have no appetite and pick at the sandwiches like a sparrow as I gaze at the expanse of sand in front of me, empty now and yet so full of memories.

I picture the girls racing from the water to warm themselves on the blanket, building a kingdom of golden sand, giggling as they work to stem the flow of the tide and defend their fortress. Then they would listen to Nellie's stories of sailing across vast oceans to foreign countries, and I would doze happily in the sun and wonder which bits were true and which Nellie had made up to amuse the girls.

I can still see them, dressed in matching bathing suits, their hair styled the same; mirrors of each other when they were clearly anything but. "Let them become their own people, Celestine," I'd urged. But she wouldn't listen. My daughter had inherited her father's flamboyant temperament: stubborn to a fault, certain she knew best. I wonder, now, if her insistence on dressing them the same as children was partly the cause of them being so determined to be different as adults.

"How do you think they'll manage, spending so much time together?" Henrietta asks, pulling me back to the present. "Do they really hate each other?"

I think about that for a moment. "No, they don't understand each other is the problem and, well, life is complicated. Anyway, they're not back yet, so it can't be a complete disaster, I suppose. I just hope that whatever bridges they build between them are strong enough to remain when they come home."

"I don't think I'd like to travel," Henrietta muses as she combs her fingers through the sand. "I'd be afraid I wouldn't like things as much when I got back."

I'd certainly returned from Venice with a sense of longing for what I'd left behind, and an understanding that life would never be the same. As I stare at the ocean, I wonder how different things would have been if I'd returned home with Margaret that summer as planned, rather than staying in Venice with Matthias for the extra month.

I tire quickly and ask Henrietta to take me back to the house. There is something I need to read again, words I must have read a hundred times, and yet call to me still.

I rummage in my desk until I find what I'm looking for: the letter Matthias wrote to me in reply all those years ago, the gracious way he'd accepted my news. I run my fingertips over his writing and my heart lurches back over the decades until I am standing in the Piazza San Marco and he twirls me around in an impromptu waltz, and everything is perfect.

I wonder what he looks like now. If his eyes are still full of mischief and passion. I wonder how he will react to hearing my name, and most of all, what will happen when Clara and Madeleine discover the truth of my past. My past—and their present.

Maddie

❧

$\mathcal{T}$he morning of our departure, Clara and I said goodbye to the hotel concierge, farewell to the glittering Seine, and so long to beautiful, enchanting Paris. Within the hour we found ourselves standing on another train station platform. I could hardly believe we'd already finished the first leg of our trip. It had passed so quickly—too quickly. Though I was sad to leave Paris, I loved the sense of change, and the anticipation of what lay ahead.

Clara fidgeted beside me, checking the station clock every few minutes. She was ready to board and to get to our next destination. I suspected part of her eagerness had a lot to do with Edward Arnold. How deliciously awful of her, daring to meet her art tutor in Venice while she was away from her fiancé! A behavior I wouldn't necessarily condone—unless the fiancé in question was Charles Hancock. Perhaps I'd misjudged her. Perhaps there was more to perfect, sensible Clara Sommers than I'd given her credit for, and although being a third wheel in the Arnolds' struggling marriage wasn't really something to be encouraged, if Edward could distract her from Charles, and help her see him for what he truly was, that could only be a good thing. In the meantime, we would enjoy our ride on the Orient Express.

As we waited to board, I admired the famous train that would whisk us away, southbound across France to the Simplon Tunnel carved through the Alps, and on, to Venice. The cars were a sleek midnight blue and beige with a gold crest that said Compagnie Internationale des Wagons-Lits. Stewards stood poised in front of open carriage doors. They were smartly dressed in royal blue livery trimmed with gold, and little hats strapped to their heads that gave them an official air. Well-dressed women gathered on the platform in Chanel coats and gloves, their hair pinned in neat curls beneath fancy hats. Their male companions wore the latest fashion in gray checks and brown double-breasted suits, none of which I would have noticed before I'd spent time with Clara on the Champs-Élysées. Porters dashed about, shouting good-naturedly to each other while the baggage was handled, and the low rumble of conversation competed with the train engine as it roared to life.

"It's quite exciting, isn't it?" Clara said. She looked beautiful in her pearl-gray travel dress. "I can hardly wait to see Venice."

I slapped her affectionately on the shoulder as I bounded up the steps. "That's the spirit, Sis. Come on!"

As we made our way through the train cars to our sleeper compartment, I took in every exquisite detail: the luxurious wood paneling, the scent of fresh flowers and brass polish that filled the air. Our accommodation was spacious and equally opulent with more inlaid paneling, polished to a shine and bringing a warm richness to the room. I glanced up at the ceiling, lined with smoked glass, and then at a small en suite bathroom fitted with pearly white tiles.

Clara declared it delightful as she settled on a cream-colored sofa, beside which two small chairs, upholstered in teal velvet, were arranged around a glass-topped table, bolted to the floor. Brilliant sunlight poured through a set of large windows nearby, casting a golden glow over Clara and the entire room.

We spent a little time unpacking, again. Or rather, Clara did while I quickly shoved the contents of my bags into a few drawers and hung the two dresses I'd brought.

"It's more like a luxury hotel than a train," I mused as I continued my way around the sleeper car to inspect the details, opening a cabinet or two and eyeing a set of shelves cleverly designed with a thin rod to hold the glasses steady.

A shrill whistle signaled our departure, the train lurched, and we both stumbled slightly, laughing.

"Here we go!" I said.

While Clara continued to unpack her things, I took in the view from the window, enjoying the slight sway of the carriage and the forward motion as we gained speed. Memories of Paris drifted through my head, and the farewell we'd exchanged with Daniel. He really was a decent man. He'd never been threatened by my passionate nature, and we'd had very enjoyable conversations—politics, history, literature, our flagging careers—and we'd also laughed a lot. Clara liked him, too, though she'd been slower to come around. I felt a tug of regret that I hadn't exchanged addresses or telephone numbers with him, but it had seemed silly to ask, and he hadn't seemed inclined to ask me for mine.

Distracted by my thoughts, I left the window and the views and sprawled on my bed. I soon drifted off, sleepy after the early morning wake-up call.

When it was time for lunch to be served, Clara woke me and we made our way together to the dining car. We'd skipped breakfast and it felt like I had a crater where my stomach should be.

We were shown to a table with fine white linen, a crystal decanter and glasses, and napkins shaped into rosettes. I laughed as I plucked mine from the center of the plate and smoothed it over my lap. "I wonder whose job it is to do that. It must take them hours."

"It's the little touches that matter," Clara said as she admired the decorative place setting. She let the waiter unfold her napkin and drape it across her lap, as was the proper way. "I wish Violet could see this. Wouldn't she adore it?"

"She would. Yes."

I wondered how Violet was faring. Still stubbornly hobbling out to the garden each day, insisting on card games and visits from her friends, or laid up in bed for the duration? What must it be like to face death as your health diminished before your eyes? As exciting as the trip had been so far, it was important to remember why we were here.

"Good afternoon, ladies. How can I be of service?" The waiter bent gallantly over the table as he filled our crystal glassware with water. He was attired in crisply ironed livery, and moved as stiffly as his uniform looked.

Clara smiled politely at him as I lit a cigarette and leaned back in my chair.

"What've you got for us, fine sir?" I asked. "I could eat a whole roasted elephant, I'm so hungry!"

He looked a little taken aback. "Indeed, miss."

Clara kicked my foot under the table as he rattled off the lunch special of duck à l'orange with whipped potatoes, grilled onions, and haricots verts.

"That sounds wonderful, thank you," Clara interjected before I could reply with some other silly comment.

"Shall I bring you both an aperitif while you wait?" he asked.

"Perhaps you should bring two," I replied.

His eyes widened. He looked from me to Clara and back to me again.

"I meant one for me and one for my sister," I said, smothering a laugh.

"Very good, mesdames."

Clara leaned forward when he'd gone. "Roasted elephant? Really, Madeleine?"

"Did you see his face?"

She rolled her eyes but a smile tugged at her lips.

After we finished the excellent meal, as fine as anything we'd eaten in Paris, we took a digestif into the lounge where several couples played bridge and others read novels, or engaged in hushed conversations.

When a gentleman beside us folded his newspaper and stood to go, I asked if I might take a look.

"Of course, please help yourself," he said, though his eyes were on Clara. She blushed at his open stare.

"Thanks." I snatched the newspaper up and slid into an empty chair.

"You're not going to read that now, are you?" Clara asked. "I haven't brought my book."

"I'll just take a quick look through the headlines, and save the rest for later. Sit down. You're making me nervous."

She took the seat opposite mine and picked up a magazine as I thumbed through the edition of the *New York Times,* already nearly a week old. There wasn't much of interest until page five. My eyes widened as I read the headline.

Hancock Enterprises to Buy City Block, Build by Autumn

Charles was going through with his development! I skimmed the article rapidly.

"It will be a magnificent building and will help clean up the neighborhood on the fringes of the financial district," Charles Hancock of Hancock Enterprises said on Thursday morning outside his office on Fifth Avenue. "We'll be employing dozens of new architects and engineers."

Nowhere did the article mention the hundreds of poor people who would be displaced because of his new building. They would likely move to Hooverville, the shantytown in Central Park that had continued to grow since the big market crash several years ago.

"That absolute pig!" I said aloud, catching Clara's attention.

"What?" She looked up from the French fashion magazine she'd taken from the pile on the table.

I hesitated, debating whether or not to tell her, but decided against it. I didn't want to start another fight between us, and this most certainly would.

"Nothing," I replied. "Just some political nonsense. I'll finish this later."

As I folded the paper, my mind raced. If Clara went through with the wedding, the Sommers family would be linked with the Hancocks, and with all of their projects—and misdeeds. My stomach churned at the thought. Our family was known for philanthropy and generosity. The Hancocks were known for their mansions and Fifth Avenue society projects, and, more recently, for Charles's success in business. This latest development of his would affect our good name by association.

I smoothed the newspaper, pausing as I was struck by an idea. What if I wrote an exposé about the displaced people suffering because of Hancock Enterprises? Since Charles's business dealings were already hitting the headlines, it would be the perfect time to pitch it. It was a great idea! I reached for my journal to take down a few notes.

"Struck by inspiration?" Clara asked as she picked up another magazine from the table.

I nodded. "Something like that."

My pen hovered over the page. Charles was Clara's fiancé, whether I liked it or not. Could I do it? Could I really expose the man my sister was going to marry? An article like this could be my way in, a real career break, but at what cost?

"Well, go on then," she prompted.

I looked up as happy chatter floated toward us from a circle of chairs near the window.

"It'll wait," I said as I put my pen and journal away, and put Charles Hancock out of mind for the time being. I motioned to the group beside the window. "Let's introduce ourselves. Maybe we'll meet some interesting people."

"Must we always be in search of interesting people?" Clara asked. "I'd be happy to sit quietly and read, or sketch. I can go back to the room and grab my things."

I told her she was no fun and that the best part of traveling was meeting new people.

"People like Daniel Miller?" she teased.

"Or like Edward Arnold?" I countered.

She cast me a warning look. "He's an old *friend,* and I would leave it there if I were you."

She begrudgingly followed me over to the group, where we were introduced to a Dr. and Mrs. Culpepper, an English couple headed to Venice and then on to Naples where Mrs. Culpepper hoped to recuperate from her gout. When they left, we enjoyed coffee with an elegant couple from Philadelphia named Mr. and Mrs. Wainwright, on a trip with their adolescent daughters, Eliza and Juliette. Clara enjoyed the young ladies' company, chatting animatedly with them about her art and promising to draw each of the young girls' portraits as a memento of their trip, while I had a rousing conversation with Mr. Wainwright. Though he seemed to disregard his wife's opinions—to my annoyance—he shared my passion for politics and current affairs.

"Young lady, I'm surprised by your interest in such things," he said, straightening his spine and puffing out his chest. "The Depression, the stock exchange. It really isn't a usual topic of conversation for women, especially of your class and wealth."

"I'm a journalist, sir. I follow the news diligently," I insisted for the second time. "I don't see how class or wealth have anything to do with the truth. Or compassion for others."

His eyebrows raised in surprise. "Well, I suppose I can see your point."

Growing irritated, I changed the subject. "What do you think of Hitler? Do you believe Germany will go to war?"

He nodded thoughtfully as he added more tobacco to his pipe. "Hitler will make a move soon, I suspect. Invade Austria, perhaps France. It seems likely, even to an observer from the United States."

"And what about Italy?" I asked, curious about Mussolini and the mark he was leaving on the country. Would there be visible signs of his rule when we arrived? I wondered.

Mr. Wainwright puffed on his pipe a moment, contemplating my question. "Mussolini is power hungry, too. According to an editorial I read the other day, he's threatened by the republican movement sweeping the country. Dictators do not believe in men's rights, after all."

"You mean men's *and* women's rights," I added.

Mr. Wainwright didn't reply and took a long drag on his pipe before he met my eye. Clara cast me a warning look from the chair opposite. Judging by both of their expressions, it was clearly time to move on.

"Well, sir, we'd better be going." I held out my hand to shake his, while Clara said her farewells to his family.

Surprised by the gesture of a woman offering a handshake, he hesitated before finally accepting and shaking my hand vigorously.

"I enjoyed our discussion," I said. "I hope to see you again tomorrow evening after dinner. I'll have caught up with the latest news by then and we can embark on round two!"

Though he clearly disapproved of a woman's interest in politics overall, he seemed open to the idea of being challenged, and smiled.

"That suits me just fine, young lady. I look forward to it."

I returned his smile. "As do I, sir. We might both learn something from each other."

He chuckled. "You say what you mean, don't you."

"Always."

As we left, Clara shot me an exasperated look. "You say what you mean, don't you," she said, mimicking Mr. Wainwright's deep voice. "If he only knew."

"But don't you see, Clara? Not everyone is offended by a person who says what they think or feel. It's freeing, actually. You should try it."

"Perhaps."

"By the way"—I grinned—"that was an excellent imitation. I think you might have a future in comedy."

We looked at each other and burst into laughter.

Clara

The Orient Express was everything I'd hoped it would be, and so much more. There was an artful elegance about it, every last attention to detail carefully considered. I felt perfectly at home as the locomotive sped across the French countryside, the motion rocking me gently from side to side as my thoughts raced over the colorful patchwork of vineyards and fields, and jumped ahead to the canals of Venice.

I pictured the city through the eyes of the artists I admired: the soft pinks and blues of Monet's *Le Grand Canal,* Renoir's dappled depictions of the crumbling buildings, Sargent's bold brushstrokes, da Vinci's use of perspective, and Canaletto's almost photographic details. My fingers itched to capture the iconic scenes myself. I relished the prospect of having the freedom to indulge my creative instincts. Would I paint in watercolor or pick up some more pastels? Sketch the gondoliers in charcoal, perhaps? I needed more paper, certainly, and a couple more brushes would be useful, too. I looked forward to an idle morning shopping for art supplies.

As the train hurtled along, the words in Violet's latest letter flitted through my mind: *It's as if I knew I had to go there, that I knew Matthias was waiting for me.* I felt the same sense of destiny as the rhythm of the locomotive matched the thoughts circling in my mind: *Edward and Charles, Edward and Charles, Edward and Charles,* on and on, each turn of the wheels taking me closer to the rendezvous with Edward and farther away from the man I would soon marry.

My emotions swayed from excitement to dread, hope to despair. I wasn't used to feeling so conflicted. My life had always been one of predictable milestones, dutifully adhering to the path of expectations set out for me when I was born the eldest daughter of an affluent New Yorker. To even think about Edward in any way other than a friend was shocking to me, and yet, that was precisely how I thought about him now. What dangerous game was I playing?

Between the carefully ordered schedule of dining, I took out the watercolors Edward had given me and painted the finer details of the train's decor: the filigree door handles and the gilded cornice, the intricate lace trim on the linen tablecloths, the elegant embellishment on the handle of the sugar tongs. I was drawn to smaller details, to the things others might easily miss. It was why I liked capturing expressions and faces. There was so much to see if you really paid attention to a person.

"What are you working on?" Madeleine asked, peering over my shoulder as I sat beside the window in our compartment.

"Pretty, dainty, elegant things," I said. "And you're blocking my light."

"And we must never put dear Clara in the shadows." She picked up her journal from the writing desk. "I'm having coffee with Mr. Wainwright. I'll leave you to it."

I gave her one of my disapproving looks. "Off to talk Nazis and politics, I suppose? Be careful, Madeleine. He could be a spy for the Nazi Party for all you know. He'll have you locked up in a gulag for writing unkind things about them."

She told me to stop being so worried all the time. "Besides," she added as she peered around the door, "the gulags are in Russia."

"Well, be careful you don't end up there, then."

"Why? Would you miss me?" she teased as she closed the door behind her.

I returned to my work, enjoying the sweep of the fine brush across the page, and the way the watercolors blended and softened, running into each other like old friends. Edward had patiently encouraged me to experiment with different techniques: to use a palette knife rather than a brush, to try Expressionism rather than the Impressionist style I always favored, to use watercolors and pastels rather than oils. As I worked, my mind returned to our conversation in the art gallery, the day before my departure.

"What do you see?" he'd asked as we studied a print of *Les parapluies* by Renoir, one of my favorite pieces of Impressionist art, depicting a group of Parisians in a rain shower.

"I see lots of umbrellas." I'd laughed as a rain shower pattered against the gallery window. "But I don't actually see any rain."

"Precisely! And that's the genius. The rain is implied. We don't have to see raindrops to know that it's raining. Art is as much about what is left out as what is added." He looked at me from beneath a lock of wavy hair. "It is often what is left unsaid that conveys the clearest message, is it not?"

I remembered how I'd instinctively covered my engagement ring with my other hand. Whether consciously or subconsciously I wasn't sure, but the unspoken implication was obvious to us both. I was engaged to Charles, the sort of man I had always been expected to marry, and yet it was the man beside me, his hands speckled with paint, who'd set my mind on fire and my pulse racing.

A knock at the compartment door interrupted my thoughts.

"A gift for you, Miss Sommers," a stewardess said as I opened the door. She pressed a small package into my hands.

I thanked her, sat at the writing desk, and untied the string. I was surprised to see a selection of tubes of oil paint and a palette knife. I turned over the enclosed note card.

My dearest girl,

Something to help you indulge in your little hobby while you are so cruelly distant from me. I thought oils would be best for doing some proper painting. That other style is so wishy-washy.
    Take care, darling. I miss you madly.

Charles

The gift was a thoughtful gesture, and yet as I looked at my just-painted watercolor drying beside the window, I could hear Charles calling it wishy-washy. I knew he'd sent oils because he preferred them to watercolors. But what he didn't know was that oils were impractical, and almost impossible to use properly while traveling, something he would have understood if he took more interest in my hobby.

But was it only a hobby?

I thought of Madeleine and her singular determination. She had serious ambitions, a sense of purpose, while I had only a sense of obligation. I'd never considered the possibility of art becoming my profession. I'd never considered having a profession at all, aside from arranging charitable luncheons and hosting parties for my husband's business colleagues. But with the Wainwright daughters each asking for a portrait, and Mr. Wainwright insisting he pay a fair rate for my time and talent, I wondered if I was capable of more than I'd believed. Was it possible for me to pursue a different life from the one I'd always assumed someone like me must live?

My hands steady, I folded Charles's gift back into the tissue paper and placed them it the drawer.

THAT EVENING, AFTER a lavish meal and too many glasses of after-dinner sherry with the Wainwrights and the Culpeppers, Madeleine and I settled into our own interests: her words, my art. I recognized the signs now when she was deep in concentration, the way her brow crinkled and how she chewed the end of her pencil while she was searching for the right word. As I watched her, it occurred to me that perhaps we weren't so different after all. I painted with color. She painted in words. In truth, our skills complemented each other, something I'd never considered before. I was too busy being angry at her, but now . . .

"I have an idea," I said as a thought struck me. "We should put my sketches with your descriptions. Create a sort of travel journal as a gift for Violet."

Madeleine looked up from her page, surprise showing on her face. "You mean, create something . . . together?" She clasped her hands to her chest in faux shock. "Oh, Clara! I thought you'd never ask."

I scrunched up a sheet of paper and threw it at her. "Well? It makes sense, don't you think?"

"It does. And I think it's a lovely idea, actually. Are you sure you're feeling alright?"

It was getting late and I closed my sketchbook for the night, a smile on my face. I was getting used to Madeleine's sense of humor again, remembering how easily she could make me laugh.

A little while later, as I began my bedtime routine—cleansing my face and pinning my hair at the vanity—the train came to a sudden stop. My pots of face cream and bottles of perfume skidded across the polished wood, and Madeleine toppled from her chair.

"What on earth's going on?" I rushed to the window to see what was happening, but it was pitch-black outside. "Why have we stopped?"

Madeleine joined me, peering out of the wide window and rubbing our breath from the glass.

"Maybe we're being kidnapped," she said. "Or arrested for talking to strangers about Nazis."

I flicked my hand against her arm. "It's nothing to joke about. We're in the middle of nowhere in the middle of the night. We might be in very grave danger."

Madeleine laughed. "Let's hope so!" She grabbed her coat, shoved her feet into her slippers, and opened the compartment door.

"Where are you going?" I whispered, instinctively lowering my voice. "You can't go wandering around at this time of night, especially not in your pajamas, or whatever that is you're wearing."

"Actually, I can go wandering around whenever and wherever I choose," she replied, a mischievous smirk at her lips.

"Well, I'd prefer it if you didn't."

Seeing my concern, her expression softened a little. "Finish your beauty routine and get some sleep. It's probably just an electrical fault and nothing to worry about. I'm sure we'll be on our way again soon."

I hoped she was right. As she closed the door behind her, and I slipped into bed, I had only one thought on my mind: we couldn't get to Venice soon enough.

Maddie

I stepped out of the room to find the corridors empty and the usually bright sconces dimmed. Either most of the passengers had already gone to bed, or more likely, wouldn't be caught dead walking around in striped pajamas and slippers. Ah, well. I wasn't known for my fashion sense, and my journalist's nose smelled drama.

I shivered as I moved from one train car to the next, glad I'd at least had the common sense to throw on my coat over my pajamas. To think I'd just begun reading *Murder on the Orient Express* only yesterday. Clara had said it was inviting trouble, but I thought reading it while on the train itself was perfect. Now, the smallest ounce of regret prickled over my skin as my imagination ran wild. Dark passageways, train cars filled with strangers, a mysterious and abrupt halt on the tracks in the middle of the night. Would Mussolini's men stop the train to search it? Or perhaps there were bandits that lived scattered throughout the Alps, planning to rob the wealthy patrons on board.

Even as I dismissed the thoughts as silly, I tiptoed forward, across another car toward the lounge, where voices drifted through the door that was slightly ajar. The low light of table lamps flickered in the dark. I pushed the door open just enough to step quietly inside.

The lounge was empty except for one gentleman, still dressed in his suit from dinner, and a bartender he was speaking to in hushed tones. They both had their backs to me, so I crept a little closer and ducked behind a chair.

"A herd of goats?" I heard the man say with a light chuckle. "Is that all?"

"They must have been spooked by something," the bartender replied. "The conductor said we'd be on our way again shortly."

I wanted to laugh. So my wild imaginings of bandits was only a pack of wayward goats. My shoulders eased, but I couldn't help being a little disappointed. I'd at least hoped for a bit of danger.

As I stood up and turned to go, the bartender spotted me.

"Can I help you, miss?"

"No, thank you. I just wanted to see what had caused the train to stop. It sounds harmless."

"Nothing to worry about," he agreed.

At the sound of my voice, the other man turned around, and I froze. I knew that pair of broad shoulders, the curls of dark hair, the long sloping nose.

"Daniel?" I almost shouted. "What are *you* doing here?"

A sheepish grin crossed his face as he pushed his hands into his pockets. "Hello, Madeleine. I wondered when we might bump into each other. Try as I might to remain inconspicuous, the train isn't all that large."

"Inconspicuous? Tell me why you're here," I demanded as I folded my arms. "Because this clearly isn't a coincidence." Every

instance when I'd run into him in Paris raced through my mind.
Had they all been planned? My anger began to rise, and yet part
of me was happy to see him again.

Daniel's smile faded, and his expression turned to one of guilty
admission as he walked toward me.

"If I tell you something, will you promise not to share it with
Clara?"

My eyes narrowed. "I'm not promising a single damned thing
to a man who has suspiciously turned up on every mode of transportation I've taken since leaving New York."

The hopeful look in his eyes vanished. "Maddie—"

"Miss Sommers, to you," I interrupted.

He sighed. "You have every right to be angry. I haven't been
entirely honest with you, but please let me explain. Over a brandy,
perhaps?"

"Fine," I conceded. "And make it a large one."

We sat at the bar, ordered two brandies, and I swallowed mine
in one great gulp. Daniel, on the other hand, took the smallest of
guilty sips.

"Well? Spill it, Miller," I said. "The truth. All of it."

"I'm not actually a theater critic," he said, exhaling. "Nor was
I visiting a cousin in Paris." At least he had the decency to look
ashamed. "I work for Charles Hancock." He paused, waiting for
my reaction. "Your sister's fiancé."

Whatever I'd been expecting him to say, it certainly wasn't
that. I stared at him a moment, speechless.

"You work for Hancock?"

He nodded. "I'm employed as an architect in his office in New
York."

"The drawings . . ." I thought about our conversation in the hotel in Paris, the detailed buildings he'd sketched and which I'd admired. Hadn't I even suggested he consider work as an architect? "But that still doesn't explain what you're doing on the Orient Express."

He ran his hands through his hair. "Charles asked me to discreetly escort his fiancé and her sister through Europe. Make sure everything went swimmingly, and report back on any difficulties, or misdemeanors."

"Misdemeanors!" Now I was furious. "He asked you to 'discreetly escort' us?" I couldn't believe it. I laughed, it was all so ridiculous. "Who in the hell does he think he is?"

"He's Charles Hancock. He thinks he can control everything. Everyone."

"Well, you're right about that." I thought of Clara, of how upset she would be when I told her, and yet part of me was glad to have some evidence of Charles's unpleasant behavior, beyond my personal opinion. "So, what's in it for you?" I challenged. "Or do you have a habit of following young ladies around Europe while they're delivering letters for their dying grandmother?"

He shook his head. "Don't, Maddie. When you put it like that it sounds dreadful."

"That's because it *is* dreadful. It's downright insulting! As if we can't take care of ourselves."

"Charles has offered me a management position when I return."

"Ahh. I see. Power and ambition. The things that make the world go around." I peered at this man who I'd thought was a friend and was now nothing but an imposter. "Is your name even Daniel Miller?"

He nodded and held out a hand in a gesture of defeat, or apology, I wasn't sure. I leaned farther away from him on my stool.

"Please, Maddie, try to understand. Charles was worried about Clara and wanted to make sure you wouldn't get into any trouble while abroad. It's a long journey, and with the unrest rumbling through Europe on all sides . . . I can see his reasoning. Never mind the way the two of you argue."

"My relationship with my sister is none of your business," I said crossly. "Or his." Yet even as I said it, I realized it would become Charles's business when he and Clara were married. And I would become his sister-in-law. I couldn't bear to think about it.

"You're right," Daniel conceded. "It isn't my business. But my relationship with you, is."

"Relationship? What relationship? There isn't . . . I don't . . ."

"I admire you, Maddie. I hardly know you, but what I do know of you, I like. Very much. And . . . well, here we both are, stuck on a train in the middle of nowhere."

"Mademoiselle, another brandy?" the bartender asked.

"No, thank you. I was just leaving." I stood up and tightened the belt on my coat. "Stay away from us, Daniel. I mean it. We don't need anyone to keep an eye on us." Even Violet and Margaret had traveled through Europe alone, nearly fifty years ago! "I'll send Hancock a telegram to tell him exactly what I think of his little scheme."

"Please, Maddie, I—"

"Goodbye, Daniel." I stormed away, furious for trusting this man who wasn't who he said he was and furious with Charles for not trusting Clara. And what was this business about misdemeanors? This was about keeping Clara under his thumb, just as he always had. He'd encouraged her to maintain friendships with a shallow group of financiers' daughters, instructed her "gently" on what to wear, always ordered for her at the table. I'd tried to tell her he was a controlling, stuck-up, no-good . . . chump! And now there was also the matter of his purchasing the tenements. I should tell Clara exactly what I thought about that, too, even though she wouldn't want to hear it.

I fumed as I made my way back to our sleeper car, anxious to tell Clara everything, but as I stepped inside the room, I paused in the doorway. My sister's lovely dark hair cascaded over her pillow as she slept. She looked like the little girl I remembered, asleep in the bed beside mine. My fury with Charles and Daniel was replaced by a fondness for her; by a need to protect her.

She stirred as I tossed my coat over the chair and kicked off my slippers.

"Oh, you're back. Did you find out why we stopped?" She sat up, propping herself against her pillows. "What on earth's wrong?" she asked. "You look like you've swallowed a swarm of bees."

"You'll never guess who's on the train."

She tucked a lock of hair behind her ear. "Who?"

I was so angry, so disappointed for her. "This isn't easy to say."

"Well, go on," she pressed. "Don't leave me in suspense."

Her tone was gentler toward me, more tolerant than usual. I hesitated, hating to be the one to show her just how unpleasant Charles was.

"Daniel is here," I said as I sat on the edge of her bed. "Daniel Miller."

"What? Again?" She sat up straighter. "Why is *he* here?"

I took a deep breath, poured us both a large sherry from the decanter, and began to explain.

Clara

I didn't sleep a wink for the rest of the night. I couldn't fully grasp what Madeleine had told me: that Charles had hired someone to follow us, and that Daniel Miller wasn't a theater critic at all, but an architect in Charles's firm and some sort of part-time amateur spy. I thought about all the conversations I'd had with Daniel—on the *Queen Mary*, outside Notre-Dame cathedral, over lunch in Amiens, during the balloon ride—and all the occasions he'd unexpectedly become a part of our plans. Now I understood why.

I was furious, hurt, confused. How many other lies and schemes were we yet to uncover? It didn't make any sense, and I didn't want to believe that Charles was capable of planning something so sneaky. I knew Charles used his power and money to influence his business transactions, but I'd never thought he would go as far as this, using people—*me!*—as if they were stocks or shares or a building to be acquired. He'd made me feel as if I were just another of his deals.

Madeleine woke me the following morning with a cup of coffee she'd ordered to the room. I forced myself to drink it and made myself presentable for breakfast, but found I had no appetite when we were seated at our table in the dining car.

I pushed my elegantly fanned melon slices around my plate.

"Pass them here," Madeleine said. "I'll put them out of their misery."

I pushed my plate toward her. "How could Charles do such a thing? I might not be as tough as you or Auntie Nellie, but I'm not some silly fragile woman, incapable of traveling through Europe without a man to assist me. Even if you're right about political instability and the Nazis, I'm quite capable of taking care of myself."

"Yes, Clara. You are. We all are. And I'm glad you've come to realize it."

I blinked back a tear, refusing to give in to my anger and confusion. "I'm sure his intentions were good"—at this, Madeleine raised an eyebrow—"but I hate the way he's gone about it with all these lies and people following us. It's unseemly."

"Unseemly!" Madeleine leaned back in her chair. "I'd say it's downright dastardly. I'd like to give him a piece of my mind."

"Who? Charles, or Daniel?"

"Both of them."

We talked about nothing else all morning, but while we shared our recollections of things Daniel had said and done, which we now saw in an entirely different light, what I didn't say out loud to Madeleine was the thing bothering me the most: that Charles didn't trust me, understand me, or respect me.

As the train hurtled along, past the snowcapped peaks of the Swiss Alps, shock and hurt turned to anger and resentment, and there, among it all, was Edward, rushing through the crowds at the dockside in New York, quietly pressing his thoughtful gift into my hands. He'd taught me to understand that while every artist's intention was to capture an image perfectly, whether the wildest storm or the mirrorlike surface of a calm sea, few ever managed to get it just right. "We aim for perfection, Clara, but must often settle for something less," he'd once said.

Did the same apply to matters of love? Charles had his flaws—more, evidently, than I'd thought—but perhaps he was the "something less" I would have to settle for. Was I seeking a perfect marriage that didn't exist? I gazed numbly through the compartment window, the passing scenery muddled and blurred. This journey kept asking me questions. I hoped Venice would provide some answers.

LATER THAT MORNING, I went to the lounge car to sketch a portrait for Eliza Wainwright, as I'd promised. I'd enjoyed the process of capturing the girls' individuality in a close-up study of their faces and expressions. They would take the mementos with them as a reminder of their Grand European Tour and their time on the Orient Express—if I could get the details right. My frustration at Charles and Daniel seemed to bleed into my concentration and I couldn't capture Eliza's expression that morning at all. Her face was petite and yet full of quiet resolve, not as obviously pretty as her sister's and yet far more compelling.

"Is something the matter?" Eliza asked, sensing my hesitation. "Is it my features? Mother says they're irregular."

"Your features are perfectly regular and very lovely," I replied, trying to hide my irritability by offering her a reassuring smile. "And your mother shouldn't say such things. I'm just a little tired this morning. Perhaps we should continue later."

I could tell she was disappointed but she agreed that we might both perform better after a break.

Part of me also wanted to track down that scoundrel Daniel Miller and tell him what I thought of him. It wouldn't change anything, but it would be a load off my mind, at least.

My chance presented itself sooner than I'd anticipated. As I was packing away my materials, a familiar voice interrupted me.

"Ah, Miss Sommers. I was hoping to run into you."

I stood up straight and squared my shoulders. "Mr. Miller. What a surprise, or should I say, not a surprise in the least." I glared at him.

He looked deeply uncomfortable. "Ah. Madeleine told you."

"Of course she told me. She's my sister. We tell each other everything."

My words caught me by surprise. We used to tell each other everything, and I realized that I'd missed having her to turn to for advice and reassurance.

He stood awkwardly, his hands in his pockets. "Of course. And I'm sure you're furious, and you have every right to be."

"I have every right to alert the police and inform them you've been making a nuisance of yourself." I paused, for dramatic effect. "But I won't. Not yet, anyway. First, I want you to tell me exactly how the arrangement with Charles came about. Exactly what was said." I sat back down and motioned for Daniel to take the seat opposite.

The details of the scheme were as absurd and insulting as I'd expected. Charles had essentially bribed Daniel into following us and had given him specific instructions to report back regularly, to make sure we weren't mixing with anyone disreputable, and so on and so on.

"I think I've heard enough," I said after listening for five minutes. "I presume you'll leave us alone once we arrive in Venice. There's little point in tailing us now that we know who you really are."

"Of course. You won't be seeing me again."

I wasn't sure if I believed him.

He mumbled another apology before leaving me to work out what on earth I would do next. Should I write to Charles to tell him I knew about his spying? Should I send a message to Edward's hotel to let him know when I'd arrived, or should I tell him it would be better if we didn't meet after all and encourage him to patch things up with his wife?

I decided to ask Madeleine for her advice.

"If it were me, I'd ditch the pair of them," she said, "but you're not me."

She passed me a handkerchief as I dabbed at the tears that threatened to come in great torrents if I didn't keep myself in check.

"Sometimes I wish I was you," I said. "That I didn't care about men at all."

"It does keep life simpler," Madeleine agreed. "But you're not me, Clara. You're you, and neither Charles—nor Edward—should ever make you question that."

She was right, of course.

"Anyway, I say we book ourselves into a different hotel when we arrive," she continued. "Charles must have asked Violet to share the whole damned itinerary with him. Hopefully, we'll lose Daniel completely, and we can concentrate on finding Matthias Morelli. Enjoy Venice and get on with what we came here to do. What do you say to that?"

I offered a weary half smile and thought, again, of the pocket watch Violet had given to me as a good luck talisman for the journey.

"I say never turn back. Onward, we go."

Maddie

As morning dawned, I stood at the window to watch the sunrise over beautiful Italy. Golden rays illuminated the newly green pastures and rolling hills and the tender vines that would soon be bursting with grapes. Cypress trees dotted the landscape in shoots of dark green that reached for the sky. There was still so much excitement ahead, so much to learn and see and do. And, in truth, I also had a more serious intention while I was here. I wanted to study Mussolini's fascist regime up close, to take stock of how he molded and shaped the Italian people, and to see if there was any real connection to what I'd read about the Nazi Party.

With only a few hours left aboard the Orient Express, I dressed quickly. Clara set out to finish her sketch of Eliza Wainwright, while I headed to the dining car to meet Mr. Wainwright for breakfast. We'd come to something of an understanding since our first meeting, and I enjoyed talking with him. I'd learned he was a retired English professor, and that he'd dabbled in a little writing himself. He'd asked if he might see some of my writing, and promised to share his thoughts with me. His wife, Mary, had thanked me for taking him off her hands for a while, and for keeping him entertained.

I took a seat at a table beside the window and ordered a café au lait and a chocolate croissant.

"No elephants today, miss?" the waiter asked. He'd come to know me, and my sense of humor.

I smiled. "A lady never eats elephant for breakfast!"

My stomach jittered with nerves as I waited for Mr. Wainwright to arrive. I was anxious to hear what he thought of the article I'd shared with him. For all intents and purposes, he was something of an expert after years of teaching literature and composition classes, and I couldn't imagine what he would think of my lean style of writing, which, I liked to think, echoed Hemingway's—or Nellie's—but with its own flair. Besides, I hadn't shared my work with anyone other than Violet since Billy had proved himself to be such a lout. I hoped Mr. Wainwright would let me down gently. Better that than be falsely supportive.

When the coffee arrived, I stirred sugar into the strong brew, and placed Violet's notebook on the table. I reread some of my favorite clippings of Nellie's articles, noting the voice and tone of each, and studying the headlines.

Nellie Bly Describes War Horrors

Nellie Bly Finds a Home and Father for Little Waif

Nellie Bly: Inside the Madhouse

The range of her journalism was far more impressive than most people realized. I continued to be amazed by her, even after all these years.

A long shadow fell across my page, and I looked up, startled back to the present.

"What's that you're reading?" Mr. Wainwright said as he pulled out a chair and sat down. "It looks interesting."

"Good morning, sir." I smiled, noticing his blue eyes were filled with good humor. "I was just looking through my grandmother's old notebook. She was a great admirer of Nellie Bly."

"Ah, yes. Miss Bly was quite the journalist," he said, waving the waiter over and ordering his breakfast and an espresso. "I imagine she is something of a heroine of yours."

"She's the reason I'm a writer," I replied. "She was a family friend. In fact, Clara and I called her Auntie Nellie."

"Is that so? Well, she was clever, if a little too outspoken at times, at least for some."

I laughed. "She was certainly outspoken, but what good journalist isn't? She encouraged me to write, much to my father's frustration," I continued. "He didn't agree with his young daughter exploring such manly pursuits."

The waiter returned and set a plate of cured hams and cheeses in front of Mr. Wainwright. "It's a difficult thing to be the father of girls," he continued between bites. "We men are stuffy awkward beings and don't always understand the fairer sex. But our intentions are only to do the best we can for our daughters. I expect your father only wanted the same."

While I wasn't entirely sure about that, I decided to take Mr. Wainwright's words in the spirit in which they were intended.

"Nellie told me to always write from the heart and with conviction. 'Don't let others dissuade you, Madeleine,' she would say. 'Trust your gut.'"

"Sound advice, I'd say." He sliced another bite of ham and seemed intent on finishing his meal without further conversation.

I longed to ask him about my article, but for once, found my forward nature failed me and my courage fled. As he ate, I sipped my coffee and thought about the varied nature of Nellie's stories. She'd reported from the Front during the Great War, worked as a foreign correspondent in Mexico for six months, exposed the state of orphanages and found homes for orphans. She'd even posed as a madwoman for ten days in a New York City asylum to challenge a system that punished women, simply because society didn't understand them. She'd braved so much, just for the story. But that was it—it was never *just* a story. She covered issues and events that defined people's lives. She brought injustices to light. She was exactly the type of journalist I longed to be.

"Perhaps you'll be another Nellie Bly one day," Mr. Wainwright offered as he put down his knife and fork and patted his mouth with his napkin. "In fact, I'd say you're well on your way, Miss Sommers."

He reached inside his jacket pocket and pulled out a piece of paper, carefully rolled so as not to crease it. My article. I'd given him my finished piece on Hancock Enterprises, exposing the truth about the tenement buildings and the displacement of hundreds of occupants.

"This is very good," he said. "Very good, indeed. You write with conviction. Your arguments are well researched and maturely constructed, if you'll pardon the pun."

A lump rose in my throat. "Thank you, sir. I . . . thank you." I couldn't explain how much his compliments meant to me, coming from a gentleman who was clearly very well read, and not always easily persuaded by an argument.

"Do you have anyone you can send this to?" he asked. "It seems to me that people need to know what this Hancock fellow is up to."

I thought about the encouraging note I'd received from the editor at the *New York Herald Tribune*.

"I do actually, yes. I know exactly who I'll send it to." I just needed to talk to Clara about the content of the article first.

"Good. And I wish you luck with it. You know," he said, stroking his mustache, "if you'd ever like to share anything else, I'd be happy to take a look and offer suggestions. And perhaps I could share some chapters from my novel with you?"

Pride, excitement, and gratitude followed in rapid succession. "I'd like that very much!"

He gave me a business card. "I'd be delighted to hear from you."

"Thank you, Walter. Sorry, Mr. Wainwright."

He patted my hand. "Walter will do just fine. I consider you a friend now, and I can never be bothered with all those dreadful formalities."

After another cup of coffee, we said our farewells, and I made my way back to our accommodation, still pondering his praise.

Wishing Clara a hasty good morning, I rushed to the desk, flipped open my notebook, and, heart racing, hand flying over the page, wrote down several new ideas.

Has gaining the right to vote truly changed women's roles in society?

*How much autonomy is too much for sisters, wives, or
    mothers?*
*Should a husband decide if his wife may join the
    workforce?*
*Will the number of women in the workplace eventually
    exceed those who are homemakers?*

My hands shook with excitement as I jotted down additional thoughts beneath each idea.

"Did your muse find you today?" Clara remarked as she observed my flurry of activity.

I sat back in my chair. "Hmm?"

"Your muse? Has she appeared?"

"Yes! She has."

"I'm glad to hear it," she said with a smile. "But I think we've arrived."

I threw the last of my things into my suitcase as the train pulled into the station with a final huff of steam and shuddered to a stop.

As we made our way through the ornate corridors for the last time, I envied those passengers, like the Wainwrights, who were continuing on to the exotic delights of Istanbul.

As we descended the steps to the station platform, Eliza and Juliette Wainwright raced over to us, giggling and flushed, clearly excited for the next stage of their journey.

"I hope you have a wonderful time in Istanbul," Clara said, giving them each their miniature portraits. She smiled as they admired the finished items, comparing one with the other, and commenting on the remarkable likenesses.

I was proud of my sister for the work she'd done, and for accepting the payment she deserved for it, although she'd insisted it wasn't necessary.

"You are a very talented pair," Mr. Wainwright boomed as he approached me and Clara and shook our hands enthusiastically. "Enjoy your differences. Don't always push against them."

We looked at each other in a way that implied we would try.

I promised to write to him soon, and Clara quietly thanked him as he tipped his hat, bid us farewell, and went to gather up his flock of twittering young ladies who had rushed off to show their portraits to their mother.

As they left, I caught sight of Daniel, standing on the platform several paces away, his eyes searching the crowds of disembarking passengers. He was looking for us, no doubt. Though I was still furious about his shocking revelation, I was mostly disappointed he'd turned out to be like all the others, just as I'd started to believe he was different. The fact that I was still thinking about him and what he'd said—that he admired me and liked me, very much—irritated me more than anything.

"There he is." I scowled.

"Who?" Clara stood at my elbow, following my gaze.

"Dastardly Daniel. Good riddance to him, I say."

Yet when his gaze met mine, his expression softened to one of apology. I stared back at him defiantly. He shrugged and held up his hands in surrender.

I wanted to speak to him one last time, but refused to give him the satisfaction of apologizing again.

"Let's go, Clara," I said, looping my arm through hers. "Let's see what Venice has in store for us."

Clara

After the bustling boulevards and narrow streets of Paris, Venice was a gentle, glorious sigh. It was like nowhere else on earth. The sun dappled the water as a vaporetto conveyed us to the hotel where we would now be staying, rather than the venue Violet had arranged. Daniel had promised to leave us alone, but he was still in Venice, and neither of us trusted him. We certainly didn't want to stay in the same hotel as him. Our new accommodation was also closer to the Rialto Bridge and Matthias Morelli's gallery.

I pushed everything else from my mind as I gazed at the beautiful palazzos and buildings that seemed to tumble into the water, their reflections captured so perfectly. Sleek black gondolas glided past us, while others were moored to rows of posts along the jetties and down narrow side canals. It was all so enchanting.

"Isn't it just beautiful," I said as I pointed out a bright ocher-colored building that housed a florist. Buckets of lilies and irises and roses hugged the storefront, and artful greenery crept over the doorframe.

"It's lovely," Madeleine agreed, although she seemed distracted.

"You don't sound too sure."

"I am sure. Ignore me, I'm just . . ." Her words trailed off as she turned the page of an Italian newspaper she'd picked up at the station.

"You're not seriously going to read that while we're on the Grand Canal are you?"

She looked at me and nodded. "Sure am."

I shook my head, exasperated, and turned my back to her to focus on the sights.

It really was a stunning cityscape, and I didn't want to miss a moment of it. For the next wonderful thirty minutes, my mind was too full of Venice's beauty to be occupied with the ugly business of Charles's deceit, but the prospect of Edward's imminent arrival pulled at my thoughts as I gazed at the reflections in the water. Washed by the wake of the passing boats, the images of the faded old buildings shifted and changed, the palette of pastel colors blurring into each other. *Find the true colors,* Edward would say. *The sky isn't blue at all when you look at it. It is grays and purples, pinks and lavender.* What were the true colors of my future? I wondered. What would it look like when the image was complete?

THE WATER TAXI deposited us at a jetty beside a run-down-looking establishment.

"*Bella casa!*" the driver joked as we both stepped off the boat.

"This is it?" I took in the terrible sight in front of us. "This is where we're staying?"

Madeleine consulted the piece of paper onto which she'd written the name and address of the hotel. It had been hastily recommended to her by one of the station porters as we'd left the Orient Express. He'd assured her it was one of Venice's finest establishments.

"Apparently so," she replied. "Let's hope it's better inside."

I muttered that it couldn't be much worse and followed her inside, only to be greeted by ladders and scaffolding and complete disarray. Dark water stains ran along the bottom half of the walls.

"*Buongiorno!*" A pleasant-looking woman approached us from a side door. She glanced at our outfits and the small cases we each carried. The rest of the luggage was to be brought on later. "Ah, tourists," she added, throwing her hands into the air.

"Yes," Madeleine replied, brightly. "We were hoping to stay?"

The woman shook her head. "No rooms. I am sorry. The *acqua alta*. The floods. They damage too much."

"Oh. I see." Madeleine turned to me. She looked as fed up as I felt. "What do we do now?"

"Could you recommend somewhere?" I asked, throwing the woman a hopeful glance. "We're tired after a long journey."

"Yes, yes. *Un momento.*" She scribbled something onto a piece of paper and handed it to me. "This is *molto bella*! Perfect for two ladies."

I read the name of the hotel she'd inscribed on the page. Hotel Giovanni. The hotel Violet had arranged for us. I sighed and showed it to Madeleine.

"Looks like we might not be such seasoned travelers after all," I said as we thanked the woman, wished her good luck with her repairs, and began the short walk to the Hotel Giovanni, a few streets away.

"Well, at least we tried," Madeleine said, striding ahead. "All the best explorers have to be prepared to make new plans on the fly."

"But we're not making new plans," I countered as I scurried after her. "We're just reverting to the old plan."

Hotel Giovanni was like a palace in comparison to the establishment we'd just left. I was so relieved to see its gleaming marble floors and gilt picture frames. Well-dressed attendants instantly greeted us and assured us they would arrange for our luggage to be collected from the other hotel. I hardly cared that Daniel Miller might appear from behind a parlor fern at any moment.

Our suite was well appointed, as we had come to expect from Violet's exquisite taste. It offered spectacular views across the Grand Canal and made me more eager than ever to get outside and capture the famous Venetian light on paper.

"Shouldn't we track down Matthias first?" Madeleine asked as I gathered up my pastel pencils and other supplies. "His gallery isn't far, and I'm dying to know who he is."

"Later," I said. "Let's just be tourists for a couple of hours first. I can go on my own if you'd rather rest?"

"Rest? In Venice? Are you mad?" Madeleine laughed. "Sometimes I think you hardly know me at all. Besides," she continued as she picked up her gloves and hat, "Venice is notorious for its winding streets, and for getting people lost. Best stick together. Safety in numbers."

"I thought you were the one who liked to seek out danger. Or are you going to tell me Mussolini might arrest us for having the wrong political ideals?"

She gave me one of her knowing looks. "It's nothing to joke about, Clara. If you took a moment to read a newspaper or ask me about things, you might not be so casual about it. You don't realize how precarious the situation is here."

"Fine. I'll stay by your side." And while I pretended to be indifferent about it, I was pleased that we would sightsee together, unlike in Paris, where we had instantly gone our separate ways. Perhaps we were making some progress after all.

Being with Madeleine made sense, even if we found fault with each other and disagreed too easily. The farther we'd traveled from New York, the more I'd found myself wanting to spend time with her, to share things with her, ask for her advice and opinion. Since finding out about Charles and Daniel's scheme, I'd come close to confronting Charles about it. But I'd held back. My bride-to-be nerves had developed into nagging whispers of doubt that seemed to grow louder with every mile traveled. But part of me wanted to hear Charles's side of the story. I wanted him to explain it wasn't how it seemed, that he'd only had my best interests at heart, and that he was acting from an urge to protect me rather than from any sense of mistrust.

Just as we were about to leave the suite, a bellboy delivered a small packet addressed to me.

I took it from him and opened it. Inside was a lapel pin, and a note.

Darling girl! I took the liberty of signing you up! Mrs. Charles Hancock is now a member of the yacht club. I thought you might like to wear the pin next to your heart, to keep me close while you are far away.

C

I returned the pin to the packet and placed it on the table. Membership of the yacht club as Mrs. Charles Hancock. Was that what my life was to become?

"Another gift from Charles?" Madeleine asked as she grabbed her scarf and dashed into her bedroom to change her shoes.

I couldn't hold back a heavy sigh. "Yes," I called in reply. "But I'd rather not discuss it."

I turned to the desk to pick up my gloves, and saw the postcards I'd bought at the train station and written to Mother and Violet. As I picked them up, I noticed Madeleine also had two letters to mail: one addressed to her roommate, Jenny, in Manhattan, and another to a Mr. Gerald McDougal at the *New York Herald Tribune*. She was so determined to be published, she was submitting articles all the way from Venice? Good for her. I sealed the envelope, noticing that she'd forgotten to, and put everything into my handbag. We could stop by the *ufficio postale* on the way to Matthias Morelli's gallery.

"Are you ready?" I called.

Madeleine emerged from the bedroom with a grin. "Yes. I now have appropriate footwear. Let's get lost somewhere."

MADELEINE BOUGHT GELATO from a stand while I ducked into the post office, and after browsing the markets together, and stopping for espresso and *cantuccini biscotti* while I made a few quick sketches, we made our way back to Calle del Toscana and, hopefully, to Matthias. Although we knew we weren't far from his gallery, we became hopelessly lost through the ancient winding streets and had to retrace our steps several times before we eventually found our way nearly two hours later. By then, my feet were aching and my enthusiasm for our task had waned.

Morelli's was exactly where Violet had told us it would be, in a narrow side street close to the Rialto Bridge, beneath an arched walkway. Clearly, she remembered it well, despite the many years since she'd been here.

A *pasticceria,* a pretty little pastry shop, stood on one side of the gallery, while on the other side was a shop that specialized in the famous Venetian Carnevale masks.

"I've always wanted to experience Carnevale in Venice," Madeleine said as she stopped to admire the ornate masks. "Wouldn't a masked ball be exciting?"

"You've read too many novels," I replied, pulling her away from the window.

"There's no such thing as too many novels," she replied.

As I tentatively pushed open the door to the art gallery, a small bell danced on a wire overhead. The light jingle was cheery and welcoming and helped to ease my apprehension a little. I wasn't sure what to expect, or how this man from Violet's past would take to two American women arriving unannounced with a letter from someone he hadn't seen in almost fifty years.

A woman emerged from a back room and said something in Italian that neither of us understood.

"*Buongiorno, signora,*" I said, noting the wedding ring on her finger. "My name is Clara Sommers, and this is my sister, Madeleine. We're visiting from America. We are looking for a Signor Morelli? Matthias. Do you speak English?"

The woman studied us both carefully. "Lucia Lambretti,"

she said in perfect English as she offered her hand in greeting. "Matthias Morelli is my uncle."

I shook her hand. Madeleine stepped forward to do the same as I continued.

"I'm sorry for the intrusion, but our grandmother is—was—a friend of your uncle's. She isn't well and has asked us to deliver a letter to him on her behalf." I placed Violet's letter on the countertop, admiring her elegant script and the name written on the front of the envelope: *Matthias*. "Her name is Violet."

"Violet?" At the name, Lucia frowned as if searching her memory.

"Yes. Violet Bell. Although he would have known her by her maiden name, Violet Lawson," I added.

A black cat slinked through a window and wound around Lucia's legs. She bent to pick it up and nestled her pet in her arms.

"I've never heard of a Violet Lawson. I'm very sorry, but I don't think I can help you."

I glanced at Madeleine. She looked as disappointed as I felt.

"Well, hopefully your uncle will remember her?" I prompted. "Our grandmother was very eager for Matthias to read her words." I reached for the letter and returned it to my pocket. "It means an awful lot to her."

"My uncle is visiting relatives in the country."

"Do you know when he might be back?" Madeleine asked.

Lucia shook her head. "I'm sorry, I cannot be sure. Perhaps he will return this afternoon. Perhaps he will return tomorrow. My uncle does not like to make plans. He lives on impulse."

She put the cat down and shooed it away into the next room.

Madeleine cast me a look that I recognized. She was preparing to dig her heels in and ask difficult questions. I reached for her arm, indicating we should leave. We would have to return later, and perhaps often, to meet this Matthias, but at least we knew he was still alive.

"We'll stop by again the next time we are passing," I said.

"You could leave the letter with me?" Lucia suggested. "I can pass it to my uncle when he returns. Save you the need to come back?"

"Thank you, but we would rather give it to him in person," Madeleine said. "Violet was very insistent on that. She wanted us to meet him. Thank you for your time."

We left the gallery, disappointed not to have seen Matthias.

"Well, that didn't go very well, did it," Madeleine said once we were outside the gallery. "Let's just hope he returns while we're still here. Otherwise, we'll have to leave the letter for him, and hope for the best."

"At least we found the right place," I agreed. "We can go back tomorrow."

I tried to sound optimistic, but just as with Grandpa Frank, it seemed that finding Matthias Morelli wouldn't be straightforward. I couldn't help feeling there was more to Matthias than Violet had implied, and I wondered if he might have had something to do with the falling out between Violet and Margaret. I glanced at Madeleine, who was as lost in thought as I was. Perhaps she was thinking the same.

We were already halfway through our trip, and there was still so much to discover.

Maddie

*D*eflated by missing Matthias, we cheered ourselves up with a box of cakes and delicate pastries from the *pasticceria* beside the gallery and strolled back along the maze of winding streets, toward the Piazza San Marco.

Venezia, the Floating City, was as beautiful as Paris, but in its own unique way. I wished I'd studied Italian in school, but to my surprise, I found it somewhat similar to French and could make out signs and menus without much trouble. The trouble I did have was keeping my article about Charles a secret. I had to bite my tongue to keep from mentioning it to Clara. And though I was truly excited by the prospect of it being accepted, the promise of publication was tempered by the risk of ruining things between us—again. I thought of the envelope on the table in our suite, already addressed though not yet sealed. A mark of my lingering indecision. I'd need to decide what to do soon, or the opportunity would be lost.

The Piazza San Marco was a large open square in the center of the old town, a place Violet had not only instructed us to visit, but a location associated with so many of her fondest memories of the city. We found a table at a café beneath the ornate arches, and while Clara added to her sketchbook, I studied a map of the area, the cluster of many islands making up the historic city, and the canals that washed into the Adriatic Sea. I was fond of Venice already, but almost as important as the things I'd seen was the thing I hadn't: Daniel Miller. It seemed he'd been respectful enough to keep his promise, and his distance. Perhaps he really didn't enjoy the task Charles had sent him to do after all, and he was mortified by how upset he'd made Clara and me. I mused over the thought for a while as I watched people stride through the piazza, anxious to get somewhere, and others who strolled languorously beside a friend.

When I had only a few sips of coffee left, I pulled out my journal to detail my first impressions of *bella* Venezia.

VENICE

I can see why Violet fell in love here. The scent of delicious fritole—already my favorite Venetian treat of fried dough dusted with sugar—wafts from a nearby doorway, and an endless flotilla of boats and gondolas slip by on the Grand Canal. The piazza is magnificent with the Doge's Palace and the impressive Basilica di San Marco standing watch at the easternmost edge. Laughing children gather near the bell tower while enjoying a break from classes.

I continued writing for a while, lost in my thoughts and my words, until the clock tower chimed the hour. I snapped my journal closed and reached for my scarf.

"Time to get going. Come on. Let's see if we can climb that bell tower."

Clara shook her head as she stared up at the tall tower in front of the Basilica. "First the balloon ascent, and now that?"

"I bet the view is worth it, and Violet would want you to climb it," I said, hoping to guilt her into coming with me.

She hesitated, but only for a moment. Suddenly, she stood up and, jaw set in determination, she headed toward the bell tower.

I raced to catch up with her. "That was a lot easier than I thought it would be."

"I'm tired of being afraid," she said, hitching up her skirt. "I want to *do* things, Madeleine. I don't want to be left behind, too afraid to try."

But as we reached the bottom of the tower, we found the door was locked.

"Perhaps it isn't possible to climb it," Clara said, a look of relief on her face.

"Well, that's a pity," I replied. "Especially with you all fired up for once."

At that moment, the door opened and an elderly woman appeared. She looked at us both, and said something in Italian neither of us understood.

Never one to miss an opportunity, I stepped forward.

"Excuse me. I wonder if you can help us. We were hoping to climb the tower steps? See the view?" I pointed to the top of the tower, hoping she understood. "Go up?" I said, placing my hands into a prayer.

"Tourists? the woman asked.

We both nodded.

"We will be very quick," I added. "My sister. It is her birthday. Felicitations?"

The woman seemed to understand, although Clara glared at me.

"Only quick," the woman said, as she unlocked the door. "Very quick."

I grabbed her hands, thanked her profusely, and turned to Clara.

"Come on, then. You heard the woman. Very quick. Let's get going!"

The steps were narrow and winding, and apparently endless. Breathing heavily, we eventually emerged into the belfry and daylight, and stood a moment, hands on our hips, to catch our breath. A cool breeze tugged at my hair as I looked out over the amazing view.

"Open your eyes, Clara! It's glorious."

Her eyes narrowed, and gripping my hand tightly, she inched forward.

I felt a familiar togetherness as she stood beside me. Clara's was the hand I'd reached for in the dark of our bedroom during a thunderstorm, or when we ran together on the sand as young girls. I'd always sought the reassurance and approval of my big sister, and I, in turn, had patiently encouraged her to let go of the fears and doubts that threatened to hold her back.

"Have you decided if you'll meet Edward yet?" I asked as we admired the view.

Clara looked at me, puzzled. "That came out of nowhere."

"You know me, full of questions." I knew the best way to get a real answer was to ask a question when people weren't prepared for it. I'd learned this early on when I'd begun to turn toward journalism.

"I'm not sure," Clara said cagily. "At least I have a way to contact him now that I have the letter back."

She still hadn't forgiven me.

"What would *you* do?" she continued.

I paused, and glanced at her, surprised she'd asked for my opinion.

"Oh, I'd most likely have a torrid love affair and then send him back to his wife while I settled in Venice, and spent my days sipping espresso and writing erotic romance novels."

Clara laughed lightly. "Seriously, Madeleine. What *would* you do?"

I turned to look at her. "Seriously, I think you should stop worrying about what *I* would do and do what *you* want to do. What harm can come from meeting him? We could go together if you like, so there would be no suggestion of anything . . . inappropriate. No room for any *misdemeanors*."

Her cheeks reddened. "I never intended for anything inappropriate to happen."

But I recognized her little tells and didn't believe her for a second. And so what if she was thinking inappropriate thoughts? Good for her. She wasn't married yet. Sometimes she acted as if she was an old dowager with her best years already behind her.

Standing at the edge of the belfry, I imagined a young Violet, standing in the same spot, gazing out over the piazza. I leaned forward, soaking up every detail to share with her when we returned. The vivid sky, people clustering in front of colorful shops, and the glistening water beyond.

And then I saw them.

Mussolini's soldiers, in black uniforms, marched into the square and fanned out at several posts at each corner, guns at their sides. Their ominous presence immediately changed the happy to-and-fro of the passersby below, and I knew that everything I'd read in the newspapers was true: Europe was on the cusp of a dramatic change.

I pulled on Clara's hand. "Come on. I think that's enough sightseeing for one day."

"But we only just got up here," she said, having finally relaxed enough to enjoy being so high above the city.

"We need to go. Now," I said, voice stern.

Alerted by the change in my tone, Clara looked at me, saw what must have been a grim expression, and quickly followed me down the stairs without a word. After thanking the woman again, we hurried back to the safety of the hotel.

THE NEXT MORNING, we woke to a dense Venetian fog that seemed to rise from the water. It lent an otherworldly atmosphere to the city, muffling the calls of the gondoliers and market traders as I peered out of the lattice window of the living room in our suite. The city felt mysterious, like the Venice I'd imagined, with masquerade balls and courtiers and hooded figures moving through the mist. The only problem was, I couldn't see a damn thing.

"There won't be much sightseeing today," I said as I let the lace curtain fall into place over the window.

"Oh, I think it's romantic," Clara replied. "No wonder so many artists painted scenes of Venetian fogs. There's something so alluring about it."

"How could they even see what they were painting?" I replied.

Clara shook her head. "Imagination. They painted an impression of the city. That's why it's called Impressionism. I think it's magical."

I grumbled under my breath and walked to the desk, intent on giving my article about Charles Hancock one last read. I'd already decided today was the day: send it, or shred it and come up with a new idea that wouldn't effectively destroy my relationship with Clara. But as I reached the desk, I paused. My mail wasn't there. Frowning, I pulled open the drawers and looked beneath the desk. I did a quick search through my journal and handbag, and even sorted through my clothing drawers. The envelope was nowhere to be seen.

"Clara?" I tried to control the panic in my voice.

"Mmm?" she said, distracted by the watercolor she was working on.

"There was an envelope, here on the desk. It was addressed but wasn't sealed. It was an article I planned to read over one last time before I mailed it. Have you seen it?"

"Oh, yes. I mailed it with the postcards yesterday. That, and a letter to Jenny, your roommate."

I squeezed my eyes closed. The article was gone. Already on its way to the editor. And if he decided it was worthy of print, I'd have to come clean to Clara for sure.

Clara looked apologetic. "I'm sorry. I thought I was being helpful."

I blew out a breath. "It's fine. I—"

A knock at the door interrupted us.

I opened the door to a bellboy, who handed me an envelope mailed from America. I recognized Violet's handwriting immediately.

"What is it?" Clara asked.

"A letter. From Violet, I think."

I sat at the desk, opened the envelope, and unfolded a page of the lilac-scented stationery I'd come to know so well.

"What does she say?" Clara prompted, joining me at the desk.

I began to read the letter aloud.

My dearest girls,

I hope your journey so far has been as full of wonder as mine was all those years ago, but I hope, more than anything, you're enjoying each other's company. Nothing would make me happier than to see my girls put their silly squabbles aside, and to become friends again. You are family, and what could matter more than that?

Did you deliver my letter to Matthias yet? I wonder. Of course I must be prepared for the news that he died some years ago. I would be sorry not to have the chance to say what I so desperately want to, or for you not to meet him, but fate will decide what should and should not be.

I miss you, girls! I must admit, it seems as though the farther away from me you travel, the more I ache for you both to return. I find myself lacking the energy to go outside, to eat, to read. The doctor says it is a natural development of my disease, but I think I am just an old woman, eager to see her granddaughters.

Don't fret, or even think about turning back (remember the inscription on the pocket watch, Clara), but know that I am looking forward to seeing you on your return.

All my love to you both,
Violet
X

My mood careened like a bicycle with a popped tire. Violet had been unwell for months, but she'd never stopped going outside. Her precious gardens, the sand and sea, called to her in any season, the way my writing called to me. There was nothing she hated more than playing the invalid. I pictured her flitting among the roses and peonies, or walking the beach in search of sea glass. Things she couldn't do now, and perhaps never would again.

I folded the letter and returned it to the envelope.

I could scarcely imagine a world without Violet in it.

Clara

*W*e were both deeply affected by Violet's letter.

A somber mood enveloped us as we quietly dressed and prepared to return to Morelli's gallery. We felt a renewed sense of urgency to deliver Violet's last two letters and return home as soon as possible. Her words had also forced me to confront my current indecision. Violet was facing up to her life's joys and regrets, preparing to say her goodbyes, while I dithered and dallied over whether to contact Edward at his hotel. Her letter, and its reminder that life is, in the end, always too short, gave me the courage to send him a short note, informing him of the address of our hotel and suggesting he send word of when and where he would like to meet. I left the note with the concierge, hesitating for just a moment before I let go of the envelope.

"You are sure you want it to be delivered?" the concierge asked, dark brows raised.

I laughed nervously, realizing he could see my hesitation. "I'm sure. And as quickly as possible. *Grazie*."

Hoping to have more luck in meeting Matthias, we retraced the path under the bridge and down a winding alley. We walked in silence, my thoughts filled with images of home and of Violet, patiently waiting for our return.

This time when we entered the gallery, Lucia was behind the counter, sorting through a stack of art books and paperwork. She stood up when she saw us and smiled.

"*Buongiorno!* You came back already!"

"We did. Is he here?" My tone was a little brusque, steered by my sense of urgency.

Lucia looked surprised at the directness of my question. As did Madeleine.

"Yes, he is here," Lucia replied. "You are in luck! He returned late last night."

"Oh, thank goodness." I smiled at Madeleine. "He's here!"

"So I heard," Madeleine replied, returning my smile.

"But I'm afraid he's still sleeping," Lucia added.

"Oh." My hands fell to my sides as I turned to Madeleine again. "Maybe we should leave Violet's letter. We shouldn't disturb him."

"You shouldn't disturb who?" An elderly man appeared from a back room. "And what's this about a letter?"

Matthias Morelli stared at us, a look of bemusement on his face. His white hair sat in a ring around his balding head, and his shoulders were hunched, but his eyes were passionate and fierce. He was short and a little stout, but striking, even in his later years.

"Hello, sir," Madeleine began. "We're very pleased to meet you. My name is Madeleine, and this is my sister, Clara. We are visiting from America, on behalf of our grandmother."

He looked at us intently, his eyes flickering from Madeleine to me and back again. "Well I never," he said as he studied us both.

"You can leave us, Lucia," he continued. "I will speak to these young women."

Lucia eyed us curiously then headed into the back room, her dark hair swinging in a ponytail behind her.

"Mr. Morelli—" I began.

"Matthias," he interrupted, his features softening into a smile. "What is it I can do for you, ladies?"

Madeleine glanced at me and I knew she had the same thought: How would we even begin to explain who we were and why we'd come to find him?

"This may all come as a shock, but do you remember a woman named Violet? Violet Lawson?" Madeleine asked.

He smiled at the name. "Violet Lawson. Of course. How could I ever forget her?"

Encouraged to discover that he remembered Violet, I continued the explanation. "We are Violet's granddaughters. She wanted us to deliver a letter to you on her behalf." I presented Violet's letter. "Unfortunately, she isn't well enough to make the journey herself."

Intrigue stamped Matthias's face as he looked at us again, picked up the envelope, and ran his fingertips over his name, written in Violet's elegant handwriting. "Violet Lawson," he whispered. "After all this time."

We stood in silence, giving him a moment to process his memories

"Violet Lawson," he repeated. "I'm so sorry to hear she isn't well." He shook his head.

"I'm glad you remember her," I said. "We were worried you might not."

He glanced up at this, his eyes wistful. "I adored Violet from the moment I saw her. She was so vibrant and beautiful with her dark hair and the most beautiful eyes I ever saw. Light blue, almost gray, like the Adriatic on a stormy day. She loved life more than anyone I'd ever met. She was a glorious reckless summer in a lifetime of quiet winters." He looked at us both, a sense of longing in his eyes. "Violet was a treasure, but she wasn't mine to keep."

I stared at Madeleine, my eyes wide. Like me, she was struck by this vibrant man whose feelings for our grandmother were clear, but I felt as if we were intruding and was uncomfortable to see him become emotional.

"We don't wish to impose," I said quietly. "We just wanted to deliver the letter. We should go."

"No. Please, stay. I would like to talk to you both." He turned the shop sign to *Chiuso* and locked the door before directing us to a back room. "Come with me," he said. "I should explain everything fully."

Whatever I'd expected from Matthias Morelli wasn't what we'd found. The frail old man I'd imagined, dozing in a chair beside the fire, was actually a sprightly fellow, suntanned and animated. He led us past easels and frames and dozens of exquisite watercolors of the canals, oil paintings of the piazzas, and canvases painted in the style of pointillism.

We followed him down a narrow flight of uneven stone steps where we all ducked to avoid bumping our heads on a low beam. Entering a small room at the bottom of the steps, Matthias pushed aside piles of books and paper and pulled two chairs forward.

"Come. Sit," he insisted. "If you can find room!"

We did as we were instructed.

"So, you are the girls!" he said, unable to take his eyes from us. "And you," he said, turning his attention to me. "You are her mirror."

"Violet?" I asked.

He nodded. "Just the same. *Bellissima!*"

"And you," he added, turning his attention to Madeleine. "You are a passionate soul. I can see it." He placed a hand to his heart. "Like me."

Madeleine smiled. "It's true, sir."

"Now, tell me about Violet," he said.

"She wanted to tell you something important," I explained, "so she wrote it all in a letter. She insisted we deliver it to you in person."

"She also wanted us to follow in her footsteps," Madeleine added. "To see Paris and Venice, just as she and her sister, Margaret, did many years ago."

Matthias leaned forward at the mention of our aunt Margaret. "And she is well?" he asked, his eyes darting from one of us to the other. "Margaret?"

"We're not entirely sure," I explained. "Violet has written a letter to her, too. We're heading to Austria next to visit her."

He nodded, as if he understood, and tucked Violet's letter into his shirt pocket. "For later," he said. "In private."

"Of course," Madeleine replied, although I could tell she was itching to know what Violet had said.

In truth, so was I.

Lucia returned with coffee for the three of us.

"Aha! And now we can all relax and get to know each other properly," Matthias said. "Nothing better than a fresh pot of coffee for making new friends. Apart, perhaps, from a glass of grappa at the end of the evening!"

"How did you know Violet?" I asked as I dipped a hard *cantuccini* biscuit into the rich coffee to soften it.

Matthias hesitated before letting out a long sigh. "It all seems so very long ago, and yet the memories are right here." He tapped his head. "And here," he added, indicating his heart. "I first saw Violet in the Piazza San Marco. She was the most beautiful woman I'd ever seen." He explained how he'd felt compelled to paint her as she sat alone at a café. "She wore a dress the color of Chianti. Everything else seemed to fade to gray around her. I couldn't resist." I nodded, recognizing that artist's urge, the desire to capture a perfect moment on the page. "She looked so alone, so vulnerable, and beautiful," he continued. "Of course I had the confidence of a much younger man then. When I'd finished the piece, I walked right up to her table, showed her the likeness, and asked if I might buy her another espresso. She was surprised, and more than a little delighted. We went dancing together that night and, well . . . You know what it's like to be young and in love."

A smile danced across his lips. I could almost see that younger man in his eyes.

"Did you meet Margaret, too?" Madeleine asked, following my own line of thinking. "We don't know much about her. Violet doesn't talk about her often."

"Violet was never far from Margaret's side. The two of them were inseparable. Wherever Violet and I went, Margaret came, too. They were the best of friends. It is a shame things changed between them."

He stood up suddenly and rummaged in a drawer before pulling something out and placing it in my hands.

"This is how I remember Violet," he said.

I stared at a painting of a beautiful young woman, the Doge's Palace and the Grand Canal caught in a golden sunset behind her.

"This is Violet? She's beautiful."

"You painted this?" Madeleine asked as she peered at the painting.

He nodded. "I painted her more than any other woman. She was my muse. My *musa*. My Lucrezia."

"Did you paint Margaret as well?" I asked, charmed by him and his lilting accent.

"There wasn't time. Margaret returned to America as planned. She was a gifted violinist and had a place to study music with a respected tutor. Violet chose to remain in Venice. We spent a wonderful summer together before her mother insisted she return home. She asked me to go with her, but I was a young fool with an art degree to complete and a family I couldn't bear to leave. I had to stay in Italy." At this he took a deep breath and leaned back in his chair, smoothing the silvery whiskers of his mustache. "I have questioned that decision many times over the years, when things became hard, but we choose the life we're destined to lead, don't we. And there are good things and bad, no matter the course."

His words hung in the air: *we choose the life we're destined to lead, don't we*. He spoke with such wisdom, such gentle honesty.

"I only wish I'd had more time with your grandmother," he continued. "But I'm just an old man, speaking in hindsight."

The room fell silent. For once, I wished Madeleine would ask a question, but she was as spellbound as I was.

Matthias leaned forward suddenly, reaching for both of our hands. "Violet wrote to me after she'd returned to America, and a couple of times after the birth."

"Birth?" we asked in unison.

He nodded. "Your grandmother returned home carrying my child, a little girl."

My mouth fell open.

I looked at Madeleine, whose eyes were wide with surprise. Had Violet raised the baby, or had she given it up for adoption? If she'd kept the baby . . . we both understood what it meant.

Matthias stood up and disappeared briefly into a side room, returning a minute or so later.

"Here," he said, holding out a faded old envelope. "You can read the letter she sent to me."

"Are you sure?" I asked. "Isn't it very private?"

He nodded. "It's part of your family now. Please. Read it. Then you will understand."

I took the envelope from him and pulled out a sheet of paper.

Veneto, East Hampton
May 1891

My dearest Mattie,

I wasn't sure how to tell you this, or whether I should, but I believe you have a right to know.

I had a child, Mattie. Our child. A daughter. I named her Celestine, after the woman in the painting we both admired. She was made with such love and passion and it feels unbearable to think she may never know you. I wish you could see her, hold her, smell the almond-sweet scent of her hair. She is my greatest masterpiece and I would not change a thing about her.

I expect nothing of you, Mattie. I understand your reasons for staying in Italy, truly, I do. What we had was perfect, and I'd like to preserve it in my heart just as it was.

I cannot give up my home, and family, and neither can you. I only wish for you to know about Celestine, to know what we made together. Society may gossip and stare and know the truth about her father, and my sister may accuse me of bringing our family name into disrepute, but when I look at my dear little girl, I cannot regret it. Not for one moment.

Perhaps we will see each other again one day, you and I? Perhaps our story was only ever meant to be fleeting. And I am thankful for what we had, and for what we have been given.

As you always told me the Italians say, it isn't goodbye, but arrivederci. "Until we meet again."

Violet

Matthias's eyes filled with tears as the weight of Violet's words reached out to us, and we understood.

"Your mother is my daughter," he said. "And you, dearest girls, are my beautiful grandchildren."

Maddie

$\mathcal{I}$ stared at Matthias Morelli, moments ago a stranger, and now a man whose life was suddenly such a significant part of my own. Was there a family resemblance in those wide eyes and aquiline nose? Did I recognize our mother's cheekbones and artful brow?

He was our grandfather. Our mother's father. We had Italian blood. Italian family! I thought about Grandpa Frank. Did he know? And what about Mother. Had Violet told her the truth about her birth, and if so, had she ever wanted to travel to Italy to meet her real father?

I had so many questions.

I swallowed hard and looked at Clara. She looked as stunned as I felt.

"You are shocked, I can see," Matthias said when he noticed our expressions. "You already have a grandfather. I know. Violet married a very good man. She wrote to me, told me how happy she was to marry Frank Bell. He raised and loved your mother as his own child. Not all men would do that."

I pictured Grandpa Frank, the man I'd known and loved as my

grandfather. Violet had said he was the love of her life, and that she'd cherished every minute of the years they'd spent together. And I believed it, even now, after this revelation about the summer of passion she'd shared with Matthias. And yet my mind still reeled from the discovery.

Hours passed as Matthias told us as much as he could remember. He asked us to share stories of Violet, too, and to tell him about our travels over the last few weeks.

"It's very good, very kind what you're doing for your grandmother," he said. "I'm sure Margaret will enjoy meeting you. She and Violet were such good friends when I knew them. I'm only sorry you will leave Venice so soon." His voice was full of regret. He looked at us both in turn, taking us in, trying to make sense of us in the same way we were trying to make sense of him. "Would you stop by again? Tomorrow, for coffee, perhaps? I'd like to show you the gallery properly. And the other paintings of your grandmother."

Clara leaned forward. "There are others?"

He chuckled and nodded. "Many more. I became—how would you say—obsessed!"

We exchanged kisses on each cheek, the Italian way, and promised to return the next day.

We'd hardly closed the door behind us when I blurted out, "Can you believe this, Clara? Our strict, straitlaced mother is the love child of a brilliant Italian artist!"

Clara shook her head. "I can't believe it. What a life Violet had! It must have scandalized the entire family. Imagine being pregnant and unmarried. It must have been so awful for her."

"There must be more to the story," I said, always interested in digging deeper. "On Margaret's side. Perhaps she was envious. Perhaps she secretly loved Matthias, too."

"You've always got the journalist's nose, don't you?" Clara said with a smile.

"Things are never as black and white as they seem. There's usually another side to the story, sometimes many sides. Anyway, life is interesting. We can definitely say that."

We talked the whole way through dinner that evening, musing aloud about what life would have been like had Violet married Matthias. We would have been Italian, not American, and who knew how our lives might have looked.

"A love affair, an illegitimate child, an estranged sister. I wouldn't have guessed any of it," Clara said as we returned to our hotel suite.

"I wonder if Father knew he'd married a woman who was half Italian? He was always so proudly American." I sat on the edge of the sofa and kicked off my shoes. "I wish he'd shared more with us, about his life. Though I guess I always had trouble talking with him. Less talking, really. More like shouting."

To my surprise, Clara sat beside me and covered my hands with hers. "He loved you, you know, despite your disagreements and differences," she said earnestly. "I think he was hard on you because he saw your talents. He only wanted the best for you. For us both."

I stared at her hands on mine. She used to be affectionate with me, and I with her, but we'd been so at odds with each other I'd almost forgotten what it was like. It was nice, and in that moment not only did I miss Father, but I realized how much I missed this—this closeness with my sister.

"Thank you," I replied softly, squeezing Clara's hand. "I wish I could have had more time with him. Made him proud of me."

"He *was* proud of you. He just had trouble saying it." She paused for a moment as she made her way to the bathroom, turning in the doorway. "I'm proud of you, too."

I made a face of mock horror. "Could you repeat that, please? I must have misheard."

She snatched a tube of lipstick from the counter and threw it at me.

I laughed and scooted beneath the covers just in time.

As Clara attended to her protracted toilette, I turned on the bedside lamp and reached for my notebook to record the day's incredible events, but as I put pen to paper, a thought flickered through my head, and I paused. I wondered when the editor at the *New York Herald Tribune* would receive my article, and whether Mr. McDougal would consider it worthy enough to print. If the article ran, Charles would be sure to see it—that was certainly my intention—but Clara would be furious with me for writing a scathing article about her future husband. It would undoubtedly cause bad feeling between us, but in the end, I wasn't sorry I'd written the article, or that it had been sent. There was a truth that needed to be told about Charles Hancock, even if he *was* marrying my sister.

I returned my gaze to the blank page, but the words wouldn't come. How could I document the events of the day? How could I adequately express how it felt to discover that my family was not what I'd thought it was?

I flipped idly through the pages, reading my entries from previous days, reliving the memories of our trip so far with a smile on

my lips, until I saw his name, and my smile faded: Daniel winning at poker. Daniel's suggestion of a pen name. Daniel helping
Clara on the hot air balloon. He was peppered throughout the
entire journey.

I still couldn't believe he was nothing but a hired hand, paid to
spy on us, and that all of the conversations and lovely afternoons
Clara and I had spent with him were a lie. But rather than be
furious, I felt a twinge of sadness. I assumed he'd returned to
New York now that the truth was out, but as I uncapped my pen
and wrote the date and location at the top of the page, part of me
hoped I was wrong.

A knock at the door broke the silence.

"I'll get it," Clara called as she finally emerged from the bathroom.

A moment later, she poked her head into my bedroom. She
held a note in her hand.

"What is it?" I asked, sitting up taller in the bed.

"It's Edward," she said, her cheeks flushed. "He's asked me to
meet him for lunch tomorrow."

Clara

*V*iolet once told me there are moments in life when we can take a leap into the unknown or turn back toward the familiar. Discovering that she'd had a child out of wedlock, and had taken that leap herself, gave me the courage to take my own.

I woke early and reread Edward's letter. His words affected me deeply. My reaction to them stirred a memory of the dizzy anticipation I'd felt when I'd first met Charles: a light-headedness, a sense of longing to be with him. Yet now when I thought about Charles, it was with a sense of hesitation and uncertainty that went far beyond any bride-to-be jitters. It was Edward who set my pulse racing, and it wasn't just the words in his letter, or the moment we'd shared in his gallery the morning before I'd departed; there were other moments—a glance, a pause, a shared appreciation of a new piece of art, the suggestion of something else, something more, waiting to be said or done.

As I'd left the gallery that last morning, Edward had encouraged me to use the trip to explore new techniques and styles. "Don't be confined by what you think you ought to be doing, Clara. Our best work comes when we set our imagination free."

His words spoke to me now. What I *ought* to be doing was looking forward to my wedding. What I *ought* to be doing was writing a few lines to Charles to tell him how much I missed him and loved him. But what I ought to be doing and what I *was* doing were increasingly becoming very different things. Of course, the proper thing to do would be to send a telegram to Edward's hotel to explain that I wouldn't be able to meet him after all. But for the first time in my life, I didn't want to be proper or do the proper thing. I wanted to do the unexpected thing, the brave and exciting thing. I wanted to take a leap.

Flustered and indecisive, I changed my dress three times and my shoes twice and I fussed and fiddled with a head of hair that insisted on acting like an obstinate child.

"Good luck," Madeleine offered when I was finally ready to go. "Are you sure you don't want me to come with you?" she added. "Act as a chaperone?"

"I need to do this alone," I replied. "Besides, two's company."

"And three's a crowd." She offered an encouraging smile. "Good for you. I'm going to take Matthias up on his invitation to take me for the best coffee in Venice."

"Send him my regards. I won't be long. I'll be back by midafternoon."

I picked up my gloves and closed the door behind me.

If only it could be as simple as I'd made it sound.

I walked with uncertain steps toward the Rialto Bridge, where Edward had asked me to meet him, every stride tugging at my conscience. I'd set off much too early and slowed my steps. Not wishing to appear too eager, or to arrive before Edward, I stopped for a while and watched the gondolas slip beneath an arched stone bridge. The gentle roll of the water below was soothing. I envied its ability to wend and weave in whichever direction it wanted to go, rather than following expectation and convention.

As the wake of a passing vaporetto calmed, I caught my reflection and was reminded of something Violet had said as I'd prepared to leave for this trip. "There are two versions of every woman, Clara: the version we present to the world with a polite smile, and the real version, the one we conceal from others and show only to ourselves when we look in the mirror." I wondered which version of myself I would take back home, to America.

As a distant church clock chimed noon, I continued on my way, my pulse racing, my heart pounding. I'd thought about Edward so often since leaving America. I'd replayed, over and over, our last exchange on the dockside in New York City, and imagined him in his gallery admiring a new piece, his head tilted slightly to one side as he ran his hands through his hair, sending it this way and that. He was so vivid, so real in my mind that when I looked up and saw him leaning against a lamppost without a care in the world, I had to stop and take a breath. The twists and turns of fate that had led us both to this beautiful city at the same time were about to be unraveled.

I paused. His back was to me, so he hadn't yet seen me. I could still turn and walk away, or I could continue and let fate decide how things would play out.

I thought of Nellie's pocket watch: *Never turn back.*

I stepped forward.

When I was close enough for him to hear, I coughed. "*Buon-giorno, signor.*"

He turned around, a smile spreading across his face as his eyes settled on mine.

"*Buongiorno, signorina.*"

We stood in silence, each of us searching for the next thing to say until his smile broke into a quiet laugh.

"I'm afraid that's the extent of my Italian," he said. "Apart from *bella*. You look radiant, Clara. Truly."

I smiled, suddenly shy to be in his company, away from the usual limitations of the art gallery and our roles as tutor and student, and without a wife and fiancé waiting for us to return.

"Don't worry," I replied, letting his compliment pass. "Venetians speak exceptionally good English. It makes one feel ashamed, to be honest. They also have wonderful coffee and the best gelato in Italy."

"Well, we must have both, immediately. What better way for two friends to spend an afternoon."

Friends.

Given our respective relationship situations, it was all we ever could be, but was it enough?

My initial reservations about meeting Edward soon dissipated, and my conscience quieted as we chatted animatedly over coffee. I told him about our journey so far, our time in Paris and on the Orient Express, my joy in painting the miniature portraits for the Wainwright girls, and our newly discovered grandfather.

"He and Violet had a passionate love affair while she was in Venice, but she returned to America, and he stayed in Venice, and they never saw each other again," I explained.

Edward was more charmed by the story than shocked. "And yet, after all those years apart, Violet still cared for him enough to send you both to meet him. He must have meant a lot to her," he said.

"He really did. It's very romantic, isn't it."

As I stirred sugar into a second cup of coffee, Edward reached for my hand.

"I can't tell you how pleased I am to see you, Clara. I wasn't sure how you would respond to my letter. I just . . . well, I couldn't bear to see you leave without saying what I did, and since I was coming here . . ."

His skin was warm against mine and prompted a rush of heat up my neck. Instinctively, I pulled my hand away, then apologized, then apologized for apologizing.

Edward smiled gently. "I should apologize, not you. I'm sorry if I've made you uncomfortable. It's just, you look so happy, Clara. You look . . ." He paused as he fished about for the right word. "You look so alive. And this city! Look at it!" He leaned forward. "Doesn't it make you want to be reckless?"

His enthusiasm was infectious, his eyes sparkling like flecks of amber, lit by the reflection of the sun off the canal. I did want to be reckless, and yet I held back. I was sensible, dutiful, predictable Clara. I didn't know *how* to be reckless.

His question lingered, unanswered in the air around us, and I was relieved when he changed the topic of conversation and told me about the exhibition he'd been working on. Art was familiar ground. I felt more comfortable there.

"So, where to next, Miss Sommers?" he asked when we'd finished our coffee and he helped me into my coat. The spring air still carried a chill when the sun slipped behind a cloud. "The Doge's Palace? The Rialto markets?"

"Art, of course, Mr. Arnold. The Gallerie dell'Accademia."

"Of course," he said with a beautiful smile that made my heart skip a beat.

We made our way by vaporetto to the Scuola della Carità on the south bank. I was surprised at how quickly I'd become familiar with the different areas of the city—the *sestieri*—and felt confident as our guide.

The building itself was beautiful and we walked in hushed appreciation, each of us taking turns to show one another a piece we admired. I was drawn to the work of Paolo Veronese and Tintoretto. Edward's eye leaned toward Carpaccio and Canaletto.

"Look at the use of light and color," he whispered. "The shadows and depth are remarkable."

I found myself as captivated by Edward's remarks as I was by the paintings themselves, but despite the beauty of the place and the brilliance of the art, my mind wandered, and doubt and guilt stood at my shoulder.

"Is everything alright?" Edward asked, noticing that I'd fallen silent. "You look like you're a million miles away." Concern etched his face.

I turned to him. "I'm sorry. I *am* a million miles away."

"Might I join you there?" he asked, and it was such a gentle, tender question that it took all my resolve not to fall into his arms and stay there forever.

"I should go to meet Madeleine," I said. "It's getting late."

Maddie

After Clara had left for her rendezvous with Edward, I set off to meet Matthias for coffee, as promised. As I stepped outside the hotel and turned the corner, I saw a group of soldiers gathering in the street. With their polished boots, pristine uniforms, and guns, they were a stark contrast to the city's ancient beauty and charm, and the atmosphere shifted dramatically in their presence. People darted inside their homes, or hurried off in the opposite direction. I wondered what had happened to make everyone so fearful. An incident, perhaps, that had not made the news? I was certain there were plenty of those. I couldn't deny the sight of them made me uneasy.

Picking up my pace, I ducked through the maze of streets, my eye drawn to posters of Mussolini that were pinned to doors and storefronts. It was clear this dictator had a firm grip on Venice, and most assuredly all of Italy.

But as I approached the Morelli gallery, I calmed again, feeling a little safer to be with a local, and one who I could now call family. The notion still filled me with surprise.

Matthias was delighted to see me and insisted on taking me

to his favorite café. He led me through the winding streets to a quaint little place tucked away in a quiet corner.

"I would never have found this on my own," I said as we took a table beside the water.

"Venice is full of secrets," Matthias replied, with a wink.

A waiter brought us two steaming cups of cappuccino and a couple of frosted almond pastries that looked too delicious to ignore, despite the large breakfast I'd had. I'd finished Clara's meal as well as my own, since she was too nervous about seeing Edward to eat.

"Clara is meeting her friend today?" Matthias asked.

"Yes. Edward Arnold. Her art tutor," I said, licking hot milk from my top lip. "Perhaps he might be more than a friend when she returns."

Matthias raised an eyebrow. "Aha. There is a story behind this rendezvous?"

"Probably not. I shouldn't have said anything."

He chuckled at my remark. "Venice makes lovers of strangers. You think your sister may fall in love with her . . . friend, yes?"

I wasn't sure what I thought, apart from that I wanted Clara to make her own choices. I wanted her to be happy, and if that meant falling for someone else so that she didn't marry the wrong man—even with the pain and difficulty that might entail—then I would be beside her every step of the way.

"We do strange things for love, don't we?" Matthias continued.

I shook my head. "I wouldn't know, sir."

The truth was I'd never been in love. Not properly. I'd only experienced a schoolgirl's crush while in college, but it didn't last.

The object of my affections hadn't been able to keep up with me and my industrious mind, he'd said. In fact, I was pretty sure he'd been afraid of me, in a way.

"You wouldn't know about love?" Matthias's dark eyes twinkled. "But you are a passionate one, yes? I noticed it the moment I met you. Passion like yours, like mine, intimidates some people. They don't know what to make of it. I have given this much thought over the years. What they are really afraid of is not having that same passion, not allowing themselves to be swept away by their emotions and their dreams, because it might bring them pain." He paused a moment. "But what *we* know—you and me—is that, in the end, there is only more pain if we don't follow what's in here." He pointed to his chest.

"Yes," I replied softly, awed by the truth of his statement and by how alike we were in our thinking. It struck me, once again, that this man was my grandfather. My family. It was *his* passion I'd inherited, and suddenly I was filled with gratitude for Violet's gift of sending us to him, for helping me realize my voracious mind wasn't what separated me from my family or friends, but what set me apart.

I touched his hand lightly. "Thank you, Matthias. I'm so happy we found you."

"As am I, Madeleine. As am I."

He was a fiery man, full of ideas, and I found myself rapt by his stories. He, in turn, wasn't put off by my many questions and instead seemed delighted to answer them.

As I drained the last of my coffee, a man wearing what appeared to be a beat-up uniform jacket from the Great War approached the table. He carried a satchel of pamphlets. He nodded to Matthias in a polite gesture, and said, *"È per loro,"* before leaving a pamphlet on the table and circling the patio to make sure each patron received one.

"What did he say?" I asked.

"This is for us," he said, picking up the pamphlet. "Ah. He is against Mussolini."

So the man was distributing antifascist propaganda. While his cause was noble, I wondered if he shouldn't pass around his literature so openly, given everything I'd read about Mussolini's secret police. They'd become notorious after his rise to power in the last decade, threatening or jailing the opposition at the merest hint of dissent. This man's life could be at risk. So could my grandfather's. I picked up the leaflet and put it into my handbag.

"Matthias," I said, lowering my voice and leaning toward him. "What do you think of Mussolini?"

He rubbed his chin a moment as if weighing how to respond. "I think he has brought some stability to our country but taken much more in the process. People are afraid of him and his men, and they have good reason to be. We are not free to say what we feel or think. And he appears to be supporting Hitler. Since the Great War, I worry about Germany. They're making noise like they may incite another conflict."

"Do you think Italy will be drawn into a war, if Hitler invades Austria, or Poland?"

He shook his head. "I don't know, but if we are supporting Hitler's agenda, it cannot be good."

I felt a rush of protectiveness for this kind, gentle man. We would leave Venice in a few more days, continue our journey to Austria and leave this all behind, but Matthias must face the uncertainty each day. Though we'd only just met him, I didn't like the idea of leaving him here, in a country run by a dangerous man.

"I hope you will write to us when we've returned to America," I said. "Should there be any trouble at all, we would help in any way we can."

"*Si, cara,* I will write. You are my family now."

But even so, I already knew there wouldn't be much we could do if things did escalate to war. What I could do, though, was ensure the American public understood what was happening in Europe, and how it affected us. Suddenly, I was more determined than ever to finish the articles I'd begun, and send them out as soon as possible. Surely some newspaper would find the topics worthy of print, especially coming from a person who'd seen the situation firsthand.

Matthias had given me a lot to think about. Even as we moved on to other topics of conversation and eventually said our goodbyes with a kiss on each cheek and a promise to meet again tomorrow, my heart felt unusually heavy. I watched him walk away with the awful knowledge that time was not on our side.

CLARA HADN'T RETURNED to the hotel by the time I made my way back after an enjoyable afternoon of sightseeing, so I caught up with the day's news and added a few more pages to my journal while I waited for her. This time, I didn't hold back and recorded more than just the pretty things I'd seen and the delicious food I'd enjoyed.

I only wonder what will become of this beautiful city—and Italy itself—should Mussolini take the country to war. Signs forbid unsanctioned gatherings. Headlines speak of Mussolini and his edicts. Posters and pamphlets praise him as if he were some sort of Messiah. Will he continue to look to Hitler should the Germans invade? Time will tell, but for now, it appears as if Mussolini is fortifying his country for war.

Eventually Clara joined me at our table for dinner, as instructed on the note I'd left for her in our suite.

She apologized profusely, out of breath as she took her seat.

"How did it go then?" I asked. "Very well, I presume, given the time?"

She blushed. "I don't know . . . I . . . it went well. It was nice to see him."

"Nice? Is that all?"

"Yes. Nice."

"You'd forgotten how handsome he is, hadn't you?" I teased. "Did he kiss you?"

"*Madeleine!*" Her face was almost scarlet she was so flustered.

I laughed. "And the museums and galleries? Did they live up to your expectations?"

"They were magical! All those masterpieces." She picked up a menu and studied it intently.

I longed to ask her what had happened between her and

Edward, but I could tell she didn't want to discuss it. For once, I decided I would respect her wishes and not pry.

Smiling, I filled both our glasses with a fine Sangiovese before raising mine to hers. "To you."

"To me?"

"For doing something unexpected. I'm proud of you."

She laughed as she clinked her glass against mine.

We ordered fresh gnocchi served with a rich lamb ragù and ate contentedly as we watched the boats rush past and admired the golden light on the buildings that lined the water's edge.

"Let's take a gondola ride," I suggested once we'd finished our meal. "Have the full Venetian experience."

"And at sunset," Clara said, peering at the sun as it began to sink behind the buildings, casting a rich glow over everything.

"Perfect," I agreed. "Just as Violet suggested."

We walked along the embankment, where the gondoliers waited patiently for tourists to wander by, calling and whistling at any women who passed.

"Signorinas? Go for a ride?" A handsome gondolier removed his black beret, held it over his heart, and gestured to his boat.

"*Si, signor,*" I said, laughing as I grabbed Clara's hand and pulled her toward him.

He helped us into the gondola, and we sat opposite each other on a pair of rich brown cushions. We glided over the water silently for some time, turning down a labyrinth of smaller side canals beside houses where window shutters were open, and neighbors gossiped to one another above our heads. We passed a pair of lovers locked in an embrace on the famous Bridge of Sighs, a small stone bridge that arched over the water between two sides of the Doge's Palace. I wanted to call out and tell them they were missing all the beautiful sights, but Clara told me to leave them alone.

"You've no heart, Madeleine Sommers," she said. "Who needs beautiful sights when you have a lover's eyes to stare into!"

After almost an hour, the gondolier turned back toward the Grand Canal, passing under several small bridges on the way. As we approached one of the bridges, my attention was caught by a figure standing in the middle, peering out at the water.

As we drew closer, I frowned.

It couldn't be.

But it was.

Once again, I recognized the dark hair, the thick shoulders, and a grin that—I hated to admit—had grown on me.

I tipped my face up and glowered at him as the gondola slipped beneath the bridge.

Clara turned in her seat. "That wasn't who I thought it was, was it?"

I folded my arms crossly. "Afraid so. Dastardly Daniel Miller."

"Madeleine?" he called as we emerged on the other side of the bridge. "Madeleine!"

"Just ignore him," Clara said.

I focused on the surface of the water ahead, no longer seeing the beautiful buildings that were hundreds of years old, or the cobbled roads that ran alongside the canal.

Daniel called out again. "Madeleine Sommers, I need to talk to you!"

"Well *I* don't need to talk to *you*," I shouted back.

As we sailed under another bridge, Daniel ran alongside to keep pace with us.

In spite of myself, I smiled. "He's making such a fool of himself."

"He'll fall in if he's not careful," Clara added, and we both started to laugh at the thought.

"We stop here, signorinas," the gondolier said, pointing ahead as he steadily steered us toward a jetty.

Daniel raced ahead, stepping onto the jetty as we pulled up beside it.

"You have to admire his persistence," Clara remarked.

"I'm glad I saw you," he shouted. "There's something I wanted to say."

The gondolier raised an eyebrow as he stepped onto the jetty and began to tie the gondola to the post.

"Beat it, Miller!" I replied. "You're not the person I thought you were." I stood up quickly, prepared to make a dash for it to get away from him. I stumbled as the gondola rocked from side to side, disturbed by the wake of a passing vaporetto.

"Maddie!" Clara called. "You're rocking the boat. Sit down!"

Her warning came too late as a larger wave tipped the gondola again, this time, more violently.

I lost my footing, leaned too far to one side to try to balance myself—and crashed into the lagoon below.

Clara shrieked.

The shock of cold water stole the breath from my lungs. I shot to the surface, sputtering and reaching for my hat that floated beside me, but as my clothes grew heavy with water, my skirt tangled around my legs and I was pulled under the water again. I told myself not to panic and pushed to the surface, just as I had so often as a child. Father had insisted we know what to do should our sailboat capsize.

Something splashed into the water beside me. I turned to see Daniel's head emerge and without hesitation, he reached for my arm.

"Let me help you," he called.

"I don't need your help," I gasped, pushing him away as I swam to the jetty and hauled myself clumsily out of the water. Cold rivulets ran down my legs and pooled around my sodden shoes.

"For God's sake, Maddie, why wouldn't you let me help you?" Daniel said as he climbed out of the water and fell into a heap beside me.

I fixed him with a glare. "I don't need your help. That's why. I don't need *anyone's* help."

He pulled off his shoes and started to wring out his socks. "You're infuriating," he said as he turned to me and let his eyes settle on mine.

We looked so absurd, the two of us. I felt a smile tug at my lips but managed to maintain a furious scowl.

"I wanted to say I'm sorry," he began. "I know it seems as if I'm not the person you got to know on the ship and in Paris, but I *am*."

"I don't really care who you are, Daniel. I just want you to leave me—us—alone."

Even as I said it, I knew it was a lie, but I was angry and still felt betrayed.

Clara, having successfully stepped off the gondola without falling into the water, rushed toward me and placed her coat around my shoulders.

"Goodness, Maddie! You could have drowned!" She cast a deathly glare at Daniel before turning her back to him. "Come along. We need to get you back to the hotel and into a warm bath. Lord knows what filth you've swallowed."

I shivered all the way back to our hotel, leaning on the one thing that had been constant my whole life, even when we'd fought and disagreed and hated each other for a time.

My sister.

Clara

As much as I'd enjoyed my time with Edward, it had left me more confused and uncertain than ever. Madeleine's tumble into the Grand Canal was an almost welcome distraction from the relentless seesawing in my mind.

We hurried back to the hotel, and after prescribing a warm bath and hot tea, I insisted she rest. She complained of a headache and a light fever, but it was hard to know with Madeleine whether she was really sick or pretending. She was known for her ability to fall suddenly ill to get out of school or one of Father's dinner party recitals. But as the evening wore on and nighttime enveloped the city, her cheeks became flushed and she couldn't stop shivering. I spent most of the night listening to her coughing, or going to check on her and make her more comfortable as I willed the sun to rise.

I must have eventually dozed off in the chair beside her bed. I woke at first light to discover she had worsened significantly.

"I'm sending for the doctor," I said as I pressed my hand to her forehead. My concern intensified at the searing heat I felt there.

"Don't fuss, Clara. I've just caught a chill."

Ignoring her, I rushed down to the lobby and asked the concierge to send for the doctor straightaway.

He arrived mercifully quickly.

"Your sister must have picked up an infection from the water," he confirmed after taking her temperature. He reminded me a little of our family doctor at home and I was glad I'd made the decision to send for him. "Her temperature is *molto alto*. Very high," he cautioned. "You will need to sponge her down, encourage her to drink, and hope the fever breaks within a day or two."

"A day or two?"

He packed away his stethoscope into a black medical bag. "After which she will need bed rest for several days more. Send for me if she worsens, or if there is no improvement in twenty-four hours. Is there anyone in the city you can ask for help? Family? Friends?"

"Not really—although, yes, actually."

He looked confused.

"It's complicated," I said, "but yes, there are people I can ask to help."

As Madeleine groaned and rolled over, I looked at her. I'd never seen her so ill, and it frightened me. In that moment, I felt very far from home and horribly alone in a strange city. I would be glad of someone's help, or at least I would be glad of their company and reassurance.

But who to ask? I didn't want to involve Edward. Meeting him had already caused me enough emotional turmoil, and I worried that it might seem a little forward of me if I asked him to come to our hotel suite. Matthias was an old man, and I didn't want to worry him. Besides, we'd already given him enough of a shock showing up out of the blue. There was little point in calling

Mother since she was so far away and would only worry terribly, and Charles would already be on his way to Austria, a thought that left me feeling increasingly panicked. The only other person I knew in Venice was Daniel Miller, and he was right here, in the same hotel.

It didn't take me long to settle on asking him to come. Madeleine might pretend to be furious with him, but I knew her better than that, and I would do whatever it took to help her recover.

I left an urgent message for him at reception and within the half hour he was knocking on the door to our suite.

"I came as soon as I heard," he said as I invited him inside. "I was doing a little shopping for my sisters, picking up some gifts for them before I return home. How is she?"

"She's very sick. An infection picked up in the water, according to the doctor." I swallowed my pride in an effort to be polite. "Thank you for coming. I know we didn't part on the best of terms."

"I'm so sorry, Miss Sommers. It's my fault Madeleine took a tumble. I was silly to chase you and bother you. What can I do to help? I brought some books to help pass the time. I can sit with her if you like, while you get some rest."

His manner was frantic, but he was so full of concern that I couldn't sustain my anger with him for long. Even if it was partly his fault that Madeleine was in her current condition, it wasn't his fault that Charles was deceitful and distrusting.

"I suppose your journey will be somewhat curtailed now," Daniel said as I took his coat and hat. "Will you go straight home when Madeleine's better?"

"I'm not sure," I said. "We're supposed to go on to Austria next, to visit my grandmother's sister." I looked at him. "But I suppose you already knew that."

He looked embarrassed. "I did, yes. And I also know that Charles is due to meet you there."

I huffed out a breath and poured us both a large brandy.

"I haven't told him that you know about our little scheme," he continued. "I've explained your silence by telling him you're busy with Violet's messages, and sightseeing."

There was that to be grateful for, at least.

"So, tell me, Mr. Miller. How does someone like you end up on a spying mission for a man like Charles Hancock? Please, enlighten me."

"It seems rather ridiculous now that I've met you both and gotten to know you a little. Charles spoke to me in confidence about your grandmother's idea. He was concerned about two women making the journey alone, but he knew your grandmother would insist, and that—despite some initial hesitation—you would go in the end. He always assumed Madeleine would jump at the chance."

"He was right about that. But what's in it for you? Why would you come all this way to follow us?"

He leaned back in his chair, his handsome features knotted into a frown.

"As you know, your fiancé is a very persuasive man."

"He can be, yes." I shifted uneasily in my chair at the mention of the term "fiancé." A reminder of my impending wedding.

"I was looking for a promotion, and for an opportunity to travel to European cities to study the architecture there, and Charles had the perfect way to offer me both. And since you and

I had never met, Charles knew you wouldn't recognize me. He said he wanted a man on the ground whom he could trust. And that man was me. We're college friends. I'm not sure if you were aware of that?"

"I wasn't. It seems there is a lot I'm not aware of when it comes to Charles Hancock."

We spoke at length about the arrangement the two men had come to and the sort of information Daniel had sent back, mostly an account of our progress, and to report on our safety.

"I suppose you told him about our disagreement over the letter Madeleine had concealed from me?" I asked. I was afraid Daniel would have mentioned it to Charles, or might even have seen Edward give me his gift before we'd boarded the *Queen Mary*. I presumed Daniel had already been watching us even then.

"I did not," he said, looking down for an instant. "I'd come to know you both a little by then and I could see you were uncertain about . . . things. I decided it was none of my business who your letters were from. Or Charles's business, for that matter."

At this, I felt great relief.

"All Charles knows is that you and Madeleine are both in Venice on schedule, as planned," he continued. "It might have taken a trip halfway around the world to realize it, and I apologize if this causes any offense, Miss Sommers, but I've decided that I don't care to put my fate, my career, or my future in the hands of a man like Charles Hancock." He offered an apologetic smile and raised his glass. "To creating our own destiny, Miss Sommers?"

The question lingered, but only for a moment.

I raised my glass to his and, although I didn't say anything in reply, the bright clink of crystal against crystal cut through any remaining doubt as Daniel's words swirled in my mind until they became my own: *I don't care to put my fate, my career, or my future in the hands of a man like Charles Hancock.*

A cough from the adjoining room made us both stand.

"I'll go," I said, placing my glass on the table. "Madeleine might be sick, but she could still wallop you if she sees you."

At this, Daniel laughed warmly. "Indeed!"

Maddie

Strange dreams of missing my train, boating accidents, and terrifying newspaper headlines followed me from one delirious night to another until at last the fever broke. I woke to find Clara at my bedside, pressing a cool cloth to my forehead and my cheeks, her brown eyes full of concern.

"Hello, you." She smiled. "Welcome back."

I sat up slowly. "How long have I been sick? You look different."

"I look exhausted, I'm sure," she said as she plumped my pillows and helped me to get comfortable. "You've been sick for several days and need to stay in bed for the rest of the week. Doctor's orders."

I groaned. "But we were supposed to leave for Austria. Did we miss the train?"

She sat beside me on the bed. "Yes. We should have left yesterday, but I made the decision for us to stay in Venice a little longer, to give you a chance to get better. I booked tickets on the train to Vienna for next week."

I wasn't even sure what day it was, but I knew we'd only had a couple of days left in Venice before I'd fallen ill. "But that will give us only a few days in Vienna. Will it be long enough?"

"Hopefully. Either way, we can't reschedule our tickets for the *Hindenburg*. It will depart from the airfield in Frankfurt on the evening of May third, and we will be on board, come what may."

I knew she was right, but I was disappointed to waste time stuck in bed. Why did I have to fall into the canal like a clumsy oaf, and in front of Daniel Miller of all people? I cringed at the memory of scrambling out of the water. Also, spending so little time in Vienna meant less chance of finding Margaret and less time scouting for story ideas. Austria was where I really hoped to get beneath the skin of the Nazi Party, perhaps even attend a rally to see what it was all about, especially after my conversation with Matthias.

"I thought, since Matthias is here," Clara continued, "it would be better to spend most of our remaining time in Venice."

She was right. Getting to know Matthias was more important than any news story. I was instantly comfortable in his presence and already liked him a great deal. I looked forward to spending a little more time with him.

"Fine, yes. That makes sense." I reached for the glass of water on the bedside table. "I'm glad you were here, Clara. Thank you for taking care of me. I wasn't going to die, was I?"

"Not unless I decided I couldn't stand another moment with you, no! You were sick enough to give us a fright, though."

"Us?"

A soft knock came at the bedroom door.

Clara stood up. "Yes. Us." She cleared her throat, and looked a little nervous. "There's someone who'd like to see you. Don't be mad at me, but I didn't know what else to do, and . . . well . . . Daniel's here."

I felt myself flush. "Daniel? Here? Why? But . . . I look a mess."

"You've been ill, Madeleine. No one expects you to look like a fashion plate! Besides, I wouldn't have thought you'd care about being a mess in front of someone you don't even like."

I ignored her teasing and looked at my blue silk pajama set to make sure I hadn't dribbled soup or tea down the front. Reaching frantically for my brush and hand mirror from the bedside table, I combed the snarls from my long, tangled hair. Just as my curls were tamed into soft waves, Clara opened the door and Daniel stepped inside.

"Hello, Maddie," he said. In his arms, he carried a small box wrapped in blue-and-gold paper.

"Daniel," I said, forcing my tone to be formal, but in truth, I was glad to see him.

"Well you look a lot better than you did yesterday."

"Yesterday?" I stared at Clara. "You were here yesterday?"

"Daniel has been here every day," she explained. "He has been a tremendous help, actually. And on that note, I'll leave you to your conversation." She stepped from the bedroom but left the door open.

"How are you feeling?" he asked.

"Much better. Clara won't let me leave the hotel, but I feel fine." I indicated that he should take the chair beside the window. "You might as well sit down, if you're staying."

"You mean, in this chair, where I've sat most of the night for the past couple of days?"

"You've been here every night?" I felt my cheeks heat again, as I thought of him seeing me in such a state. What was Clara thinking? And why did I keep blushing around Daniel?

He laughed. "Don't worry. It was all very proper. I read, mostly. And thought a lot." He perched on the edge of the chair and fidgeted with the box in his hands.

"Is that for me?" I asked, eyeing the gift.

He held out the package. "Perhaps it will say what I've been trying to."

I accepted the gift and opened it carefully to preserve the beautiful paper. Inside, was a fountain pen, a set of colored inks, and an elegant stamp with the inscription *M. Sommers* in curled script. My hand covered my mouth in surprise. It was so beautiful. So thoughtful.

"Daniel, it's . . . thank you. It's perfect."

"I'm glad you like it," he said, a hint of a blush coloring his olive skin.

I studied his thick wavy hair, the dimple in his right cheek. His face was open and expressive, his humor affable. He was handsome; there was no other way to look at it, or him. He was a handsome . . . friend.

"I love it." I stuck out my hand. "Truce?"

"Truce." He shook my hand firmly, holding it a little longer than necessary.

I squirmed inwardly at the surprisingly pleasant sensation of his warm hand in mine, not sure what to make of it all, of his perfect gift or of his being at my bedside while I was feverish.

"Since I can't leave this room," I said, looking down as he gently pulled his hand from mine, "I suppose you might as well tell me who you really are, and all about those sisters of yours."

He spoke fondly about his five sisters, most still living near one another, even after marriage. They seemed to be a happy, tightly knit family group.

"I can't believe you have so many sisters," I said, when the conversation lulled. "And you the youngest, and only son."

"It's why I'm so sensitive." He waggled his eyebrows.

I rolled my eyes at him dramatically and then laughed.

"You really are getting better," he said, a gleam of good humor in his eyes.

"Not fast enough. I'm missing the sights. I wanted to see Vienna, too, but it looks like that trip will have to be cut short. We can't change our tickets to return home on the *Hindenburg,* and that's an experience I definitely don't want to miss."

"Something I've been looking forward to myself," he said, his features becoming animated. "A marvel of engineering and modern science."

Of course! Daniel would be returning on the *Hindenburg,* too. Charles really had thought of everything. And he, no doubt, had a ticket for himself, too. Suddenly, my excitement dampened.

"Clara's dreading it," I replied. "She's terrified of heights. I keep telling her there's nothing to be afraid of, that it's perfectly safe. You might say the same if you get the chance."

I reached for one of the books Daniel had brought. "I think I'd like to read a little while and get some more rest."

"Of course." He stood. "I'll check in on you tomorrow. If that's alright?"

I shrugged and hid my smile behind the book. "I guess."

"Is there anything I can bring you?"

I thought for a moment. "There is actually. I was hoping to pick up some more newspapers, or literature about Mussolini." Daniel raised an eyebrow, but before he could reply I added, "I know it's a little obscure, but it's research for a piece I have in mind."

He shrugged. "To be honest, I'd have been more surprised if you'd asked for a romance novel."

"Why so?"

"Well, you don't seem the kind of woman for romance. Novels, I mean."

"Oh? What kind of woman do I seem?"

He shoved his hands into his pockets. "One of a kind. You are most definitely one of a kind, Madeleine Sommers."

My stomach somersaulted at what I knew was meant as a compliment.

"I'll see you tomorrow," he added, before leaving the room.

A moment later, I heard the door closing behind him.

"That seemed to go well," Clara said as she peered around the doorframe. "Considering you can't stand the man."

I threw a pillow at her and slid beneath the covers.

She caught the pillow and threw it straight back. "Oh, Madeleine. Just admit it. You like him."

"I don't!" I shouted, my voice muffled by the bedcovers. "Go away."

She laughed as she closed the bedroom door.

When she'd gone, I emerged from beneath the covers and picked up the beautiful inks and stamp. A huge smile spread across my face. *M. Sommers.* One of a kind.

Clara

With Madeleine falling ill, I hadn't been able to spend as much time with Edward or Matthias as I'd hoped. I'd sent messages to them both to explain what had happened, and that I wouldn't be able to meet them, and added an apology to Edward for not being able to attend the opening day of his exhibition. He arrived at the hotel with a beautiful but simple spray of sunflowers, and offered to help in any way he could.

"I don't wish to intrude, Clara, but I wanted to let you know I am thinking of you both. And much as I would love to spend more time with you, I know that your sister is your priority now. You know where to reach me if you need me."

Edward understood, better than most, the strain that existed between me and Madeleine. I'd spoken to him about it often, just as he'd spoken to me about the strain between him and Annabel. I knew it saddened him greatly that they'd grown apart, and that she increasingly pulled in a different direction. "I try to make her happy, but it seems I only irritate her more and more," he'd said one fall afternoon as we'd painted the

Manhattan skyline together. "She says I have my head in the clouds and that if I spent half as much time attending to our business affairs as I did to my damned paintings, we might fare better."

Perhaps they were conversations we shouldn't have had, private thoughts we shouldn't have shared. Still, we took comfort in the exchange even though there wasn't a great deal either of us could do to help the other.

Being alone in the hotel suite, watching over Madeleine, had given me time to think, especially in the silent hours of the night. There, I searched my heart, asking question after question, demanding only the truth in my replies. I'd thought a lot about Charles, about how we'd met, and how quickly everything had happened. The son of my father's lawyer, Charles Hancock ticked all the boxes. Mother had quietly encouraged the relationship. She believed Charles would be a good husband who would give me a good life. Marrying him was the sensible thing to do, she said. The proper thing to do. Violet, on the other hand, was more challenging. "Do you love him?" she'd asked when I'd shown her the engagement ring. I'd laughed and said of course I did. "Truly, Clara?" she'd pressed. "Do you love him with all your heart, until it aches?" I hadn't answered her then, but I knew the answer now.

When Madeleine had improved enough for me to leave her on her own, I'd come closer to knowing how I wanted my life, my journey, to continue when I returned home, yet I still hesitated as I prepared to leave the hotel the following morning.

"Are you sure you'll be alright?" I asked, fussing with Madeleine's pillows before I pulled on a pair of cotton gloves. "I don't have to see Edward today. I'm perfectly happy to stay here."

"Yes, you do have to see Edward today. I insist. Go, please. I feel much better. It's bad enough that one of us is cooped up here, there's no point in both of us missing out. Besides, I know how much you want to see him."

It was true. I did.

I'd finally told her everything: my reservations about Charles, my confusion over my feelings for Edward, the tangle of emotions I could barely make sense of. She hadn't teased or mocked or made me feel uncomfortable. She'd listened and offered advice where she could.

"I'll be back to check on you later," I said. "Don't do anything silly."

Once again, as I waited beside the Rialto Bridge, I found myself drawn to the water, comforted by the gentle motion of the little waves that licked the edge of the wooden struts beneath the bridge. As I watched the world slip by, a conversation I'd had with Violet the previous summer came to mind. We were painting a still life of peonies together, side by side on our lawn chairs, our faces shaded by floppy straw hats.

"You should see Venice one day," she'd said, out of the blue. "It's such a wonderful place to fall in love."

I'd laughed and told her I planned to fall in love with a handsome American, not an Italian. "Tell me about Venice. Is it as beautiful as they say?" I'd asked.

Violet often talked about the past while she painted. The process seemed to unlock some deeply private part of her as her brushstrokes painted her memories onto the canvas in shades of plum and cobalt.

"It's as if the city carries a sort of magic in the water," she'd continued. "The reflections make two of everything, so that I always felt it was reminding me we're not meant to be alone. It's hard to explain until you've experienced it for yourself—and I hope you will, one day."

Her tears had caught me by surprise.

"Oh, Violet. I'm so sorry. I didn't mean to upset you."

She'd brushed the tears from her cheeks and waved my sympathy away. "You didn't upset me, dear girl. I'm being silly. Time spent lamenting what wasn't, and was never meant to be, is time wasted. Trust me. I'm an old woman. I know about such things."

With each day more that I spent in Venice, I was beginning to understand what Violet had meant. Venice *was* the perfect place to fall in love. It was also a city that was easy to fall in love *with*. I felt different here, lighter. I felt more sure of myself.

"I hope you're not planning on taking a swim, too?"

I smiled as Edward's face joined mine in the rippled reflections.

"Not today," I replied. "I'll leave the impromptu swimming in the canals to Madeleine."

"How is she?"

"Better. Complaining about missing out on all the sightseeing!"

His shoulder brushed against mine as we peered down into the water at our reflections.

"So, your last few days here. It's a shame your visit was so brief."

"Yes. It has all gone far too quickly, and so much has happened.

I found a grandfather, for a start!" We both laughed at the remark. "You're lucky to have another few weeks here," I added.

"What if you could stay?" he asked suddenly. "What if you didn't have to leave?"

His question caught me by surprise. "There is no 'what if.' I *can't* stay. We have the final letter to deliver to Violet's sister in Vienna, and then . . . Well. Then I need to go home."

Edward turned away from the water and leaned back against the bridge, his face tipped toward the sun. "But if you *could* live anywhere in the world, make a choice without consequences, wouldn't Venice be a marvelous place to call home?"

He was beginning to speak in riddles.

"I suppose it would, yes." A sense of unease crept over me. "You're not planning to move here are you?"

He shrugged. "Perhaps."

"What does Annabel say?"

He pushed his hands into his pockets. "Annabel doesn't know. *I* didn't know until a few days ago. Besides, she'll never leave America. She would hate it here, so far away from her family. And she doesn't like ice cream. Or coffee. And frankly, she's not much for art, either."

He offered a tired smile. The strains of his marriage were clear to see in the gray hairs at his temples.

"I can't imagine ever moving away from New York for good, as lovely as Venice is." I fussed with my gloves and adjusted my hat. "Do you miss her?" I asked. "Annabel?"

"I miss the old Annabel. I miss the girl I married. The girl I loved, and who I thought loved me back." He turned to look at me. "You know, she told me recently she'd always had reservations, that she wasn't sure she should have married me in the first place but was too afraid to do anything about it at the time."

"Do you wish she had?" I asked. "Done something about it? Called it off?"

"I wish she'd been honest with herself, yes. 'Til death us do part is a very long time, Clara. Too long to be with the wrong person."

His words struck me so hard, I felt myself sway a little beneath their power. For a moment, we both fell silent.

"Well, this has all turned a bit serious," he said, offering a smile. "Come on. Let's forget about all that. How about we paint together in the Piazza San Marco?"

The setting in the Piazza San Marco was perfect, but I struggled to concentrate. My color choices were poor, and my shading was all wrong. Although I loved spending time with Edward, I couldn't shake the feeling that I was betraying Charles, or that Edward was betraying Annabel. We weren't at liberty to do as we pleased. There were others involved, whether we liked it or not. After a couple of hours, I grew frustrated with my art and anxious to return to Madeleine.

"I should go," I said, picking up my things, half afraid of what might happen if I stayed any longer and half afraid of preventing it.

"Until tomorrow," Edward said as we parted, both of us hesitating, unsure of how to say goodbye. "If you have time, that is? I know you plan to meet your grandfather again."

I nodded. "Tomorrow."

And suddenly it struck me that perhaps tomorrow was where

Edward and I were always meant to meet. A day that would never come around, that was never quite within my grasp.

AFTER CHECKING ON Madeleine, who was happily playing chess with Daniel and seemed almost disappointed to see me back so soon, I headed out again. I hoped to catch Matthias for an afternoon aperitif.

I was in luck, and found him pottering around the gallery. He was very pleased to see me again. We were instantly comfortable in each other's company, picking up where we'd left off during our first meeting. The conversation flowed easily, both of us exchanging memories and stories with a sense of urgency, and delighted to discover our shared taste in art. His eyes danced as he spoke, and my heart felt full, even as I considered the dilemma and decisions I faced in the coming days.

I was a little shy asking if he would sit for a portrait, but he was more than happy to oblige.

"It's for her, isn't it?" he said as my fingers moved deftly across the page. "For Violet."

I looked up at him and smiled. "How did you know?"

"Because you're very like her. And that's exactly what she would have done."

"Would you change anything?" I asked as my hand stilled. "If you could go back in time, have another chance?"

He smiled ruefully. "A month with the most lovely creature I've ever met? Wouldn't change a second of it, although I am sorry that it caused her family so much pain in the end. And I'm sorry that I haven't known my daughter or my granddaughters—until now! But Violet met a good man, and I met a wonderful woman, and here we are, back where it all started. Life goes on, my dear girl. We can only ever do what feels right in the moment. There is little to be gained by regret."

When the portrait was finished, he disappeared into the back room. I listened to him rummaging around as I packed away my pastels, until he eventually emerged with several sheets of paper in his hands.

"For you," he said, spreading the pages out on the table in front of me. "I will keep one or two. To remember her. But I would like you to have them now."

The images were all of Violet, and they were so beautiful. Violet caught in a ray of light beside a window. Violet leaning against a striped gondola post. Violet laughing and reclining among tousled bedsheets.

"You drew these?" I asked. "They're stunning."

"She made it easy. Violet made everything feel right. That's how it should be with someone you love, isn't it?"

His words gave me pause. "Yes. I suppose it is."

"She had such taste and class, even then, when she was so young," he said, his eyes fixed on the sketch of Violet laughing.

"She still has taste and class," I said, with a smile. "You had so much talent," I added as I admired his techniques.

"Yes, I showed great promise. I often wonder what I might have done with all that talent if I'd stuck with it."

"Why didn't you?"

"The war, dear girl. I was dispatched as an official artist to the Front. When I came back . . . well, when you've seen the things I saw and put it all on canvas, all the joy had gone from it. I haven't picked up a paintbrush since."

"I'm so sorry," I offered, yet my sympathy didn't seem nearly enough.

"That's why I love this little shop and gallery so much. I can still admire the work of others, even if I can't find any joy in it myself."

"I would like to have learned from you," I added.

"And it is never too late to start! Come, let me show you."

Happy hours passed as Matthias showed me his techniques for capturing light and shading to add depth and immediacy to a piece. He was a patient teacher and I was an eager student. When he grew tired, I took my cue to leave.

"Perhaps you and Madeleine would join me for lunch on Sunday, before you leave?" he said. "We have a big family meal every Sunday afternoon at my son's home. It's not far from the city. In Mirano, in the country. We stay until the food and wine runs out, and there is always plenty of both!"

"We would love to join you," I said, hoping Madeleine would be fully recovered. Madeleine being Madeleine, she would insist on going anyway. "If you're sure we won't be intruding?"

He waved his hand. "My daughter-in-law would feed the whole village if we let her! Besides, after all these years I've finally met two beautiful granddaughters I didn't know I had. This will make everything complete. My American and Italian families together! And please, bring along your gentlemen friends: Daniel and, Edward, is it?"

I blushed at the mention of Edward's name. "Yes. My art tutor. He's visiting for an exhibition. It's really quite a coincidence that we're here at the same time."

Matthias studied me a moment, then nodded. "Venice is a strange city, Clara. It makes lovers of friends. Like the fogs and the *acqua alta*, we cannot fight it. Nature, and fate, will find a way."

As I returned to the hotel, I felt the bittersweet sting of being given this wonderful opportunity to meet the grandfather I didn't know I had and the knowledge that we would have to leave him, and Venice, far too soon.

Maddie

After over a week stuck indoors, I finally felt well enough to get out of bed and get dressed. I spent my last few days in Venice fitting in as much as I could to make up for lost time. I met Matthias for coffee each morning, both of us relishing the opportunity to pick over the morning's news together and discuss the issues raised. I visited the museums Clara had already seen, and enjoyed walking with Daniel, who taught me a lot about Venetian architecture and the history of the city. He truly had a passion for his profession, and I found his interest contagious.

When Sunday arrived—our final day in Italy—I hummed happily as I got ready for the Morelli family luncheon in the country. It had been a wonderful trip, outside of the canal incident, and I could see by Clara's glow she was happy, too. I wondered if she was still unsure of what to do about Charles, and couldn't help but worry about her. She was far more fragile than I was, more easily hurt. I didn't know if she had the courage to call things off with Charles, if that was what she decided to do. In the end, I wasn't sure Edward was the right choice for her, either, and yet, what did I know? I was hardly experienced in the matter of relationships.

Rather than reach for my favorite slacks, I decided on a green shirtwaist dress. It wasn't overly feminine in silk or a floral print, but it was pretty and had a scalloped collar and ivory buttons, and it brought out the color of my eyes. After so many days of looking a mess while sick, I felt inspired to put on something special to meet our Italian family.

"The dress suits you," Clara said, and added slyly, "I'm sure Daniel will agree."

I turned quickly from the mirror. "I don't care what Daniel thinks. Anyway, I'm sure he won't notice."

But to my irritation, I did care what Daniel thought. And I hoped he *would* notice.

Clara at least had the tact not to tease me as she stood beside me at the mirror and fussed with her hair. She'd decided not to pin it so tightly for a change and to let her chestnut locks fall in waves around her face instead, like a Hollywood movie star. She looked like a drop of sunshine in a yellow silk dress that floated around her legs. Rather than the envy I used to feel when I compared my wild hair and freckles to her elegant beauty, I felt a warm wave of affection.

"You look gorgeous," I said. "Happy."

She smiled at the unexpected compliment. "I *am* happy."

She'd seemed more self-assured the last couple of days, calmer and more centered. I'd also noticed she'd been painting every day. Her technique seemed to have improved after her impromptu lesson with Matthias and the time she'd spent with Edward.

"Are you ready?" I asked. "Daniel will be here with the car any minute. He's borrowed a car for the day from a colleague just outside the city."

I picked up the bouquet of mixed flowers we'd bought as a gift for Matthias's daughter-in-law, Clara grabbed the small portrait of us both she'd painted for Matthias, and we headed to the lobby.

"*Scusi, signorina?*" the concierge called from the desk when he saw me. "Miss Madeleine Sommers, there is a telegram for you."

"For me?" I cast a puzzled glance at Clara and walked to the desk, desperately hoping it wasn't bad news about Violet.

The telegram was from Jenny, my roommate back home. I'd asked her to open my mail while I was away and to contact me if there was anything important. She knew exactly what that meant: anything from editors or publications to which I'd been submitting. I'd sent a telegram from each hotel to let her know our location, and yet I hadn't quite believed she would ever need to get in touch.

I read the message quickly.

Maddie,

Gerald McDougal from the *New York Herald Tribune*
sent you a note. The article you sent him is going
to be published! Will save several copies for you.
Congratulations!
Be safe and see you soon.

Jenny

I shrieked, then quickly covered my mouth with my hand. I felt as if my heart would burst. At last, after one measly article placed over the years, and enough rejections to fill my entire apartment, I was going to be published by a distinguished newspaper.

"What is it?" Clara asked. "Is everything alright at home?"

"Everything's fine!" I said. "More than fine. I'm going to have an article published—in the *New York Herald Tribune*! Can you believe it?"

"Oh, Madeleine! That's wonderful news! I'm so proud of you!" She wrapped me in a fierce embrace and then pulled back, her face shining with happiness for me. "What's the article about?"

And then it hit me.

My article was about her fiancé's desire to put profit before people, and the way his company took advantage of the less fortunate. My article was about to change my life for the better, and potentially make hers very difficult.

"What's all the excitement about?" Daniel asked as he walked over to us.

"Madeleine's going to have an article published," Clara explained. "In a *real* newspaper."

"I knew you would do it," he said, his face a picture of genuine delight. "I didn't have the slightest doubt."

At that moment Edward arrived, saving me—for now—from the need to explain to Clara what the article was about.

"Thank you, Daniel," I said sincerely. "For your encouragement."

"I mean it, Maddie, you deserve this." His tone was earnest and I felt a rush of pleasure at his faith in me.

Clara called over her shoulder. "We should get going."

"After you, ladies," Daniel said, stepping aside as he held the door open. "And you look like a handful of trouble in that dress, Maddie," he whispered as I walked past.

"Haven't you learned yet that trouble is what I'm all about, Mr. Miller?"

He laughed and followed me outside.

It was a stunning spring day in late April, warmer than usual, we were told. I could almost feel the hint of early summer in the air as we took our seats in the water taxi.

After picking up the car, as we left the city, the four of us talked amiably about the weather and the passing sights, but soon our chatter diverted into two more private conversations.

I glanced in the rearview mirror from my place in the front seat. Clara's and Edward's heads were inclined toward each other as they discussed some artwork they'd seen at a gallery. Edward looked handsome in a light linen suit. I'd never really noticed his looks before, but with his face lightly suntanned and flecks of gray at his temples, I could see why Clara was attracted to him.

Daniel patiently steered us along the narrow winding roads that dipped and twisted through the verdant countryside. As we turned around a bend, we came upon a field of wild poppies in full bloom.

"Look at those flowers!" I said. "Can we stop the car? I'd like to walk a little in the fields. Stretch my legs."

"Do we have time?" Clara asked.

Daniel glanced at his wristwatch. "We don't have much time, but we could take a quick look." He steered the car onto the side of the road.

Without waiting for anyone else, I dashed from the car and out into the field. As I walked among the happy red blooms, I thought again of my article. I felt my shoulders drop and the tension in my neck release as a sense of validation settled over me. I had something to say, and a newspaper editor thought so, too. I was on my way, at last! I squeezed my eyes shut and let the sensation wash over me. Nellie would have been proud, and I liked to think Father would be, too. I could hardly wait to tell Violet.

Daniel joined me at my side as I stopped to take in the view.

"It's beautiful, isn't it?" he said.

I looked at the luscious fields. The bright sunlight made the petals look ablaze and the dust in the air glistened like floating specks of gold. "It's unbelievable!"

I turned to him and smiled. Behind him I saw Clara and Edward, leaning against the car, laughing at something one of them had said.

"Still processing your good news?" Daniel asked.

I nodded. "I don't think I'll really believe it until I see it in print with my own eyes."

"I have some news of my own, actually," he said, clasping his hands behind his back as we walked on.

"Oh?"

"I've resigned from Hancock's company. I sent a telegram to Charles at his hotel in Vienna yesterday."

Surprised, I didn't reply at first. I'd thought he might try to work things out with Charles, but this was much better.

"Well good for you! I bet he was furious."

"I told him I would see out this 'arrangement' but wouldn't be taking the promised promotion. In other words, he still doesn't know you and Clara are aware of his scheme."

"Will you stay in New York, then, or move back to Boston?" I asked, trying to keep my voice even, surprised I cared so much about where he planned to be.

He studied my expression an instant before returning his eyes to the fields around us.

"I need to be in New York if I want to make a real go of being an architect. I've made a list of firms I'd like to apply to, and I have an idea for a new building, on the southwestern side of Central Park. I've also set up a meeting with a possible investor the week after we get back."

I let out a breath I didn't realize I'd been holding. "It sounds like you have it all figured out."

"I know what I want," he said, and the look he gave me made my stomach turn cartwheels.

"Do you?" I said, voice hoarse.

We stared at each other, broad smiles on our faces. Golden light spilled over his shoulders and lit his face.

"Your hair looks like flames," he said, gently brushing a strand from my cheek.

My breath caught in my throat at the sensation of his touch, the look in his eyes.

He searched my face as if looking for a sign. What he saw there made him step closer.

"Maddie." My name came out as a sigh. My heart thumped wildly as he cupped my face in his hands. "You're the most infuriating, brave, fascinating woman I've ever met, did you know that? Not to mention beautiful."

A sense of falling overtook me as I gazed back at him. How had we gotten here? How had I lost my resolve to keep him where a man belonged: at a distance, as a friend.

At last I managed a reply. "Are you sure you have the right girl?"

He laughed softly, the amber in his brown eyes dancing. "I'm more than sure."

And in that moment he leaned in slowly, pausing only an instant to peer into my face before he lightly brushed his lips over mine.

All my reservations disappeared as I wound my arms around his neck. He kissed me again, tenderly at first, and then more insistently, until we both gasped for air.

When we finally managed to pull away, I rested my forehead against his.

"Well then," I said.

He laughed softly. "Well then." He ran a finger gently down my cheek.

"That was . . . we should probably go back to the car."

Daniel grinned and held out his arm. "Shall we?"

I linked my arm through his and we strolled together to the car, where Clara and Edward were still deep in conversation, sitting beside each other on the hood. Clara had her knees tucked up to her chest and rested her cheek on her arms. Whether she'd seen the kiss or not, her face was inscrutable.

We drove the rest of the way in silence, the windows rolled down and the wind in our hair.

That kiss! The way I'd leaned into Daniel instantly. I could still feel his lips on mine. As I sneaked a look at him, he felt my eyes on him and winked.

I didn't know where any of this would lead, with the trip soon coming to an end. I still wasn't sure I wanted it to lead anywhere because of my career ambitions, but right now, on a beautiful day beneath a vivid Italian sky, I was happy to just be, to live in the moment.

I would worry about the future tomorrow.

EVENTUALLY, WE PULLED up to a charming old villa with a stucco façade and terra-cotta roof. It was surrounded by open fields dotted with trees, and a modest garden flanked the side of the house. A couple burst from the door instantly and met us at the car, all smiles. We were greeted by a middle-aged man who was the spitting image of Matthias, and a lovely woman with light eyes and hair who, I presumed, was his wife.

"*Buongiorno*," he said. "I am Giani and this is my wife, Isabella. Welcome, please make yourself at home. You are family!"

We followed the pair around the back of the house to a wide terrace where a table was covered with a linen cloth, set with dishes, and finished with vases of brightly colored flowers. Children raced after a ball through the yard, and at least a dozen adults sat on mismatched chairs and stools, or stood in small clusters, talking to each other. We met Isabella's sisters and their spouses, who all greeted us with smiles.

"I planned to eat indoors, but we are lucky today," Isabella said. "It's very warm for spring."

It was lovely to sit outside in the sun. Soon we'd leave this all behind for the much cooler climes of Austria and the final part of our trip.

Matthias appeared suddenly, planting a kiss on each cheek. "Ciao! Ciao! How happy I am to see you, girls. Come, sit beside me."

He sat at the head of the table, Clara and I on either side of him, followed by Daniel and Edward, and everyone else.

Matthias leaned close to me. "Your boyfriend seems very nice," he whispered.

"Friend," I replied with a smile. "Just a friend."

Matthias chuckled. "Of course. Just a friend."

Clara and I told stories of our days on the beach in East Hampton as children, and the many times I'd made trouble in school or at home. Matthias shared anecdotes about his children: Giani, the eldest, and his youngest son, Pietro, who now lived in Rome; and he talked fondly of his deceased wife, Maria. We feasted on *crostini toscani* and grilled *bistecca,* piles of fresh asparagus in olive oil and lemon, a platter of cheeses, and Italian cookies picked up from the bakery in town that morning. Our wineglasses were refilled the moment they were emptied.

Spending time with Matthias and his family was an unexpected gift. I couldn't have known how much the Morellis and their boisterous love and laughter would make me long for the same. It made me appreciate my sister and my mother, and even my memories of Father, whose ambition, stubbornness, and sense of justice I'd inherited. Now I understood why he'd pushed me so hard. It wasn't that he didn't believe in me, it was that I didn't believe enough in myself, and he thought he could help me see that, in his own flawed way. For the first time, I felt at peace with it all. With who I was, and who I was yet to be.

I smiled and raised a glass in another toast to *la famiglia,* followed by a chorus of "more wine."

A long, lazy afternoon stretched wonderfully ahead.

Clara

I raised my glass to Edward's as Matthias called for another toast.

"To family," I joined in the chorus, glancing across the table to catch Madeleine's eye, but she was deep in conversation with Daniel.

It was lovely to spend time with Matthias's family. *Our* family. It was still strange to think of them that way and would take some getting used to. Our American family was small, and social gatherings had often been soured by the simmering tension between one or the other of us. After Father's death and my estrangement from Madeleine, family had become something of a curiosity I observed among my friends. I hadn't craved it for myself, but rather accepted that it was something I would never truly understand: the clatter and chatter of shared memories, a fondness formed over many years. Now that it was all around me, I understood how important it was and what I'd been missing.

I watched Madeleine and Daniel closely during the luncheon. Their delight in being together, and the connection between them, was impossible to ignore. They sparked off each other, neither one more dominant or more infatuated than the other. They were a perfect match, everything in harmony. I hadn't mentioned their passionate kiss in the poppy field when Madeleine had returned to the car, but I would enjoy teasing her about it later.

"They get along very well, don't they," Edward remarked. "Amazing really, when you consider how short a time they've known each other."

"I don't think it matters how long you know someone," I replied. "When it's right, it's right. You must have felt that with Annabel."

I hadn't meant to bring her up again, but part of me was testing the water, checking exactly what, if anything, he still felt for her.

He put down his fork and studied me. "I did, yes. But I was young and naive and too eager to fall in love. And people change within a relationship. It's a fluid thing, like this wine." He swirled the rich red liquid around his glass. "Feelings, plans, hopes . . . they all change. Don't you agree?"

His question was framed as an invitation of sorts.

"I think we should enjoy our lunch," I replied as Madeleine glanced over to me, her cheeks wonderfully flushed from sunshine and wine.

After a delicious dessert and rich coffee, and an Italian liqueur called limoncello, I dabbed my lips with my napkin and excused myself from the table. Madeleine was so absorbed by Matthias, who, just like Violet, was capable of holding an entire room captivated with his stories, that she didn't notice me leave.

Edward, however, did.

He caught up with me as I walked beneath the dappled shade of the lemon trees.

"Do you mind if I join you? I need to walk off some of that delicious food."

"Of course." I didn't mind at all. In fact, I'd hoped he would follow me.

"Your grandfather has a beautiful home," he remarked, his steps falling in sync with mine.

"He does," I agreed. "I only wish we could spend more time with him, with all of them."

"I wish you could stay longer, too. I've been happier here in Italy, than I have been for years."

We stopped walking as Edward reached for my hand, a smile in his eyes. As I looked at him, the intensity of my feelings burned like a fierce summer sun. I imagined his lips on mine, imagined how easy it would be to fall into his arms, to fall in love with this kind, humble man. It would be the perfect culmination to this wonderful day, to this journey I was taking, and yet something in me held back.

"Love is complicated, isn't it?" I said, my voice calm despite the rush of adrenaline I felt. "To fall in love, or not. To be with this person, or that person. It is full of layers and depth, like a painting we see more detail in every time we look at it."

Edward tilted his head to one side and looked at me with such fondness. "Spoken like a true artist."

I returned his smile. "I had the best tutor."

"And I had the finest student."

Tutor and student. The words settled around me, and in that moment, doubt lifted from my mind, blown away by a light breeze that ruffled the leaves on the cypress trees and sent curls dancing around my face. I understood that my feelings for Edward didn't mean he had to become my lover, or my husband. He had come into my life to teach me about art, but had taught me about love, too. He had shown me what was possible, even if our being together was impossible.

"You know, Violet once told me that life, in the end, falls into two halves: the things we got right, and the things we got wrong," I said. "She believes there's no point wishing any of it were different."

Edward nodded. "She's a wise woman. And what is it you think you've got right, so far?"

I smiled. "Coming here. Knowing you. Spending time together. I got that right."

He placed his hand gently against my cheek. "We both got that right. And yet . . ."

"And yet."

A slight inclination of his head toward mine showed me that he understood: what we'd both gotten wrong, through no fault of our own, was the timing of our lives intersecting.

We lingered a moment longer, knowing that as soon as we returned to the others, what might have been was all we would ever be.

He held out his arm. "Could I walk you back, Miss Clara Sommers?"

My arm in his, as we walked back to the luncheon, I remembered what Violet had said on the morning of my departure. "Traveling is the best way to discover what's important, Clara, to find out what you need to take with you in life, and what you can manage without. One good dress and a heart full of belief in oneself is more than enough to see anyone around the world."

The others had hardly noticed we'd gone as wineglasses were refilled and conversations continued. Everything was just as we'd left it a few moments ago, and yet as I took my seat and Edward took his, we looked at each other and smiled, and only the two of us knew how much had changed.

THE AFTERNOON PASSED quickly. As dusk settled over the landscape, we drove back toward the city, full of good food and good wine, and a sense of contentment.

I left Madeleine and Daniel to say their goodnights in private, while Edward walked me to the door of the hotel. We paused at the bottom of the steps.

"Don't look so sad," he said. "You have so much to look forward to. So much life ahead of you. Don't spend it doing the wrong things with the wrong people. Spend it with people who make your heart full. Nothing less." He leaned forward, kissed my cheek, and whispered, "Arrivederci, dear Clara."

As I watched him go, I touched my hand to my cheek, and felt a surge of confidence and independence and I knew we had made the right decision, even if my heart longed for it to be the wrong one.

"No time for loitering," Madeleine said as she bounded past me. "Best get packing. Austria awaits!"

Back in our suite, we packed our trunks and smaller bags for the final stage of our journey.

"I guess we should read Violet's next letter," Madeleine said. "See what's in store for us?"

I picked up the final sealed envelope, tied with red ribbon. Inside, was a folded sheet of Violet's stationery, a newspaper clipping, and a photograph I knew well: Violet and Aunt Margaret, arms around each other, the Piazza San Marco in the background. The photograph had always sat on the bedside table in Violet's bedroom. I'd often admired it. The headline of the newspaper article read: "Two Sisters Take on the World."

"Look at this," I said, showing it to Madeleine. "It was written by Auntie Nellie."

Madeleine read the article out loud.

When I set out on my journey to circumnavigate the globe, I wanted to break a world record. But I also wanted to prove that women don't need a male escort to accompany them on such a trip, and that we are capable of doing anything a man might do abroad. Little did I know how much my foray into the world would come to mean to two sisters, Margaret and Violet Lawson.

I slid the items back into the envelope and unfolded the sheet of stationery next. Violet's final letter to us.

Dear Clara and Madeleine,

How are your travels? I hope you've had the most wonderful time in Venice.

Now it is time to move on to Austria, a country I have never seen. I longed to travel there one day to see my sister, but alas, it was not meant to be. You must become my eyes and ears, my voice.

By now, assuming you found dear Matthias, you will understand why Venice has always held such a special place in my heart, but you might not yet understand why Margaret and I have been estranged for so many years.

My pregnancy brought disgrace on our family. Margaret found it especially upsetting to have friends and neighbors whispering about me behind my back. It made things difficult for her in the circles she moved in: high society does not tolerate such scandal. After she moved to Austria to focus on her music, we simply drifted apart.

I hope she will meet you both, and that your presence will help us come together again, as sisters should. Please know this won't be easy. With so many years gone and too many things left unsaid, I might be asking too much of her. I only ask you to deliver my final letter and hope that I have said enough.

Love each other and travel safely. I can't wait to see you both very soon.

With all my love to you,
Violet

"Do you think Margaret will see us?" I asked, slipping the paper back into the envelope. "I can't bear to disappoint Violet now."

"I don't know," Madeleine replied. "But we'll do our best."

A knock at the door disturbed us. Madeleine answered it.

"For you," she said, returning with a telegram.

I took it from her and sank onto the bed as I read the message.

Darling Clara. Arrived safely in Vienna. Can hardly wait
to see you. Tell Madeleine she'll be staying alone. I've
reserved a suite for the two of us at the Hotel Brauner.

Charles

"What is it?" Madeleine asked as she sat beside me.

"It's Charles. He's in Austria." I folded the telegram and placed it on the table. "I can't put it off any longer, can I? I need to make a decision."

She put her arm around my shoulder. "If you have to ask the question, I suspect you've already made your decision."

She was right. I had.

I'd decided I wasn't ready to settle into a life as Charles Hancock's well-mannered, dutiful wife, or as anyone else's for that matter. Marriage implied an end to Miss Clara Sommers, and she was only just beginning.

PART THREE

Auf Wiedersehen

Violet

❧

Veneto Estate, East Hampton, New York
April 1937

They tell me I must rest, that I must listen to the doctors, but I don't find it easy to do. I want to be outside, to live the last of my days rather than watch them pass in a cycle of concerned faces and rattling pill bottles. I tell Celestine the boredom will kill me far quicker than the cancer. She offers a rueful smile and tells me I'm a terrible patient as she plumps my pillows. Everyone plumps my pillows. I think it gives them something to do, a way to feel useful.

"I'll have to pay Henrietta double this week if you keep up this grumbling," she says. "The poor girl."

"Poor girl nothing," I reply. "She enjoys my company. She likes my stories. She told me so."

"I suspect she is just being polite," Celestine remarks as she walks to the window and opens the shutters.

The light catches her hair in a way that reminds me of a Rossetti painting. Sometimes I love her so much I could burst. My surprise daughter, created with such passion, and yet the cause of such pain and distress. I catch glimpses of him sometimes, in her eyes and full lips. She took the news hard when I first told her about her real father, but her anger had faded quickly as Frank reassured her of his love for her, of the bond between them that would never be broken regardless of biology.

"Pfft. People spend too much time being polite," I reply. "Saying the right thing. Doing the right thing. When you're at the end of it all, what really matters is that you've been honest, with others, yes, but mostly with yourself."

Celestine studies me a moment. "What is it, Mom? What's bothering you?"

I fuss with the bed linen and then look her straight in the eye. "Clara's wedding is what's bothering me. I don't care for that Hancock fellow. I don't trust him. There. I've said it."

She turns and folds her arms. "Yes. You most certainly have said it." She lets out a long sigh. "Charles has his faults, but he's smart, and handsome, and comes from a very good family. He gives Clara everything she could possibly want, and he's clearly very taken with her. You've seen the way he looks at her."

"The way he watches her, you mean. To make sure she's not talking to another man, or having too much fun."

Celestine rolls her eyes. "If she's happy, then *we* should be, too."

"*If* she's happy, she has my blessing," I add. "But it looks like a big 'if' from where I'm sitting."

Celestine plumps my pillows again. "Anyway, it's too late now. It's all arranged. Now, I have some errands to run. Can I get you anything before I go?"

I think for a moment. "A glass of champagne, please. And a handsome young man. And the morning papers."

She laughs, kisses my forehead, and says she'll bring the papers.

"And the champagne," I call after her. "The good stuff."

I close my eyes and prop myself up in bed. I listen to the sound of the ocean beyond the window, the tide seeming to whisper the echo of distant secrets and difficult conversations. I think of Clara and Madeleine's last stop in Vienna and know they will face another difficult conversation there, assuming they find Margaret.

My sister's reaction to the news of my pregnancy was the worst. She'd left Venice a month before me that summer in 1890, to return to her beloved music lessons. Soon, the society crowd would be planning their holiday parties and she'd wanted to be hired as a premier violinist. I'd stayed behind, lured by my love for Venice, and by the promise of spending another month with Matthias. We hadn't meant to fall in love, but when you leave home and everything familiar behind, things don't always go as planned. Still, it was my homecoming that I remember most. The urge to see my sister again, to tell her how wonderful my month with Matthias had been, how we'd fallen madly in love, and that it was the most thrilling time of my life. But Margaret was distracted, intent on her rehearsals.

"You'll have forgotten all about Matthias Morelli by the fall," she'd said. "It was a holiday romance, Violet. That's all."

Neither of us yet knew how wrong she was, that a new life was already blooming within me. The following months brought waves of nausea, missed periods, and an acid burn in my throat, confirming what I'd begun to suspect: I'd returned home carrying Matthias's child.

It was Margaret I turned to first for help. I wanted her advice and the comfort only a sister could offer. But when I needed her the most, Margaret turned away from me, telling me I would ruin everything if I had the baby, as I'd told her I intended to.

"An unmarried mother! An illegitimate child! Don't be ridiculous, Violet! Everyone will gossip and you'll bring the family name into ruin. We'll never be taken seriously again."

She was right. Everyone gossiped, and one by one, all of Margaret's carefully planned performances for the social season were canceled. As my stomach swelled and the reality of my condition could no longer be concealed, she could hardly bear to look at me. By Christmas that year, we were hardly speaking. I had the support of my mother, at least, if not of my father or my sister. And then there was Frank, my childhood friend; my soul mate. How willingly he'd seen the solution to my problem when he'd arrived with a Christmas basket, as he did every year.

"Marry me," he'd said while we ate gingerbread on the boardwalk, wrapped in heavy coats and hats. "Marry me, Violet Lawson, and make me the happiest man in America. I'll raise the child as my own, and who knows how many more we might have."

I'll never forget the look in his eyes: so calm, so tender. I wasn't surprised by the marriage proposal—part of me had always known I would marry Frank—it was how sure he was that surprised me. When everyone else was accusing me of bringing the family name into disrepute and ruining their lives along with mine, Frank Bell simply asked me to marry him, and promised to love me and the child he would raise as his own.

Margaret left for Vienna before Celestine was born, intent on studying under one of the best violinists in Europe. She never returned to New York, and her letters home grew few and far between. Even Frank knew it was a subject he shouldn't bring up. Birthdays and Christmases and other anniversaries came and went with a quiet wondering: What was she doing? Did she ever think of me at all?

I picture her bright smile now, her long chestnut hair swirling around her shoulders as we bent over candlelight in our bedroom as children, telling stories and laughing, invoking our mother's anger for being up well past our bedtime. The pain of her rejection still hurts after all these years, and as my final days approach, a longing to see her once more is stronger than ever.

I wonder if Clara and Madeleine are getting along, if they've managed to find those I needed to say my goodbyes to. For them, it isn't so much about the journey—the miles traveled or the sights they might have seen—it has always been about learning to understand each other better, to let go of old disagreements and embrace a new connection. I know the pain of losing a sister and can't bear for history to repeat itself.

A knock at the bedroom door interrupts my thoughts.

"Come in. I'm awake," I call.

Henrietta carries in a lunch tray and slides it carefully onto my lap. The fragrance of chicken broth and vegetables wafts around me and for the first time in days, I feel hungry.

"I brought the newspapers," she says, "and one more thing." She steps from the room and returns a moment later. "A chilled glass of champagne for madam."

I smile and lift the glass to my lips. The bubbles tickle my nose.

"What day is it?" I ask.

"Friday. The girls will be home in little more than a week's time."

Their impending return gives me strength.

I finish the bowl of broth and drink half the glass of champagne as I pick idly through the newspapers. But one headline in the *New York Herald Tribune* makes me stop.

Hancock Enterprises: Shocking Human Cost of New Development

Exclusive by M. Sommers

I read on, devouring the words of Madeleine's shocking exposé about Charles Hancock's heartless plans, and while I know it will hurt Clara deeply, it is a truth far better exposed now than later.

"Atta girl, Maddie," I whisper, raising my glass in a toast to my clever granddaughter. "Atta girl."

Maddie

Vienna
April 1937

$\mathcal{I}$ watched Venice slide away as the train carried us toward Austria and our elusive great-aunt Margaret. It seemed impossible that our trip had gone so quickly, and I found myself wishing we could be on the road longer, exploring more of Europe together. And yet, as the train raced toward the distant snowcapped mountains, my thoughts turned to the kind gentleman from the *Queen Mary*, Mr. Klein, and his palpable fear of what might be waiting for him in Austria. I also remembered Matthias's parting words: *Be careful in Austria. There are sure to be Nazi soldiers afoot, and if the rumors are to be believed, they look for any reason to cause trouble.*

I'd read several German newspapers and reports about the Nazi Party, highlighting passages and taking notes in the evenings, trying to understand Hitler's ideology. His persecution of Jewish people was chilling. He'd even stated outright the very thing many Austrians feared: that the German-speaking country

should be annexed to Germany. I thought about the fascist propaganda pamphlets and antifascist posters I'd collected in Venice,
and wondered how long it would be before Hitler or Mussolini
made a move.

The train rattled on through the night, and at dawn, I awoke
with a start. It had been a restless sleep in the cramped quarters
of the express train we'd been forced to take when we'd changed
our plans. As Clara slid from her bunk, she glanced down at her
dress and laughed. Neither of us had changed into our nightwear,
and now she looked like a wadded-up tissue.

I stretched and stood, wondering if Daniel had slept better in
his bunk a few cars away. It was fitting that he would complete
the journey with us, although it was far nicer not to be followed
in secret.

I peered through the window to catch the sunrise. We had already crossed the border from Italy into Austria, but still had some
way to go, Vienna being closer to Austria's borders with Czecho-
slovakia and Hungary than with Italy. Thick forest stretched over
the alpine mountains, the peaks still dusted with snow. In the
distance, a lake glistened beneath the morning sun. Austria was
so much more inviting than I'd expected and entirely unlike the
other places we'd visited. I'd pictured the country as cold and
sterile, not lush and beautiful and alive. I regretted instantly that
our journey would soon end, without much time to explore.

Eventually, we arrived at the train station in Vienna. As I
stepped onto the platform and stretched my aching limbs, Daniel
appeared and wished me good morning.

He took his own luggage and helped the porter with Clara's
enormous trunks.

"I'll see you at the hotel, later?" he asked.

I nodded. "We can make a plan for lunch or something?"

"Perfect." He planted a kiss on my cheek, eliciting a smile from Clara and a warm flush across my face.

Daniel was gracious enough to give me and Clara the time we needed together, and although Clara enjoyed teasing me about my *boyfriend*, I was keen to prove to her that I was no different for enjoying his company, and his affections.

The taxicab set out for the hotel Violet had arranged for us, Clara having firmly ignored the message from Charles and his instruction for her to abandon me and join him at a different hotel. I thought of nothing but a strong cup of coffee and a brisk walk through the city to shake off my tiredness. Traveling, I'd discovered, was filled with adventure and excitement, but it also wore me out.

"Do you think we should send a telegram to Margaret to warn her before we visit tomorrow?" I asked. "As a courtesy? Maybe she'll be more likely to see us if we give her time to prepare."

Clara shook her head. "I think we should go without any warning. She'll know what we've come to discuss and may turn us away. Violet warned us this would be the most difficult of the three visits. She hasn't seen Margaret for so many years. Remember how strained Violet said it was between them when Margaret had last visited America?"

"She doesn't sound like the type to bury grievances easily, does she?" I said.

"She doesn't, but I hope we can persuade her."

Lost in thought, I watched the city of Vienna speed by through the window: the half-timbered houses with lattice frameworks;

the famed Theater an der Wien, where Beethoven's Fifth and Sixth Symphonies had once premiered; and the lush Danube River that twisted through the heart of the city in one long, green-gray ribbon. I couldn't help noticing how different the architecture was from the buildings in France and Italy. I imagined Daniel would be noticing the same.

Daniel. It surprised me, the way my thoughts turned so easily to him. I thoroughly enjoyed our conversations, relishing his thoughts about topics from working women to the best plate of pasta in New York. His view of the world was bright, optimistic. He inspired me, but I worried what the future would bring when our lives returned to normal and we went our separate ways—and that was only a few days away. I wasn't certain where Daniel would be in that mix, or if I even wanted him to be a part of things in any real way. Perhaps this was a holiday romance, just as Matthias had been for Violet, and I should leave it at that.

When we reached the Freyung, home to some of the oldest Christmas markets in the world, several policemen stepped in front of the flow of traffic and promptly set up wooden barriers.

Our driver came to a sudden stop.

Across the square, a makeshift stage had been set up, and around it, dozens of people were gathering.

"What's happening?" Clara asked.

"It looks like some sort of show," I replied, squinting to make out the signs.

The crowd parted, making way for a row of soldiers in gray uniforms, marching in unison. In an orderly fashion, they stationed themselves on either side of the stage.

I leaned forward in my seat. "Are they Nazi soldiers?"

At my question, the driver glanced over his shoulder and in heavily accented English said, "Yes. The Nazis. They meet, stop traffic. Make a mess of things."

I returned my attention to the scene outside, fascinated to see one of the rallies I'd read so much about. The crowd pushed closer to the stage as two soldiers climbed the steps. In their hands, they raised a red-and-white flag with a black swastika, the symbol of the Nazi Party. A sense of injustice burned through me as I thought about everything I'd read, and how they didn't accept Jewish people, or anyone else who failed to support their cause. This wasn't even their country, and they were trying to stake their claim.

Our driver swore under his breath as policemen blew whistles and gestured aggressively for us to turn around. We managed to make a U-turn, narrowly missing the wooden barriers. As we rode away from the square, I turned to peer out of the back window.

In that instant, the roar of voices reverberated against the buildings behind us, and the crowd saluted as several more soldiers made their way to the stage.

The sight left a bad taste in my mouth and yet I itched to document what we'd seen. I glanced at Clara. Her face was etched with concern.

"That was disturbing," she said.

"Very," I agreed, my mind already racing.

It had taken all my resolve not to rush from the car and see what was happening up close. If I came across another rally, I would do exactly that.

A somber mood settled over us as we drove the rest of the way to the hotel, contemplating what we'd just seen. The headlines

I'd read for months were no longer words on a page, but real. Dangerous. And whether or not Clara read the papers as often as I did, she sensed it, too. I could see it in her clenched jaw.

As the taxicab pulled up outside our hotel, I turned to her.

"How about we unpack our things and then go for a walk? See a little of the city and clear our heads."

"That sounds perfect."

Grateful to be staying some distance away from the Nazi rally we'd just seen, we enjoyed a long walk through the wide avenues and pretty side streets, and beside the river, stopping to buy gifts for Violet and Mother. We ended our first evening in Vienna with a satisfying dinner of bratwurst and sauerkraut, and a glass of slivovitz, a popular plum brandy. In the morning, we would visit Margaret, and while I looked forward to meeting our elusive great-aunt, I found myself on edge. The pinnacle of our trip had come at last, and I worried it wouldn't bring about the reunion Violet so dearly hoped for.

Clara

*V*ienna's sharp edges and political tensions were a stark contrast to the soft spring light of Paris and the glistening waters of Venice, but perhaps my reluctance to embrace Vienna in the same way as the other cities was more to do with what I'd left behind than what I found when I arrived. The long train journey had given me time to think about Edward—too much time, perhaps. The way we'd parted was the only possible resolution to our feelings, and yet there was a yearning in my heart, a longing for things to be different. It tainted everything with a sense of regret and left me restless.

Our encounter with the Nazi Party before we'd even arrived at our hotel hadn't helped. I felt hesitant and uncertain as I looked out of the window of our pretty room in Gasthaus Helene the following morning. Beyond the window, charming confectioners' shops and bakeries made for a pleasant scene, and yet I had no enthusiasm for capturing it on the page. Vienna didn't tug on my heart the way Paris and Venice had. It nagged, like an uncomfortable itch I couldn't scratch.

As our journey neared its end, it felt as if there was far more at stake than there had been when we'd boarded the *Queen Mary* in

New York, with Violet's letters in our luggage and enough friction between me and Madeleine to light a match. Everything was reaching its culmination: the imminent meeting with Margaret and the looming confrontation with Charles.

Madeleine was at the desk, scribbling furiously in her notebook. It had felt good to tell her how I felt about Charles, to confide in her the way we used to confide in each other as teenage girls, and yet it still saddened me that things had come to this; that Charles wasn't the man I'd wanted to believe he was. I felt sick to my stomach when I imagined the look on his face as I returned his ring. People didn't turn Charles Hancock down, women especially.

"We should probably get going," I said, checking myself in the mirror. I'd chosen a blue skirt and jacket, and a red pillbox hat with navy ribbon. "Is this too much?" I asked, as much to my reflection as to Madeleine. "Is it a bit formal?"

What did one wear to meet a reclusive great-aunt?

"It's perfectly fine. How do you always look so pretty, and I, well, don't?"

Madeleine was wearing one of her curious slacks-blouse-and-oxfords ensembles again.

"You have your own . . . style," I said. "You shouldn't apologize for it."

We both responded to my remark with stunned silence, knowing that a month ago I would have found her appearance embarrassing. "Although," I added, "I think your black slacks would go better with those shoes."

Sometimes it struck me how far we'd come together, and not

just in miles traveled. I thought back to the January morning when Violet had announced her plan to send us to Europe, how I'd bristled at the sound of Madeleine's voice. I'd been reluctant to embark on this trip with her, but I now found myself reluctant for it to end. We'd traveled so far from home, and yet the distance between us had narrowed so that we were now able to forgive, even if we weren't always prepared to forget.

"Are you nervous?" I asked. "About meeting Margaret?"

"A little? You?"

I nodded. "It feels like there's so much riding on this last meeting."

We exchanged an uneasy glance as I picked up Violet's letter from the table. *Margaret* was written on the front. I wondered what Violet had felt as she'd sealed the envelope, and sealed her last chance of reconciliation with it.

We took a tram across the city and walked the last block to Margaret's home, a neat town house at the end of a crescent of a dozen houses. Each had pretty flower boxes adorning the front windows, white façades with brown shutters, and blue trim.

We walked up the steps and I rapped the knocker.

After a moment or two, the sound of footsteps inside confirmed someone was home. A thin woman with brown hair and large brown eyes opened the door. She studied us as she wiped her hands on her apron.

"*Guten Morgen.*"

"Good morning," I replied. "Margaret?"

The woman shook her head and said something else in German.

"Do you speak English?" I asked.

"*Ja,* a little. What can I do for you?"

"I'm Clara Sommers," I said, "and this is my sister, Madeleine. We're here to see Margaret. Margaret Lawson? She's our grandmother's sister."

The woman flinched a little, surprise etched across her face. "Your grandmother's sister?"

"Yes, Violet. Violet Bell. Lawson, before she was married."

At this, the woman's face changed from surprise to something of a frown. "I see. Is Margaret expecting you?"

I shook my head. "We don't think so. But we have something very important to pass on to her. From Violet."

"You had better come inside. I'll let Margaret know you are here. I am Fräulein Meyer. Helga."

We were shown to a neat little parlor, decorated with floral sofas and wooden cabinets displaying glassware and china. The room smelled strongly of pine and lemon. We waited in silence as an ornate cuckoo clock ticked ominously above the fireplace.

"Do you think she'll see us?" Madeleine whispered.

I shrugged. "Let's hope so."

After a short while, the woman returned.

"Follow me," she said. "Margaret is in the back room. She is very busy, so you cannot stay long. She has her final performance tomorrow."

It certainly wasn't a warm welcome, but then we hadn't really expected one.

We were shown into a smaller room. It took a moment for my eyes to adjust to the dim light and then I saw her, our great-aunt Margaret. She was busy at a desk, sheets of music strewn around her. She sipped a cup of coffee as she hummed to herself.

Helga—a maid, perhaps—moved behind the chair in a protective manner, and said something to her.

Margaret looked up at us and nodded tersely. "Please, sit down."

She didn't offer even the faintest of smiles.

We perched awkwardly on the sofa, inches apart.

I cleared my throat. "I'm Clara Sommers and this is my sister, Madeleine. We've come on behalf of your sister, Violet. She is our grandmother."

"Yes, so I hear," Margaret said.

Madeleine and I exchanged looks. She was *not* pleased to meet us.

Madeleine rushed to fill the silence.

"Violet sent us on a trip to Europe. Sisters on the road together, just like the two of you all those years ago, when you won Nellie Bly's guessing contest."

"Young women, discovering the world on their own," I added.

When Margaret didn't reply, my eyes darted over the decorative touches in her sitting room. I noticed several photographs of a woman with a violin, and others of a large orchestra. There was one image, older than the rest, that I recognized instantly. Three women caught in a moment of laughter: Nellie Bly, Violet, and Margaret. So she hadn't banished Violet from her life entirely, and it appeared she hadn't forgotten Nellie, either.

"There's another reason we are here," I added, eager to explain everything fully. "Violet wanted us to deliver a message to you. A letter." I held the letter in my hand. "If you could read it I'm sure . . ."

"I see the two of you looking at me with hope in your eyes," Margaret said. "Violet nearly ruined my career, all because of a man she hardly knew."

I was taken aback by the tone of her voice, the resentment and anger still there after all these years. With the slightest movement, I nudged Madeleine.

"Madam," Madeleine began. "Great-aunt Margaret . . ." At the name, the old woman's eyes flickered. "We aren't here to counsel you. We're here to explain that Violet is—well, she is . . ."

"Dying," I interjected. My voice cracked as I spoke. "Your sister is dying."

Margaret looked directly at me for the first time. She resembled Violet with her gray eyes and the determined set of her jaw, but that was where the similarities ended. Where Violet was all warmth and vivacity, Margaret was as brittle as glass. I studied the rigid set of her shoulders, her hands curled with arthritis. Time hadn't been kind to her.

"Dying?" she repeated as her eyes fluttered closed a moment before she opened them and returned her gaze to us. "And she sent you all the way to Vienna to tell me this?"

"She sent us here to say goodbye," I explained. "It would mean so much to her if you would read her letter."

"Have you been to see him as well?" Margaret asked at last. "Matthias?"

"We have, yes," I said. "He asked after you. He wished you well."

"Is that so?"

Madeleine and I exchanged another glance. Clearly, she still held bad feelings toward him, too.

"So you are Celestine's daughters." She studied us a moment. "You don't look like sisters. So different."

I smiled. "We are different in every possible way."

"But discovering our similarities," Madeleine added.

Margaret stared into the fire. "Yes, a long trip will show the best and the worst of people. You must have been on the road for quite some time."

I explained how we'd started our journey in Paris to find Grandpa Frank, and gave a short synopsis of our trip since. "You are our final destination. Next, we travel to Frankfurt to take the *Hindenburg* home."

She sat quietly as I spoke. Helga perched in a chair beside the fire, prodding it now and again with a poker.

Eventually Margaret spoke again. "How long does she have?"

I fiddled with my gloves on my lap. "Not long. Months, at best."

At this she flinched.

"Helga, I'm suddenly very tired." Margaret exchanged a knowing glance with the woman who had shown us inside.

"We'll let you rest," I said, indicating to Madeleine that we should go. "Perhaps we could call on you again tomorrow? I'm afraid we're only staying another two days."

"Such an unexpected intrusion isn't good for an old woman's nerves," Margaret replied.

"You've had a shock," Madeleine agreed. "We'll leave the letter for you."

I placed it on a mahogany table beside the sofa.

"We are glad to have met you, Margaret," I offered as Helga ushered us from the room, but Margaret kept her gaze fixed firmly on the fire and said nothing in reply, not even goodbye.

Maddie

Clara and I were so disappointed to discover that our long-lost great-aunt was a bitter old woman, so different from our vivacious, generous Violet. Her lingering resentment and cold reaction had surprised us both and left us feeling subdued.

We walked for a while until we found a neighborhood garden several blocks away and sat together on a park bench to talk about what had just happened. We couldn't believe how rude Margaret had been, even with Violet's warning to us before we'd left. She'd anticipated the difficulty we would face with her estranged sister. She wasn't wrong.

"I knew it wasn't going to be easy, but I'd hoped for a little more forgiveness on Margaret's part," Clara said. "Do you think she'll even read the letter? I have a horrible feeling she'll throw it in the fire."

"Me too," I replied. "She still blames Violet for having 'nearly ruined' her career but did you see all the certificates on the wall? Margaret has been honored at least half a dozen times from various music halls," I said, rolling my eyes.

"It's so disappointing," Clara agreed. "This whole thing has gone on far too long. Violet is dying! What possible reason could Margaret have to still not want to forgive and forget?"

I rubbed my hands together for warmth. It was cloudy, and much colder than it had been yesterday. I was glad Clara had insisted I wear my overcoat.

"I think we should go back tomorrow," I said. "Try again. We might get a better response after she's had time to read Violet's letter."

Clara shook her head. "It will probably be more of the same. Or worse. Maybe it's just too late for her to change."

"But it may not be," I pressed. "And I don't want to go home to Violet without trying every last option. Even if it's awkward and uncomfortable."

A crisp breeze stirred the tender new leaves on the trees around us.

"Are you sure you're warm enough?" Clara asked. "I don't want you to get sick again."

"I'm fine!" I brushed off her concern but was secretly glad for it. It had been a long time since someone had fussed over me the way Clara did.

"Alright," Clara said at last. "Let's try again tomorrow. Maybe once the shock of seeing us has passed, Margaret will be more open to talking with us."

"Exactly." I stood up as a church bell across the park chimed noon. "For now, I'm going to meet Daniel for lunch. And I might pay Mr. Klein a visit after," I added.

Clara let out a long sigh. "I wish I could come with you, but I can't put this off any longer, can I?"

I shook my head. "No. You can't."

Her rendezvous with Charles weighed as heavily on my mind as I knew it did on hers. I presumed someone in his office had told him about my article, even if he hadn't seen it yet. He wouldn't hold back his anger, and neither would Clara when she found out about it. I bit my lip. This was my last chance to tell her.

"Clara, there's something I need to say before you meet Charles."

She pulled her coat collar up as a light rain began to fall. "Well, hurry up and tell me then before we both get soaked—again!"

She looked so pretty in her red hat, and so sure of herself, despite her nerves. If I told her now, she might not go through with her confrontation with Charles. I hesitated. Maybe now wasn't the time.

"I can go with you. If you need me to," I offered, scrambling for something to say. "It might be easier if I'm there. Less . . . emotional?"

It wasn't the worst idea. If Charles did know about the article, I was more than ready to defend myself against him and to explain my reasons to Clara.

She took a deep breath. "Thank you, but this is something I need to do on my own."

"If you're sure?"

"I'm sure."

We parted with a hug for encouragement. I held on to her a moment longer than usual, wrapping a silent apology around her for what she was about to discover. We rushed off then in opposite directions as the rain began to fall in earnest.

WHEN I ARRIVED back at the hotel, somewhat worse for wear from the weather, and with damp feet, I found Daniel waiting for me in the lobby.

"Is everything alright?" he asked, concern in his eyes. I was both comforted and a little alarmed at how well he was able to read my expressions. How well he already seemed to know me. "Did you meet Margaret?"

"Oh, we met Margaret," I said as I shook out my coat.

He steered me to a chair beside a large open fireplace in the restaurant lobby and ordered a hot cup of tea. Somehow, he always knew what to do without asking.

I recounted the way Margaret had behaved and how upsetting it would be to tell Violet we'd been unable to get through to her sister.

"I feel like we've failed." I sighed. "That we're letting her down."

"She sounds like a bitter old woman. Perhaps it's too late to change her mind about things."

"Apparently so," I said, relaxing a little as the tea wound a warm path through my body. "At least we were able to find Grandpa Frank's grave and deliver her message to Matthias, so it hasn't all been a waste. And I have a dozen new ideas for articles. I'll be busy when I go home."

He looked disappointed. "Yes, you'll be busy."

I had the distinct feeling I'd said something wrong. I looked down as I moved the teacup around on its saucer.

"Are you hungry?" I asked.

"Starved."

"Me too."

We decided to dine at a cozy little tavern across from the hotel. Over a steaming plate of fried schnitzel covered in a thick, rich gravy, Daniel explained where he'd been all morning.

"I met with Charles. He insisted on speaking in person after receiving my telegram. I thought it would be the professional thing to do, so I agreed."

I paused, setting my fork on the edge of the plate. The food had done me some good and I was able to put the events with Margaret out of my mind for the moment. "And?"

"He did his best to talk me out of resigning."

"Of course he did. He's persistent. Always seems to get what he wants."

Daniel nodded. "He threatened to withhold a letter of recommendation, but I called his bluff. At any rate, thanks to my experience before I joined his firm, I should be able to find another position, with or without his help."

"Well, anyone would be lucky to have you."

A smile crossed his face. "Even you?"

I made an uncomfortable sound that was something between a cough and a laugh.

He reached for my hand and covered it with his. "You've come to mean a great deal to me, Maddie. I hope you know that. When we return to New York, I'd like to see you. We could have dinner, or go to museums, see movies. I'll meet you for lunch on Newspaper Row if you can fit me in between important meetings! What do you say?"

My stomach churned at his directness, but I smiled and tapped the half-empty glass in front of me. "Oh come now, a lady never makes promises. Why don't we wait and see."

He shrugged, as if my reply was fine, and ordered two more beers from a passing waiter, but I hadn't missed his look of disappointment.

Somewhere inside me, I knew that if I couldn't allow myself to trust this thing developing between us I would regret it. And yet. I still couldn't bring myself to say the words he wanted me to say. Not today, not now.

"I have some other news," he said, changing the subject, his tone becoming more serious. "I was waiting for the right time to tell you."

"Well, don't keep me in suspense. What is it?"

"Charles knows about your article. His secretary sent an urgent telegram to his hotel." His expression changed. I saw concern in his eyes. "He is absolutely furious, Maddie."

"Good. He brought it on himself," I said, sticking out my chin stubbornly. "I did nothing wrong. I merely reported what I'd discovered. If he doesn't want articles written about him, he should stop being such a . . ." I stopped, realizing my tone was acidic, and it shouldn't be directed at Daniel.

"You're right," he said, holding up his hands. "If Charles doesn't want negative press, he should behave accordingly." He leaned forward. "Have you told Clara?"

I shook my head, and a rising wave of panic washed over me. Once again, I'd put my relationship with her in the crosshairs.

"I have to go," I said, standing suddenly. "I need to tell Clara right now, before he does."

I rushed for the door and raced to the Hotel Brauner, with one thought on my mind: talk to my sister before Charles Hancock got to her first.

Clara

The light drizzle quickly turned to rain as I left the park and made my way to meet Charles at his hotel. My mood was already gloomy after the disappointing visit with Margaret and the prospect of the difficult conversation ahead, and the weather didn't help. Still, I was beginning to accept that life often didn't go the way you wanted or expected it to, and that I had to be more willing to confront, not avoid, whatever challenges came my way.

My stomach tumbled and my pulse raced as I rounded a corner and saw the hotel. My planned speech turned over and over in my mind. I hoped I wouldn't falter when I saw him. Charles had a talent for disarming even the most determined opponent.

I ducked into the ladies' bathroom before going to find him. Madeleine had told me I looked perfect but I added a slick of lipstick for good measure and checked myself in the mirror.

I'd envied Madeleine as I'd watched her walk away, a spring in her step as she headed off for her lunch with Daniel. I envied the excitement of first lunch dates, the promise of everything still to come. Was it really only a year since I'd been that same excited young woman, waiting for Charles to pull up outside to take me on another extravagant date? I was so impressed by him, so in awe of him, but I had never loved him. I thought about something Matthias had said as I'd sketched his portrait: *She made it easy. Violet made everything feel right. That's how it should be with someone you love.* It had taken a trip of thousands of miles to realize that I'd never truly loved Charles. Not in the way I wanted to love the man I would marry.

I looked at myself in the bathroom mirror one last time, took a deep breath, and went to find him.

He was waiting for me in the lobby bar, his back to me as he sat on a stool, his eyes trained on the pages of a newspaper. I took a moment to study him, to check my reaction, relieved to discover there was no flicker of passion still lingering.

"Hello, Charles."

He turned, then stood and walked toward me. He reached for me instantly and pressed his lips to mine.

"Darling Clara. How I've missed you!" He pulled back to study me. "And how pretty you've made yourself for me!" He kissed me again with a low moan of desire.

I stood like a statue, my arms hanging like fire irons at my sides before I pulled away and suggested we sit down.

"So, you survived!" He laughed as we took our seats at a window table, and he ordered two scotch and sodas. "My brave little Clara, traveling around the world!"

"I'll actually have a negroni," I corrected, smiling at the waiter. "Thank you."

Charles stared at me. "I see your journey has already changed your tastes."

"I never cared for scotch and soda," I countered as I took off my gloves. "And yes, my tastes *have* changed. Very much."

"Did you like your gifts?" he asked. "I thought they would act as a reminder of my love while you were gone, so you wouldn't forget me. I was sorry to only hear from you once. You must have been very busy squabbling with your sister." He stuck out his bottom lip in a fake childish pout.

"They were nice gifts," I said. "Very thoughtful of you, but entirely unnecessary."

"Nothing is unnecessary when it comes to my Clara." He leaned forward and took my hand in his. "You, my darling, are *entirely* necessary." He paused and leaned toward me to steal another kiss as our drinks arrived.

I took a long sip of my negroni, enjoying the warm bolstering buzz from the alcohol as I summoned the courage to tell him.

"So," he continued, leaning back in his chair, "we can spend the last two nights together and return home triumphantly on the mighty *Hindenburg*! They say she's quite something. And then we can get on with the wedding. Mother has been remarkable while you've been away. She has everything organized. There's really nothing left for you to worry about."

I heard him speak, but the words seemed to float above me, as if he was talking about someone else's wedding. I sat patiently while he went on and on, until I couldn't stand it any longer.

"Stop, Charles. Please, just stop."

He paused, midsentence. "Whatever's the matter?"

"There won't be a wedding, Charles. I can't marry you. I'm sorry." I blurted it out in a rush, my carefully rehearsed speech disintegrating.

He laughed, too loudly. "What are you talking about? Of course there'll be a wedding. Darling, I . . ."

I leaned back in my chair. "No, Charles. There won't." I felt suddenly calm, as if an enormous weight had lifted from me. "I know all about your scheme with Daniel Miller. I know you arranged for him to follow us."

At this, he looked taken aback. "I see. He didn't mention it."

"Didn't mention what? That we'd found out? That I'd discovered your plan to keep an eye on me in case of any 'misdemeanors'? What were you thinking, Charles? *Spying* on me?"

He laughed. "It wasn't spying! You're being a little melodramatic, don't you think?"

"Am I?" I took a deep breath and another long sip of my drink.

"I only wanted to make sure you didn't come to any harm, darling. I only ever want the best for you."

"You don't know what's best for me, though. You smother me, Charles. You order my meals. You decide on my drink. You tell me when and where we are having dinner, and with whom. You even decided on our wedding venue. Did it ever occur to you that I might not want to get married at the yacht club? That I might have set my heart on other places? And as for your gifts, I don't like roses, and my favorite perfume is Chanel. You *think* you know what's best for me, Charles, without ever trying to know *me* at all."

My voice was raised, catching the attention of the other guests.

"Clara, you're making a scene." Now he looked shocked, and angry. "And where's your engagement ring?"

I'd wondered when he might notice that. "Don't worry," I said, lowering my voice. "I didn't throw it into the Grand Canal. I know how much it's worth."

I took a small envelope from my handbag and pushed it across the table toward him.

He stared at the envelope. "You're really going to call off our engagement over a silly misunderstanding?"

"This is about far more than a silly misunderstanding. You don't truly know me, know my heart. You only see me as an extension of you. Things don't feel easy with you, Charles. And they *should* feel easy with the person you're planning to spend the rest of your life with."

His cheeks flushed with anger. "I can give you a good life, Clara. You would want for nothing."

I shook my head. "What I want is to be happy."

He picked the envelope up roughly and pushed it into the inside pocket of his jacket. "I suppose I shouldn't be surprised. No doubt your sister has tried to turn you against me the entire time you've been away. She never did like me, but even I didn't think she would stoop this low."

"What do you mean?" I asked.

"Your sister's exposé. About Hancock Enterprises. Front page news back home."

My mind raced. An exposé? About Hancock Enterprises? So that was why Madeleine hadn't told me what her article was about. It was about Charles.

He watched me carefully, swirling the ice in his glass as he waited for my reaction. I knew he intended to shock me, to turn me against Madeleine again.

"You look surprised," he said, his voice mocking. "Didn't she tell you?"

And just like that, he was back in control.

"No. She didn't tell me."

I couldn't think straight. I was confused and hurt. I was furious with Madeleine for putting me on the spot and furious with Charles for turning the conversation around.

"Apparently it was mailed to the editor of the *New York Herald Tribune* from Venice," he continued, a look of smug delight on his face. "Oops. I suppose I've just made more trouble between the two of you. I assumed you knew about it since you've become such good friends."

I stood up, fumbling as I picked up my hat and gloves. "I need to go. I need . . ."

"Clara!"

I turned to see my sister rushing toward me. She stopped as I turned around, then she looked from me to Charles and back again.

Charles grinned. "Well, hello, Madeleine. We were just talking about you, weren't we, Clara? I was updating her on your inventive storytelling."

Her face fell as she saw my expression.

"I'm sorry, Clara. I was going to tell you about the article, but I wanted you to make up your mind about Charles first."

"You're each as bad as the other," I snapped, looking at them both. "Trying to protect me. Deciding what's best for me. How could you, Madeleine? After everything? I opened up to you, told you exactly how I felt about things." I stared at her, searching those green eyes for the sister I thought I'd come to understand. "You'll never change, will you? No matter how far you travel around the world or how many cities you visit, you'll always come back to you. Putting the story before everything, and everyone, else. I'm sorry I ever let myself believe you'd changed."

At this, she looked wounded, but I didn't regret a word.

"I hadn't decided if I would send the article," she explained. "But you mailed it from Venice, along with the postcards and letters."

"And you wrote it behind my back!" I reached into my handbag and pulled out Nellie's pocket watch. "Here," I said, thrusting it at her. "I was planning to give this to you on our way home. You might as well have it now, because I don't even want to *see* you on the *Hindenburg*."

She stared at me as she took the pocket watch. "But this is yours. Violet gave it to you."

"And I know how much Auntie Nellie meant to you. I wanted to give it to you. As a gift. From your sister." The words caught in my throat, emotion overwhelming me.

Charles stepped forward and reached for my arm. "Darling. Calm down. We can talk more about this . . ."

I stepped out of his way. "And I don't want to see *you* on the *Hindenburg,* either. If you really care for me as much as you say you do, then prove it, and let me go home alone. My decision is made, Charles. You can't use one of your negotiating techniques to change my mind."

I turned then and walked away from them both, tears of anger and frustration stinging my eyes.

I jumped into a taxi and looked straight ahead as the car pulled into traffic. My heart raced from the confrontation and from the exhilaration of standing up to a man who thought he could tell me what to do, and who to be. From now on, I would make my own decisions, forge my own path.

As the car tracked the curve of the Danube, I asked the driver to pull over.

"I'll walk the rest of the way. It isn't far."

As I had so often, I turned to the water for comfort. Inhaling deeply, I peered over the bridge and looked at my reflection. *There are two of us,* Violet had said. *The version we present to the world behind the polite smiles, and the private person we really are.*

From now on, I would live the life I really wanted, be the real me, without apology, or hesitation.

Maddie

❖

There was no point in running after Clara. The damage was done, and now I had to give her time to heal, to calm down, so that she might listen to my side of the story.

Perhaps she was right in saying I would never change, but perhaps she was wrong to want me to. I hadn't written my article from a place of spite or vengeance. I'd written it because I cared about the people Charles's company would be displacing. I cared about making a difference through my journalism. An opportunist like Charles Hancock didn't think about those on the other end of his transactions. It wasn't personal to him. And that, in my view, was wrong.

"This is all your fault," Charles seethed as soon as Clara had gone. "Turning Clara against me with your so-called journalistic morals. I bet you've poisoned her mind at every opportunity."

I laughed, incredulous. "Clara didn't need me to say a damned word. She is perfectly capable of making up her own mind, although you would never give her the credit for that, would you?"

He shook, he was so furious. "How dare you charge me with ridiculous accusations that entirely miss the point of what I'm trying to accomplish. This article could do irreparable damage to my reputation. To my career. I can't believe you even had the nerve to attack your future brother-in-law! I—"

"*Ex*-future brother-in-law," I corrected, crossing my arms defiantly. "And I know exactly what you're trying to accomplish, Charles. You care about nothing but yourself. Do you have any idea what you've done to the people who will be forced to move? They'll end up in the shantytown in Central Park, or worse. Meanwhile, you'll go back to your mansion on the beach or your penthouse in midtown."

His face was red with anger. "Who cares? They're just collateral. It happens all the time. This is business, the progression of industry. But of course you'd never understand that." He downed his drink in one gulp, and shouted to the bartender to bring another. "You'd better write a retraction, Madeleine, or I'll slap you and the newspaper with a lawsuit and you'll never write another damn word again."

I knew he was bluffing. He had many more reasons not to pursue a lawsuit than to make an enemy of a prime newspaper or of journalists in New York City. I'd be damned if I'd retract a single thing I'd ever thought or written about Charles Hancock.

I straightened my shoulders and met his eye, determined not to let him rattle me. "I'm so glad Clara wants nothing more to do with you. She deserves better. You never cared much about her anyway, did you? Only that she made you look good. You can be on your way, Chuck," I said. "Clara will get along without you just fine."

I started for the door and refused to look back. Charles Hancock could go to hell.

Clutching the pocket watch in my hand, I went straight back to the hotel, hoping to find Clara there. The only thing that mattered now was to make amends with my sister, to explain why I'd written what I had and how important it was, even if the truth was difficult to accept. Because the truth was almost always difficult. Something I'd learned the hard way these last few weeks.

Clara wasn't at the hotel, so I put the pocket watch in the drawer, grabbed my journal, and decided to get some air.

I walked to the Stephansplatz, where I stood for a while, admiring the Stephansdom, Vienna's Gothic cathedral. I continued up the Graben, the famous street packed with boutiques and vendors, and suddenly remembered Mr. Klein's office was located nearby. Given that Clara was nowhere to be found, now was as good a time as any to stop in and say hello, especially since tomorrow was our last day in the city.

I dug out his business card to check the address and studied the street map the concierge had given me. I walked across the square, and down several side streets. As I reached Mr. Klein's address, I began to cross the street, but stopped.

Three soldiers stood outside his office door. Nazi soldiers. I paused, taking in their uniforms, their demeanor. I'd read so much about them I was strangely fascinated by their physical presence. And then the reality of what I was seeing hit me. Nazi soldiers were standing outside of Mr. Klein's office—a kind Jewish gentleman's office—with guns.

I recalled Mr. Klein's warnings and the conversations we'd had on the *Queen Mary*. He'd been so worried about what was to come for his family and his country, and now I could see all too clearly what that meant.

Immediately on the defensive, I continued across the street.

One of the soldiers met my eye and nodded. I noticed his hand rested on the hilt of a gun at his side. Pulse pounding in my ears, I forced a polite nod in reply.

Another soldier gestured at a man walking toward them in a dark suit. He walked with the assistance of a cane. I recognized him instantly.

"Mr. Klein!" I called, waving my hand in greeting.

Mr. Klein's footsteps faltered as one of the soldiers barked an order at him in German. He replied and tried to continue past the soldiers to his office door, but one of the soldiers grabbed him by the lapels and shook him violently. His cane clattered on the cobblestones as it fell. As Mr. Klein cried out, the soldier punched him squarely in the face. The elderly man grunted and crumpled to the ground.

I gasped, horrified as the soldiers began to kick his ribs several times, shouting and taunting him before sauntering away. I had to do something, but I stood frozen in place, too shocked to move.

Mr. Klein waited for the soldiers to go before sitting up. His face was deathly pale, his eye already bruising and swollen. Several people glanced his way, but walked by, as if he were invisible.

Then, his eyes met mine.

I exhaled a breath and ran to help him. He called out something in German, his hand seeming to wave me away. He didn't want my help, or perhaps he thought I would be in danger? I didn't stop. I had to help him anyway.

"Are you hurt? Here, let me help you," I said, offering my hand and pulling a handkerchief from my pocket to stem the flow of blood from his nose. "It's Madeleine. Madeleine Sommers. From the *Queen Mary*. I was coming to visit you."

"You are very kind, Miss Sommers, but you shouldn't be here."

As I helped Mr. Klein to his feet, someone shouted. I turned to see one of the soldiers gesturing to the others. The trio started back toward us.

Mr. Klein shot me a warning look as he pulled himself up, fumbled in his pocket, and turned the key in the lock. "Be careful, Miss Sommers. It isn't safe." He slipped inside his office, locking the door behind him.

I didn't know whether to flee, or wait to hear what the soldiers had to say. If I ran it would make me look guilty of something, which I wasn't. And my instinct was to stay and protect Mr. Klein. Still, my heart pounded as they approached.

"Fräulein!" one of them barked, and continued to say something I didn't understand.

"*Ich spreche nicht Deutsch,*" I said, shrugging nonchalantly in spite of my thumping pulse.

The soldier who appeared to be in charge—or was at least the biggest bully of the three—eyed my handbag. "Papers, please," he said in heavily accented English.

"My passport is at the hotel. I'm a tourist. Visiting from America."

"How do you know that man? Klein."

"I don't," I said. I could see where this was going and didn't like it one bit. "I met him briefly on the *Queen Mary,* traveling from the United States. I saw that he was hurt and wanted to help."

"Are you a Jew?" one of the other soldiers asked, his bright blue eyes filled with disgust.

I stuck out my chin. "No, not that it's any of your business. I'm not Austrian, either, and in my country we can be whatever we want."

I instantly regretted provoking them, but I never could hold my tongue, and I wasn't about to start now.

The man in charge grabbed my arm and yanked my handbag away.

"That's mine," I said, reaching for the bag, but I was too late.

He turned it over and dumped its contents onto the ground. Coins and writing utensils scattered, and my lipstick rolled into the drain. My journal thudded to the ground. When he picked it up and fanned through it, the newspaper clippings and antifascist propaganda leaflets I'd collected during the trip fell from its pages and settled all over the street.

Heart racing, I bent to collect them, but the soldier in charge pushed me away and shouted something at one of the others. He gripped my arm again and dragged me upright.

"That hurts!" I said, trying to pull away.

As the two others flipped through the articles, they sneered.

"I see we are famous, no?" the leader said, gesturing to the dozens of headlines and photographs I'd kept about the Nazi Party. "You want a Nazi man, fräulein?"

The men laughed.

I wanted to slap him in his smug face, for me and for Mr. Klein, and for every other Jewish person he'd laid his hands on or insulted.

"If by famous, you mean most hated, then yes. The Nazis are reviled everywhere." At the look on the soldier's face, my mouth snapped shut. I couldn't believe I'd said that.

He let go of me, pushing me hard enough to make me stumble and nearly fall.

"Go back to America where you came from," he said. "Next time I won't be so nice."

They sauntered off, laughing and talking among themselves.

My hands shaking, my breathing shallow, I stooped to collect my things and then turned to check again on Mr. Klein. He had seen everything from the window. He offered a small smile of gratitude and motioned urgently with his hands for me to go.

I hurried away. The image of Mr. Klein's bloody nose was imprinted in my mind, and the odor of the soldier's breath still lingered.

Vienna had turned out to be unpredictable and volatile, in spite of its picturesque homes, stunning architecture, and the beautiful river winding through the city. I was glad we were leaving soon. We'd visit Margaret one last time tomorrow, pack up our things, and go.

I was never so anxious to be back among the frenetic but happy bustle of New York, where a person's religion didn't matter, and a woman could help an elderly gentleman without getting into trouble. But one thing was for certain: those Nazi bullies had firmed my resolve to write about them and expose them for what they truly were. I owed it to Mr. Klein and his family, and to every other person suffering from their despicable show of force.

Still shaking, I walked quickly back to the hotel. For the first time since we were young girls, the only person I wanted to see, to offer some reassurance and a sense of normality, was my sister.

Clara

While I'd assumed that calling off my engagement would be the most distressing thing to happen that day, it was the discovery of Madeleine's article about Charles that upset me the most. After everything we'd been through together, she still hadn't been honest with me, hadn't valued the connection I'd thought we'd established. My delight for her in getting published was now tempered by my anger at the manner in which she'd done it. But even though I wasn't yet prepared to admit it to her, I accepted that it wasn't Madeleine who'd ruined Charles's reputation. Charles had done that all by himself.

We spent a frosty evening together at the hotel and went to bed early. Madeleine muttered something about running into Nazi soldiers and I could tell she was rattled by whatever had happened, but I wasn't in the mood to offer any sympathy. Perhaps getting a fright would knock some sense into her head.

The following morning, as we dressed to go to Margaret's house one last time, Madeleine broke the ice.

"Are we talking again, or not?" she asked.

"Not," I replied.

She flopped onto her bed and let out a weary sigh. "I wanted to tell you about the article, Clara. Truly. You've no idea the number of times I almost confided in you, but I didn't see the point in causing an argument between us, not when the piece was unlikely to be printed anyway. Or at least, that's what I thought."

I turned to her, my hands on my hips. "You caused an argument between us anyway, so that didn't work out too well, did it?"

Her expression contrite, she shrugged and then winced as she rubbed her arm.

"How is it?" I asked.

"Still bruised, but I'm more concerned about Mr. Klein. They really gave him a horrible beating. I hope they didn't crack his ribs, poor man. I really think we should go and check on him."

Her run-in with the Nazi soldiers had really shaken her, but besides leaving a bruise on her arm, it had also left the telltale steely resolve in her eyes that I'd come to recognize.

"Be careful, Madeleine. Don't go meddling in things you don't understand."

"But that's my job, Clara. To do exactly that."

I decided to let the conversation drop. There was no talking to her when she was in one of her stubborn moods.

I dressed in a dusty rose silk shirtwaist with a wildflower print and pinned a few curls to the crown of my head, leaving the rest of my hair loose around my shoulders. I wanted to look my best for Margaret and needed the extra boost of confidence to confront her again.

Meeting Margaret had affected us both. It was the culmination of the entire trip, an end point we'd been heading toward since the moment we'd departed from New York. With so much happening along the way, so many twists and turns, I'd almost forgotten how much depended on reaching Margaret and passing on Violet's final letter. It wasn't just the end of our journey, it was the *purpose* of our journey. One thing was clear: a satisfying conclusion would not come wrapped up in a pretty bow. It looked as though the end would be as messy and disjointed as the beginning had been.

"Let's hope she's more welcoming today," I said as we set out. "If she's read Violet's letter and it has stirred old resentments, she might not even let us in."

"Helga might see us off the premises with a bratwurst," Madeleine added.

I tried to conceal my laughter as a cough, but she heard it.

"Good to know I can still make you laugh," she said, as she started to laugh, too.

I tried to compose myself, but the image of Helga wielding a sausage was too funny. "You're infuriating, Madeleine Sommers. You do know that."

"But you still like me," she replied. "Even if you'd prefer not to."

"Maybe," I said, smiling.

Helga wasn't quite as frosty as we'd anticipated when she opened the door to us the second time.

"Ah. You are back," she said.

"We did say we would come back today," I replied, "but if . . ."

"Come inside," she added. "Margaret has been expecting you."

I threw a hopeful glance at Madeleine as we followed Helga into the now-familiar little home.

This time, Margaret was sitting in a different chair. The window shutters were open, letting in a soft light that settled around her.

Her hair was neater than it had been the day before and there was a little rouge on her cheeks. She wore a matching skirt and cardigan, finished with a string of pearls. She looked much more like Violet.

"Hello, girls." She offered a thin smile as we entered the room. "Sit. Please. Will we have some tea?"

We both nodded. "That would be lovely," I replied. "Thank you."

This was already much better than the unenthusiastic reception we'd received yesterday.

"I wasn't sure you would come back," she added. "I'm afraid I was unwelcoming."

"Not at all," I replied. "We must have given you quite a shock, arriving unannounced and bringing up difficult memories."

At this, she nodded. "It was a little unexpected, yes. But I'm glad you came."

"So are we," Madeleine said. "We were so keen to finally meet our great-aunt."

Margaret's smile reappeared briefly. "I don't know anything about you. Tell me more about your trip. Your lives."

I breathed a sigh of relief. She was trying, at least.

As Helga returned with a beautiful tea tray, we shared tales from the Orient Express and the *Queen Mary,* and our lives back in New York. We talked about Violet and her famous garden parties, the charities she ran with Mother, and excursions we'd taken with her and Nellie Bly.

"She kept in touch with Nellie?" Margaret asked, her blue eyes alight.

"We called her Auntie Nellie," Madeleine explained. "We spent a lot of time with her when we were little girls. She liked to shock us with her stories and her view on life."

"She was a remarkable woman. So confident and self-assured. And courageous," Margaret replied. "I've never met anyone like her, full of energy and that devil-may-care attitude of hers. Violet followed her around-the-world race so meticulously, it was no surprise she guessed the closest time in the competition!" She paused for a moment and stirred her tea absentmindedly, as if her thoughts were far away. "Violet was so starstruck when we first met Nellie that January after her return, she could hardly speak. She thought Nellie Bly was the absolute bee's knees. 'Nellie this' and 'Nellie that'! When Violet eventually returned from Venice, we met Nellie again. She wrote about us in her newspaper, what the trip had meant to us, and how we'd changed."

"Yes, Violet gave us a copy of the article," Madeleine said.

Margaret looked surprised. "She did? She'd kept it all this time?"

"Violet has kept everything," I added.

"I met Nellie again, in Austria, shortly before the outbreak of war," Margaret continued. "She came here with her husband's business but soon had her hand in all sorts of things. And then war broke out, and she went to report from the front line. The newspapers were shocked and said it was no place for a woman. Nellie's response to that was typical of her."

"What did she say?" Madeleine asked.

"She said the front line was no place for a man, either, but there they were all the same." She smiled at the memory. "I think some people are meant to be in your life for a long time, the way Nellie was in mine and Violet's. Others only stay briefly. Some aren't meant to be there at all," she added quietly.

I agreed as I thought fleetingly about Charles, but felt a pang of regret as an image of Edward immediately followed.

Margaret saw Madeleine's eyes settle on a stack of greeting cards on the dresser behind her.

"Christmas cards," she said. "From Violet." She picked up the bundle and held them toward me. "She sends a Christmas card every year to tell me about you all. I enjoy reading all the news and seeing the occasional photograph." She dabbed at her eyes with a lace handkerchief. "I kept them all, but of course I was too stubborn to reply. And then . . ." She glanced at Helga, who offered an encouraging smile. "Well, the tea is going cold. Shall we?"

When at last the sweet rolls were eaten and the tea drunk, Margaret broached the subject we'd all been avoiding.

"I suppose you're wondering if I read Violet's letter." She reached for the envelope on the table beside her. I saw it had been opened.

"You read it?" Madeleine asked.

Margaret nodded. She rubbed her fingers lightly over the envelope. "Many times," she said. "It is not a letter you can read only once." She held it out to me. "Read it. It might help you understand."

I hesitated, but she nodded her encouragement.

Picking up the envelope, I removed the folded sheets of paper inside, cleared my throat, and began to read.

My dearest Maggie,

Where should I begin? What can I say after all these years? Every time I put pen to paper it never seems to be enough. I wish I could see you, that I could take your hand and look into those blue eyes of yours and tell you what I want to say in person. But age and geography are not my allies, so I must try to find the words and hope against hope you will understand what I am trying to tell you.

I still remember, so vividly, when we were the best of friends. It has been so many years since we talked and laughed together, and yet I remember it all as clearly as if you were here beside me. I think of you all the time, wonder what you're doing and where you are, what you look like now, what you think about when you look out of the window at the start of a new day. You always used to look for shapes in the clouds. Do you still? I wonder.

I cannot say I'm sorry for what happened between me and Matthias. We didn't mean to fall in love, nor did I plan on becoming pregnant. And yet, if I hadn't returned home carrying his child, that little girl would not have grown up to be my beloved Celestine, who married a good man and had two beautiful daughters of her own: Clara and Madeleine. My three girls are my world. I cannot possibly regret them. But I do regret that I caused you embarrassment and shame, and most of all, I regret that we have been separated all these years because of it.

I wrote to you each Christmas. A few lines to pass on our

news and to ask how you were. You never sent a reply, but I kept writing. If I stopped, it would mean I had given up, and I will never give up on you, Maggie. As long as there is breath in my lungs, my arms are open and waiting for you.

There is very little time left for me. It will mean everything if I can go with your understanding. What I want to tell you is that I love you, as only a sister can. I hope you are happy and that life has been kind to you.

Auf Wiedersehen, my dear sister. To seeing you again, one day.

Violet

The room fell silent as I refolded the pages, returned the letter to the envelope, and placed it back on the table beside Margaret.

"I've missed her so much," Margaret said. "I started so many letters but threw them all into the fire, half-written. I wasn't sure, you see, if I could tell her."

"Tell her what?" Madeleine asked.

Margaret glanced again at Helga, who offered an encouraging smile and a slight nod of her head.

"I was afraid to reconnect with my family not because of Violet's child," Margaret continued, "but because of the life I have made here, in Vienna, with Helga."

As she reached for Helga's hand, the impact of her words, of the two women's gentle gesture, settled around the room. I was shocked, and could tell Madeleine was, too, but suddenly it all made sense, and I was pleased to know there was a reason beyond Violet's pregnancy for Margaret's silence all these years.

"So here we are," she continued. "Years spent without each

other, Violet and me, because I was too stubborn, and then too frightened, to do anything about it."

I leaned forward and took Margaret's hand.

"She so desperately wants your understanding, your forgiveness, if that's the right word. And I know she would give you hers in an instant."

Margaret squeezed my hand and shook her head. "Too much time has passed, Clara. It is too late." When she looked at me, I saw such sorrow in her eyes. "Perhaps we were meant to travel different paths, Violet and I. To journey apart, rather than together."

I glanced at Madeleine, who shook her head lightly, indicating we had done our best.

"We should go," I said as I stood. I leaned forward and kissed Margaret lightly on the cheek as Madeleine began to gather our things. "Thank you for inviting us into your home."

"Before you go, I have something for you both." Margaret rose from her chair. "I'm being honored tonight at the opera house. They're giving me an achievement award after my final performance." She reached inside the drawer of the lamp table, produced an envelope, and handed it to me.

"I've secured two tickets, orchestra seats in the third row. I do hope you can come. It would be a shame to come all the way to Vienna and not visit the opera."

"I couldn't agree more," Madeleine said enthusiastically. "Thank you."

"We'd love to," I added.

"Well then." Margaret smiled. "I look forward to seeing you tonight."

We made our goodbyes but as we started to leave, Margaret grabbed my hand.

"She will always be my sister, no matter the things that have come between us."

I nodded. Perhaps more than she would ever know, I understood.

Madeleine and I traveled back to the *gasthaus* in silence, our conversation stolen by the lingering discord between us, and by the awful realization that although Margaret had made peace with Violet, she still didn't intend to contact her. Some things, it seemed, were simply too broken to mend.

"So, that's that," Madeleine said as she stared out of the window of the tram.

"Not quite," I replied. "I hate to see how Violet and Margaret have ended up. Let's not make the same mistake."

She turned to me, a smile on her face. "Really? So you forgive me?"

"'Forgive' might be too strong a word. But I *am* prepared to forget and move on. It seems that while I'm free to choose who I do, or don't, marry, I am stuck with you, dear Madeleine. For better or worse."

My sister smiled, and for a moment, the world felt right.

It seemed fitting our last night in Vienna—and the final day of our European tour—would conclude with a grand symphony.

Clara and I enjoyed an early meal with Daniel, where Clara filled him in on the news of her break from Charles, and I explained what had happened to poor Mr. Klein and the despicable soldiers who had roughed me up when I'd tried to help him. Daniel was shocked to hear how the men had treated us both.

"I wish I'd been there," he said. "I'd have given *them* a kick in the ribs."

"I handled myself just fine," I replied.

"I know you did. It's just . . . well . . . It doesn't matter." He looked away, the muscle in his jaw twitching.

I smiled into my glass as Clara nudged my foot under the table. Even if I didn't need a man in my life, it was nice to know someone was prepared to leap to my defense.

"Why don't I go back to check on him while you're at the opera?" Daniel offered.

"Would you?" I said. "It would put my mind at ease. He must

at least have some bad bruises, if not a cracked rib. They kicked him pretty hard, and he's not the youngest of men."

"It's ghastly." Clara's face was a mask of concern. "That would be very decent of you, Daniel. He was such a kind soul."

"I'll look in on him at his office, and if he isn't there, I'll leave him a note." Daniel motioned to the waiter to bring the check, having already insisted on treating us to our last dinner.

After our meal, Daniel left us with a promise to meet in the morning for the early train to Frankfurt. From there, we would take a car to the airfield from where the *Hindenburg* would launch and we would be on our way home to Violet, at last.

We packed our things, laid out a change of clothes and a few toiletries for the morning, and slipped into our finest clothes. Clara wore a stunning silver gown that poured over her frame like water, and I wore crushed green velvet that tucked and swirled in a way that accentuated my tall, lean figure. We were a sight to behold together, different but complementary, as we'd always been.

I was relieved Clara and I had made amends. We needed each other, even if we weren't always prepared to admit it. Since we'd left New York, our views of the world—and of ourselves—had changed, and for the better. I was proud of Clara for making difficult decisions, and I was proud of myself for not only taking the next step in my career by also making a difficult decision, but for opening up to a vulnerability I'd never felt comfortable embracing until now.

I buttoned my coat over my gown to protect myself against the cold Austrian spring night.

"I wonder what Violet will say when we tell her about Margaret and Helga?" I said. "Do you think she'll be shocked?"

Clara put on red lipstick and reached for a handbag matching the dazzling silver of her gown. "It takes a lot to shock Violet. I think she'll be pleased to know that Margaret found happiness. Sisters have a way of instinctively knowing things about each other, even if they don't say them aloud. Perhaps she suspected Margaret was hiding something else all along."

I lost myself in deep thought as we wound through the streets until our taxi dropped us at the entrance of the Vienna State Opera, an elegant building in the Renaissance Revival style. I smiled to myself to notice how Daniel's influence had rubbed off on me.

"It's beautiful," Clara said as we stepped from the taxi.

"Did you know this opera house premiered with Mozart's *Don Giovanni*?" I said, following her inside.

She laughed. "Always full of facts, aren't you! If the writing doesn't work out, you could always have a career as a tour guide!"

I stuck my tongue out at her and we laughed.

Inside, as we waited for the performance to begin, I looked around at the impressive building, the stunning chandelier that hung from the domed ceiling, the gilded balconies, the sumptuous decor of burgundy velvet seats with gold trim, and the beautifully clad patrons dressed in fine gowns and furs and tuxedos. It was wild to think our great-aunt Margaret had performed here for years with the Vienna Philharmonic, and was being honored by them tonight.

When the curtains went up and the lights dimmed, the crowd hushed, and we were both instantly mesmerized by the performance, the rise and fall of the music sending a shiver along my skin. It was powerful and yet so beautiful, it brought me to tears. Clara smiled and passed me a handkerchief.

As the intermission concluded and we returned to our seats, the director of the opera, along with the conductor, called Margaret forward. She wore a plain but pretty black gown, and the gold barrettes in her hair gleamed in the light. In her hands, she held her beloved violin. The director delivered a short speech, and though we couldn't understand the language, we knew his remarks were wonderful. Margaret beamed in the glow of the stage lights, bowed to a thundering audience, and at last made her way back to her seat in the orchestra as first violinist.

"It's so lovely, isn't it?" Clara said, while we stood and clapped to honor her. "Listen to that applause!"

It was incredible. To see Margaret so revered and loved by her fellow musicians. Yet, as happy as the occasion was, I couldn't help feeling such sadness that Violet wasn't here to see what her sister had achieved, and couldn't celebrate with her.

We sat when the lights dimmed again and enjoyed the rest of the performance. As the rousing grand finale reverberated through the majestic walls of the opera house, my body filled again with the beautiful music and I was swept away by its power and its magic. I squeezed Clara's hand, and she returned the gesture.

After the performance, we joined Margaret and Helga, along with several of their friends, for a celebration with champagne and plenty of good stories.

Too soon, the night came to an end.

"Any last word for Violet?" I prompted as we kissed Margaret goodbye. "It would mean so much to her."

Margaret looked wistful and pressed her hands to mine. "Tell her to look at the clouds," she said with a smile. "Ask her what she sees there."

As Clara and I made our way back to the hotel, exhausted but happy, I thought about all we'd done and seen the last few weeks. I smiled at the memories; from arguments to contented strolls through the cities we'd visited, dodging suspicious men who spied on us, surviving pickpockets, and run-ins with nasty soldiers, and navigating our way through difficult breakups and new relationships. We'd helped each other through it all. And I wouldn't change a moment of it.

Back at the hotel, I shared a nightcap with Daniel. I was relieved to hear he'd managed to speak with Mr. Klein.

"He wanted me to assure you he is well, considering, and that apart from some bruising, he'll make a full recovery. He also wanted me to thank you for intervening."

"I didn't really intervene," I said. "I mostly stood there, frozen in shock."

"Well, whatever you did, it made a difference. And he is grateful for that."

And although the entire event still troubled me, if I *had* made a difference, then I was pleased. To make a difference, to take a stand for what I believed, was more important to me than anything.

WHATEVER THE DISTANCE or the duration, there is a point at which every journey must come to an end. I thought of how true that was with Clara and Charles, with Matthias and Violet, and soon, with Violet and me. My heart grew heavy. I didn't know how I'd face my grandmother's death, or how I would part company with Clara as our lives continued in different directions. I'd grown used to her soft snores in the night, her hard-won laughter and bright conversation.

And then there was Daniel. I certainly liked him; I just didn't know what came next. I had dreams, plans, goals, and I didn't yet know where he fit into this new, more confident version of myself. Yet, I found myself peering through the crowd, searching for his fedora, his thick shoulders. How funny to think I didn't even know him a few weeks ago, then briefly hated him, and now felt a little unmoored when he wasn't within sight. When I spotted him, there was no denying the happy leap in my heart.

I turned and squinted at the sun perched near the horizon. It cast a golden haze over the airfield, but soon, all would be engulfed in cool twilight. The gleaming zeppelin behemoth that would fly us across the Atlantic was a beast with a metal rib cage, overlaid with a fabric skin, held aloft by hydrogen gas. A true marvel of science, engineering, and modern machinery. The name *Hindenburg* stretched across the hull in proud red lettering, and the swastika emblem I'd come to recognize all too well adorned the tail fins of the airship. The *Hindenburg* was a German vessel, which meant it also belonged to the Nazi Party.

Still, it was an impressive end to our adventures.

Whether sparked by worries of spies, or merely by Nazi protocol, officials checked all baggage several times before letting anyone board, making the passengers restless.

"Will they ever finish with our luggage?" Clara huffed, breaking the silence.

"They've already searched them three times," I said, rolling my eyes. "Do they think we've packed bombs in there along with our cuckoo clocks and schnapps?"

I couldn't say I was sad to leave Europe in its current unsettled state, but I would miss beautiful Paris and Venice. In just three days, we would land in New Jersey and take a car to Long Island. I pictured Violet's loving face, lined with years of laughter and a hint of regret, which I now understood. I only hoped she could hold on long enough for us to say a proper goodbye.

Clara looked past me at the line, scrutinizing the faces of the assembled passengers. I knew she was looking for Charles.

"You don't think he'll come, do you?" I asked.

She shook her head. "I have a feeling he listened to me for once. Besides, he hates being humiliated. Pride won't allow him to come."

"Good. It would have been awkward as hell trying to avoid him while trapped on a giant balloon together above the ocean for three days."

Clara's clear, unencumbered laughter made me smile.

As the crew eventually signaled that it was time for us to board, an excited murmur rippled through the crowd. I glanced over my shoulder at the line spiraling behind us. There were only thirty-six passengers if I'd counted correctly, an exclusive group, plus nearly twice the number of crew, a fact that would hopefully soothe Clara's nerves.

"Ready?" I asked as we stepped forward.

She looked at me with large brown eyes that drew men to her like bees to a flower. Her lips were trembling but she stubbornly tipped her chin and lifted the edge of her skirt to ascend the steps.

"I've always been ready, Madeleine. It's you who dithers and dallies all the time."

I laughed. It wouldn't be true anymore. I'd not waste time believing the worst about myself. I was a proper journalist now, and I had solid ideas. I'd find a way to follow my heart and my dreams. I'd already started down that path.

Daniel put his hand on my back, but I shooed him along ahead of me while I took a moment. I thought about how far I'd come, how much I'd changed. But if I'd learned anything these last few weeks, it was that the end of one journey always meant the start of another. The promise of even greater adventures always lay ahead.

"Madeleine! Come on." Clara stood at the top of the steps, her hands on her hips. "The captain won't come back for you if you're left behind, and neither will I."

I grinned. "Yes you will! You can't bear to be without me, Clara Sommers!"

I took a last lingering look behind me, and stepped aboard.

Clara

The Hindenburg was the fastest and most luxurious way to travel from Europe to America, and a fitting end to our journey. Violet had chosen our modes of transport carefully. From the *Queen Mary* to the Orient Express and now this, she had given us the very best of modern transportation, and I would be forever grateful for the experience.

I tried to suppress my nerves as I stepped into the spacious lobby area of A deck. In different circumstances, I would have preferred to return home on the *Queen Mary,* even if it meant putting up with a week of horrible seasickness again, but a week felt like such a long time with Violet so ill. I would stand on the wings of a plane if it was what Violet wished, and if it could get me back to her sooner.

A handsome young steward in full uniform approached us and in nearly perfect English said, "Welcome aboard the *Hindenburg.* I will escort you to your cabin."

He led us down a long corridor, pleasantly decorated in creams and scarlets.

"She's surprisingly spacious," I remarked.

I'd worried the airship would be horribly claustrophobic, but it wasn't at all.

"She's a wonder, miss. The passenger accommodation is built within the hull, rather than in the gondola like on most airships. That's what gives her the extra space. And there's additional accommodation for crew on B deck below."

The steward pointed out the port and starboard promenade decks, the dining room, and a writing room.

"You'll be able to finish your next damning article, Madeleine," I said over my shoulder. "Bring some other poor unsuspecting businessman to his knees."

"I thought you'd agreed to forget about that."

"Did I? I'm sure I can squeeze a few more days of torture out of it before we arrive home."

The steward paused in front of a cabin door and stared at us.

"We're sisters," I explained. "It's what we do."

He shrugged his shoulders and opened the door to our accommodation. It was decorated in a very clean and modern style. My lips curled into a smile. It would do just fine.

"You can contact a member of the crew by pressing this button," he said as he turned to leave. "Have a pleasant journey, ladies. Not many people get to travel on the *Hindenburg*. It is a special treat to do it with your sister."

"Thank you," I said, pressing a roll of dollar bills into his hand. "What's your name?"

"Lehmann," he replied. "Walter Lehmann."

"Well, Walter Lehmann, thank you for your assistance. You have a wise head for young shoulders."

"I also had a sister, miss. She died last year. It makes you see things differently."

He tipped the peak of his cap and closed the door behind him, leaving a poignant silence in his wake.

THE IMPRESSIVE DINING room occupied the length of the port side of A deck. Chairs upholstered in red velvet stood in neat rows alongside dining tables draped with linen tablecloths. Silk wallpaper shimmered beneath the lights and the waitstaff were dressed immaculately in chef's whites. No expense had been spared.

With a barely discernible bump, we took off a short while later and were finally airborne. I didn't even mind looking out of the windows in the generous viewing galleries that ran along each side of the craft. The sun had almost set and night would soon begin its descent over the landscape below.

"It's more like floating than flying, isn't it?" Daniel remarked as he joined me at the window.

"It's certainly not as terrifying as a hot air balloon," I replied. "Goodness. How long ago that seems."

Daniel laughed lightly. "At least you and Madeleine aren't squabbling in midair."

I grimaced at the memory. "Don't remind me!"

But his comment prompted memories of Edward's letter and the ache of our parting in Venice. I gazed out of the window and felt, again, the relief of going home without an engagement ring on my finger. I was quietly grateful to Charles for not showing up. Although I'd asked him not to, he was a man who made up his own mind. Perhaps something of what I'd said to him in the hotel had left its mark, or perhaps the sting of Madeleine's article was still too sore. Whatever it was, I was grateful for his absence. Now I could relax, forget, and look ahead.

"It's really none of my business," Daniel continued, "other than the fact that I've come to know you both these past months and have grown terribly fond of your sister, but, for what it's worth, I'm pleased you're going home as friends."

I looked at him. "You really care for her, don't you."

He nodded. "More than she knows. Your sister is a very special woman. One of a kind. I hope she might give me—us—a chance when we're back on terra firma."

It still amused me to observe Madeleine being so enraptured by Daniel while she adamantly claimed not to be. "I'm sure she will. After all, it's not often you get to fall for a spy!"

At this he laughed and excused himself.

I understood why Madeleine was having such a hard time trying not to fall in love with him, and yet I didn't envy her one bit. She was welcome to it, all the heartache and dizzy delight. I was done with all that for now. I felt hopeful. Excited for the possibilities of what my future might bring.

I spent the rest of the evening happily alone in the lounge, capturing the scene in my sketchbook so I could show Violet. How she would love to be here, among such grandeur. I imagined her sitting across from me, dressed in powder blue and rose pink, a smile at her lips as she quietly watched the other passengers and sipped her glass of champagne. *Never miss an opportunity to drink champagne, darling, and only ever drink real champagne. The best you can find. They say the bubbles help to keep one young and vivacious.*

She had lived life to the fullest, and I intended to do the same.

I caught the attention of a passing waiter.

"Yes, miss. What can I get for you?"

"Champagne, please. A glass of your very best."

He smiled. "Certainly, miss. Are we celebrating a special occasion?"

I returned his smile and thought for a moment. "Yes. I am celebrating a fresh start. I think that's a special occasion, don't you?"

"Absolutely, miss. Then you will need a Dom Pérignon. I'll be right back."

"Actually, could you bring two glasses?"

"Two, miss?" He looked at the empty seat opposite me.

"Yes. The other one is for my grandmother."

Maddie

The first two days on the *Hindenburg* flew by without a hitch; the service on board was second to none, our sleeping quarters were comfortable, and we dined like royalty. To add to my winning streak, I indulged in after-dinner poker and beat Daniel in every game but one. Clara and I worked together happily, finishing the remaining pages of Violet's gift—the book of our journey—and in my remaining time, I took in the view from the windows, marveling at the way we soared through the sky over a glimmering swathe of dark blue ocean. It was all so easy, so enjoyable.

On the third and final day of our journey, concerns about the weather started to circulate among the passengers. We'd finally arrived in the United States but were several hours late, delayed by intense headwinds over the Atlantic, and now the weather was too unfavorable in New Jersey to land. I told Clara not to worry, that these things happened.

Daniel and I headed to the lounge to pass the time while we waited.

"We'll have to circle until we can land safely," a stewardess calmly informed us. "There's no need to worry."

A murmur arose among the small gathering in the lounge as the stewardess repeated her instruction among the rest of the passengers.

"See," Daniel said with a smile and a gentle squeeze of my arm. "Nothing to worry about. I'm going to pack the last of my things. See you when we land?"

I nodded. "See you when we land."

I heaved a sigh and moved to the window. We turned, circling northward over New York City. I looked down at the sprawl of Manhattan below, so close and yet so small from a distance. The sprawling city was flanked by miles of countryside on one side and by water lapping at its shores on the other. I hoped the storms would let up soon.

"It doesn't look real from up here, does it?"

A cloud of Clara's favorite perfume enveloped me as she joined me at the window, grabbing my arm for reassurance.

"I can't wait to be home," I replied. "After we visit with Violet, I'm going to buy a knish from the stand on Eighth Avenue, grab a stack of newspapers, and find a bench in Bryant Park. And then I'll write myself into a stupor. What will you do?"

"After seeing Violet? I'm going to take stock of all my paintings and sketches, organize them in a way that makes sense, and then I'm going to start a new collection with a theme: Women on the Move. I'm hoping I might show it in a gallery somewhere in the city when I'm finished."

I was happy for her and proud of her. Proud of us both.

"I think we're turning again," Clara said, pointing to the shifting landscape far below us.

"I hope that's good news."

"I'm sure it is," she replied. "I'm going to freshen up before we land."

I watched her go and turned back to the window.

Dark clouds crowded the sky and the sea tossed in a murky haze below. When at last we veered away from the shoreline toward the landing strip in Lakehurst, New Jersey, I breathed a sigh of relief. But as we grew close enough to make out the tiny figures of people on the ground preparing for our landing, the airship tilted sharply sideways. Passengers cried out as glasses slid from the tables and crashed to the floor. Several crew members raced around the room, helping to clean up the mess and calming everyone as they went. It was just the storm, they assured us. We'd be on the ground shortly, they insisted.

And yet I sensed danger. My instincts told me to find Clara.

Heart pounding, I walked quickly through the lounge toward our cabin, trying to quell the erratic thoughts in my head. Everything was fine. It was only the wind.

When I didn't find Clara in the cabin, I hurried back down the corridor, toward the dining room.

The airship jerked sharply again. I braced myself against a table, and made my way to the other side of the room. And there she was, with Daniel. A wave of relief washed over me. They turned and saw me at the same moment and rushed toward me.

A lump gathered in my throat as Clara reached for my hand. "Maddie, I'm scared."

I closed my fingers around hers and squeezed them tightly, just as I had when we were little girls. "It's fine. I think we're just about to land. They'll be dropping the mooring ropes."

We exchanged a nervous smile. My heart lurched as I looked

at Daniel, but my attention was caught by something flickering outside the window. It looked like a blue flame.

"Is that—"

"Fire!" Daniel shouted, reaching for my hand.

But at that moment, a muffled blast rocked the airship violently and knocked me off my feet.

The last thing I heard was Clara's scream.

Clara

*T*he airship reared up from its tail, sending us all tumbling like rag dolls. For a second, I managed to hold on to Madeleine's hand, but another sudden lurch ripped us apart and I let out a scream as I skittered and rolled across the floor, my arms and legs banging against tables and fallen chairs that tumbled alongside me.

The noise was terrifying. Shattered glass and dinnerware rained down on me, leaving cuts and lacerations on my skin as I fell roughly against a wooden bench. Several other passengers landed on top of me, pinning me against the wall.

I pushed and kicked at them as I felt myself being suffocated. "Maddie!" I screamed her name as the ship rolled to one side and everyone fell again, releasing me. I grabbed a curtain and pulled myself up against the incline, peering through a wall of flames and choking black smoke that had filled the airship in seconds. I hardly knew which way was up.

"Maddie! Where are you?" I shouted, my voice wild with terror.

There was no sign of her, or Daniel, although they'd been beside me just a second earlier.

All around me, people screamed in terror and pain. Names of loved ones were called in desperation. I covered my mouth with my hand as the smoke began to choke me. My eyes smarted and stung. The heat from the fire was overwhelming. I couldn't think straight. For a moment I froze, unable to comprehend what was happening. The ship was on fire. We were crashing to the ground—and I didn't know where my sister was.

"Madeleine!" I screamed again.

"Jump, miss!" A young man grabbed roughly at my coat sleeve as he ran past me. "You'll have to jump for it." I recognized him as the steward who'd shown us to our cabin just a few days ago. He dragged me after him, his fingers gripping my arm. "Hurry, miss. It's our only chance."

Ahead of me, I watched in horror as men and women leaped through the shattered gallery windows.

"I can't!" I screamed. "My sister is in here."

"You have to jump, miss." He turned to look at me, a wild, terrified look in his eyes. "Or you'll be burned alive."

I ran to the shattered edge of the airship, the metal frame and the fabric covering a tangled, terrifying mess. I looked down. We were dropping rapidly, only a few meters now from the ground, but it was still too high to jump. My mind spun wildly as I peered through the smoke and flames at what was left of the dining room. Had Maddie already jumped?

"You have to go now!" the steward shouted over the roar of fire that now consumed the vessel we'd trusted to bring us safely home.

"We'll be killed!" I screamed. "I can't."

"You can, miss. You must."

And with that, he jumped, and as the heat from the fire engulfing the airship became unbearable, I closed my eyes, stepped out into the air, and fell.

Violet

❧

Veneto Estate, East Hampton, New York
May 1937

I thought I'd cried my final tears, folded away the last of my grief and regret.

I was mistaken.

I watch, helplessly, as Celestine paces across the floor, stirring the diaphanous curtains at the windows as she sweeps past. Henrietta has transferred me to the sofa in the sunroom so that I might find distraction in the distant ocean and my beautiful gardens, but their loveliness wanes beneath the dreadful news we've received. The vivid life I've known for seventy-three years has suddenly lost all its color.

We heard the news through the evening newspaper. The *Hindenburg*, carrying my precious granddaughters home to me at last, had suffered a catastrophic fire and crashed, just moments from landing.

Celestine's frantic calls to the hospitals have yet to yield any news. Clara and Madeleine are still missing, not yet confirmed among those who have tragically lost their lives, and not yet counted among those recovering. It is as if they are suspended somewhere between life and death, and my heart feels as if it will tear in two.

Hours creep slowly by. Food comes and goes, brought by Henrietta on a tray that I ignore. Anxious glances and questions without answers hang in the air whenever anyone comes to comfort me. Angry clouds march across the sky and blossoms fly from the trees, snatched away by the wind as if it knows beauty isn't welcome on such a dark day.

Finally, as the last of the daylight sinks into the ocean, Celestine returns from another round of frantic telephone calls and takes my hand, her eyes searching mine.

"You have news?" I ask. "Did they make it?"

She wraps her fingers around mine.

I take a deep breath as my life, with all its moments of exquisite beauty and unimaginable pain, comes down to this one moment, one word. Yes, or no?

Clara

Manchester, New Jersey
May 1937

J woke to sunlight streaming through a sheer curtain, people coming and going all around me. I tried to sit up, but I couldn't.

"Hello?" My voice was raspy and dry. I coughed to clear my throat, but it was too painful. And then I remembered. The fire. The crash.

"Madeleine?" I called out. "Maddie, are you here? Where are you?"

Where was I?

A voice approached at my side. "You're in the hospital, miss. In New Jersey."

I stared up at a kind face. A nurse.

She smiled. "It's good to have you back."

"Am I hurt?" I asked.

"Cuts and bruises. Shock, mostly. You were one of the lucky ones. It's a miracle anyone got out alive. You need to rest now. Drink plenty of fluids. Get your strength back."

"Is my sister here?" I asked. "Madeleine Sommers. There was a friend of ours on the airship, too. Daniel Miller."

The nurse reassured me she would check. "You rest up now. I'll do my best to find them. Oh, and we found this in your coat pocket."

She handed me my sketchbook, my illustrations now interspersed with Madeleine's beautiful descriptions. Our gift for Violet. It didn't have a single mark on it.

"Oh! My mother and grandmother? Have they been informed? They'll be so worried. We were on our way home."

"Let me check. There are many families to contact. Many who've lost loved ones."

Panic and fear washed over me. The horror of what I'd seen and heard. "How many?" I asked, trying to steady the tremble in my hand. "How many died?"

"We can't be sure yet. Around thirty-five, we think. It's a miracle anyone survived at all, but over sixty of you did."

It was too many deaths. I couldn't bear to think of Madeleine among them.

I lay back on my pillow and stared at the ceiling. Numb. Broken. My mind turned over images and memories of Madeleine, and then of Violet. Fragments of conversations, moments of laughter, all of it jumbled together until I felt I would drown in despair.

Beyond the hospital window, life carried on. I closed my eyes and listened to the familiar sounds of motorcars and sirens, construction sites and laughter. I was back home, our journey complete, and I was terrified I'd lost everything that was dear to me, that I'd lost my sister after finding her again.

In a moment, all our differences and disagreements became nothing, and all I saw was our similarities, the connections within our story, not the divisions and gaps. I wanted to turn back time. I wanted to pause every silly squabble and hold Madeleine's hand and laugh with her. All those thousands of miles traveled. All those opportunities grasped and chances taken, memories made and regrets formed, and in the end it came down to a small room in a New Jersey hospital. I had never felt more alone, or more desperate.

I whispered her name to the clouds beyond the open window and prayed that she might hear me. Tears slipped down my cheeks.

"Madeleine."

My sister. My traveling companion. My friend. The words to my pictures. How could I possibly face life without her?

Hours passed as I drifted in and out of sleep. Nurses came and went, engaging me in snatches of conversation. I wasn't sure if they were real or part of a dream.

Eventually, I was helped from my bed and taken in a wheelchair down a long corridor to another room in the hospital, to the side of another hospital bed.

"She's resting," the nurse whispered to me as she tended the patient's tubes and checked a chart at the foot of the bed. "The medication for the pain makes her very sleepy. She was lucky, pulled away from the flames by a gentleman, apparently. He stayed with her all the way to the hospital, even though he was injured himself." She lay her hand on my shoulder for a moment. "Stay with her as long as you wish."

I don't remember what I said, only that I gasped and wept and shook with relief when I saw her.

My sister.

Alive.

I focused on Madeleine's breathing: slow steady breaths, in and out, as the bedcovers rose and fell with her. Life. Breath. My sister had survived the dreadful inferno. I took her hand in mine, remembering how I'd done the same just moments before the crash, seeking her reassurance. Except now all I asked of her was to get better.

"I'm here, Maddie," I whispered. "It's Clara. We're in the hospital. We made it home."

Tears fell down my cheeks as relief and horror washed over me again. She'd suffered burns and had a concussion from the fall when she'd jumped. Like me, she'd leaped into nothing.

I sat with Madeleine until I fell asleep and my dreams took me back to my childhood, my sister always beside me, laughing, wondering, finding our way together, and when a hand gently shook my arm to wake me, it was Madeleine's eyes that met mine, her voice that whispered my name, her hopeful smile that told me everything would be alright, because whatever life had in store for us from that moment on, we would take every step together.

Maddie

$\mathcal{T}$he muffled sound of voices edged their way into my consciousness as I tumbled through darkness, scrambling to make sense of where I was, what had happened. And then I heard Clara's voice.

"Maddie. You're going to be alright. I'm here. We're together."

My eyes slowly opened to a strange room: light blue walls, a vase of red roses, everything else stark white. The odor of medicine and bleach stung my nose, and the memory of what we'd endured flooded my mind. The *Hindenburg*. The fire. I turned my head slowly to the left, wincing at the pain, and there she was, perched at my side in a wheelchair.

"Clara?" I croaked, my voice hoarse from the smoke I'd inhaled. "You're hurt. Are you alright?"

"I'm alive and so are you, and that's all that matters."

Tears ran a twisting course down her cheeks. One eye was swollen and there was a nasty cut on her chin. I reached for her hand, careful not to move too much, not yet certain where all of the aches and injuries were on my body.

"Yes," I whispered as I squeezed her hand and my own tears fell to match hers. "That's all that matters."

I looked down at my body to assess the damage. My left arm was covered in a burn salve, but my writing hand had been saved. I breathed a sigh of relief. But my head. It felt as if someone was hitting me with a sledgehammer.

"I know I said we should go out with a bang, but this wasn't exactly what I had in mind," I attempted a feeble joke, falling back on old habits. I didn't know how else to process what had happened.

Clara wiped her eyes. "Even now, when I thought I'd lost you, you try to make me smile." She winced and cradled her sore cheek. "It hurts too much."

It did hurt too much—the injuries, the horror of everything we'd seen, the terrifying prospect of losing everything I held dear: my sister. Daniel.

My mind flashed back to the moment of the crash, and the last question I had for Clara sat, unasked, on the tip of my tongue. Had I seen Daniel's face in the midst of the chaos of ambulances and doctors? Who was it who had pulled me away from the fire? It was all such a muddle, I couldn't be sure.

Emotion rose in waves until I felt dizzy. I squinted beneath the glare of the bright hospital lights, my head in searing pain as I tried to remember exactly what had happened after I'd jumped. I'd landed on the grass and rolled, just as Daniel had told me to. "When we hit the ground, try to tuck and roll. It will help break the fall," he'd shouted over the unfolding chaos. I thought I'd done as he'd instructed but I couldn't be sure. The memory was blurred. It had all happened so fast.

A soft knock came at the door before it opened a crack.

A nurse stuck her head inside. "There's someone to see you, Miss Sommers, if you're up to another visitor?"

Behind her, I caught a glimpse of dark hair, broad shoulders.

As he stepped into the room, his gaze settled on mine and my heart swelled.

Limping with the help of a cane, Daniel approached the bedside, concern etched across his face. "How are you, my darling?"

I couldn't find any words but cried tears of relief at seeing him. I reached for his hand.

With his handkerchief, he gently dabbed my cheeks. "You don't need to say anything."

I looked at Clara and then at this wonderful man who I'd met over a game of poker and whose life had intersected with mine in the most unfathomable way, and I knew, with a certainty I'd never felt before, that life was better with him in it. That I loved him.

Daniel took the chair on the other side of the bed, and we talked for a long time about what had happened, and how fortunate we were, and the terrible loss of so many lives. When the nurse came to tend to my dressings, he brushed his lips to my forehead.

"Get some rest so we can get you home. You still haven't shown me your poker tricks, and I can't let you keep on beating me."

I smiled weakly but he looked into my eyes and saw the truth laid bare within them.

As the pull of sleep enveloped me, I surrendered to its healing calm, safe in the knowledge that the two people who meant the most to me were still with me. We had stared death in the face, all three of us, and I knew we would never look at life the same way again.

Clara

Veneto Estate, East Hampton
May 1937

The ocean led us home, the road beneath the Lincoln twisting and turning as I pressed my foot to the accelerator. Every minute on the road felt like precious moments we should be spending with Violet. Beside me, Maddie rested, her eyes closed. She was still recovering, but nothing would stop her making the trip to Veneto with me.

The *Hindenburg* tragedy had provided a much-needed reminder that life was too short. There was no time to spend any of it going in the wrong direction, or putting up with things that didn't make your heart sing. From now on, I would follow my passions, and I would spend time with people who filled my life with love and joy, not misery and doubt.

People like Edward Arnold.

He'd visited me in the hospital, rushing back to America as soon as he'd heard the dreadful news of the accident. I'd often wondered how I would feel when I saw him again, and something about the fragility of it all—the hospital room, my injuries, the shocking events of the crash—left no room for hesitation. When he'd quietly told me Annabel had left him, I'd reached for his hand and felt anchored for the first time in my life.

"She's moved back to the south, to be closer to her mother and sisters in Virginia," he'd explained. "She said there was no point denying that we made each other miserable."

"And where will you go?" I asked.

"I'm not entirely sure. Possibly back to Venice."

"What about the gallery? Will you sell it?"

He'd smiled and given me a small silver key with a lavender ribbon tied to it. "I wondered if you might consider taking over the gallery?"

"Me?"

"*Yes, you!* It would mean so much to me to know it's in capable hands. I can't think of anyone better."

It was the greatest gift he could give me: not just the gallery, but the encouragement to fulfill my ambitions. I would start my Women on the Move collection there. It was perfect.

"And perhaps, in time, you could visit me, in Venice?" he'd offered. "We never did get to the Doge's Palace."

I'd smiled and told him I would like that. Very much. In time.

Maddie yawned beside me. "Are we there?" she asked, opening a sleepy eye as I turned into the driveway, came to a stop, and killed the engine.

I nodded. "Home."

We stepped from the car and linked arms as we walked inside the house together. I breathed in the familiar scent of tea roses and hyacinth, but looked with new eyes at the familiar paintings and vases, and I relished the creak of the old floorboards with new and purposeful steps. Everything was so familiar and yet so different.

"It feels smaller, doesn't it?" Maddie whispered beside me.

"I think we are the ones who have grown," I replied.

In the entrance hall, the grandfather clock ticked the minutes idly away with its gilded hands, just as it had since I was a little girl, staring up at its ivory face. For a moment, I felt as if we'd never left home, and nothing had changed.

We paused outside the sitting room.

"Ready?" I asked.

Maddie nodded. "Ready."

We pushed open the door and stepped inside, our breathing in sync, our steps matching each other's as we crossed the continents and oceans of wooden boards and Persian rugs and mapped our way steadily back to our beloved grandmother.

She was resting, her face turned to the window and the ocean beyond, a slight smile at her lips, a touch of rouge in the apple of her cheeks.

We sat quietly, one on each side of her. Maddie took her left hand. I took her right.

I closed my eyes and took a long, deep breath. Everything was in balance, everything as it should be, and then the lightest touch against my hand, a gentle squeeze.

"My girls," she said as her hand tightened around mine.

"You came back to me." She let out a long sigh. "Two sets of sisters, together again."

I glanced at Maddie, her face as puzzled as mine.

"Two, Violet? I think you mean one."

She shook her head as the door opened behind us, and I turned to see a familiar face.

"Margaret?"

I watched in awe as our great-aunt Margaret crossed the room and bent in front of Violet, resting her hands on top of each of ours.

"You reminded me how much I'd missed my sister," she said. "You reminded me how important family is."

The sound of more footsteps caused me to turn around again.

"Helga?"

She smiled at me, walked to Margaret, and placed a reassuring hand on her shoulder. And in that moment, I understood that Margaret had come to say goodbye, but also to ask for Violet's blessing. For all we'd seen and done during our journey, for all the exciting departures and arrivals, nothing mattered more than to have brought Violet's sister back to her.

"We have a gift for you, Violet," I said, motioning to Maddie, who placed our journal in Violet's outstretched hands. "A memento of our trip, so that you can experience it for yourself, just as if you were right there with us."

The journal was tied with a ribbon we'd chosen together from a shop in Venice. I'd illustrated the title page with images of steamships and locomotives, hot air balloons and airships. And on the first page, Madeleine had added a quote from the book Nellie Bly had written about her remarkable race around the world.

They can talk of the companionship of men, the splendor of the sun, the softness of moonlight, the beauty of music, but give me a willow chair on a quiet deck, the world with its worries and noise and prejudices lost in distance, the glare of the sun, the cold light of the moon blotted out by the dense blackness of night. Let me rest rocked gently by the rolling sea, in a nest of velvety darkness, my only light the soft twinkling of the myriads of stars in the quiet sky above; my music, the sound of the kissing waters, cooling the brain and easing the pulse; my companionship, dreaming my own dreams. Give me that and I have happiness in its perfection.

For hours we talked, telling Violet everything about finding Grandpa Frank, and the time we'd spent with Matthias and his family. She sat quietly, absorbing it all, asking occasional questions and sharing a memory or two of her own. When she grew tired, we left her to rest awhile, Margaret beside her, their heads bent together as they watched the ocean.

Madeleine and I walked along the stone path to the place where we used to stand as little girls, searching for shapes in the clouds.

"Where to next?" Madeleine asked as she bumped my shoulder gently with hers. "What's our next adventure going to be?"

I linked my arm through hers and we turned our faces toward

the horizon. As the sun glittered on the water beyond the garden, I understood that the real journey wasn't out there, in Paris or Venice or some other distant place. The real journey, the most important of all, was right here, within the maps and contours of our everyday lives, among the friends and family who traveled alongside us.

In the end, that was what really mattered.

Adventure was everywhere. We just needed the courage to look for it.

Epilogue

〜❈〜

NEW YORK TIMES, DECEMBER 4, 1942

Excerpt from "Women Lead the Charge to Keep America Running"

By M. Sommers, special war correspondent

They tell us to stay home, that our duties as homemakers mean we must forgo our passions and dreams. Yet roughly one-quarter of all women are already in the workforce as typists and teachers and seamstresses, and in rare cases, jobs typically filled by men. Now, as our brothers, fathers, and husbands face the enemy abroad, we're given a new opportunity. A chance to prove that we can work as hard, and as well, as our male counterparts.

Hundreds of thousands of women are now employed in a variety of positions in factories, defense plants, and the aircraft industry. We are being called to war as nurses and operators and support personnel. We are needed. We are valued.

This is a dark time as we watch our loved ones battle an evil regime and mourn the devastating loss of innocent lives at the hands of a cruel dictator. But for many women, it is also a time of great change. We are ready to do our duty for our country, for ourselves, and for our mothers and grandmothers, who paved the way, and for whom such opportunities were denied.

In these turbulent days, I am reminded of a brave young woman, a talented journalist and family friend, and an inspiration to us all: Nellie Bly. As one of the few female journalists to report from the Eastern Front during the Great War, she believed the public had a right to know what we were fighting for, and what it truly meant to be at war. She also fought for women's suffrage, for divorce law reform, for social justice.

In her groundbreaking 1885 letter to the editor of the *Pittsburgh Dispatch,* in which she anonymously replied to a reader's question "What shall we do with our girls?" Nellie Bly answered as follows: "Instead of gathering up 'the real smart young men,' gather up the real smart girls, pull them out of the mire, give them a shove up the ladder of life, and be amply repaid both by their success and unforgetfulness of those that held out the helping hand."

Nellie Bly showed us exactly what girls are good for—and now it is our turn to carry that legacy on. Let us unite in a common cause, for a brighter, and more equal, future. One and all.

Sisters, together.

Acknowledgments

*W*riting a book during the Coronavirus pandemic of 2020 was an enormous challenge, to say the least, but if our previous two books together had taught us anything, it was that even when socially distant, it is entirely possible to cowrite a book. We were well-rehearsed, but the struggle was still very real. Worry, distraction, disruption, homeschooling, other writing projects all conspired to make this, at times, feel like an impossible task, but we prevailed! This is why we dedicated *Three Words for Goodbye* to each other. Cowriting comes with a huge amount of trust and teamwork. We have often been each other's greatest cheerleader over the past year, a shoulder to cry on, and a friend to laugh with when the going got tougher than ever.

In the end, we felt fortunate to be able to escape from reality, to continue to do the job we love, and to travel the world between our pages at a time when we could hardly leave the house. It was a gift to lose ourselves among the streets of Paris and the canals of Venice, and to sit in the audience of a Viennese opera house. For all that, we have to thank our wonderful editor, Lucia Macro, who believed in us, and took this journey with us, as our story morphed and changed. As all the best editors do, she helped us shape this into the best book it could be.

As always, we are indebted to the many, many book bloggers, Instagrammers, booksellers, and librarians who support us and spread the word about our books. Many of you have become our friends, and we thank you from the bottom of our hearts.

To our families, who replenish the coffee and wine and administer essential hugs regularly, and to our fellow authors who understand the struggle of the soggy middle, the waking in a panic in the middle of the night, and the bravery it takes to share your art with the world—thank you all. You are our tribe, and our constant inspiration.

To our superstar agent, Michelle Brower, without whose support and constant encouragement we would—like Clara and Madeleine in Venice—be hopelessly lost! Thank you for everything.

And finally, we are especially grateful to you, our readers. Thank you for trusting us, and for spending time with our stories. It means the absolute world.

About the authors

About the book

Insights,
Interviews
& More . . .

Meet Hazel Gaynor

Deasy Photographic

HAZEL GAYNOR is the *New York Times* and *USA Today* bestselling author of *A Memory of Violets* and *The Girl Who Came Home,* for which she received the 2015 Romantic Novelists' Association Historical Romantic Novel of the Year award. Her third novel, *The Girl from The Savoy,* was an *Irish Times* and *Globe and Mail* bestseller, and was shortlisted for the Irish Book Awards Popular Fiction Book of the Year. In 2017, she published *The Cottingley Secret* and *Last Christmas in Paris* (cowritten with Heather Webb). Both novels hit bestseller lists, and *Last Christmas in Paris* won the 2018 Women's Fiction Writers Association Star Award. *The Lighthouse Keeper's Daughter* was an *Irish Times* and *USA Today* bestseller, and was shortlisted for the 2019 Historical Writers' Association Gold Crown Award. *Meet Me in Monaco* (cowritten with Heather Webb) was shortlisted for the 2020 Romantic Novelists' Association Historical Romantic Novel award. Hazel's most recent novel, *When We Were Young & Brave* (*The Bird in the Bamboo Cage*) was an *Irish Times* bestseller, and was shortlisted for the 2020 Irish Book Awards Popular Fiction Novel of the Year. Hazel was selected by *Library Journal* as one of Ten Big Breakout Authors for 2015. Her work has been translated into seventeen languages and is published in twenty-three countries to date. Hazel lives in Ireland with her husband and two children. ᢙ

Meet Heather Webb

Courtesy of the author

HEATHER WEBB is the *USA Today* bestselling, award-winning author of *Rodin's Lover* and *Becoming Josephine,* as well as *Last Christmas in Paris* and *Meet Me in Monaco* (cowritten with Hazel Gaynor), both of which were award finalists and winners. Her upcoming novel, *The Next Ship Home,* about the dark secrets of Ellis Island and two unlikely friends who confront a corrupt system, releases in early 2022. Heather's works have been translated into over a dozen languages. She lives in New England with her family and one feisty rabbit. ∾

Authors' Note

The day we knew we had to write
a book inspired by Nellie Bly's trip
around the world, we were sitting in
a brasserie in Nice, France (which is a
great place to find inspiration, by the
way). We'd just returned from a long
day of research for *Meet Me in Monaco*.
We were beat, but we were also buzzing
with that creative energy that comes
from filling ourselves to the brim
with fascinating sights, smells, and
sounds. What could be better to
accomplish that task than travel?
This got us to thinking—were there
trailblazing women who enjoyed travel
as much as we did? For many centuries,
it was unseemly for women to travel
alone—or at all—but we knew if we
looked hard enough, we'd find a woman
who stood out from the rest, one who
broke the rules of stuffy convention.
Such women are always there if you
look hard enough. We like to believe
they are waiting for their stories to be
told; for their voices to be heard again.

After a lovely meal of fried squash
blossoms and salades Niçoises, and one
or two Aperol spritz cocktails (when in
France!), we pulled out our cellphones
to do a quick search. One name flashed
across our screens at exactly the same
time, and we knew instantly she was
the one to inspire us: Nellie Bly.

Born Elizabeth Cochran, and eventually taking Nellie Bly as her pseudonym, Nellie was a trailblazer in many aspects of her life and career. She is perhaps best known for her groundbreaking report on the Blackwell's Island asylum in New York City, for which she had herself declared insane in order to be committed so that she could witness the terrible conditions up close, but it was her trip around the world in 1889 that got us excited. Nellie Bly circumnavigated the globe in seventy-two days, alone and with one dress. Why? So that she could break the carefully calculated fictional record set by Jules Verne's character, Phileas Fogg, in his 1872 novel, *Around the World in Eighty Days*. What a woman! She even inspired another female journalist, Elizabeth Bisland, to challenge the record herself. Bisland wrote for *Cosmopolitan* magazine, a very different publication then from the one we know now, and set off to race around the world in the opposite direction, only hours after Nellie! But Nellie was not to be beaten and she returned triumphantly to a New Jersey train station seventy-two days later.

What was especially interesting to us about this whole adventure was not so much the places Nellie traveled to, or what happened to her along the way (having rushed through the countries she visited, she'd actually observed ▶

Authors' Note *(continued)*

very little of the local culture or sights);
it was the hysteria her trip created in
America that really caught our attention.
The newspapers followed Nellie's
progress carefully, turning her into
something of a celebrity and household
name, and many thousands of Americans
entered a competition to guess the time
it would take for Nellie to circumnavigate
the globe. The person who guessed the
closest to the actual time it took her
would win a trip to Europe as their
prize. This is where history becomes
fiction: who might have won that trip,
we wondered? Why did they enter, and
what impact did a trip to Europe have
on the individual who had become
so invested in Nellie's journey? These
questions formed the basis of Violet's
story, and the legacy of her experience
in Europe became her granddaughters'
story, and that, in turn, became the
book you are holding in your hands.

Our research trip to France came to
an end over a bottle of chilled Provençal
rosé, *Meet Me in Monaco* was published
to great acclaim the following summer,
and the words of our new book began
to find their way slowly onto the page
soon after. When we started writing
Three Words for Goodbye, we first delved
into lots of research about Nellie Bly's
trip, and then about the golden age
of travel. We became excited by the
prospect of sending our characters on

an unforgettable journey to Europe aboard some of the most famous and luxurious modes of transportation. The iconic *Queen Mary,* an ocean liner renowned for her opulence and which also played an integral role during World War II, was the perfect place for us to start. Then came the Orient Express, a train made famous by its unparalleled elegance and tales of Nazi spies, and of course, Agatha Christie's murder mystery novel. We were excited to place our characters within these lush and intriguing settings, but it was the *Hindenburg,* the world's grandest airship, the *Titanic* of the skies, that fixed our story in time. The *Hindenburg* tragedy of May 1937 would be where our story ended, and that, in turn, meant that our sisters would be travelling through a Europe on the brink of war, and already under the threat of Nazi invasion.

In our first cowritten book, *Last Christmas in Paris,* we took the points of view of a man and a woman, childhood friends separated by war. In our second novel, *Meet Me in Monaco,* we had another pair of male and female narrators, James and Sophie, two strangers thrown together by fate and by the wedding of the century. For this, our third cowritten book, we wanted to tell a story of generations of women, of family connections, and of sisters—but not just a pair of ordinary ▶

Authors' Note *(continued)*

sisters. We wanted a story of two sisters who can't stand the sight of each other when we first meet them, a story that follows them on a journey that begins as a last request from their dying grandmother, but which becomes about their relationship with each other, with the men in their lives, and so much more along the way.

Clara and Madeleine Sommers jumped onto the page sometime in late 2019 and pulled us along after them as they hopped from ocean liner, to steam train, to airship. Within their petty squabbles and irritations, and among all that they see and experience on their journey, we hope to entertain, to enchant, and to shine a light on the golden age of interwar travel, a time when *how* you traveled mattered as much as *where* you traveled to. As we rush onto budget airlines, and break into a sweat while trying to cram our cabin baggage into the overhead compartment, we might all feel a little wistful for how things used to be. And since we haven't yet invented a time travel machine, we hope that our words have taken you back in time instead.

Nellie's legacy lives on through novels, films, and other mediums, each inspired by her accomplishments and bravery. In the final chapter of our book, we have a lovely quote by Nellie Bly, which we found in her book titled *Around the World in Seventy-Two Days and Other Writings*. In early 2020, it was announced that a statue of Nellie Bly will be erected in her birthplace of Pittsburgh, beside George Washington and Pittsburgh football star Franco Harris, in the Pittsburgh International Airport. She will also be honored in a stunning monument called *The Girl Puzzle,* named for her first published article. It will consist of large mirrored spheres, an elegant walkway, and four seven-foot faces cast in bronze. This is a nod to the women of the asylum she wanted to help through her investigative reporting and exposé, along with a statue of Nellie's own face, and will be installed on Roosevelt Island (formerly Blackwell's Island) in New York. Should you find yourself in New York City, we hope you'll take the little tram from Midtown across the river to pay respects to one of the most vivacious, fascinating, and tenacious women in American history. ⌒

Reading Group Guide

1. The golden age of travel happened as a result of the invention of steam power, the expansion of railroads, and advancements in German engineering. Suddenly the world became accessible, at least to those who could afford such luxuries and those who were brave enough to venture out. How has our view of travel changed today?

2. What impact has the COVID-19 pandemic had on your own travel plans? Have you looked for ways to travel fictitiously, through books, TV, movies, et cetera?

3. What parallels can you draw between the two sets of sisters: Violet and Margaret, and Clara and Maddie? How did their paths diverge?

4. Clara is a gifted artist, but has trouble truly seeing her desires and feels restricted by societal expectations. How did you respond to her dilemma about her wedding to Charles and her feelings for Edward?

5. Maddie seems to believe she can't pursue a career if she falls in love; that a man in her life will only derail her. Has a relationship ever come between you and your career or passion?

6. All families come with a few skeletons in the closet and secrets from the past. What was your reaction to discovering Matthias was Clara and Maddie's grandfather? Do you think Margaret was justified in her reaction to Violet's pregnancy?

7. What secrets have been shared within your own family, and what reaction did that cause?

8. Have you ever traveled on an ocean liner? If so, where did you travel to? Did it contain the incredible array of activities, dining experiences, and elegance as the *Queen Mary* depicted in this story?

9. What infamous stories have you read or heard about the Orient Express? As it's still in operation today, would you ever book a trip aboard it, given the opportunity? ▶

10. What, if anything, did you know about the *Hindenburg* crash? Given its frightening fire and destruction, did you realize people survived? Has a fear of accidental disaster prevented you from travel in the past? ⮌

Discover great authors, exclusive offers, and more at hc.com.